The yellowbacks... classics of popular fiction

The yellowjackets or yellowbacks were a great series of bestselling adventure and crime thrillers that had its origins in the mid to late 19th century following on from the 'penny dreadfuls'. They virtually began the mass market revolution of the early 20th century with a clear standard format and imprint/series livery (what would today be called branding). Hodder & Stoughton published the yellow jackets in two main series with series run dates of: 1923-1939 and later 1949-1957.

As the tagline ('where thrillers really began') on the back cover implies, the imprint and series focused on thrillers that were the bestsellers of their time. This current reissue or retro revival if you will, brings back many of these masterpieces, now classics in their own way and extends it further by including key titles from that period that were either great crime or thriller or even general commercial fiction (including sub-genres of noir, horror, gothic, romance, westerns etc) influences of their time. There are some perennial favourites and many rarities either lost or not easily available being revived in the current series. Writers and characters ranged from adventure heroes like Bulldog Drummond, Allan Quatermain, Richard Hannay or the Saint through thriller grandmasters Edgar Wallace and E. Phillips Oppenheim, crime and mystery maestros like Patricia Wentworth, GK Chesterton, Agatha Christie and the Detection club, to western and swashbucklers like Zane Grey, Max Brand, Captain Blood and even romance or general fiction classics like Hermina Black, Denise Robins, Marie Corelli or Stella Morton. These were books that had storytelling at their heart and always entertained.

The yellowbacks had both hardback (with varying design elements) and paperback (which built the series look) versions with the latter still carrying the imprint 'yellowjacket'. The current reissues pay tribute to both and use an amalgam of elements from both editions while retaining the complete yellow (or 'mustard-plaster') livery with the author's name in blue beveled type with a 'simulated emboss' effect and a white outer 'outline', and the book title in black. These reissues retain the distinctive size of the original mass market paperback and follow the three main category variations— the thrillers (crime, westerns, mystery, adventure) had blue lettering for the author's name, while Romance and 'softer general fiction had red; and other categories like humour had green.

For more detail and a full list of titles visit https://www.hachetteindia.com/home/yellowbacks

THE COMPLETE MARTIN HEWITT COLLECTION

VOLUME 1

THE COMPLETE MARTIN HEWITT COLLECTION

Arthur George Morrison (1863–1945) was an English author and journalist, known for his realistic novels about London's East End and for his detective stories. In 1890, he left his job as a clerk at the People's Palace and joined the editorial staff of the Evening Globe newspaper. The following year, he published a story titled 'A Street', which was subsequently published in book form in *Tales of Mean Streets* (1894). Around this time, Morrison was also producing detective short stories which emulated those of Conan Doyle about Sherlock Holmes. Three volumes of Martin Hewitt stories were published before the publication of the novel for which Morrison is most famous: *A Child of the Jago* (1896). Other less well-received novels and stories followed, until Morrison effectively retired from writing fiction around 1913. Between then and his death, he seems to have concentrated on building his collection of Japanese prints and paintings.

Amongst his other works are *Martin Hewitt: Investigator* (1894), Zig-Zags at the Zoo (1894), *Chronicles of Martin Hewitt* (1895), *Adventures of Martin Hewitt* (1896), and *The Hole in the Wall* (1902).

THE
COMPLETE MARTIN
HEWITT COLLECTION

Arthur Morrison

VOLUME 1

Martin Hewitt, Investigator
Chronicles of Martin Hewitt

The Complete Martin Hewitt
Martin Hewitt first appeared in The Strand magazine in March 1894
Martin Hewitt, Investigator. Originally published: 1895
Chronicles of Martin Hewitt Published by Ward Lock and Bowden in 1896

This Hodder Yellowback edition © Hachette India 2023
(Registered Name: Hachette Book Publishing India Pvt. Ltd.)
An Hachette UK Company www.hachetteindia.com

1

All rights reserved. No part of the publication may be reproduced, stored in a retrieval system (including but not limited to computers, disks, external drives, electronic or digital devices, e-readers, websites), or transmitted in any form or by any means (including but not limited to cyclostyling, photocopying, docutech or other reprographic reproductions, mechanical, recording, electronic, digital versions) without the prior written permission of the publisher, nor be otherwise circulated in any form of binding or cover other than that in which it is published and without a similar condition being imposed on the subsequent purchaser.

The texts in these editions in most cases have been reprinted as is, with minimal editorial changes and by and large no bowdlerizing for political correctness; though in some editions, a few words and phrases considered archaic, or those considered offensive now, along with archaic punctuation may have been modified in places to make the text more accessible to today's readers. The narratives, language, beliefs, social mores and/or cultural depictions, in these volumes are a reflection of their times and must be viewed as such. They may also contain certain cultural, racial and gender prejudices and stereotypes that may be outdated or clearly wrong then and wrong today; but their removal would be tantamount to claiming these prejudices never existed. The Publisher does not endorse or support those depictions or stereotypes; and these books have been made available for a discerning audience that will read it for entertainment value and a chronicle/record of popular fiction of past times.

Cover design by Priya Singh adapted from the original classic yellowjacket by Hodder & Stoughton.

Cover illustration by Ishan Trivedi.

Series note: Some of the books in the series (unless otherwise credited) may have cover or inside illustrations from the original yellowbacks or early editions, and while full restoration has been attempted, some images may be grainy or faded due to the condition of the original material. The end notes or bonus material or blurb details may have been sourced from the public domain or free use publications such as Wikipedia and attribution is hereby made also allowing similar free use reproduction from here. Sources requiring further specific attribution may write in and further detailing and/or corrections shall be made in subsequent printings/editions.

Reprint specifications may be subject to change including but not limited to finishes, paper, colour sections.

ISBN: 978-93-5731-216-5

Hachette Book Publishing India Pvt. Ltd.
4th & 5th Floors, Corporate Centre,
Plot No. 94, Sector 44, Gurugram - 122 003, India

Typeset in Electra LT STD 10/12.5 pt by Manipal Technologies Limited, Manipal

Printed and bound in India by Manipal Technologies Limited, Manipal

CONTENTS

1. Martin Hewitt, Investigator   1
2. Chronicles of Martin Hewitt   177

Martin Hewitt, Investigator

CONTENTS

1.	The Lenton Croft Robberies	5
2.	The Loss of Sammy Crockett	32
3.	The Case of Mr Foggatt	58
4.	The Case of the Dixon Torpedo	82
5.	The Quinton Jewel Affair	105
6.	The Stanway Cameo Mystery	131
7.	The Affair of the Tortoise	156

1

THE LENTON CROFT ROBBERIES

Those who retain any memory of the great law cases of fifteen or twenty years back will remember, at least, the title of that extraordinary will case, "Bartley *v.* Bartley and others," which occupied the Probate Court for some weeks on end, and caused an amount of public interest rarely accorded to any but the cases considered in the other division of the same court. The case itself was noted for the large quantity of remarkable and unusual evidence presented by the plaintiff's side—evidence that took the other party completely by surprise, and overthrew their case like a house of cards. The affair will, perhaps, be more readily recalled as the occasion of the sudden rise to eminence in their profession of Messrs. Crellan, Hunt & Crellan, solicitors for the plaintiff—a result due entirely to the wonderful ability shown in this case of building up, apparently out of nothing, a smashing weight of irresistible evidence. That the firm has since maintained—indeed enhanced—the position it then won for itself need scarcely be said here; its name is familiar to everybody. But there are not many of the outside public who know that the credit of the whole performance was primarily due to a young clerk in the employ of Messrs. Crellan, who had been given charge of the seemingly desperate task of collecting evidence in the case.

This Mr Martin Hewitt had, however, full credit and reward for his exploit from his firm and from their client, and more than one other firm of lawyers engaged in contentious work made good offers to entice Hewitt to change his employers. Instead of this, however, he determined to work independently for the future, having conceived the idea of making a regular business of doing, on behalf of such clients as might retain him, similar work to that he had just done with such conspicuous success for Messrs. Crellan, Hunt & Crellan. This was the beginning of the private detective business of Martin Hewitt, and his action at that time has been completely justified by the brilliant professional successes he has since achieved.

His business has always been conducted in the most private manner, and he has always declined the help of professional assistants, preferring to carry out himself such of the many investigations offered him as he could manage. He has always maintained that he has never lost by this policy, since the chance of his refusing a case begets competition for his services, and his fees rise by a natural process. At the same time, no man could know better how to employ casual assistance at the right time.

Some curiosity has been expressed as to Mr Martin Hewitt's system, and, as he himself always consistently maintains that he has no system beyond a judicious use of ordinary faculties, I intend setting forth in detail a few of the more interesting of his cases in order that the public may judge for itself if I am right in estimating Mr Hewitt's "ordinary faculties" as faculties very extraordinary indeed. He is not a man who has made many friendships (this, probably, for professional reasons), notwithstanding his genial and companionable manners. I myself first made his acquaintance as a result of an accident resulting in a fire at the old house in which Hewitt's office was situated, and in an upper floor of which I occupied bachelor chambers. I was able to help in saving a quantity of extremely important papers relating to his business, and, while repairs were being made, allowed him to lock them in an old wall-safe in one of my rooms which the fire had scarcely damaged.

The acquaintance thus begun has lasted many years, and has become a rather close friendship. I have even accompanied Hewitt on some of his expeditions, and, in a humble way, helped him. Such of the cases, however, as I personally saw nothing of I have put into narrative form from the particulars given me.

"I consider you, Brett," he said, addressing me, "the most remarkable journalist alive. Not because you're particularly clever, you know, because, between ourselves, I hope you'll admit you're not; but because you have known something of me and my doings for some years, and have never yet been guilty of giving away any of my little business secrets you may have become acquainted with. I'm afraid you're not so enterprising a journalist as some, Brett. But now, since you ask, you shall write something—if you think it worth while."

This he said, as he said most things, with a cheery, chaffing goodnature that would have been, perhaps, surprising to a stranger who thought of him only as a grim and mysterious discoverer of secrets and crimes. Indeed, the man had always as little of the aspect of the conventional detective as may be imagined. Nobody could appear more cordial or less observant in manner, although there was to be seen a certain sharpness of the eye—which might, after all, only be the twinkle of good humor.

I *did* think it worthwhile to write something of Martin Hewitt's investigations, and a description of one of his adventures follows.

At the head of the first flight of a dingy staircase leading up from an ever-open portal in a street by the Strand stood a door, the dusty ground-glass upper panel of which carried in its center the single word "Hewitt," while at its right-hand lower corner, in smaller letters, "Clerk's Office" appeared. On a morning when the clerks in the ground-floor offices had barely hung up their hats, a short, well-dressed young man, wearing spectacles, hastening to open the dusty door, ran into the arms of another man who suddenly issued from it.

"I beg pardon," the first said. "Is this Hewitt's Detective Agency Office?"

"Yes, I believe you will find it so," the other replied. He was a stoutish, clean-shaven man, of middle height, and of a cheerful, round countenance. "You'd better speak to the clerk."

In the little outer office the visitor was met by a sharp lad with inky fingers, who presented him with a pen and a printed slip. The printed slip having been filled with the visitor's name and present business, and conveyed through an inner door, the lad reappeared with an invitation to the private office. There, behind a writing-table, sat the stoutish man himself, who had only just advised an appeal to the clerk.

"Good morning, Mr Lloyd—Mr Vernon Lloyd," he said, affably, looking again at the slip. "You'll excuse my care to start even with my visitors—I must, you know. You come from Sir James Norris, I see."

"Yes; I am his secretary. I have only to ask you to go straight to Lenton Croft at once, if you can, on very important business. Sir James would have wired, but had not your precise address. Can you go by the next train? Eleven-thirty is the first available from Paddington."

"Quite possibly. Do you know any thing of the business?"

"It is a case of a robbery in the house, or, rather, I fancy, of several robberies. Jewelry has been stolen from rooms occupied by visitors to the Croft. The first case occurred some months ago—nearly a year ago, in fact. Last night there was another. But I think you had better get the details on the spot. Sir James has told me to telegraph if you are coming, so that he may meet you himself at the station; and I must hurry, as his drive to the station will be rather a long one. Then I take it you will go, Mr Hewitt? Twyford is the station."

"Yes, I shall come, and by the 11.30. Are you going by that train yourself?"

"No, I have several things to attend to now I am in town. Good morning; I shall wire at once."

Mr Martin Hewitt locked the drawer of his table and sent his clerk for a cab.

At Twyford Station Sir James Norris was waiting with a dog-cart. Sir James was a tall, florid man of fifty or thereabout, known away from home as something of a county historian, and nearer his own parts as a great supporter of the hunt, and a gentleman much troubled with poachers. As soon as he and Hewitt had found one another the baronet hurried the detective into his dog-cart. "We've something over seven miles to drive," he said, "and I can tell you all about this wretched business as we go. That is why I came for you myself, and alone."

Hewitt nodded.

"I have sent for you, as Lloyd probably told you, because of a robbery at my place last evening. It appears, as far as I can guess, to be one of three by the same hand, or by the same gang. Late yesterday afternoon—"

"Pardon me, Sir James," Hewitt interrupted, "but I think I must ask you to begin at the first robbery and tell me the whole tale in proper order. It makes things clearer, and sets them in their proper shape."

"Very well! Eleven months ago, or thereabout, I had rather a large party of visitors, and among them Colonel Heath and Mrs Heath—the lady being a relative of my own late wife. Colonel Heath has not been long retired, you know—used to be political resident in an Indian native state. Mrs Heath had rather a good stock of jewelry of one sort and another, about the most valuable piece being a bracelet set with a particularly fine pearl—quite an exceptional pearl, in fact—that had been one of a heap of presents from the maharajah of his state when Heath left India.

"It was a very noticeable bracelet, the gold setting being a mere feather-weight piece of native filigree work—almost too fragile to trust on the wrist—and the pearl being, as I have said, of a size and quality not often seen. Well, Heath and his wife arrived late one evening, and after lunch the following day, most of the men being off by themselves—shooting, I think— my daughter, my sister (who is very often down here), and Mrs Heath took it into their heads to go walking—fern-hunting, and so on. My sister was rather long dressing, and, while they waited, my daughter went into Mrs Heath's room, where Mrs Heath turned over all her treasures to show her, as women do, you know. When my sister was at last ready, they came straight away, leaving the things littering about the room rather than stay longer to pack them up. The bracelet, with other things, was on the dressing-table then."

"One moment. As to the door?"

"They locked it. As they came away my daughter suggested turning the key, as we had one or two new servants about."

"And the window?"

"That they left open, as I was going to tell you. Well, they went on their walk and came back, with Lloyd (whom they had met somewhere) carrying their ferns for them. It was dusk and almost dinner-time. Mrs Heath went straight to her room, and—the bracelet was gone."

"Was the room disturbed?"

"Not a bit. Everything was precisely where it had been left, except the bracelet. The door hadn't been tampered with, but of course the window was open, as I have told you."

"You called the police, of course?"

"Yes, and had a man from Scotland Yard down in the morning. He seemed a pretty smart fellow, and the first thing he noticed on the dressing-table, within an inch or two of where the bracelet had been, was a match, which had been lit and thrown down. Now nobody about the house had had occasion to use a match in that room that day, and, if they had, certainly wouldn't have thrown it on the cover of the dressing-table. So that, presuming the thief to have used that match, the robbery must have been committed when the room was getting dark—immediately before Mrs Heath returned, in fact. The thief had evidently struck the match, passed it hurriedly over the various trinkets lying about, and taken the most valuable."

"Nothing else was even moved?"

"Nothing at all. Then the thief must have escaped by the window, although it was not quite clear how. The walking party approached the house with a full view of the window, but saw nothing, although the robbery must have been actually taking place a moment or two before they turned up.

"There was no water-pipe within any practicable distance of the window, but a ladder usually kept in the stable-yard was found lying along the edge of the lawn. The gardener explained, however, that he had put the ladder there after using it himself early in the afternoon."

"Of course it might easily have been used again after that and put back."

"Just what the Scotland Yard man said. He was pretty sharp, too, on the gardener, but very soon decided that he knew nothing of it. No stranger had been seen in the neighborhood, nor had passed the lodge gates. Besides, as the detective said, it scarcely seemed the work of a stranger. A stranger could scarcely have known enough to go straight to the room where a lady—only arrived the day before—had left a valuable jewel, and away again without being seen. So all the people about the house were suspected in turn. The servants offered, in a body, to have their boxes searched, and this was done; everything was turned over, from the butler's to the new kitchen maid's. I don't know that I should have had this carried quite so far if I had been the loser myself, but it was my guest, and I was in such a horrible position. Well, there's little more to be said about that, unfortunately. Nothing came of it all, and the thing's as great a mystery now as ever. I believe the Scotland Yard man got as far as suspecting *me* before he gave it up altogether, but give it up he did in the end. I think that's all I know about the first robbery. Is it clear?"

"Oh, yes; I shall probably want to ask a few questions when I have seen the place, but they can wait. What next?"

"Well," Sir James pursued, "the next was a very trumpery affair, that I should have forgotten all about, probably, if it hadn't been for one circumstance. Even now I hardly think it could have been the work of the same hand. Four months or thereabout after Mrs Heath's disaster—in February of this year, in fact—Mrs Armitage, a young widow, who had been a schoolfellow of my daughter's, stayed with us for a week or so. The girls don't trouble about the London season, you know, and I have no town house, so they were glad to have their old friend here for a little in the dull time. Mrs Armitage is a very active young lady, and was scarcely in the house half an hour before she arranged a drive in a pony-cart with Eva—my daughter—to look up old people in the village that she used to know before she was married. So they set off in the afternoon, and made such a round of it that they were late for dinner. Mrs Armitage had a small plain gold brooch—not at all valuable, you know; two or three pounds, I suppose—which she used to pin up a cloak or anything of that sort. Before she went out she stuck this in the pin-cushion on her dressing-table, and left a ring—rather a good one, I believe—lying close by."

"This," asked Hewitt, "was not in the room that Mrs Heath had occupied, I take it?"

"No; this was in another part of the building. Well, the brooch went—taken, evidently, by someone in a deuce of a hurry, for, when Mrs Armitage got back to her room, there was the pin-cushion with a little tear in it, where the brooch had been simply snatched off. But the curious thing was that the ring—worth a dozen of the brooch—was left where it had been put. Mrs Armitage didn't remember whether or not she had locked the door herself, although she found it locked when she returned; but my niece, who was indoors all the time, went and tried it once—because she remembered that a gas-fitter was at work on the landing near by—and found it safely locked. The gas-fitter, whom we didn't know at the time, but who since seems to be quite an honest fellow, was ready to swear that nobody but my niece had been to the door while he was in sight of it—which was almost all the time. As to the window, the sash-line had broken that very morning, and Mrs Armitage had propped open the bottom half about eight or ten inches with a brush; and, when she returned, that brush, sash, and all were exactly as she had left them. Now I scarcely need tell *you* what an awkward job it must have been for anybody to get noiselessly in at that unsupported window; and how unlikely he would have been to replace it, with the brush, exactly as he found it."

"Just so. I suppose the brooch, was really gone? I mean, there was no chance of Mrs Armitage having mislaid it?"

"Oh, none at all! There was a most careful search."

"Then, as to getting in at the window, would it have been easy?"

"Well, yes," Sir James replied; "yes, perhaps it would. It was a first-floor window, and it looks over the roof and skylight of the billiard-room. I built the billiard-room myself—built it out from a smoking-room just at this corner. It would be easy enough to get at the window from the billiard-room roof. But, then," he added, "that couldn't have been the way. Somebody or other was in the billiard-room the whole time, and nobody could have got over the roof (which is nearly all skylight) without being seen and heard. I was there myself for an hour or two, taking a little practice."

"Well, was anything done?"

"Strict inquiry was made among the servants, of course, but nothing came of it. It was such a small matter that Mrs Armitage wouldn't hear of my calling in the police or anything of that sort, although I felt pretty certain that there must be a dishonest servant about somewhere. A servant might take a plain brooch, you know, who would feel afraid of a valuable ring, the loss of which would be made a greater matter of."

"Well, yes, perhaps so, in the case of an inexperienced thief, who also would be likely to snatch up whatever she took in a hurry. But I'm doubtful. What made you connect these two robberies together?"

"Nothing whatever—for some months. They seemed quite of a different sort. But scarcely more than a month ago I met Mrs Armitage at Brighton, and we talked, among other things, of the previous robbery—that of Mrs Heath's bracelet. I described the circumstances pretty minutely, and, when I mentioned the match found on the table, she said: 'How strange! Why, *my* thief left a match on the dressing-table when he took my poor little brooch!'"

Hewitt nodded. "Yes," he said. "A spent match, of course?"

"Yes, of course, a spent match. She noticed it lying close by the pin-cushion, but threw it away without mentioning the circumstance. Still, it seemed rather curious to me that a match should be lit and dropped, in each case, on the dressing-cover an inch from where the article was taken. I mentioned it to Lloyd when I got back, and he agreed that it seemed significant."

"Scarcely," said Hewitt, shaking his head. "Scarcely, so far, to be called significant, although worth following up. Everybody uses matches in the dark, you know."

"Well, at any rate, the coincidence appealed to me so far that it struck me it might be worthwhile to describe the brooch to the police in order that they could trace it if it had been pawned. They had tried that, of course, over the bracelet without any result, but I fancied the shot might be worth making, and might possibly lead us on the track of the more serious robbery."

"Quite so. It was the right thing to do. Well?"

"Well, they found it. A woman had pawned it in London — at a shop in Chelsea. But that was some time before, and the pawnbroker had clean forgotten all about the woman's appearance. The name and address she gave were false. So that was the end of that business."

"Had any of the servants left you between the time the brooch was lost and the date of the pawn ticket?"

"No."

"Were all your servants at home on the day the brooch was pawned?"

"Oh, yes! I made that inquiry myself."

"Very good! What next?"

"Yesterday — and this is what made me send for you. My late wife's sister came here last Tuesday, and we gave her the room from which Mrs Heath lost her bracelet. She had with her a very old-fashioned brooch, containing a miniature of her father, and set in front with three very fine brilliants and a few smaller stones. Here we are, though, at the Croft. I'll tell you the rest indoors."

Hewitt laid his hand on the baronet's arm. "Don't pull up, Sir James," he said. "Drive a little farther. I should like to have a general idea of the whole case before we go in."

"Very good!" Sir James Norris straightened the horse's head again and went on. "Late yesterday afternoon, as my sister-in-law was changing her dress, she left her room for a moment to speak to my daughter in her room, almost adjoining. She was gone no more than three minutes, or five at most, but on her return the brooch, which had been left on the table, had gone. Now the window was shut fast, and had not been tampered with. Of course the door was open, but so was my daughter's, and anybody walking near must have been heard. But the strangest circumstance, and one that almost makes me wonder whether I have been awake today or not, was that there lay *a used match* on the very spot, as nearly as possible, where the brooch had been—and it was broad daylight!"

Hewitt rubbed his nose and looked thoughtfully before him. "Um—curious, certainly," he said, "Anything else?"

"Nothing more than you shall see for yourself. I have had the room locked and watched till you could examine it. My sister-in-law had heard of your name, and suggested that you should be called in; so, of course, I did exactly as she wanted. That she should have lost that brooch, of all things, in my house is most unfortunate; you see, there was some small difference about the thing between my late wife and her sister when their mother died and left it. It's almost worse than the Heaths' bracelet business, and altogether I'm not pleased with things, I can assure you. See what a position it is for me! Here are three ladies, in the space of one year, robbed one after another in this mysterious fashion in my house, and I can't find the thief! It's horrible! People will be afraid to come near the place. And I can do nothing!"

"Ah, well, we'll see. Perhaps we had better turn back now. By-the-by, were you thinking of having any alterations or additions made to your house?"

"No. What makes you ask?"

"I think you might at least consider the question of painting and decorating, Sir James—or, say, putting up another coach-house, or something. Because I should like to be (to the servants) the architect—or the builder, if you please—come to look around. You haven't told any of them about this business?"

"Not a word. Nobody knows but my relatives and Lloyd. I took every precaution myself, at once. As to your little disguise, be the architect by all means, and do as you please. If you can only find this thief and put an end to this horrible state of affairs, you'll do me the greatest service I've ever asked for—and as to your fee, I'll gladly make it whatever is usual, and three hundred in addition."

Martin Hewitt bowed. "You're very generous, Sir James, and you may be sure I'll do what I can. As a professional man, of course, a good fee always stimulates my interest, although this case of yours certainly seems interesting enough by itself."

"Most extraordinary! Don't you think so? Here are three persons, all ladies, all in my house, two even in the same room, each successively robbed of a piece of jewelry, each from a dressing-table, and a used match left behind in every case. All in the most difficult—one would say impossible—circumstances for a thief, and yet there is no clue!"

"Well, we won't say that just yet, Sir James; we must see. And we must guard against any undue predisposition to consider the robberies in a lump. Here we are at the lodge gate again. Is that your gardener—the man who left the ladder by the lawn on the first occasion you spoke of?"

Mr Hewitt nodded in the direction of a man who was clipping a box border.

"Yes; will you ask him anything?"

"No, no; at any rate, not now. Remember the building alterations. I think, if there is no objection, I will look first at the room that the lady—Mrs.—" Hewitt looked up, inquiringly.

"My sister-in-law? Mrs Cazenove. Oh, yes! you shall come to her room at once."

"Thank you. And I think Mrs Cazenove had better be there."

They alighted, and a boy from the lodge led the horse and dog-cart away.

Mrs Cazenove was a thin and faded, but quick and energetic, lady of middle age. She bent her head very slightly on learning Martin Hewitt's name, and said: "I must thank you, Mr Hewitt, for your very prompt attention. I need scarcely say that any help you can afford in tracing the thief who has my property—whoever it may be—will make me most grateful. My room is quite ready for you to examine."

The room was on the second floor—the top floor at that part of the building. Some slight confusion of small articles of dress was observable in parts of the room.

"This, I take it," inquired Hewitt, "is exactly as it was at the time the brooch was missed?"

"Precisely," Mrs Cazenove answered. "I have used another room, and put myself to some other inconveniences, to avoid any disturbance."

Hewitt stood before the dressing-table. "Then this is the used match," he observed, "exactly where it was found?"

"Yes."

"Where was the brooch?"

"I should say almost on the very same spot. Certainly no more than a very few inches away."

Hewitt examined the match closely. "It is burned very little," he remarked. "It would appear to have gone out at once. Could you hear it struck?"

"I heard nothing whatever; absolutely nothing."

"If you will step into Miss Norris' room now for a moment," Hewitt suggested, "we will try an experiment. Tell me if you hear matches struck, and how many. Where is the match-stand?"

The match-stand proved to be empty, but matches were found in Miss Norris' room, and the test was made. Each striking could be heard distinctly, even with one of the doors pushed to.

"Both your own door and Miss Norris' were open, I understand; the window shut and fastened inside as it is now, and nothing but the brooch was disturbed?"

"Yes, that was so."

"Thank you, Mrs Cazenove. I don't think I need trouble you any further just at present. I think, Sir James," Hewitt added, turning to the baronet, who was standing by the door—"I think we will see the other room and take a walk outside the house, if you please. I suppose, by the by, that there is no getting at the matches left behind on the first and second occasions?"

"No," Sir James answered. "Certainly not here. The Scotland Yard man may have kept his."

The room that Mrs Armitage had occupied presented no peculiar feature. A few feet below the window the roof of the billiard-room was visible, consisting largely of skylight. Hewitt glanced casually about the walls, ascertained that the furniture and hangings had not been materially changed since the second robbery, and expressed his desire to see the windows from the outside. Before leaving the room, however, he wished to know the names of any persons who were known to have been about the house on the occasions of all three robberies.

"Just carry your mind back, Sir James," he said. "Begin with yourself, for instance. Where were you at these times?"

"When Mrs Heath lost her bracelet, I was in Tagley Wood all the afternoon. When Mrs Armitage was robbed, I believe I was somewhere about the place most of the time she was out. Yesterday I was down at the farm." Sir James' face broadened. "I don't know whether you call those suspicious movements," he added, and laughed.

"Not at all; I only asked you so that, remembering your own movements, you might the better recall those of the rest of the household. Was anybody, to your knowledge—*anybody*, mind—in the house on all three occasions?"

"Well, you know, it's quite impossible to answer for all the servants. You'll only get that by direct questioning—I can't possibly remember things of that sort. As to the family and visitors—why, you don't suspect any of them, do you?"

"I don't suspect a soul, Sir James," Hewitt answered, beaming genially, "not a soul. You see, I can't suspect people till I know something about where they were. It's quite possible there will be independent evidence enough as it is, but you must help me if you can. The visitors, now. Was there any visitor here each time—or even on the first and last occasions only?"

"No, not one. And my own sister, perhaps you will be pleased to know, was only there at the time of the first robbery."

"Just so! And your daughter, as I have gathered, was clearly absent from the spot each time—indeed, was in company with the party robbed. Your niece, now?"

"Why hang it all, Mr Hewitt, I can't talk of my niece as a suspected criminal! The poor girl's under my protection, and I really can't allow—"

Hewitt raised his hand, and shook his head deprecatingly.

"My dear sir, haven't I said that I don't suspect a soul? *Do* let me know how the people were distributed, as nearly as possible. Let me see. It was your, niece, I think, who found that Mrs Armitage's door was locked—this door, in fact—on the day she lost her brooch?"

"Yes, it was."

"Just so—at the time when Mrs Armitage herself had forgotten whether she locked it or not. And yesterday—was she out then?"

"No, I think not. Indeed, she goes out very little—her health is usually bad. She was indoors, too, at the time of the Heath robbery, since you ask. But come, now, I don't like this. It's ridiculous to suppose that *she* knows anything of it."

"I don't suppose it, as I have said. I am only asking for information. That is all your resident family, I take it, and you know nothing of anybody else's movements—except, perhaps, Mr Lloyd's?"

"Lloyd? Well, you know yourself that he was out with the ladies when the first robbery took place. As to the others, I don't remember. Yesterday he was probably in his room, writing. I think that acquits *him*, eh?" Sir James looked quizzically into the broad face of the affable detective, who smiled and replied:

"Oh, of course nobody can be in two places at once, else what would become of the *alibi* as an institution? But, as I have said, I am only setting my facts in order. Now, you see, we get down to the servants—unless some stranger is the party wanted. Shall we go outside now?"

Lenton Croft was a large, desultory sort of house, nowhere more than three floors high, and mostly only two. It had been added to bit by bit, till it zigzagged about its site, as Sir James Norris expressed it, "like a game of dominoes." Hewitt scrutinized its external features carefully as they strolled around, and stopped some little while before the windows of the two bedrooms he had just seen from the inside. Presently they approached the stables and coach-house, where a groom was washing the wheels of the dog-cart.

"Do you mind my smoking?" Hewitt asked Sir James. "Perhaps you will take a cigar yourself—they are not so bad, I think. I will ask your man for a light."

Sir James felt for his own matchbox, but Hewitt had gone, and was lighting his cigar with a match from a box handed him by the groom. A smart little terrier was trotting about by the coach-house, and Hewitt stooped to rub its head. Then he made some observation about the dog, which enlisted the groom's interest, and was soon absorbed in a chat with the man. Sir James, waiting a little way off, tapped the stones rather impatiently with his foot, and presently moved away.

For full a quarter of an hour Hewitt chatted with the groom, and, when at last he came away and overtook Sir James, that gentleman was about re-entering the house.

"I beg your pardon, Sir James," Hewitt said, "for leaving you in that unceremonious fashion to talk to your groom, but a dog, Sir James—a good dog—will draw me anywhere."

"Oh!" replied Sir James, shortly.

"There is one other thing," Hewitt went on, disregarding the other's curtness, "that I should like to know: There are two windows directly below that of the room occupied yesterday by Mrs Cazenove—one on each floor. What rooms do they light?"

"That on the ground floor is the morning-room; the other is Mr Lloyd's—my secretary. A sort of study or sitting-room."

"Now you will see at once, Sir James," Hewitt pursued, with an affable determination to win the baronet back to good-humor—"you will see at once that, if a ladder had been used in Mrs Heath's case, anybody looking from either of these rooms would have seen it."

"Of course! The Scotland Yard man questioned everybody as to that, but nobody seemed to have been in either of the rooms when the thing occurred; at any rate, nobody saw anything."

"Still, I think I should like to look out of those windows myself; it will, at least, give me an idea of what *was* in view and what was not, if anybody had been there."

Sir James Norris led the way to the morning-room. As they reached the door a young lady, carrying a book and walking very languidly, came out. Hewitt stepped aside to let her pass, and afterward said interrogatively: "Miss Norris, your daughter, Sir James?"

"No, my niece. Do you want to ask her anything? Dora, my dear," Sir James added, following her in the corridor, "this is Mr Hewitt, who is investigating these wretched robberies for me. I think he would like to hear if you remember anything happening at any of the three times."

The lady bowed slightly, and said in a plaintive drawl: "I, uncle? Really, I don't remember anything; nothing at all."

"You found Mrs Armitage's door locked, I believe," asked Hewitt, "when you tried it, on the afternoon when she lost her brooch?"

"Oh, yes; I believe it was locked. Yes, it was."

"Had the key been left in?"

"The key? Oh, no! I think not; no."

"Do you remember anything out of the common happening—anything whatever, no matter how trivial—on the day Mrs Heath lost her bracelet?"

"No, really, I don't. I can't remember at all."

"Nor yesterday?"

"No, nothing. I don't remember anything."

"Thank you," said Hewitt, hastily; "thank you. Now the morning-room, Sir James."

In the morning-room Hewitt stayed but a few seconds, doing little more than casually glance out of the windows. In the room above he took a little longer time. It was a comfortable room, but with rather effeminate indications about its contents. Little pieces of draped silk-work hung about the furniture, and Japanese silk fans decorated the mantelpiece. Near the window was a cage containing a gray parrot, and the writing-table was decorated with two vases of flowers.

"Lloyd makes himself pretty comfortable, eh?" Sir James observed. "But it isn't likely anybody would be here while he was out, at the time that bracelet went."

"No," replied Hewitt, meditatively. "No, I suppose not."

He stared thoughtfully out of the window, and then, still deep in thought, rattled at the wires of the cage with a quill toothpick and played a moment with the parrot. Then, looking up at the window again, he said: "That is Mr Lloyd, isn't it, coming back in a fly?"

"Yes, I think so. Is there anything else you would care to see here?"

"No, thank you," Hewitt replied; "I don't think there is."

They went down to the smoking-room, and Sir James went away to speak to his secretary. When he returned, Hewitt said quietly: "I think, Sir James—I *think* that I shall be able to give you your thief presently."

"What! Have you a clue? Who do you think? I began to believe you were hopelessly stumped."

"Well, yes. I have rather a good clue, although I can't tell you much about it just yet. But it is so good a clue that I should like to know now whether you are determined to prosecute when you have the criminal?"

"Why, bless me, of course," Sir James replied, with surprise. "It doesn't rest with me, you know—the property belongs to my friends. And even if they were disposed to let the thing slide, I shouldn't allow it—I couldn't, after they had been robbed in my house."

"Of course, of course! Then, if I can, I should like to send a message to Twyford by somebody perfectly trustworthy—not a servant. Could anybody go?"

"Well, there's Lloyd, although he's only just back from his journey. But, if it's important, he'll go."

"It is important. The fact is we must have a policeman or two here this evening, and I'd like Mr Lloyd to fetch them without telling anybody else."

Sir James rang, and, in response to his message, Mr Lloyd appeared. While Sir James gave his secretary his instructions, Hewitt strolled to the door of the smoking-room, and intercepted the latter as he came out.

"I'm sorry to give you this trouble, Mr Lloyd," he said, "but I must stay here myself for a little, and somebody who can be trusted must go. Will you just bring back a police constable with you? or rather two—two would be better. That is all that is wanted. You won't let the servants know, will you? Of course there will be a female searcher at the Twyford police-station? Ah—of course. Well, you needn't bring her, you know. That sort of thing is done at the station." And, chatting thus confidentially, Martin Hewitt saw him off.

When Hewitt returned to the smoking-room, Sir James said, suddenly: "Why, bless my soul, Mr Hewitt, we haven't fed you! I'm awfully sorry. We came in rather late for lunch, you know, and this business has bothered me so I clean forgot everything else. There's no dinner till seven, so you'd better let me give you something now. I'm really sorry. Come along."

"Thank you, Sir James," Hewitt replied; "I won't take much. A few biscuits, perhaps, or something of that sort. And, by the by, if you don't mind, I rather think I should like to take it alone. The fact is I want to go over this case thoroughly by myself. Can you put me in a room?"

"Any room you like. Where will you go? The dining-room's rather large, but there's my study, that's pretty snug, or—"

"Perhaps I can go into Mr Lloyd's room for half an hour or so; I don't think he'll mind, and it's pretty comfortable."

"Certainly, if you'd like. I'll tell them to send you whatever they've got."

"Thank you very much. Perhaps they'll also send me a lump of sugar and a walnut; it's—it's a little fad of mine."

"A—what? A lump of sugar and a walnut?" Sir James stopped for a moment, with his hand on the bell-rope. "Oh, certainly, if you'd like it; certainly," he added, and stared after this detective with curious tastes as he left the room.

When the vehicle, bringing back the secretary and the policeman, drew up on the drive, Martin Hewitt left the room on the first floor and proceeded down-stairs. On the landing he met Sir James Norris and Mrs Cazenove, who stared with astonishment on perceiving that the detective carried in his hand the parrot-cage.

"I think our business is about brought to a head now," Hewitt remarked, on the stairs. "Here are the police officers from Twyford." The men were standing in the hall with Mr Lloyd, who, on catching sight of the cage in Hewitt's hand, paled suddenly.

"This is the person who will be charged, I think," Hewitt pursued, addressing the officers, and indicating Lloyd with his finger.

"What, Lloyd?" gasped Sir James, aghast. "No—not Lloyd—nonsense!"

"He doesn't seem to think it nonsense himself, does he?" Hewitt placidly observed. Lloyd had sank on a chair, and, gray of face, was staring blindly at the man he had run against at the office door that morning. His lips moved in spasms, but there was no sound. The wilted flower fell from his buttonhole to the floor, but he did not move.

"This is his accomplice," Hewitt went on, placing the parrot and cage on the hall table, "though I doubt whether there will be any use in charging *him*. Eh, Polly?"

The parrot put his head aside and chuckled. "Hullo, Polly!" it quietly gurgled. "Come along!"

Sir James Norris was hopelessly bewildered. "Lloyd—Lloyd," he said, under his breath. "Lloyd—and that!"

"This was his little messenger, his useful Mercury," Hewitt explained, tapping the cage complacently; "in fact, the actual lifter. Hold him up!"

The last remark referred to the wretched Lloyd, who had fallen forward with something between a sob and a loud sigh. The policemen took him by the arms and propped him in his chair.

"System?" said Hewitt, with a shrug of the shoulders, an hour or two after in Sir James' study. "I can't say I have a system. I call it nothing but common sense and a sharp pair of eyes. Nobody using these could help taking the right road in this case. I began at the match, just as the Scotland Yard man did, but I had the advantage of taking a line through three cases. To begin with, it was plain that that match, being left there in daylight, in Mrs Cazenove's room, could not have been used to light the table-top, in the full glare of the window; therefore it had been used for some other purpose—*what* purpose I could not, at the moment, guess. Habitual thieves, you know, often have curious superstitions, and some will never take anything without leaving something behind—a pebble or a piece of coal, or something like that—in the premises they have been robbing. It seemed at first extremely likely that this was a case of that kind. The match had clearly been *brought in*—because, when I asked for matches, there were none in the stand, not even an empty box, and the room had not been disturbed. Also the match probably had not been struck there, nothing having been heard, although, of course, a mistake in this matter was just possible. This match, then, it was fair to assume, had been lit somewhere else and blown out immediately—I remarked at the time that it was very little burned. Plainly it could not have been treated thus for nothing, and the only possible object would have been to prevent it igniting accidentally. Following on this, it became obvious that the match was used, for whatever purpose, not *as* a match, but merely as a convenient splinter of wood.

"So far so good. But on examining the match very closely I observed, as you can see for yourself, certain rather sharp indentations in the wood. They are very small, you see, and scarcely visible, except upon narrow inspection; but there they are, and their positions are regular. See, there are two on each side, each opposite the corresponding mark of the other pair. The match, in fact, would seem to have been gripped in some fairly sharp instrument, holding it at two points above and two below—an instrument, as it may at once strike you, not unlike the beak of a bird.

"Now here was an idea. What living creature but a bird could possibly have entered Mrs Heath's window without a ladder—supposing no ladder to have been used—or could have got into Mrs Armitage's window without lifting the sash higher than the eight or ten inches it was already open? Plainly, nothing. Further, it is significant that only *one* article was stolen at a time, although others were about. A human being could have carried any reasonable number, but a bird could only take one at a time. But why should a bird carry a match in its beak? Certainly it must have been trained to do that for a purpose, and a little consideration made that purpose pretty clear. A noisy, chattering bird would probably betray itself at once. Therefore it must be trained to keep quiet both while going for and coming away with its plunder. What readier or more probably effectual way than, while teaching it to carry without dropping, to teach it also to keep quiet while carrying? The one thing would practically cover the other.

"I thought at once, of course, of a jackdaw or a magpie — these birds' thievish reputations made the guess natural. But the marks on the match were much too wide apart to have been made by the beak of either. I conjectured, therefore, that it must be a raven. So that, when we arrived near the coach-house, I seized the opportunity of a little chat with your groom on the subject of dogs and pets in general, and ascertained that there was no tame raven in the place. I also, incidentally, by getting a light from the coach-house box of matches, ascertained that the match found was of the sort generally used about the establishment — the large, thick, red-topped English match. But I further found that Mr Lloyd had a parrot which was a most intelligent pet, and had been trained into comparative quietness — for a parrot. Also, I learned that more than once the groom had met Mr Lloyd carrying his parrot under his coat, it having, as its owner explained, learned the trick of opening its cage-door and escaping.

"I said nothing, of course, to you of all this, because I had as yet nothing but a train of argument and no results. I got to Lloyd's room as soon as possible. My chief object in going there was achieved when I played with the parrot, and induced it to bite a quill toothpick.

"When you left me in the smoking-room, I compared the quill and the match very carefully, and found that the marks corresponded exactly. After this I felt very little doubt indeed. The fact of Lloyd having met the ladies walking before dark on the day of the first robbery proved nothing, because, since it was clear that the match had *not* been used to procure a light, the robbery might as easily have taken place in daylight as not—must have so taken place, in fact, if my conjectures were right. That they were right I felt no doubt. There could be no other explanation.

"When Mrs Heath left her window open and her door shut, anybody climbing upon the open sash of Lloyd's high window could have put the bird upon the sill above. The match placed in the bird's beak for the purpose I have indicated, and struck first, in case by accident it should ignite by rubbing against something and startle the bird—this match would, of course, be dropped just where the object to be removed was taken up; as you know, in every case the match was found almost upon the spot where the missing article had been left—scarcely a likely triple coincidence had the match been used by a human thief. This would have been done as soon after the ladies had left as possible, and there would then have been plenty of time for Lloyd to hurry out and meet them before dark—especially plenty of time to meet them *coming back*, as they must have been, since they were carrying their ferns. The match was an article well chosen for its purpose, as being a not altogether unlikely thing to find on a dressing-table, and, if noticed, likely to lead to the wrong conclusions adopted by the official detective.

"In Mrs Armitage's case the taking of an inferior brooch and the leaving of a more valuable ring pointed clearly either to the operator being a fool or unable to distinguish values, and certainly, from other indications, the thief seemed no fool. The door was locked, and the gas-fitter, so to speak, on guard, and the window was only eight or ten inches open and propped with a brush. A human thief entering the window would have disturbed this arrangement, and would scarcely risk discovery by attempting to replace it, especially a thief in so great a hurry as to snatch the brooch up without unfastening the pin. The bird could pass through the opening as it was, and *would have* to tear the pin-cushion to pull the brooch off, probably holding the cushion down with its claw the while.

"Now in yesterday's case we had an alteration of conditions. The window was shut and fastened, but the door was open — but only left for a few minutes, during which time no sound was heard either of coming or going. Was it not possible, then, that the thief was *already* in the room, in hiding, while Mrs Cazenove was there, and seized its first opportunity on her temporary absence? The room is full of draperies, hangings, and what not, allowing of plenty of concealment for a bird, and a bird could leave the place noiselessly and quickly. That the whole scheme was strange mattered not at all. Robberies presenting such unaccountable features must have been effected by strange means of one sort or another. There was no improbability. Consider how many hundreds of examples of infinitely higher degrees of bird-training are exhibited in the London streets every week for coppers.

"So that, on the whole, I felt pretty sure of my ground. But before taking any definite steps I resolved to see if Polly could not be persuaded to exhibit his accomplishments to an indulgent stranger. For that purpose I contrived to send Lloyd away again and have a quiet hour alone with his bird. A piece of sugar, as everybody knows, is a good parrot bribe; but a walnut, split in half, is a better — especially if the bird be used to it; so I got you to furnish me with both. Polly was shy at first, but I generally get along very well with pets, and a little perseverance soon led to a complete private performance for my benefit. Polly would take the match, mute as wax, jump on the table, pick up the brightest thing he could see, in a great hurry, leave the match behind, and scuttle away round the room; but at first wouldn't give up the plunder to *me*. It was enough. I also took the liberty, as you know, of a general look round, and discovered that little collection of Brummagem rings and trinkets that you have just seen—used in Polly's education, no doubt. When we sent Lloyd away, it struck me that he might as well be usefully employed as not, so I got him to fetch the police, deluding him a little, I fear, by talking about the servants and a female searcher. There will be no trouble about evidence; he'll confess. Of that I'm sure. I know the sort of man. But I doubt if you'll get Mrs Cazenove's brooch back. You see, he has been to London today, and by this time the swag is probably broken up."

Sir James listened to Hewitt's explanation with many expressions of assent and some of surprise. When it was over, he smoked a few whiffs and then said: "But Mrs Armitage's brooch was pawned, and by a woman."

"Exactly. I expect our friend Lloyd was rather disgusted at his small luck—probably gave the brooch to some female connection in London, and she realized on it. Such persons don't always trouble to give a correct address."

The two smoked in silence for a few minutes, and then Hewitt continued: "I don't expect our friend has had an easy job altogether with that bird. His successes at most have only been three, and I suspect he had many failures and not a few anxious moments that we know nothing of. I should judge as much merely from what the groom told me of frequently meeting Lloyd with his parrot. But the plan was not a bad one—not at all. Even if the bird had been caught in the act, it would only have been 'That mischievous parrot!' you see. And his master would only have been looking for him."

2

THE LOSS OF SAMMY CROCKETT

It was, of course, always a part of Martin Hewitt's business to be thoroughly at home among any and every class of people, and to be able to interest himself intelligently, or to appear to do so, in their various pursuits. In one of the most important cases ever placed in his hands he could have gone but a short way toward success had he not displayed some knowledge of the more sordid aspects of professional sport, and a great interest in the undertakings of a certain dealer therein.

The great case itself had nothing to do with sport, and, indeed, from a narrative point of view, was somewhat uninteresting, but the man who alone held the one piece of information wanted was a keeper, backer, or "gaffer" of professional pedestrians, and it was through the medium of his pecuniary interest in such matters that Hewitt was enabled to strike a bargain with him.

The man was a publican on the outskirts of Padfield, a northern town, pretty famous for its sporting tastes, and to Padfield, therefore, Hewitt betook himself, and, arrayed in a way to indicate some inclination of his own toward sport, he began to frequent the bar of the Hare and Hounds. Kentish, the landlord, was a stout, bull-necked man, of no great communicativeness at first; but after a little acquaintance he opened out wonderfully, became quite a jolly (and rather intelligent) companion, and came out with innumerable anecdotes of his sporting adventures. He could put a very decent dinner on the table, too, at the Hare and Hounds, and Hewitt's frequent invitation to him to join therein and divide a bottle of the best in the cellar soon put the two on the very best of terms. Good terms with Mr Kentish was Hewitt's great desire, for the information he wanted was of a sort that could never be extracted by casual questioning, but must be a matter of open communication by the publican, extracted in what way it might be.

"Look here," said Kentish one day, "I'll put you on to a good thing, my boy—a real good thing. Of course you know all about the Padfield 135 Yards Handicap being run off now?"

"Well, I haven't looked into it much," Hewitt replied. "Ran the first round of heats last Saturday and Monday, didn't they?"

"They did. Well"—Kentish spoke in a stage whisper as he leaned over and rapped the table—"I've got the final winner in this house." He nodded his head, took a puff at his cigar, and added, in his ordinary voice. "Don't say nothing."

"No, of course not. Got something on, of course?"

"Rather! What do you think? Got any price I liked. Been saving him up for this. Why, he's got twenty-one yards, and he can do even time all the way! Fact! Why, he could win runnin' back'ards. He won his heat on Monday like—like—like that!" The gaffer snapped his fingers, in default of a better illustration, and went on. "He might ha' took it a little easier, I think; it's shortened his price, of course, him jumpin' in by two yards. But you can get decent odds now, if you go about it right. You take my tip—back him for his heat next Saturday, in the second round, and for the final. You'll get a good price for the final, if you pop it down at once. But don't go makin' a song of it, will you, now? I'm givin' you a tip I wouldn't give anybody else."

"Thanks, very much; it's awfully good of you. I'll do what you advise. But isn't there a dark horse anywhere else?"

"Not dark to me, my boy, not dark to me. I know every man runnin' like a book. Old Taylor—him over at the Cop—he's got a very good lad at eighteen yards, a very good lad indeed; and he's a tryer this time, I know. But, bless you, my lad could give him ten, instead o' taking three, and beat him then! When I'm runnin' a real tryer, I'm generally runnin' something very near a winner, you bet; and this time, mind *this* time, I'm runnin' the certainest winner I *ever* run—and I don't often make a mistake. You back him."

"I shall, if you're as sure as that. But who is he?"

"Oh, Crockett's his name—Sammy Crockett. He's quite a new lad. I've got young Steggles looking after him—sticks to him like wax. Takes his little breathers in my bit o' ground at the back here. I've got a cinder-sprint path there, over behind the trees. I don't let him out o' sight much, I can tell you. He's a straight lad, and he knows it'll be worth his while to stick to me; but there's some 'ud poison him, if they thought he'd spoil their books."

Soon afterward the two strolled toward the taproom. "I expect Sammy'll be there," the landlord said, "with Steggles. I don't hide him too much—they'd think I'd got something extra on if I did."

In the taproom sat a lean, wire-drawn-looking youth, with sloping shoulders and a thin face, and by his side was a rather short, thickset man, who had an odd air, no matter what he did, of proprietorship and surveillance of the lean youth. Several other men sat about, and there was loud laughter, under which the lean youth looked sheepishly angry.

"'Tarn't no good, Sammy, lad," someone was saying, "you a-makin' after Nancy Webb—she'll ha' nowt to do with 'ee."

"Don' like 'em so thread-papery," added another. "No, Sammy, you aren't the lad for she. I see her—"

"What about Nancy Webb?" asked Kentish, pushing open the door. "Sammy's all right, any way. You keep fit, my lad, an' go on improving, and some day you'll have as good a house as me. Never mind the lasses. Had his glass o' beer, has he?" This to Raggy Steggles, who, answering in the affirmative, viewed his charge as though he were a post, and the beer a recent coat of paint.

"Has two glasses of mild a day," the landlord said to Hewitt. "Never puts on flesh, so he can stand it. Come out now." He nodded to Steggles, who rose and marched Sammy Crockett away for exercise.

On the following afternoon (it was Thursday), as Hewitt and Kentish chatted in the landlord's own snuggery, Steggles burst into the room in a great state of agitation and spluttered out: "He—he's bolted; gone away!"

"What?"

"Sammy—gone! Hooked it! *I* can't find him."

The landlord stared blankly at the trainer, who stood with a sweater dangling from his hand and stared blankly back. "What d'ye mean?" Kentish said, at last. "Don't be a fool! He's in the place somewhere. Find him!"

But this Steggles defied anybody to do. He had looked already. He had left Crockett at the cinder-path behind the trees in his running-gear, with the addition of the long overcoat and cap he used in going between the path and the house to guard against chill. "I was goin' to give him a bust or two with the pistol," the trainer explained, "but, when we got over t'other side, 'Raggy,' ses he, 'it's blawin' a bit chilly. I think I'll ha' a sweater. There's one on my box, ain't there?' So in I coomes for the sweater, and it weren't on his box, and, when I found it and got back—he weren't there. They'd seen nowt o' him in t' house, and he weren't nowhere."

Hewitt and the landlord, now thoroughly startled, searched everywhere, but to no purpose. "What should he go off the place for?" asked Kentish, in a sweat of apprehension. "'Tain't chilly a bit—it's warm. He didn't want no sweater; never wore one before. It was a piece of kid to be able to clear out. Nice thing, this is. I stand to win two years' takings over him. Here— you'll have to find him."

"Ah, but how?" exclaimed the disconcerted trainer, dancing about distractedly. "I've got all I could scrape on him myself. Where can I look?"

Here was Hewitt's opportunity. He took Kentish aside and whispered. What he said startled the landlord considerably. "Yes, I'll tell you all about that," he said, "if that's all you want. It's no good or harm to me whether I tell or no. But can you find him?"

"That I can't promise, of course. But you know who I am now, and what I'm here for. If you like to give me the information I want, I'll go into the case for you, and, of course, I shan't charge any fee. I may have luck, you know, but I can't promise, of course."

The landlord looked in Hewitt's face for a moment. Then he said: "Done! It's a deal."

"Very good," Hewitt replied; "get together the one or two papers you have, and we'll go into my business in the evening. As to Crockett, don't say a word to anybody. I'm afraid it must get out, since they all know about it in the house, but there's no use in making any unnecessary noise. Don't make hedging bets or do anything that will attract notice. Now we'll go over to the back and look at this cinder-path of yours."

Here Steggles, who was still standing near, was struck with an idea. "How about old Taylor, at the Cop, guv'nor, eh?" he said, meaningly. "His lad's good enough to win with Sammy out, and Taylor is backing him plenty. Think he knows anything o' this?"

"That's likely," Hewitt observed, before Kentish could reply. "Yes. Look here—suppose Steggles goes and keeps his eye on the Cop for an hour or two, in case there's anything to be heard of? Don't show yourself, of course."

Kentish agreed, and the trainer went. When Hewitt and Kentish arrived at the path behind the trees, Hewitt at once began examining the ground. One or two rather large holes in the cinders were made, as the publican explained, by Crockett, in practicing getting off his mark. Behind these were several fresh tracks of spiked shoes. The tracks led up to within a couple of yards of the high fence bounding the ground, and there stopped abruptly and entirely. In the fence, a little to the right of where the tracks stopped, there was a stout door. This Hewitt tried, and found ajar.

"That's always kept bolted," Kentish said. "He's gone out that way—he couldn't have gone any other without comin' through the house."

"But he isn't in the habit of making a step three yards long, is he?" Hewitt asked, pointing at the last footmark and then at the door, which was quite that distance away from it. "Besides," he added, opening the door, "there's no footprint here nor outside."

The door opened on a lane, with another fence and a thick plantation of trees at the other side. Kentish looked at the footmarks, then at the door, then down the lane, and finally back toward the house. "That's a licker!" he said.

"This is a quiet sort of lane," was Hewitt's next remark. "No houses in sight. Where does it lead?"

"That way it goes to the Old Kilns—disused. This way down to a turning off the Padfield and Catton road."

Hewitt returned to the cinder-path again, and once more examined the footmarks. He traced them back over the grass toward the house. "Certainly," he said, "he hasn't gone back to the house. Here is the double line of tracks, side by side, from the house—Steggles' ordinary boots with iron tips, and Crockett's running pumps; thus they came out. Here is

Steggles' track in the opposite direction alone, made when he went back for the sweater. Crockett remained; you see various prints in those loose cinders at the end of the path where he moved this way and that, and then two or three paces toward the fence—not directly toward the door, you notice—and there they stop dead, and there are no more, either back or forward. Now, if he had wings, I should be tempted to the opinion that he flew straight away in the air from that spot—unless the earth swallowed him and closed again without leaving a wrinkle on its face."

Kentish stared gloomily at the tracks and said nothing.

"However," Hewitt resumed, "I think I'll take a little walk now and think over it. You go into the house and show yourself at the bar. If anybody wants to know how Crockett is, he's pretty well, thank you. By the by, can I get to the Cop—this place of Taylor's—by this back lane?"

"Yes, down to the end leading to the Catton road, turn to the left and then first on the right. Any one'll show you the Cop," and Kentish shut the door behind the detective, who straightway walked—toward the Old Kilns.

In little more than an hour he was back. It was now becoming dusk, and the landlord looked out papers from a box near the side window of his snuggery, for the sake of the extra light. "I've got these papers together for you," he said, as Hewitt entered. "Any news?"

"Nothing very great. Here's a bit of handwriting I want you to recognize, if you can. Get a light."

Kentish lit a lamp, and Hewitt laid upon the table half a dozen small pieces of torn paper, evidently fragments of a letter which had been torn up, here reproduced in facsimile:

The landlord turned the scraps over, regarding them dubiously. "These aren't much to recognize, anyhow. I don't know the writing. Where did you find 'em?"

"They were lying in the lane at the back, a little way down. Plainly they are pieces of a note addressed to someone called Sammy or something very like it. See the first piece, with its 'mmy'? That is clearly from the beginning of the note, because there is no line between it and the smooth, straight edge of the paper above; also, nothing follows on the same line. Someone writes to Crockett—presuming it to be a letter addressed to him, as I do for other reasons—as Sammy. It is a pity that there is no more of the letter to be found than these pieces. I expect the person who tore it up put the rest in his pocket and dropped these by accident."

Kentish, who had been picking up and examining each piece in turn, now dolorously broke out:

"Oh, it's plain he's sold us—bolted and done us; me as took him out o' the gutter, too. Look here—'throw them over'; that's plain enough—can't mean anything else. Means throw *me* over, and my friends—me, after what I've done for him! Then 'right away'—go right away, I s'pose, as he has done. Then"—he was fiddling with the scraps and finally fitted two together—"why, look here, this one with 'lane' on it fits over the one about throwing over, and it says 'poor f' where its torn; that means 'poor fool,' I s'pose—*me*, or 'fathead,' or something like that. That's nice. Why, I'd twist his neck if I could get hold of him; and I will!"

Hewitt smiled. "Perhaps it's not quite so uncomplimentary, after all," he said. "If you can't recognize the writing, never mind. But, if he's gone away to sell you, it isn't much use finding him, is it? He won't win if he doesn't want to."

"Why, he wouldn't dare to rope under my very eyes. I'd—I'd—"

"Well, well; perhaps we'll get him to run, after all, and as well as he can. One thing is certain—he left this place of his own will. Further, I think he is in Padfield now; he went toward the town, I believe. And I don't think he means to sell you."

"Well, he shouldn't. I've made it worth his while to stick to me. I've put a fifty on for him out of my own pocket, and told him so; and, if he won, that would bring him a lump more than he'd probably get by going crooked, besides the prize money and anything I might give him over. But it seems to me he's putting me in the cart altogether."

"That we shall see. Meantime, don't mention anything I've told you to any one—not even to Steggles. He can't help us, and he might blurt things out inadvertently. Don't say anything about these pieces of paper, which I shall keep myself. By-the-by, Steggles is indoors, isn't he? Very well, keep him in. Don't let him be seen hunting about this evening. I'll stay here tonight and we'll proceed with Crockett's business in the morning. And now we'll settle *my* business, please."

In the morning Hewitt took his breakfast in the snuggery, carefully listening to any conversation that might take place at the bar. Soon after nine o'clock a fast dog-cart stopped outside, and a red-faced, loud-voiced man swaggered in, greeting Kentish with boisterous cordiality. He had a drink with the landlord, and said: "How's things? Fancy any of 'em for the sprint handicap? Got a lad o' your own in, haven't you?"

"Oh, yes," Kentish replied. "Crockett. Only a young un not got to his proper mark yet, I reckon. I think old Taylor's got No. 1 this time."

"Capital lad," the other replied, with a confidential nod. "Shouldn't wonder at all. Want to do anything yourself over it?"

"No, I don't think so. I'm not on at present. Might have a little flutter on the grounds just for fun; nothing else."

There were a few more casual remarks, and then the red-faced man drove away.

"Who was that?" asked Hewitt, who had watched the visitor through the snuggery window.

"That's Danby—bookmaker. Cute chap. He's been told Crockett's missing, I'll bet anything, and come here to pump me. No good, though. As a matter of fact, I've worked Sammy Crockett into his books for about half I'm in for altogether—through third parties, of course."

Hewitt reached for his hat. "I'm going out for half an hour now," he said. "If Steggles wants to go out before I come back, don't let him. Let him go and smooth over all those tracks on the cinder-path, very carefully. And, by the by, could you manage to have your son about the place today, in case I happen to want a little help out of doors?"

"Certainly; I'll get him to stay in. But what do you want the cinders smoothed for?"

Hewitt smiled, and patted his host's shoulder. "I'll explain all my tricks when the job's done," he said, and went out.

On the lane from Padfield to Sedby village stood the Plough beer-house, wherein J. Webb was licensed to sell by retail beer to be consumed on the premises or off, as the thirsty list. Nancy Webb, with a very fine color, a very curly fringe, and a wide smiling mouth revealing a fine set of teeth, came to the bar at the summons of a stoutish old gentleman in spectacles who walked with a stick.

The stoutish old gentleman had a glass of bitter beer, and then said in the peculiarly quiet voice of a very deaf man: "Can you tell me, if you please, the way into the main Catton road?"

"Down the lane, turn to the right at the cross-roads, then first to the left."

The old gentleman waited with his hand to his ear for some few seconds after she had finished speaking, and then resumed in his whispering voice: "I'm afraid I'm very deaf this morning." He fumbled in his pocket and produced a notebook and pencil. "May I trouble you to write it down? I'm so very deaf at times that I—Thank you."

The girl wrote the direction, and the old gentleman bade her good morning and left. All down the lane he walked slowly with his stick. At the crossroads he turned, put the stick under his arm, thrust his spectacles into his pocket, and strode away in the ordinary guise of Martin Hewitt. He pulled out his notebook, examined Miss Webb's direction very carefully, and then went off another way altogether, toward the Hare and Hounds.

Kentish lounged moodily in his bar. "Well, my boy," said Hewitt, "has Steggles wiped out the tracks?"

"Not yet; I haven't told him. But he's somewhere about; I'll tell him now."

"No, don't. I don't think we'll have that done, after all. I expect he'll want to go out soon—at any rate, some time during the day. Let him go whenever he likes. I'll sit upstairs a bit in the club-room."

"Very well. But how do you know Steggles will be going out?"

"Well, he's pretty restless after his lost *protégé*, isn't he? I don't suppose he'll be able to remain idle long."

"And about Crockett. Do you give him up?"

"Oh, no! Don't you be impatient. I can't say I'm quite confident yet of laying hold of him—the time is so short, you see—but I think I shall at least have news for you by the evening."

Hewitt sat in the club-room until the afternoon, taking his lunch there. At length he saw, through the front window, Raggy Steggles walking down the road. In an instant Hewitt was downstairs and at the door. The road bent eighty yards away, and as soon as Steggles passed the bend the detective hurried after him.

All the way to Padfield town and more than half through it Hewitt dogged the trainer. In the end Steggles stopped at a corner and gave a note to a small boy who was playing near. The boy ran with the note to a bright, well-kept house at the opposite corner. Martin Hewitt was interested to observe the legend, "H. Danby, Contractor," on a board over a gate in the side wall of the garden behind this house. In five minutes a door in the side gate opened, and the head and shoulders of the red-faced man emerged. Steggles immediately hurried across and disappeared through the gate.

This was both interesting and instructive. Hewitt took up a position in the side street and waited. In ten minutes the trainer reappeared and hurried off the way he had come, along the street Hewitt had considerately left clear for him. Then Hewitt strolled toward the smart house and took a good look at it. At one corner of the small piece of forecourt garden, near the railings, a small, baize-covered, glass-fronted notice-board stood on two posts. On its top edge appeared the words, "H. Danby. Houses to be Sold or Let." But the only notice pinned to the green baize within was an old and dusty one, inviting tenants for three shops, which were suitable for any business, and which would be fitted to suit tenants. Apply within.

Hewitt pushed open the front gate and rang the doorbell. "There are some shops to let, I see," he said, when a maid appeared. "I should like to see them, if you will let me have the key."

"Master's out, sir. You can't see the shops till Monday."

"Dear me, that's unfortunate, I'm afraid I can't wait till Monday. Didn't Mr Danby leave any instructions, in case anybody should inquire?"

"Yes, sir—as I've told you. He said anybody who called about 'em must come again on Monday."

"Oh, very well, then; I suppose I must try. One of the shops is in High Street, isn't it?"

"No, sir; they're all in the new part—Granville Road."

"Ah, I'm afraid that will scarcely do. But I'll see. Good day."

Martin Hewitt walked away a couple of streets' lengths before he inquired the way to Granville Road. When at last he found that thoroughfare, in a new and muddy suburb, crowded with brick-heaps and half-finished streets, he took a slow walk along its entire length. It was a melancholy example of baffled enterprise. A row of a dozen or more shops had been built before any population had arrived to demand goods. Would-be tradesmen had taken many of these shops, and failure and disappointment stared from the windows. Some were half covered by shutters, because the scanty stock scarce sufficed to fill the remaining half. Others were shut almost altogether, the inmates only keeping open the door for their own convenience, and, perhaps, keeping down a shutter for the sake of a little light. Others, again, had not yet fallen so low, but struggled bravely still to maintain a show of business and prosperity, with very little success. Opposite the shops there still remained a dusty, ill-treated hedge and a forlorn-looking field, which an old board offered on building leases. Altogether a most depressing spot.

There was little difficulty in identifying the three shops offered for letting by Mr H. Danby. They were all together near the middle of the row, and were the only ones that appeared not yet to have been occupied. A dusty "To Let" bill hung in each window, with written directions to inquire of Mr H. Danby or at No. 7. Now No. 7 was a melancholy baker's shop, with a stock of three loaves and a plate of stale buns. The disappointed baker assured Hewitt that he usually kept the keys of the shops, but that the landlord, Mr Danby, had taken them away the day before to see how the ceilings were standing, and had not returned them. "But if you was thinking of taking a shop here," the poor baker added, with some hesitation, "I—I—if you'll excuse my advising you—I shouldn't recommend it. I've had a sickener of it myself."

Hewitt thanked the baker for his advice, wished him better luck in future, and left. To the Hare and Hounds his pace was brisk. "Come," he said, as he met Kentish's inquiring glance, "this has been a very good day, on the whole. I know where our man is now, and I think we can get him, by a little management."

"Where is he?"

"Oh, down in Padfield. As a matter of fact, he's being kept there against his will, we shall find. I see that your friend Mr Danby is a builder as well as a bookmaker."

"Not a regular builder. He speculates in a street of new houses now and again, that's all. But is he in it?"

"He's as deep in it as anybody, I think. Now, don't fly into a passion. There are a few others in it as well, but you'll do harm if you don't keep quiet."

"But go and get the police; come and fetch him, if you know where they're keeping him. Why—"

"So we will, if we can't do it without them. But it's quite possible we can, and without all the disturbance and, perhaps, delay that calling in the police would involve. Consider, now, in reference to your own arrangements. Wouldn't it pay you better to get him back quietly, without a soul knowing—perhaps not even Danby knowing—till the heat is run tomorrow?"

"Well, yes, it would, of course."

"Very good, then, so be it. Remember what I have told you about keeping your mouth shut; say nothing to Steggles or anybody. Is there a cab or brougham your son and I can have for the evening?"

"There's an old hiring landau in the stables you can shut up into a cab, if that'll do."

"Excellent. We'll run down to the town in it as soon as it's ready. But, first, a word about Crockett. What sort of a lad is he? Likely to give them trouble, show fight, and make a disturbance?"

"No, I should say not. He's no plucked un, certainly; all his manhood's in his legs, I believe. You see, he ain't a big sort o' chap at best, and he'd be pretty easy put upon—at least, I guess so."

"Very good, so much the better, for then he won't have been damaged, and they will probably only have one man to guard him. Now the carriage, please."

Young Kentish was a six-foot sergeant of grenadiers home on furlough, and luxuriating in plain clothes. He and Hewitt walked a little way toward the town, allowing the landau to catch them up. They traveled in it to within a hundred yards of the empty shops and then alighted, bidding the driver wait.

"I shall show you three empty shops," Hewitt said, as he and young Kentish walked down Granville Road. "I am pretty sure that Sammy Crockett is in one of them, and I am pretty sure that that is the middle one. Take a look as we go past."

When the shops had been slowly passed, Hewitt resumed: "Now, did you see anything about those shops that told a tale of any sort?"

"No," Sergeant Kentish replied. "I can't say I noticed anything beyond the fact that they were empty—and likely to stay so, I should think."

"We'll stroll back, and look in at the windows, if nobody's watching us," Hewitt said. "You see, it's reasonable to suppose they've put him in the middle one, because that would suit their purpose best. The shops at each side of the three are occupied, and, if the prisoner struggled, or shouted, or made an uproar, he might be heard if he were in one of the shops next those inhabited. So that the middle shop is the most likely. Now, see there," he went on, as they stopped before the window of the shop in question, "over at the back there's a staircase not yet partitioned off. It goes down below and up above. On the stairs and on the floor near them there are muddy footmarks. These must have been made today, else they would not be muddy, but dry and dusty, since there hasn't been a shower for a week till today. Move on again. Then you noticed that there were no other such marks in the shop. Consequently the man with the muddy feet did not come in by the front door, but by the back; otherwise he would have made a trail from the door. So we will go round to the back ourselves."

It was now growing dusk. The small pieces of ground behind the shops were bounded by a low fence, containing a door for each house.

"This door is bolted inside, of course," Hewitt said, "but there is no difficulty in climbing. I think we had better wait in the garden till dark. In the meantime, the jailer, whoever he is, may come out; in which case we shall pounce on him as soon as he opens the door. You have that few yards of cord in your pocket, I think? And my handkerchief, properly rolled, will make a very good gag. Now over."

They climbed the fence and quietly approached the house, placing themselves in the angle of an outhouse out of sight from the windows. There was no sound, and no light appeared. Just above the ground about a foot of window was visible, with a grating over it, apparently lighting a basement. Suddenly Hewitt touched his companion's arm and pointed toward the window. A faint rustling sound was perceptible, and, as nearly as could be discerned in the darkness, some white blind or covering was placed over the glass from the inside. Then came the sound of a striking match, and at the side edge of the window there was a faint streak of light.

"That's the place," Hewitt whispered. "Come, we'll make a push for it. You stand against the wall at one side of the door and I'll stand at the other, and we'll have him as he comes out. Quietly, now, and I'll startle them."

He took a stone from among the rubbish littering the garden and flung it crashing through the window. There was a loud exclamation from within, the blind fell, and somebody rushed to the back door and flung it open. Instantly Kentish let fly a heavy right-hander, and the man went over like a skittle. In a moment Hewitt was upon him and the gag in his mouth.

"Hold him," Hewitt whispered, hurriedly. "I'll see if there are others."

He peered down through the low window. Within Sammy Crockett, his bare legs dangling from beneath his long overcoat, sat on a packing-box, leaning with his head on his hand and his back toward the window. A guttering candle stood on the mantelpiece, and the newspaper which had been stretched across the window lay in scattered sheets on the floor. No other person besides Sammy was visible.

They led their prisoner indoors. Young Kentish recognized him as a public-house loafer and race-course ruffian, well known in the neighborhood.

"So it's you, is it, Browdie?" he said. "I've caught you one hard clump, and I've half a mind to make it a score more. But you'll get it pretty warm one way or another before this job's forgotten."

Sammy Crockett was overjoyed at his rescue. He had not been ill-treated, he explained, but had been thoroughly cowed by Browdie, who had from time to time threatened him savagely with an iron bar by way of persuading him to quietness and submission. He had been fed, and had taken no worse harm than a slight stiffness from his adventure, due to his light under-attire of jersey and knee-shorts.

Sergeant Kentish tied Browdie's elbows firmly together behind, and carried the line round the ankles, bracing all up tight. Then he ran a knot from one wrist to the other over the back of the neck, and left the prisoner, trussed and helpless, on the heap of straw that had been Sammy's bed.

"You won't be very jolly, I expect," Kentish said, "for some time. You can't shout and you can't walk, and I know you can't untie yourself. You'll get a bit hungry, too, perhaps, but that'll give you an appetite. I don't suppose you'll be disturbed till some time tomorrow, unless our friend Danby turns up in the meantime. But you can come along to jail instead, if you prefer it."

They left him where he lay, and took Sammy to the old landau. Sammy walked in slippers, carrying his spiked shoes, hanging by the lace, in his hand.

"Ah," said Hewitt, "I think I know the name of the young lady who gave you those slippers."

Crockett looked ashamed and indignant. "Yes," he said, "they've done me nicely between 'em. But I'll pay her—I'll—"

"Hush, hush!" Hewitt said; "you mustn't talk unkindly of a lady, you know. Get into this carriage, and we'll take you home. We'll see if I can tell you your adventures without making a mistake. First, you had a note from Miss Webb, telling you that you were mistaken in supposing she had slighted you, and that, as a matter of fact, she had quite done with somebody else—left him—of whom you were jealous. Isn't that so?"

"Well, yes," young Crockett answered, blushing deeply under the carriage-lamp; "but I don't see how you come to know that."

"Then she went on to ask you to get rid of Steggles on Thursday afternoon for a few minutes, and speak to her in the back lane. Now, your running pumps, with their thin soles, almost like paper, no heels and long spikes, hurt your feet horribly if you walk on hard ground, don't they?"

"Ay, that they do—enough to cripple you. I'd never go on much hard ground with 'em."

"They're not like cricket shoes, I see."

"Not a bit. Cricket shoes you can walk anywhere in!"

"Well, she knew this—I think I know who told her—and she promised to bring you a new pair of slippers, and to throw them over the fence for you to come out in."

"I s'pose she's been tellin' you all this?" Crockett said, mournfully. "You couldn't ha' seen the letter; I saw her tear it up and put the bits in her pocket. She asked me for it in the lane, in case Steggles saw it."

"Well, at any rate, you sent Steggles away, and the slippers did come over, and you went into the lane. You walked with her as far as the road at the end, and then you were seized and gagged, and put into a carriage."

"That was Browdie did that," said Crockett, "and another chap I don't know. But—why, this is Padfield High Street?" He looked through the window and regarded the familiar shops with astonishment.

"Of course it is. Where did you think it was?"

"Why, where was that place you found me in?"

"Granville Road, Padfield. I suppose they told you you were in another town?"

"Told me it was Newstead Hatch. They drove for about three or four hours, and kept me down on the floor between the seats so as I couldn't see where we was going."

"Done for two reasons," said Hewitt. "First, to mystify you, and prevent any discovery of the people directing the conspiracy; and second, to be able to put you indoors at night and unobserved. Well, I think I have told you all you know yourself now as far as the carriage.

"But there is the Hare and Hounds just in front. We'll pull up here, and I'll get out and see if the coast is clear. I fancy Mr Kentish would rather you came in unnoticed."

In a few seconds Hewitt was back, and Crockett was conveyed indoors by a side entrance. Hewitt's instructions to the landlord were few, but emphatic. "Don't tell Steggles about it," he said; "make an excuse to get rid of him, and send him out of the house. Take Crockett into some other bedroom, not his own, and let your son look after him. Then come here, and I'll tell you all about it."

Sammy Crockett was undergoing a heavy grooming with white embrocation at the hands of Sergeant Kentish when the landlord returned to Hewitt. "Does Danby know you've got him?" he asked. "How did you do it?"

"Danby doesn't know yet, and with luck he won't know till he sees Crockett running tomorrow. The man who has sold you is Steggles."

"Steggles?"

"Steggles it is. At the very first, when Steggles rushed in to report Sammy Crockett missing, I suspected him. You didn't, I suppose?"

"No. He's always been considered a straight man, and he looked as startled as anybody."

"Yes, I must say he acted it very well. But there was something suspicious in his story. What did he say? Crockett had remarked a chilliness, and asked for a sweater, which Steggles went to fetch. Now, just think. You understand these things. Would any trainer who knew his business (as Steggles does) have gone to bring out a sweater for his man to change for his jersey in the open air, at the very time the man was complaining of chilliness? Of course not. He would have taken his man indoors again and let him change there under shelter. Then supposing Steggles had really been surprised at missing Crockett, wouldn't he have looked about, found the gate open, and *told* you it was open when he first came in? He said nothing of that—we found the gate open for ourselves. So that from the beginning I had a certain opinion of Steggles."

"What you say seems pretty plain now, although it didn't strike me at the time. But, if Steggles was selling us, why couldn't he have drugged the lad? That would have been a deal simpler."

"Because Steggles is a good trainer, and has a certain reputation to keep up. It would have done him no good to have had a runner drugged while under his care; certainly it would have cooked his goose with *you*. It was much the safer thing to connive at kidnapping. That put all the active work into other hands, and left him safe, even if the trick failed. Now, you remember that we traced the prints of Crockett's spiked shoes to within a couple of yards from the fence, and that there they ceased suddenly?"

"Yes. You said it looked as though he had flown up into the air; and so it did."

"But I was sure that it was by that gate that Crockett had left, and by no other. He couldn't have got through the house without being seen, and there was no other way—let alone the evidence of the unbolted gate. Therefore, as the footprints ceased where they did, and were not repeated anywhere in the lane, I knew that he had taken his spiked shoes off—probably changed them for something else, because a runner anxious as to his chances would never risk walking on bare feet, with a chance of cutting them. Ordinary, broad, smooth-soled slippers would leave no impression on the coarse cinders bordering the track, and nothing short of spiked shoes would leave a mark on the hard path in the lane behind. The spike-tracks were leading, not directly toward the door, but in the direction of the fence, when they stopped; somebody had handed, or thrown, the slippers over the fence, and he had changed them on the spot. The enemy had calculated upon the spikes leaving a track in the lane that might lead us in our search, and had arranged accordingly.

"So far so good. I could see no footprints near the gate in the lane. You will remember that I sent Steggles off to watch at the Cop before I went out to the back—merely, of course, to get him out of the way. I went out into the lane, leaving you behind, and walked its whole length, first toward the Old Kilns and then back toward the road. I found nothing to help me except these small pieces of paper—which are here in my pocketbook, by the by. Of course this 'mmy' might have meant 'Jimmy' or 'Tommy' as possibly as 'Sammy,' but they were not to be rejected on that account. Certainly Crockett had been decoyed out of your ground, not taken by force, or there would have been marks of a scuffle in the cinders. And as his request for a sweater was probably an excuse—because it was not at all a cold afternoon—he must have previously designed going out. Inference, a letter received; and here were pieces of a letter. Now, in the light of what I have said, look at these pieces. First, there is the 'mmy'—that I have dealt with. Then see this 'throw them ov'—clearly a part of 'throw them over'; exactly what had probably been done with the slippers. Then the 'poor f,' coming just on the line before, and seen, by joining up with this other piece, might easily be a reference to 'poor feet.' These coincidences, one on the other, went far to establish the identity of the letter, and to confirm my previous impressions. But then there is something else. Two other pieces evidently mean 'left him,' and 'right away,' perhaps; but there is another, containing almost all of the words 'hate his,' with the word 'hate' underlined. Now, who writes 'hate' with the emphasis of underscoring—who but a woman? The writing is large and not very regular; it might easily be that of a half-educated woman. Here was something more—Sammy had been enticed away by a woman.

"Now, I remembered that, when we went into the taproom on Wednesday, some of his companions were chaffing Crockett about a certain Nancy Webb, and the chaff went home, as was plain to see. The woman, then, who could most easily entice Sammy Crockett away was Nancy Webb. I resolved to find who Nancy Webb was and learn more of her.

"Meantime, I took a look at the road at the end of the lane. It was damper than the lane, being lower, and overhung by trees. There were many wheel-tracks, but only one set that turned in the road and went back the way it came, toward the town; and they were narrow wheels—carriage wheels. Crockett tells me now that they drove him about for a long time before shutting him up; probably the inconvenience of taking him straight to the hiding-place didn't strike them when they first drove off.

"A few inquiries soon set me in the direction of the Plough and Miss Nancy Webb. I had the curiosity to look around the place as I approached, and there, in the garden behind the house, were Steggles and the young lady in earnest confabulation!

"Every conjecture became a certainty. Steggles was the lover of whom Crockett was jealous, and he had employed the girl to bring Sammy out. I watched Steggles home, and gave you a hint to keep him there.

"But the thing that remained was to find Steggles' employer in this business. I was glad to be in when Danby called. He came, of course, to hear if you would blurt out anything, and to learn, if possible, what steps you were taking. He failed. By way of making assurance doubly sure I took a short walk this morning in the character of a deaf gentleman, and got Miss Webb to write me a direction that comprised three of the words on these scraps of paper—'left,' 'right,' and 'lane'; see, they correspond, the peculiar 'f's,' 't's,' and all.

"Now, I felt perfectly sure that Steggles would go for his pay today. In the first place, I knew that people mixed up with shady transactions in professional pedestrianism are not apt to trust one another far—they know better. Therefore Steggles wouldn't have had his bribe first. But he would take care to get it before the Saturday heats were run, because once they were over the thing was done, and the principal conspirator might have refused to pay up, and Steggles couldn't have helped himself. Again I hinted he should not go out till I could follow him, and this afternoon, when he went, follow him I did. I saw him go into Danby's house by the side way and come away again. Danby it was, then, who had arranged the business; and nobody was more likely, considering his large pecuniary stake against Crockett's winning this race.

"But now how to find Crockett? I made up my mind he wouldn't be in Danby's own house. That would be a deal too risky, with servants about and so on. I saw that Danby was a builder, and had three shops to let—it was on a paper before his house. What more likely prison than an empty house? I knocked at Danby's door and asked for the keys of those shops. I couldn't have them. The servant told me Danby was out (a manifest lie, for I had just seen him), and that nobody could see the shops till Monday. But I got out of her the address of the shops, and that was all I wanted at the time.

"Now, why was nobody to see those shops till Monday? The interval was suspicious—just enough to enable Crockett to be sent away again and cast loose after the Saturday racing, supposing him to be kept in one of the empty buildings. I went off at once and looked at the shops, forming my conclusions as to which would be the most likely for Danby's purpose. Here I had another confirmation of my ideas. A poor, half-bankrupt baker in one of the shops had, by the bills, the custody of a set of keys; but he, too, told me I couldn't have them; Danby had taken them away—and on Thursday, the very day—with some trivial excuse, and hadn't brought them back. That was all I wanted or could expect in the way of guidance. The whole thing was plain. The rest you know all about."

"Well, you're certainly as smart as they give you credit for, I must say. But suppose Danby had taken down his 'To Let' notice, what would you have done, then?"

"We had our course, even then. We should have gone to Danby, astounded him by telling him all about his little games, terrorized him with threats of the law, and made him throw up his hand and send Crockett back. But, as it is, you see, he doesn't know at this moment—probably won't know till tomorrow afternoon—that the lad is safe and sound here. You will probably use the interval to make him pay for losing the game—by some of the ingenious financial devices you are no doubt familiar with."

"Ay, that I will. He'll give any price against Crockett now, so long as the bet don't come direct from me."

"But about Crockett, now," Hewitt went on. "Won't this confinement be likely to have damaged his speed for a day or two?"

"Ah, perhaps," the landlord replied; "but, bless ye, that won't matter. There's four more in his heat tomorrow. Two I know aren't tryers, and the other two I can hold in at a couple of quid apiece any day. The third round and final won't be till tomorrow week, and he'll be as fit as ever by then. It's as safe as ever it was. How much are you going to have on? I'll lump it on for you safe enough. This is a chance not to be missed; it's picking money up."

"Thank you; I don't think I'll have anything to do with it. This professional pedestrian business doesn't seem a pretty one at all. I don't call myself a moralist, but, if you'll excuse my saying so, the thing is scarcely the game I care to pick tap money at in any way."

"Oh, very well! if you think so, I won't persuade ye, though I don't think so much of your smartness as I did, after that. Still, we won't quarrel; you've done me a mighty good turn, that I must say, and I only feel I aren't level without doing something to pay the debt. Come, now, you've got your trade as I've got mine. Let me have the bill, and I'll pay it like a lord, and feel a deal more pleased than if you made a favor of it—not that I'm above a favor, of course. But I'd prefer paying, and that's a fact."

"My dear sir, you have paid," Hewitt said, with a smile. "You paid in advance. It was a bargain, wasn't it, that I should do your business if you would help me in mine? Very well; a bargain's a bargain, and we've both performed our parts. And you mustn't be offended at what I said just now."

"That I won't! But as to that Raggy Steggles, once those heats are over tomorrow, I'll—well—"

It was on the following Sunday week that Martin Hewitt, in his rooms in London, turned over his paper and read, under the head "Padfield Annual 135 Yards Handicap," this announcement: "Final heat: Crockett, first; Willis, second; Trewby, third; Owen, 0; Howell, 0. A runaway win by nearly three yards."

3

THE CASE OF MR FOGGATT

Almost the only dogmatism that Martin Hewitt permitted himself in regard to his professional methods was one on the matter of accumulative probabilities. Often when I have remarked upon the apparently trivial nature of the clews by which he allowed himself to be guided—sometimes, to all seeming, in the very face of all likelihood—he has replied that two trivialities, pointing in the same direction, became at once, by their mere agreement, no trivialities at all, but enormously important considerations. "If I were in search of a man," he would say, "of whom I knew nothing but that he squinted, bore a birthmark on his right hand, and limped, and I observed a man who answered to the first peculiarity, so far the clue would be trivial, because thousands of men squint. Now, if that man presently moved and exhibited a birthmark on his right hand, the value of that squint and that mark would increase at once a hundred or a thousand fold. Apart they are little; together much. The weight of evidence is not doubled merely; it would be only doubled if half the men who squinted had right-hand birthmarks; whereas the proportion, if it could be ascertained, would be, perhaps, more like one in ten thousand. The two trivialities, pointing in the same direction, become very strong evidence. And, when the man is seen to walk with a limp, that limp (another triviality), re-enforcing the others, brings the matter to the rank of a practical certainty. The Bertillon system of identification—what is it but a summary of trivialities? Thousands of men are of the same height, thousands of the same length of foot, thousands of the same girth of head—thousands correspond in any separate measurement you may name. It is when the measurements are taken *together* that you have your man identified forever. Just consider how few, if any, of your friends correspond exactly in any two personal peculiarities." Hewitt's dogma received its illustration unexpectedly close at home.

The old house wherein my chambers and Hewitt's office were situated contained, besides my own, two or three more bachelors' dens, in addition to the offices on the ground and first and second floors. At the very top of all, at the back, a fat, middle-aged man, named Foggatt, occupied a set of four rooms. It was only after a long residence, by an accidental remark of the housekeeper's, that I learned the man's name, which was not painted on his door or displayed, with all the others, on the wall of the ground-floor porch.

Mr Foggatt appeared to have few friends, but lived in something as nearly approaching luxury as an old bachelor living in chambers can live. An ascending case of champagne was a common phenomenon of the staircase, and I have more than once seen a picture, destined for the top floor, of a sort that went far to awaken green covetousness in the heart of a poor journalist.

The man himself was not altogether prepossessing. Fat as he was, he had a way of carrying his head forward on his extended neck and gazing widely about with a pair of the roundest and most prominent eyes I remember to have ever seen, except in a fish. On the whole, his appearance was rather vulgar, rather arrogant, and rather suspicious, without any very pronounced quality of any sort. But certainly he was not pretty. In the end, however, he was found shot dead in his sitting-room.

It was in this way: Hewitt and I had dined together at my club, and late in the evening had returned to my rooms to smoke and discuss whatever came uppermost. I had made a bargain that day with two speculative odd lots at a book sale, each of which contained a hidden prize. We sat talking and turning over these books while time went unperceived, when suddenly we were startled by a loud report. Clearly it was in the building. We listened for a moment, but heard nothing else, and then Hewitt expressed his opinion that the report was that of a gunshot. Gunshots in residential chambers are not common things, wherefore I got up and went to the landing, looking up the stairs and down.

At the top of the next flight I saw Mrs Clayton, the housekeeper. She appeared to be frightened, and told me that the report came from Mr Foggatt's room. She thought he might have had an accident with the pistol that usually lay on his mantelpiece. We went upstairs with her, and she knocked at Mr Foggatt's door.

There was no reply. Through the ventilating fanlight over the door it could be seen that there were lights within, a sign, Mrs Clayton maintained, that Mr Foggatt was not out. We knocked again, much more loudly, and called, but still ineffectually. The door was locked, and an application of the housekeeper's key proved that the tenant's key had been left in the lock inside. Mrs Clayton's conviction that "something had happened" became distressing, and in the end Hewitt pried open the door with a small poker.

Something *had* happened. In the sitting-room Mr Foggatt sat with his head bowed over the table, quiet and still. The head was ill to look at, and by it lay a large revolver, of the full-sized army pattern. Mrs Clayton ran back toward the landing with faint screams.

"Run, Brett!" said Hewitt; "a doctor and a policeman!"

I bounced down the stairs half a flight at a time. "First," I thought, "a doctor. He may not be dead." I could think of no doctor in the immediate neighborhood, but ran up the street away from the Strand, as being the more likely direction for the doctor, although less so for the policeman. It took me a good five minutes to find the medico, after being led astray by a red lamp at a private hotel, and another five to get back, with a policeman.

Foggatt was dead, without a doubt. Probably had shot himself, the doctor thought, from the powder-blackening and other circumstances. Certainly nobody could have left the room by the door, or he must have passed my landing, while the fact of the door being found locked from the inside made the thing impossible. There were two windows to the room, both of which were shut, one being fastened by the catch, while the catch of the other was broken—an old fracture. Below these windows was a sheer drop of fifty feet or more, without a foot or hand-hold near. The windows in the other rooms were shut and fastened. Certainly it seemed suicide— unless it were one of those accidents that will occur to people who fiddle ignorantly with firearms. Soon the rooms were in possession of the police, and we were turned out.

We looked in at the housekeeper's kitchen, where her daughter was reviving and calming Mrs Clayton with gin and water.

"You mustn't upset yourself, Mrs Clayton," Hewitt said, "or what will become of us all? The doctor thinks it was an accident."

He took a small bottle of sewing-machine oil from his pocket and handed it to the daughter, thanking her for the loan.

There was little evidence at the inquest. The shot had been heard, the body had been found—that was the practical sum of the matter. No friends or relatives of the dead man came forward. The doctor gave his opinion as to the probability of suicide or an accident, and the police evidence tended in the same direction. Nothing had been found to indicate that any other person had been near the dead man's rooms on the night of the fatality. On the other hand, his papers, bankbook, etc., proved him to be a man of considerable substance, with no apparent motive for suicide. The police had been unable to trace any relatives, or, indeed, any nearer connections than casual acquaintances, fellow-clubmen, and so on. The jury found that Mr Foggatt had died by accident.

"Well, Brett," Hewitt asked me afterward, "what do you think of the verdict?"

I said that it seemed to be the most reasonable one possible, and to square with the common-sense view of the case.

"Yes," he replied, "perhaps it does. From the point of view of the jury, and on their information, their verdict was quite reasonable. Nevertheless, Mr Foggatt did not shoot himself. He was shot by a rather tall, active young man, perhaps a sailor, but certainly a gymnast—a young man whom I think I could identify if I saw him."

"But how do you know this?"

"By the simplest possible inferences, which you may easily guess, if you will but think."

"But, then, why didn't you say this at the inquest?"

"My dear fellow, they don't want any inferences and conjectures at an inquest; they only want evidence. If I had traced the murderer, of course then I should have communicated with the police. As a matter of fact, it is quite possible that the police have observed and know as much as I do—or more. They don't give everything away at an inquest, you know. It wouldn't do."

"But, if you are right, how did the man get away?"

"Come, we are near home now. Let us take a look at the back of the house. He *couldn't* have left by Foggatt's landing door, as we know; and as he *was* there (I am certain of that), and as the chimney is out of the question—for there was a good fire in the grate—he must have gone out by the window. Only one window is possible—that with the broken catch—for all the others were fastened inside. Out of that window, then, he went."

"But how? The window is fifty feet up."

"Of course it is. But why *will* you persist in assuming that the only way of escape by a window is downward? See, now, look up there. The window is at the top floor, and it has a very broad sill. Over the window is nothing but the flat face of the gable-end; but to the right, and a foot or two above the level of the top of the window, an iron gutter ends. Observe, it is not of lead composition, but a strong iron gutter, supported, just at its end, by an iron bracket. If a tall man stood on the end of the window-sill, steadying himself by the left hand and leaning to the right, he could just touch the end of this gutter with his right hand. The full stretch, toe to finger, is seven feet three inches. I have measured it. An active gymnast, or a sailor, could catch the gutter with a slight spring, and by it draw himself upon the roof. You will say he would have to be *very* active, dexterous, and cool. So he would. And that very fact helps us, because it narrows the field of inquiry. We know the sort of man to look for. Because, being certain (as I am) that the man was in the room, I *know* that he left in the way I am telling you. He must have left in some way, and, all the other ways being impossible, this alone remains, difficult as the feat may seem. The fact of his shutting the window behind him further proves his coolness and address at so great a height from the ground."

All this was very plain, but the main point was still dark.

"You say you *know* that another man was in the room," I said; "how do you know that?"

"As I said, by an obvious inference. Come, now, you shall guess how I arrived at that inference. You often speak of your interest in my work, and the attention with which you follow it. This shall be a simple exercise for you. You saw everything in the room as plainly as I myself. Bring the scene back to your memory, and think over the various small objects littering about, and how they would affect the case. Quick observation is the first essential for my work. Did you see a newspaper, for instance?"

"Yes. There was an evening paper on the floor, but I didn't examine it."

"Anything else?"

"On the table there was a whisky decanter, taken from the tantalus-stand on the sideboard, and one glass. That, by the by," I added, "looked as though only one person were present."

"So it did, perhaps, although the inference wouldn't be very strong. Go on!"

"There was a fruit-stand on the sideboard, with a plate beside it containing a few nutshells, a piece of apple, a pair of nutcrackers, and, I think, some orange peel. There was, of course, all the ordinary furniture, but no chair pulled up to the table, except that used by Foggatt himself. That's all I noticed, I think. Stay—there was an ash-tray on the table, and a partly burned cigar near it—only one cigar, though."

"Excellent—excellent, indeed, as far as memory and simple observation go. You saw everything plainly, and you remember everything. Surely *now* you know how I found out that another man had just left?"

"No, I don't; unless there were different kinds of ash in the ash-tray."

"That is a fairly good suggestion, but there were not—there was only a single ash, corresponding in every way to that on the cigar. Don't you remember everything that I did as we went downstairs?"

"You returned a bottle of oil to the housekeeper's daughter, I think."

"I did. Doesn't that give you a hint? Come, you surely have it now?"

"I haven't."

"Then I sha'n't tell you; you don't deserve it. Think, and don't mention the subject again till you have at least one guess to make. The thing stares you in the face; you see it, you remember it, and yet you *won't* see it. I won't encourage your slovenliness of thought, my boy, by telling you what you can know for yourself if you like. Goodby—I'm off now. There's a case in hand I can't neglect."

"Don't you propose to go further into this, then?"

Hewitt shrugged his shoulders. "I'm not a policeman," he said. "The case is in very good hands. Of course, if anybody comes to me to do it as a matter of business, I'll take it up. It's very interesting, but I can't neglect my regular work for it. Naturally, I shall keep my eyes open and my memory in order. Sometimes these things come into the hands by themselves, as it were; in that case, of course, I am a loyal citizen, and ready to help the law. *Au revoir!*"

I am a busy man myself, and thought little more of Hewitt's conundrum for some time; indeed, when I did think, I saw no way to the answer. A week after the inquest I took a holiday (I had written my nightly leaders regularly every day for the past five years), and saw no more of Hewitt for six weeks. After my return, with still a few days of leave to run, one evening we together turned into Luzatti's, off Coventry Street, for dinner.

"I have been here several times lately," Hewitt said; "they feed you very well. No, not that table"—he seized my arm as I turned to an unoccupied corner—"I fancy it's draughty." He led the way to a longer table where a dark, lithe, and (as well as could be seen) tall young man already sat, and took chairs opposite him.

We had scarcely seated ourselves before Hewitt broke into a torrent of conversation on the subject of bicycling. As our previous conversation had been of a literary sort, and as I had never known Hewitt at any other time to show the slightest interest in bicycling, this rather surprised me. I had, however, such a general outsider's grasp of the subject as is usual in a journalist-of-all-work, and managed to keep the talk going from my side. As we went on I could see the face of the young man opposite brighten with interest. He was a rather fine-looking fellow, with a dark, though very clear skin, but had a hard, angry look of eye, a prominence of cheekbone, and a squareness of jaw that gave him a rather uninviting aspect. As Hewitt rattled on, however, our neighbor's expression became one of pleasant interest merely.

"Of course," Hewitt said, "we've a number of very capital men just now, but I believe a deal in the forgotten riders of five, ten, and fifteen years back. Osmond, I believe, was better than any man riding now, and I think it would puzzle some of them to beat Furnivall as he was, at his best. But poor old Cortis—really, I believe he was as good as anybody. Nobody ever beat Cortis—except—let me see—I think somebody beat Cortis once—who was it now? I can't remember."

"Liles," said the young man opposite, looking up quickly.

"Ah, yes—Liles it was; Charley Liles. Wasn't it a championship?"

"Mile championship, 1880; Cortis won the other three, though."

"Yes, so he did. I saw Cortis when he first broke the old 2.46 mile record." And straightway Hewitt plunged into a whirl of talk of bicycles, tricycles, records, racing cyclists, Hillier, and Synyer and Noel Whiting, Taylerson and Appleyard—talk wherein the young man opposite bore an animated share, while I was left in the cold.

Our new friend, it seems, had himself been a prominent racing bicyclist a few years back, and was presently, at Hewitt's request, exhibiting a neat gold medal that hung at his watch-guard. That was won, he explained, in the old tall bicycle days, the days of bad tracks, when every racing cyclist carried cinder scars on his face from numerous accidents. He pointed to a blue mark on his forehead, which, he told us, was a track scar, and described a bad fall that had cost him two teeth, and broken others. The gaps among his teeth were plain to see as he smiled.

Presently the waiter brought dessert, and the young man opposite took an apple. Nut-crackers and a fruit-knife lay on our side of the stand, and Hewitt turned the stand to offer him the knife.

"No, thanks," he said; "I only polish a good apple, never peel it. It's a mistake, except with thick-skinned foreign ones."

And he began to munch the apple as only a boy or a healthy athlete can. Presently he turned his head to order coffee. The waiter's back was turned, and he had to be called twice. To my unutterable amazement Hewitt reached swiftly across the table, snatched the half-eaten apple from the young man's plate and pocketed it, gazing immediately, with an abstracted air, at a painted Cupid on the ceiling.

Our neighbor turned again, looked doubtfully at his plate and the table-cloth about it, and then shot a keen glance in the direction of Hewitt. He said nothing, however, but took his coffee and his bill, deliberately drank the former, gazing quietly at Hewitt as he did it, paid the latter, and left.

Immediately Hewitt was on his feet and, taking an umbrella, which stood near, followed. Just as he reached the door he met our late neighbor, who had turned suddenly back.

"Your umbrella, I think?" Hewitt asked, offering it.

"Yes, thanks." But the man's eye had more than its former hardness, and his jaw muscles tightened as I looked. He turned and went. Hewitt came back to me. "Pay the bill," he said, "and go back to your rooms; I will come on later. I must follow this man — it's the Foggatt case." As he went out I heard a cab rattle away, and immediately after it another.

I paid the bill and went home. It was ten o'clock before Hewitt turned up, calling in at his office below on his way up to me.

"Mr Sidney Mason," he said, "is the gentleman the police will be wanting tomorrow, I expect, for the Foggatt murder. He is as smart a man as I remember ever meeting, and has done me rather neatly twice this evening."

"You mean the man we sat opposite at Luzatti's, of course?"

"Yes, I got his name, of course, from the reverse of that gold medal he was good enough to show me. But I fear he has bilked me over the address. He suspected me, that was plain, and left his umbrella by way of experiment to see if I were watching him sharply enough to notice the circumstance, and to avail myself of it to follow him. I was hasty and fell into the trap. He cabbed it away from Luzatti's, and I cabbed it after him. He has led me a pretty dance up and down London tonight, and two cabbies have made quite a stroke of business out of us. In the end he entered a house of which, of course, I have taken the address, but I expect he doesn't live there. He is too smart a man to lead me to his den; but the police can certainly find something of him at the house he went in at — and, I expect, left by the back way. By the way, you never guessed that simple little puzzle as to how I found that this *was* a murder, did you? You see it now, of course?"

"Something to do with that apple you stole, I suppose?"

"Something to do with it? I should think so, you worthy innocent. Just ring your bell; we'll borrow Mrs Clayton's sewing-machine oil again. On the night we broke into Foggatt's room you saw the nutshells and the bitten remains of an apple on the sideboard, and you remembered it; and yet you couldn't see that in that piece of apple possibly lay an important piece of evidence. Of course I never expected you to have arrived at any conclusion, as I had, because I had ten minutes in which to examine that apple, and to do what I did with it. But, at least, you should have seen the possibility of evidence in it.

"First, now, the apple was white. A bitten apple, as you must have observed, turns of a reddish brown color if left to stand long. Different kinds of apples brown with different rapidities, and the browning always begins at the core. This is one of the twenty thousand tiny things that few people take the trouble to notice, but which it is useful for a man in my position to know. A russet will brown quite quickly. The apple on the sideboard was, as near as I could tell, a Newtown pippin or other apple of that kind, which will brown at the core in from twenty minutes to half an hour, and in other parts in a quarter of an hour more. When we saw it, it was white, with barely a tinge of brown about the exposed core. Inference, somebody had been eating it fifteen or twenty minutes before, perhaps a little longer—an inference supported by the fact that it was only partly eaten.

"I examined that apple, and found it bore marks of very irregular teeth. While you were gone, I oiled it over, and, rushing down to my rooms, where I always have a little plaster of Paris handy for such work, took a mold of the part where the teeth had left the clearest marks. I then returned the apple to its place for the police to use if they thought fit. Looking at my mold, it was plain that the person who had bitten that apple had lost two teeth, one at top and one below, not exactly opposite, but nearly so. The other teeth, although they would appear to have been fairly sound, were irregular in size and line. Now, the dead man had, as I saw, a very excellent set of false teeth, regular and sharp, with none missing. Therefore it was plain that somebody *else* had been eating that apple. Do I make myself clear?"

"Quite! Go on!"

"There were other inferences to be made—slighter, but all pointing the same way. For instance, a man of Foggatt's age does not, as a rule, munch an unpeeled apple like a schoolboy. Inference, a young man, and healthy. Why I came to the conclusion that he was tall, active, a gymnast, and perhaps a sailor, I have already told you, when we examined the outside of Foggatt's window. It was also pretty clear that robbery was not the motive, since nothing was disturbed, and that a friendly conversation had preceded the murder—witness the drinking and the eating of the apple. Whether or not the police noticed these things I can't say. If they had had their best men on, they certainly would, I think; but the case, to a rough observer, looked so clearly one of accident or suicide that possibly they didn't.

"As I said, after the inquest I was unable to devote any immediate time to the case, but I resolved to keep my eyes open. The man to look for was tall, young, strong and active, with a very irregular set of teeth, a tooth missing from the lower jaw just to the left of the center, and another from the upper jaw a little farther still toward the left. He might possibly be a person I had seen about the premises (I have a good memory for faces), or, of course, he possibly might not.

"Just before you returned from your holiday I noticed a young man at Luzatti's whom I remembered to have seen somewhere about the offices in this building. He was tall, young, and so on, but I had a client with me, and was unable to examine him more narrowly; indeed, as I was not exactly engaged on the case, and as there are several tall young men about, I took little trouble. But today, finding the same young man with a vacant seat opposite him, I took the opportunity of making a closer acquaintance."

"You certainly managed to draw him out."

"Oh, yes; the easiest person in the world to draw out is a cyclist. The easiest cyclist to draw out is, of course, the novice, but the next easiest is the veteran. When you see a healthy, well-trained-looking man, who, nevertheless, has a slight stoop in the shoulders, and, maybe, a medal on his watch-guard, it is always a safe card to try him first with a little cycle-racing talk. I soon brought Mr Mason out of his shell, read his name on his medal, and had a chance of observing his teeth—indeed, he spoke of them himself. Now, as I observed just now, there are several tall, athletic young men about, and also there are several men who have lost teeth. But now I saw that this tall and athletic young man had lost exactly *two* teeth—one from the lower jaw, just to the left of the center, and another from the upper jaw, farther still toward the left! Trivialities, pointing in the same direction, became important considerations. More, his teeth were irregular throughout, and, as nearly as I could remember it, looked remarkably like this little plaster mold of mine."

He produced from his pocket an irregular lump of plaster, about three inches long. On one side of this appeared in relief the likeness of two irregular rows of six or eight teeth, minus one in each row, where a deep gap was seen, in the position spoken of by my friend. He proceeded:

"This was enough at least to set me after this young man. But he gave me the greatest chance of all when he turned and left his apple (eaten unpeeled, remember!—another important triviality) on his plate. I'm afraid I wasn't at all polite, and I ran the risk of arousing his suspicions, but I couldn't resist the temptation to steal it. I did, as you saw, and here it is."

He brought the apple from his coat-pocket. One bitten side, placed against the upper half of the mold, fitted precisely, a projection of apple filling exactly the deep gap. The other side similarly fitted the lower half.

"There's no getting behind that, you see," Hewitt remarked. "Merely observing the man's teeth was a guide, to some extent, but this is as plain as his signature or his thumb impression.

You'll never find two men *bite* exactly alike, no matter whether they leave distinct teeth-marks or not. Here, by the by, is Mrs Clayton's oil. We'll take another mold from this apple, and compare *them*."

He oiled the apple, heaped a little plaster in a newspaper, took my water-jug, and rapidly pulled off a hard mold. The parts corresponding to the merely broken places in the apple were, of course, dissimilar; but as to the teeth-marks, the impressions were identical.

"That will do, I think," Hewitt said. "Tomorrow morning, Brett, I shall put up these things in a small parcel, and take them round to Bow Street."

"But are they sufficient evidence?"

"Quite sufficient for the police purpose. There is the man, and all the rest — his movements on the day and so forth — are simple matters of inquiry; at any rate, that is police business."

I had scarcely sat down to my breakfast on the following morning when Hewitt came into the room and put a long letter before me.

"From our friend of last night," he said; "read it."

This letter began abruptly, and undated, and was as follows:

"TO MARTIN HEWITT, ESQ.

"SIR: I must compliment you on the adroitness you exhibited this evening in extracting from me my name. The address I was able to balk you of for the time being, although by the time you read this you will probably have found it through the *Law List*, as I am an admitted solicitor. That, however, will be of little use to you, for I am removing myself, I think, beyond the reach even of your abilities of search. I knew you well by sight, and was, perhaps, foolish to allow myself to be drawn as I did. Still, I had no idea that it would be dangerous, especially after seeing you, as a witness with very little to say, at the inquest upon the scoundrel I shot. Your somewhat discourteous seizure of my apple at first amazed me—indeed, I was a little doubtful as to whether you had really taken it—but it was my first warning that you might be playing a deep game against me, incomprehensible as the action was to my mind. I subsequently reflected that I had been eating an apple, instead of taking the drink he first offered me, in the dead wretch's rooms on the night he came to his merited end. From this I assume that your design was in some way to compare what remained of the two apples—although I do not presume to fathom the depths of your detective system. Still, I have heard of many of your cases, and profoundly admire the keenness you exhibit. I am thought to be a keen man myself, but, although I was able, to some extent, to hold my own tonight, I admit that your acumen in this case alone is something beyond me.

"I do not know by whom you are commissioned to hunt me, nor to what extent you may be acquainted with my connection with the creature I killed. I have sufficient respect for you, however, to wish that you should not regard me as a vicious criminal, and a couple of hours to spare in which to offer you an explanation that will convince you that such is not altogether the case. A hasty and violent temper I admit possessing; but even now I cannot forget the one crime it has led me into—for it is, I suppose, strictly speaking, a crime. For it was the man Foggatt who made a felon of my father before the eyes of the world, and killed him with shame. It was he who murdered my mother, and none the less murdered her because she died of a broken heart. That he was also a thief and a hypocrite might have concerned me little but for that.

"Of my father I remember very little. He must, I fear, have been a weak and incapable man in many respects. He had no business abilities—in fact, was quite unable to understand the complicated business matters in which he largely dealt. Foggatt was a consummate master of all those arts of financial jugglery that make so many fortunes, and ruin so many others, in matters of company promoting, stocks, and shares. He was unable to exercise them, however, because of a great financial disaster in which he had been mixed up a few years before, and which made his name one to be avoided in future. In these circumstances he made a sort of secret and informal partnership with my father, who, ostensibly alone in the business, acted throughout on the directions of Foggatt, understanding as little what he did, poor, simple man, as a schoolboy would have done. The transactions carried on went from small to large, and, unhappily from honorable to dishonorable. My father relied on the superior abilities of Foggatt with an absolute trust, carrying out each day the directions given him privately the previous evening, buying, selling, printing prospectuses, signing whatever had to be signed, all with sole responsibility and as sole partner, while Foggatt, behind the scenes absorbed the larger share of the profits. In brief, my unhappy and foolish father was a mere tool in the hands of the cunning scoundrel who pulled all the wires of the business, himself unseen and irresponsible. At last three companies, for the promotion of which my father was responsible, came to grief in a heap. Fraud was written large over all their history, and, while Foggatt retired with his plunder, my father was left to meet ruin, disgrace, and imprisonment. From beginning to end he, and he only, was responsible. There was no shred of evidence to connect Foggatt with the matter, and no means of escape from the net drawn about my father. He lived through three years of imprisonment, and then, entirely abandoned by the man who had made use of his simplicity, he died — of nothing but shame and a broken heart.

"Of this I knew nothing at the time. Again and again, as a small boy, I remember asking of my mother why I had no father at home, as other boys had — unconscious of the stab I thus inflicted on her gentle heart. Of her my earliest, as well as my latest, memory is that of a pale, weeping woman, who grudged to let me out of her sight.

"Little by little I learned the whole cause of my mother's grief, for she had no other confidant, and I fear my character developed early, for my first coherent remembrance of the matter is that of a childish design to take a table-knife and kill the bad man who had made my father die in prison and caused my mother to cry.

"One thing, however, I never knew — the name of that bad man. Again and again, as I grew older, I demanded to know, but my mother always withheld it from me, with a gentle reminder that vengeance was for a greater hand than mine.

"I was seventeen years of age when my mother died. I believe that nothing but her strong attachment to myself and her desire to see me safely started in life kept her alive so long. Then I found that through all those years of narrowed means she had contrived to scrape and save a little money — sufficient, as it afterward proved, to see me through the examinations for entrance to my profession, with the generous assistance of my father's old legal advisers, who gave me my articles, and who have all along treated me with extreme kindness.

"For most of the succeeding years my life does not concern the matter in hand. I was a lawyer's clerk in my benefactors' service, and afterward a qualified man among their assistants. All through the firm were careful, in pursuance of my poor mother's wishes, that I should not learn the name or whereabouts of the man who had wrecked her life and my father's. I first met the man himself at the Clifton Club, where I had gone with an acquaintance who was a member. It was not till afterward that I understood his curious awkwardness on that occasion. A week later I called (as I had frequently done) at the building in which your office is situated, on business with a solicitor who has an office on the floor above your own. On the stairs I almost ran against Mr Foggatt. He started and turned pale, exhibiting signs of alarm that I could not understand, and asked me if I wished to see him.

"'No,' I replied, 'I didn't know you lived here. I am after somebody else just now. Aren't you well?'

"He looked at me rather doubtfully, and said he was *not* very well.

"I met him twice or thrice after that, and on each occasion his manner grew more friendly, in a servile, flattering, and mean sort of way—a thing unpleasant enough in anybody, but doubly so in the intercourse of a man with another young enough to be his own son. Still, of course, I treated the man civilly enough. On one occasion he asked me into his rooms to look at a rather fine picture he had lately bought, and observed casually, lifting a large revolver from the mantelpiece:

"'You see, I am prepared for any unwelcome visitors to my little den! He! He!' Conceiving him, of course, to refer to burglars, I could not help wondering at the forced and hollow character of his laugh. As we went down the stairs he said: 'I think we know one another pretty well now, Mr Mason, eh? And if I could do anything to advance your professional prospects, I should be glad of the chance, of course. I understand the struggles of a young professional man—he! he!' It was the forced laugh again, and the man spoke nervously. 'I think,' he added, 'that if you will drop in tomorrow evening, perhaps I may have a little proposal to make. Will you?'

"I assented, wondering what this proposal could be. Perhaps this eccentric old gentleman was a good fellow, after all, anxious to do me a good turn, and his awkwardness was nothing but a natural delicacy in breaking the ice. I was not so flush of good friends as to be willing to lose one. He might be desirous of putting business in my way.

"I went, and was received with cordiality that even then seemed a little over-effusive. We sat and talked of one thing and another for a long while, and I began to wonder when Mr Foggatt was coming to the point that most interested me. Several times he invited me to drink and smoke, but long usage to athletic training has given me a distaste for both practices, and I declined. At last he began to talk about myself. He was afraid that my professional prospects in this country were not great, but he had heard that in some of the colonies— South Africa, for example—young lawyers had brilliant opportunities.

"'If you'd like to go there,' he said, 'I've no doubt, with a little capital, a clever man like you could get a grand practice together very soon. Or you might buy a share in some good established practice. I should be glad to let you have £500, or even a little more, if that wouldn't satisfy you, and—'

"I stood aghast. Why should this man, almost a stranger, offer me £500, or even more, 'if that wouldn't satisfy' me? What claim had I on him? It was very generous of him, of course, but out of the question. I was, at least, a gentleman, and had a gentleman's self-respect. Meanwhile, he had gone maundering on, in a halting sort of way, and presently let slip a sentence that struck me like a blow between the eyes.

"'I shouldn't like you to bear ill-will because of what has happened in the past,' he said. 'Your late—your late lamented mother—I'm afraid—she had unworthy suspicions—I'm sure—it was best for all parties—your father always appreciated—'

"I set back my chair and stood erect before him. This groveling wretch, forcing the words through his dry lips, was the thief who had made another of my father and had brought to miserable ends the lives of both my parents! Everything was clear. The creature went in fear of me, never imagining that I did not know him, and sought to buy me off—to buy me from the remembrance of my dead mother's broken heart for £500—£500 that he had made my father steal for him! I said not a word. But the memory of all my mother's bitter years, and a savage sense of this crowning insult to myself, took a hold upon me, and I was a tiger. Even then I verily believe that one word of repentance, one tone of honest remorse, would have saved him. But he drooped his eyes, snuffled excuses, and stammered of 'unworthy suspicions' and 'no ill-will.' I let him stammer. Presently he looked up and saw my face; and fell back in his chair, sick with terror. I snatched the pistol from the mantelpiece, and, thrusting it in his face, shot him where he sat.

"My subsequent coolness and quietness surprise me now. I took my hat and stepped toward the door. But there were voices on the stairs. The door was locked on the inside, and I left it so. I went back and quietly opened a window. Below was a clear drop into darkness, and above was plain wall; but away to one side, where the slope of the gable sprang from the roof, an iron gutter ended, supported by a strong bracket. It was the only way. I got upon the sill and carefully shut the window behind me, for people were already knocking at the lobby door. From the end of the sill, holding on by the reveal of the window with one hand, leaning and stretching my utmost, I caught the gutter, swung myself clear, and scrambled on the roof. I climbed over many roofs before I found, in an adjoining street, a ladder lashed perpendicularly against the front of a house in course of repair. This, to me, was an easy opportunity of descent, notwithstanding the boards fastened over the face of the ladder, and I availed myself of it.

"I have taken some time and trouble in order that you (so far as I am aware the only human being beside myself who knows me to be the author of Foggatt's death) shall have at least the means of appraising my crime at its just value of culpability. How much you already know of what I have told you I can not guess. I am wrong, hardened, and flagitious, I make no doubt, but I speak of the facts as they are. You see the thing, of course, from your own point of view—I from mine. And I remember my mother!

"Trusting that you will forgive the odd freak of a man—a criminal, let us say—who makes a confidant of the man set to hunt him down, I beg leave to be, sir, your obedient servant,

"SIDNEY MASON."

I read the singular document through and handed it back to Hewitt.

"How does it strike you?" Hewitt asked.

"Mason would seem to be a man of very marked character," I said. "Certainly no fool. And, if his tale is true, Foggatt is no great loss to the world."

"Just so—if the tale is true. Personally I am disposed to believe it is."

"Where was the letter posted?"

"It wasn't posted. It was handed in with the others from the front-door letter-box this morning in an unstamped envelope. He must have dropped it in himself during the night. Paper," Hewitt proceeded, holding it up to the light, "Turkey mill, ruled foolscap. Envelope, blue, official shape, Pirie's watermark. Both quite ordinary and no special marks."

"Where do you suppose he's gone?"

"Impossible to guess. Some might think he meant suicide by the expression 'beyond the reach even of your abilities of search,' but I scarcely think he is the sort of man to do that. No, there is no telling. Something may be got by inquiring at his late address, of course; but, when such a man tells you he doesn't think you will find him, you may count upon its being a difficult job. His opinion is not to be despised."

"What shall you do?"

"Put the letter in the box with the casts for the police. *Fiat justitia*, you know, without any question of sentiment. As to the apple, I really think, if the police will let me, I'll make you a present of it. Keep it somewhere as a souvenir of your absolute deficiency in reflective observation in this case, and look at it whenever you feel yourself growing dangerously conceited. It should cure you."

This is the history of the withered and almost petrified half apple that stands in my cabinet among a number of flint implements and one or two rather fine old Roman vessels. Of Mr Sidney Mason we never heard another word. The police did their best, but he had left not a track behind him. His rooms were left almost undisturbed, and he had gone without anything in the way of elaborate preparation for his journey, and without leaving a trace of his intentions.

4

THE CASE OF THE DIXON TORPEDO

Hewitt was very apt, in conversation, to dwell upon the many curious chances and coincidences that he had observed, not only in connection with his own cases, but also in matters dealt with by the official police, with whom he was on terms of pretty regular, and, indeed, friendly, acquaintanceship. He has told me many an anecdote of singular happenings to Scotland Yard officials with whom he has exchanged experiences. Of Inspector Nettings, for instance, who spent many weary months in a search for a man wanted by the American Government, and in the end found, by the merest accident (a misdirected call), that the man had been lodging next door to himself the whole of the time; just as ignorant, of course, as was the inspector himself as to the enemy at the other side of the party-wall. Also of another inspector, whose name I cannot recall, who, having been given rather meager and insufficient details of a man whom he anticipated having great difficulty in finding, went straight down the stairs of the office where he had received instructions, and actually *fell over* the man near the door, where he had stooped down to tie his shoe-lace! There were cases, too, in which, when a great and notorious crime had been committed, and various persons had been arrested on suspicion, some were found among them who had long been badly wanted for some other crime altogether. Many criminals had met their deserts by venturing out of their own particular line of crime into another; often a man who got into trouble over something comparatively small found himself in for a startlingly larger trouble, the result of some previous misdeed that otherwise would have gone unpunished. The ruble note-forger Mirsky might never have been handed over to the Russian authorities had he confined his genius to forgery alone. It was generally supposed at the time of his extradition that he had communicated with the Russian Embassy, with a view to giving himself up—a foolish proceeding on his part, it would seem, since his whereabouts, indeed even his identity as the forger, had not been suspected. He *had* communicated with the Russian Embassy, it is true, but for quite a different purpose, as Martin Hewitt well understood at the time. What that purpose was is now for the first time published.

The time was half-past one in the afternoon, and Hewitt sat in his inner office examining and comparing the handwriting of two letters by the aid of a large lens. He put down the lens and glanced at the clock on the mantelpiece with a premonition of lunch; and as he did so his clerk quietly entered the room with one of those printed slips which were kept for the announcement of unknown visitors. It was filled up in a hasty and almost illegible hand, thus:

Name of visitor: *F. Graham Dixon.*
Address: *Chancery Lane.*
Business: *Private and urgent.*

"Show Mr Dixon in," said Martin Hewitt.

Mr Dixon was a gaunt, worn-looking man of fifty or so, well, although rather carelessly, dressed, and carrying in his strong, though drawn, face and dullish eyes the look that characterizes the life-long strenuous brain-worker. He leaned forward anxiously in the chair which Hewitt offered him, and told his story with a great deal of very natural agitation.

"You may possibly have heard, Mr Hewitt—I know there are rumors—of the new locomotive torpedo which the government is about adopting; it is, in fact, the Dixon torpedo, my own invention, and in every respect—not merely in my own opinion, but in that of the government experts—by far the most efficient and certain yet produced. It will travel at least four hundred yards farther than any torpedo now made, with perfect accuracy of aim (a very great desideratum, let me tell you), and will carry an unprecedentedly heavy charge. There are other advantages—speed, simple discharge, and so forth—that I needn't bother you about. The machine is the result of many years of work and disappointment, and its design has only been arrived at by a careful balancing of principles and means, which are expressed on the only four existing sets of drawings. The whole thing, I need hardly tell you, is a profound secret, and you may judge of my present state of mind when I tell you that one set of drawings has been stolen."

"From your house?"

"From my office, in Chancery Lane, this morning. The four sets of drawings were distributed thus: Two were at the Admiralty Office, one being a finished set on thick paper, and the other a set of tracings therefrom; and the other two were at my own office, one being a penciled set, uncolored—a sort of finished draft, you understand—and the other a set of tracings similar to those at the Admiralty. It is this last set that has gone. The two sets were kept together in one drawer in my room. Both were there at ten this morning; of that I am sure, for I had to go to that very drawer for something else when I first arrived. But at twelve the tracings had vanished."

"You suspect somebody, probably?"

"I cannot. It is a most extraordinary thing. Nobody has left the office (except myself, and then only to come to you) since ten this morning, and there has been no visitor. And yet the drawings are gone!"

"But have you searched the place?"

"Of course I have! It was twelve o'clock when I first discovered my loss, and I have been turning the place upside down ever since—I and my assistants. Every drawer has been emptied, every desk and table turned over, the very carpet and linoleum have been taken up, but there is not a sign of the drawings. My men even insisted on turning all their pockets inside out, although I never for a moment suspected either of them, and it would take a pretty big pocket to hold the drawings, doubled up as small as they might be."

"You say your men—there are two, I understand—had neither left the office?"

"Neither; and they are both staying in now. Worsfold suggested that it would be more satisfactory if they did not leave till something was done toward clearing the mystery up, and, although, as I have said, I don't suspect either in the least, I acquiesced."

"Just so. Now—I am assuming that you wish me to undertake the recovery of these drawings?"

The engineer nodded hastily.

"Very good; I will go round to your office. But first perhaps you can tell me something about your assistants—something it might be awkward to tell me in their presence, you know. Mr Worsfold, for instance?"

"He is my draughtsman—a very excellent and intelligent man, a very smart man, indeed, and, I feel sure, quite beyond suspicion. He has prepared many important drawings for me (he has been with me nearly ten years now), and I have always found him trustworthy. But, of course, the temptation in this case would be enormous. Still, I cannot suspect Worsfold. Indeed, how can I suspect anybody in the circumstances?"

"The other, now?"

"His name's Ritter. He is merely a tracer, not a fully skilled draughtsman. He is quite a decent young fellow, and I have had him two years. I don't consider him particularly smart, or he would have learned a little more of his business by this time. But I don't see the least reason to suspect him. As I said before, I can't reasonably suspect anybody."

"Very well; we will get to Chancery Lane now, if you please, and you can tell me more as we go."

"I have a cab waiting. What else can I tell you?"

"I understand the position to be succinctly this: The drawings were in the office when you arrived. Nobody came out, and nobody went in; and *yet* they vanished. Is that so?"

"That is so. When I say that absolutely nobody came in, of course I except the postman. He brought a couple of letters during the morning. I mean that absolutely nobody came past the barrier in the outer office—the usual thing, you know, like a counter, with a frame of ground glass over it."

"I quite understand that. But I think you said that the drawings were in a drawer in your *own* room—not the outer office, where the draughtsmen are, I presume?"

"That is the case. It is an inner room, or, rather, a room parallel with the other, and communicating with it; just as your own room is, which we have just left."

"But, then, you say you never left your office, and yet the drawings vanished—apparently by some unseen agency—while you were there in the room?"

"Let me explain more clearly." The cab was bowling smoothly along the Strand, and the engineer took out a pocketbook and pencil. "I fear," he proceeded, "that I am a little confused in my explanation—I am naturally rather agitated. As you will see presently, my offices consist of three rooms, two at one side of a corridor, and the other opposite—thus." He made a rapid pencil sketch.

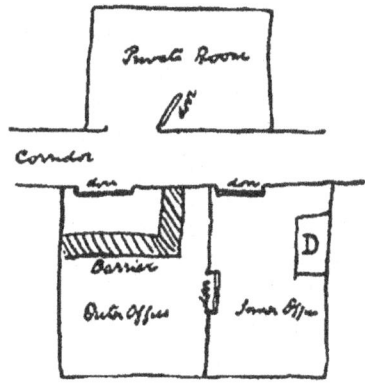

"In the outer office my men usually work. In the inner office I work myself. These rooms communicate, as you see, by a door. Our ordinary way in and out of the place is by the door of the outer office leading into the corridor, and we first pass through the usual lifting flap in the barrier. The door leading from the *inner* office to the corridor is always kept locked on the inside, and I don't suppose I unlock it once in three months. It has not been unlocked all the morning. The drawer in which the missing drawings were kept, and in which I saw them at ten o'clock this morning, is at the place marked D; it is a large chest of shallow drawers in which the plans lie flat."

"I quite understand. Then there is the private room opposite. What of that?"

"That is a sort of private sitting-room that I rarely use, except for business interviews of a very private nature. When I said I never left my office, I did not mean that I never stirred out of the inner office. I was about in one room and another, both the outer and the inner offices, and once I went into the private room for five minutes, but nobody came either in or out of any of the rooms at that time, for the door of the private room was wide open, and I was standing at the book-case (I had gone to consult a book), just inside the door, with a full view of the doors opposite. Indeed, Worsfold was at the door of the outer office most of the short time. He came to ask me a question."

"Well," Hewitt replied, "it all comes to the simple first statement. You know that nobody left the place or arrived, except the postman, who couldn't get near the drawings, and yet the drawings went. Is this your office?"

The cab had stopped before a large stone building. Mr Dixon alighted and led the way to the first-floor. Hewitt took a casual glance round each of the three rooms. There was a sort of door in the frame of ground glass over the barrier to admit of speech with visitors. This door Hewitt pushed wide open, and left so.

He and the engineer went into the inner office. "Would you like to ask Worsfold and Ritter any questions?" Mr Dixon inquired.

"Presently. Those are their coats, I take it, hanging just to the right of the outer office door, over the umbrella stand?"

"Yes, those are all their things—coats, hats, stick, and umbrella."

"And those coats were searched, you say?"

"Yes."

"And this is the drawer—thoroughly searched, of course?"

"Oh, certainly; every drawer was taken out and turned over."

"Well, of course I must assume you made no mistake in your hunt. Now tell me, did anybody know where these plans were, beyond yourself and your two men?"

"As far as I can tell, not a soul."

"You don't keep an office boy?"

"No. There would be nothing for him to do except to post a letter now and again, which Ritter does quite well for."

"As you are quite sure that the drawings were there at ten o'clock, perhaps the thing scarcely matters. But I may as well know if your men have keys of the office?"

"Neither. I have patent locks to each door and I keep all the keys myself. If Worsfold or Ritter arrive before me in the morning they have to wait to be let in; and I am always present myself when the rooms are cleaned. I have not neglected precautions, you see."

"No. I suppose the object of the theft—assuming it is a theft—is pretty plain: the thief would offer the drawings for sale to some foreign government?"

"Of course. They would probably command a great sum. I have been looking, as I need hardly tell you, to that invention to secure me a very large fortune, and I shall be ruined, indeed, if the design is taken abroad. I am under the strictest engagements to secrecy with the Admiralty, and not only should I lose all my labor, but I should lose all the confidence reposed in me at headquarters; should, in fact, be subject to penalties for breach of contract, and my career stopped forever. I can not tell you what a serious business this is for me. If you cannot help me, the consequences will be terrible. Bad for the service of the country, too, of course."

"Of course. Now tell me this: It would, I take it, be necessary for the thief to *exhibit* these drawings to anybody anxious to buy the secret—I mean, he couldn't describe the invention by word of mouth."

"Oh, no, that would be impossible. The drawings are of the most complicated description, and full of figures upon which the whole thing depends. Indeed, one would have to be a skilled expert to properly appreciate the design at all. Various principles of hydrostatics, chemistry, electricity, and pneumatics are most delicately manipulated and adjusted, and the smallest error or omission in any part would upset the whole. No, the drawings are necessary to the thing, and they are gone."

At this moment the door of the outer office was heard to open and somebody entered. The door between the two offices was ajar, and Hewitt could see right through to the glass door left open over the barrier and into the space beyond. A well-dressed, dark, bushy-bearded man stood there carrying a handbag, which he placed on the ledge before him. Hewitt raised his hand to enjoin silence. The man spoke in a rather high-pitched voice and with a slight accent. "Is Mr Dixon now within?" he asked.

"He is engaged," answered one of the draughtsmen; "very particularly engaged. I am afraid you won't be able to see him this afternoon. Can I give him any message?"

"This is two—the second time I have come today. Not two hours ago Mr Dixon himself tells me to call again. I have a very important—very excellent steam-packing to show him that is very cheap and the best of the market." The man tapped his bag. "I have just taken orders from the largest railway companies. Cannot I see him, for one second only? I will not detain him."

"Really, I'm sure you can't this afternoon; he isn't seeing anybody. But if you'll leave your name—"

"My name is Hunter; but what the good of that? He ask me to call a little later, and I come, and now he is engaged. It is a very great pity." And the man snatched up his bag and walking-stick, and stalked off, indignantly.

Hewitt stood still, gazing through the small aperture in the doorway.

"You'd scarcely expect a man with such a name as Hunter to talk with that accent, would you?" he observed, musingly. "It isn't a French accent, nor a German; but it seems foreign. You don't happen to know him, I suppose?"

"No, I don't. He called here about half-past twelve, just while we were in the middle of our search and I was frantic over the loss of the drawings. I was in the outer office myself, and told him to call later. I have lots of such agents here, anxious to sell all sorts of engineering appliances. But what will you do now? Shall you see my men?"

"I think," said Hewitt, rising—"I think I'll get you to question them yourself."

"Myself?"

"Yes, I have a reason. Will you trust me with the 'key' of the private room opposite? I will go over there for a little, while you talk to your men in this room. Bring them in here and shut the door; I can look after the office from across the corridor, you know. Ask them each to detail his exact movements about the office this morning, and get them to recall each visitor who has been here from the beginning of the week. I'll let you know the reason of this later. Come across to me in a few minutes."

Hewitt took the key and passed through the outer office into the corridor.

Ten minutes later Mr Dixon, having questioned his draughtsmen, followed him. He found Hewitt standing before the table in the private room, on which lay several drawings on tracing-paper.

"See here, Mr Dixon," said Hewitt, "I think these are the drawings you are anxious about?"

The engineer sprang toward them with a cry of delight. "Why, yes, yes," he exclaimed, turning them over, "every one of them! But where—how—they must have been in the place after all, then? What a fool I have been!"

Hewitt shook his head. "I'm afraid you're not quite so lucky as you think, Mr Dixon," he said. "These drawings have most certainly been out of the house for a little while. Never mind how—we'll talk of that after. There is no time to lose. Tell me—how long would it take a good draughtsman to copy them?"

"They couldn't possibly be traced over properly in less than two or two and a half long days of very hard work," Dixon replied with eagerness.

"Ah! then it is as I feared. These tracings have been photographed, Mr Dixon, and our task is one of every possible difficulty. If they had been copied in the ordinary way, one might hope to get hold of the copy. But photography upsets everything. Copies can be multiplied with such amazing facility that, once the thief gets a decent start, it is almost hopeless to checkmate him. The only chance is to get at the negatives before copies are taken. I must act at once; and I fear, between ourselves, it may be necessary for me to step very distinctly over the line of the law in the matter. You see, to get at those negatives may involve something very like housebreaking. There must be no delay, no waiting for legal procedure, or the mischief is done. Indeed, I very much question whether you have any legal remedy, strictly speaking."

"Mr Hewitt, I implore you, do what you can. I need not say that all I have is at your disposal. I will guarantee to hold you harmless for anything that may happen. But do, I entreat you, do everything possible. Think of what the consequences may be!"

"Well, yes, so I do," Hewitt remarked, with a smile. "The consequences to me, if I were charged with housebreaking, might be something that no amount of guarantee could mitigate. However, I will do what I can, if only from patriotic motives. Now, I must see your tracer, Ritter. He is the traitor in the camp."

"Ritter? But how?"

"Never mind that now. You are upset and agitated, and had better not know more than is necessary for a little while, in case you say or do something unguarded. With Ritter I must take a deep course; what I don't know I must appear to know, and that will seem more likely to him if I disclaim acquaintance with what I do know. But first put these tracings safely away out of sight."

Dixon slipped them behind his book-case.

"Now," Hewitt pursued, "call Mr Worsfold and give him something to do that will keep him in the inner office across the way, and tell him to send Ritter here."

Mr Dixon called his chief draughtsman and requested him to put in order the drawings in the drawers of the inner room that had been disarranged by the search, and to send Ritter, as Hewitt had suggested.

Ritter walked into the private room with an air of respectful attention. He was a puffy-faced, unhealthy-looking young man, with very small eyes and a loose, mobile mouth.

"Sit down, Mr Ritter," Hewitt said, in a stern voice. "Your recent transactions with your friend Mr Hunter are well known both to Mr Dixon and myself."

Ritter, who had at first leaned easily back in his chair, started forward at this, and paled.

"You are surprised, I observe; but you should be more careful in your movements out of doors if you do not wish your acquaintances to be known. Mr Hunter, I believe, has the drawings which Mr Dixon has lost, and, if so, I am certain that you have given them to him. That, you know, is theft, for which the law provides a severe penalty."

Ritter broke down completely and turned appealingly to Mr Dixon.

"Oh, sir," he pleaded, "it isn't so bad, I assure you. I was tempted, I confess, and hid the drawings; but they are still in the office, and I can give them to you—really, I can."

"Indeed?" Hewitt went on. "Then, in that case, perhaps you'd better get them at once. Just go and fetch them in; we won't trouble to observe your hiding-place. I'll only keep this door open, to be sure you don't lose your way, you know—down the stairs, for instance."

The wretched Ritter, with hanging head, slunk into the office opposite. Presently he reappeared, looking, if possible, ghastlier than before. He looked irresolutely down the corridor, as if meditating a run for it, but Hewitt stepped toward him and motioned him back to the private room.

"You mustn't try anymore of that sort of humbug," Hewitt said with increased severity. "The drawings are gone, and you have stolen them; you know that well enough. Now attend to me. If you received your deserts, Mr Dixon would send for a policeman this moment, and have you hauled off to the jail that is your proper place. But, unfortunately, your accomplice, who calls himself Hunter—but who has other names besides that— as I happen to know—has the drawings, and it is absolutely necessary that these should be recovered. I am afraid that it will be necessary, therefore, to come to some arrangement with this scoundrel—to square him, in fact. Now, just take that pen and paper, and write to your confederate as I dictate. You know the alternative if you cause any difficulty."

Ritter reached tremblingly for the pen.

"Address him in your usual way," Hewitt proceeded. "Say this: 'There has been an alteration in the plans.' Have you got that? 'There has been an alteration in the plans. I shall be alone here at six o'clock. Please come, without fail.' Have you got it? Very well; sign it, and address the envelope. He must come here, and then we may arrange matters. In the meantime, you will remain in the inner office opposite."

The note was written, and Martin Hewitt, without glancing at the address, thrust it into his pocket. When Ritter was safely in the inner office, however, he drew it out and read the address. "I see," he observed, "he uses the same name, Hunter; 27 Little Carton Street, Westminster, is the address, and there I shall go at once with the note. If the man comes here, I think you had better lock him in with Ritter, and send for a policeman—it may at least frighten him. My object is, of course, to get the man away, and then, if possible, to invade his house, in some way or another, and steal or smash his negatives if they are there and to be found. Stay here, in any case, till I return. And don't forget to lock up those tracings."

It was about six o'clock when Hewitt returned, alone, but with a smiling face that told of good fortune at first sight.

"First, Mr Dixon," he said, as he dropped into an easy chair in the private room, "let me ease your mind by the information that I have been most extraordinarily lucky; in fact, I think you have no further cause for anxiety. Here are the negatives. They were not all quite dry when I—well, what?—stole them, I suppose I must say; so that they have stuck together a bit, and probably the films are damaged. But you don't mind that, I suppose?"

He laid a small parcel, wrapped in a newspaper, on the table. The engineer hastily tore away the paper and took up five or six glass photographic negatives, of a half-plate size, which were damp, and stuck together by the gelatine films in couples. He held them, one after another, up to the light of the window, and glanced through them. Then, with a great sigh of relief, he placed them on the hearth and pounded them to dust and fragments with the poker.

For a few seconds neither spoke. Then Dixon, flinging himself into a chair, said:

"Mr Hewitt, I can't express my obligation to you. What would have happened if you had failed, I prefer not to think of. But what shall we do with Ritter now? The other man hasn't been here yet, by the by."

"No; the fact is I didn't deliver the letter. The worthy gentleman saved me a world of trouble by taking himself out of the way." Hewitt laughed. "I'm afraid he has rather got himself into a mess by trying two kinds of theft at once, and you may not be sorry to hear that his attempt on your torpedo plans is likely to bring him a dose of penal servitude for something else. I'll tell you what has happened.

"Little Carton Street, Westminster, I found to be a seedy sort of place—one of those old streets that have seen much better days. A good many people seem to live in each house—they are fairly large houses, by the way—and there is quite a company of bell-handles on each doorpost, all down the side like organ-stops. A barber had possession of the ground floor front of No. 27 for trade purposes, so to him I went. 'Can you tell me,' I said, 'where in this house I can find Mr Hunter?' He looked doubtful, so I went on: 'His friend will do, you know—I can't think of his name; foreign gentleman, dark, with a bushy beard.'

"The barber understood at once. 'Oh, that's Mirsky, I expect,' he said. 'Now, I come to think of it, he has had letters addressed to Hunter once or twice; I've took 'em in. Top floor back.'

"This was good so far. I had got at 'Mr Hunter's' other alias. So, by way of possessing him with the idea that I knew all about him, I determined to ask for him as Mirsky before handing over the letter addressed to him as Hunter. A little bluff of that sort is invaluable at the right time. At the top floor back I stopped at the door and tried to open it at once, but it was locked. I could hear somebody scuttling about within, as though carrying things about, and I knocked again. In a little while the door opened about a foot, and there stood Mr Hunter—or Mirsky, as you like—the man who, in the character of a traveler in steam-packing, came here twice today. He was in his shirt-sleeves, and cuddled something under his arm, hastily covered with a spotted pocket-handkerchief.

"'I have called to see M. Mirsky,' I said, 'with a confidential letter—'

"'Oh, yas, yas,' he answered hastily; 'I know—I know. Excuse me one minute.' And he rushed off downstairs with his parcel.

"Here was a noble chance. For a moment I thought of following him, in case there might be something interesting in the parcel. But I had to decide in a moment, and I decided on trying the room. I slipped inside the door, and, finding the key on the inside, locked it. It was a confused sort of room, with a little iron bedstead in one corner and a sort of rough boarded inclosure in another. This I rightly conjectured to be the photographic dark-room, and made for it at once.

"There was plenty of light within when the door was left open, and I made at once for the drying-rack that was fastened over the sink. There were a number of negatives in it, and I began hastily examining them one after another. In the middle of this our friend Mirsky returned and tried the door. He rattled violently at the handle and pushed. Then he called.

"At this moment I had come upon the first of the negatives you have just smashed. The fixing and washing had evidently only lately been completed, and the negative was drying on the rack. I seized it, of course, and the others which stood by it.

"'Who are you, there, inside?' Mirsky shouted indignantly from the landing. 'Why for you go in my room like that? Open this door at once, or I call the police!'

"I took no notice. I had got the full number of negatives, one for each drawing, but I was not by any means sure that he had not taken an extra set; so I went on hunting down the rack. There were no more, so I set to work to turn out all the undeveloped plates. It was quite possible, you see, that the other set, if it existed, had not yet been developed.

"Mirsky changed his tune. After a little more banging and shouting I could hear him kneel down and try the keyhole. I had left the key there, so that he could see nothing. But he began talking softly and rapidly through the hole in a foreign language. I did not know it in the least, but I believe it was Russian. What had led him to believe I understood Russian I could not at the time imagine, though I have a notion now. I went on ruining his stock of plates. I found several boxes, apparently of new plates, but, as there was no means of telling whether they were really unused or were merely undeveloped, but with the chemical impress of your drawings on them, I dragged everyone ruthlessly from its hiding-place and laid it out in the full glare of the sunlight—destroying it thereby, of course, whether it was unused or not.

"Mirsky left off talking, and I heard him quietly sneaking off. Perhaps his conscience was not sufficiently clear to warrant an appeal to the police, but it seemed to me rather probable at the time that that was what he was going for. So I hurried on with my work. I found three dark slides—the parts that carried the plates in the back of the camera, you know—one of them fixed in the camera itself. These I opened, and exposed the plates to ruination as before. I suppose nobody ever did so much devastation in a photographic studio in ten minutes as I managed.

"I had spoiled every plate I could find, and had the developed negatives safely in my pocket, when I happened to glance at a porcelain washing-well under the sink. There was one negative in that, and I took it up. It was *not* a negative of a drawing of yours, but of a Russian twenty-ruble note!"

This *was* a discovery. The only possible reason any man could have for photographing a bank-note was the manufacture of an etched plate for the production of forged copies. I was almost as pleased as I had been at the discovery of *your* negatives. He might bring the police now as soon as he liked; I could turn the tables on him completely. I began to hunt about for anything else relating to this negative.

"I found an inking-roller, some old pieces of blanket (used in printing from plates), and in a corner on the floor, heaped over with newspapers and rubbish, a small copying-press. There was also a dish of acid, but not an etched plate or a printed note to be seen. I was looking at the press, with the negative in one hand and the inking-roller in the other, when I became conscious of a shadow across the window. I looked up quickly, and there was Mirsky hanging over from some ledge or projection to the side of the window, and staring straight at me, with a look of unmistakable terror and apprehension.

"The face vanished immediately. I had to move a table to get at the window, and by the time I had opened it there was no sign or sound of the rightful tenant of the room. I had no doubt now of his reason for carrying a parcel downstairs. He probably mistook me for another visitor he was expecting, and, knowing he must take this visitor into his room, threw the papers and rubbish over the press, and put up his plates and papers in a bundle and secreted them somewhere downstairs, lest his occupation should be observed.

"Plainly, my duty now was to communicate with the police. So, by the help of my friend the barber downstairs, a messenger was found and a note sent over to Scotland Yard. I awaited, of course, for the arrival of the police, and occupied the interval in another look round—finding nothing important, however. When the official detective arrived, he recognized at once the importance of the case. A large number of forged Russian notes have been put into circulation on the Continent lately, it seems, and it was suspected that they came from London. The Russian Government have been sending urgent messages to the police here on the subject.

"Of course I said nothing about your business; but, while I was talking with the Scotland Yard man, a letter was left by a messenger, addressed to Mirsky. The letter will be examined, of course, by the proper authorities, but I was not a little interested to perceive that the envelope bore the Russian imperial arms above the words 'Russian Embassy.' Now, why should Mirsky communicate with the Russian Embassy? Certainly not to let the officials know that he was carrying on a very extensive and lucrative business in the manufacture of spurious Russian notes. I think it is rather more than possible that he wrote— probably before he actually got your drawings—to say that he could sell information of the highest importance, and that this letter was a reply. Further, I think it quite possible that, when I asked for him by his Russian name and spoke of 'a confidential letter,' he at once concluded that *I* had come from the embassy in answer to his letter. That would account for his addressing me in Russian through the keyhole; and, of course, an official from the Russian Embassy would be the very last person in the world whom he would like to observe any indications of his little etching experiments. But, anyhow, be that as it may," Hewitt concluded, "your drawings are safe now, and if once Mirsky is caught, and I think it likely, for a man in his shirtsleeves, with scarcely any start, and, perhaps, no money about him, hasn't a great chance to get away—if he is caught, I say, he will probably get something handsome at St. Petersburg in the way of imprisonment, or Siberia, or what not; so that you will be amply avenged."

"Yes, but I don't at all understand this business of the drawings even now. How in the world were they taken out of the place, and how in the world did you find it out?"

"Nothing could be simpler; and yet the plan was rather ingenious. I'll tell you exactly how the thing revealed itself to me. From your original description of the case many people would consider that an impossibility had been performed. Nobody had gone out and nobody had come in, and yet the drawings had been taken away. But an impossibility is an impossibility, after all, and as drawings don't run away of themselves, plainly somebody had taken them, unaccountable as it might seem. Now, as they were in your inner office, the only people who could have got at them besides yourself were your assistants, so that it was pretty clear that one of them, at least, had something to do with the business. You told me that Worsfold was an excellent and intelligent draughtsman. Well, if such a man as that meditated treachery, he would probably be able to carry away the design in his head—at any rate, a little at a time—and would be under no necessity to run the risk of stealing a set of the drawings. But Ritter, you remarked, was an inferior sort of man. 'Not particularly smart,' I think, were your words—only a mechanical sort of tracer. *He* would be unlikely to be able to carry in his head the complicated details of such designs as yours, and, being in a subordinate position, and continually overlooked, he would find it impossible to make copies of the plans in the office. So that, to begin with, I thought I saw the most probable path to start on.

"When I looked round the rooms, I pushed open the glass door of the barrier and left the door to the inner office ajar, in order to be able to see any thing that *might* happen in any part of the place, without actually expecting any definite development. While we were talking, as it happened, our friend Mirsky (or Hunter—as you please) came into the outer office, and my attention was instantly called to him by the first thing he did. Did you notice anything peculiar yourself?"

"No, really, I can't say I did. He seemed to behave much as any traveler or agent might."

"Well, what I noticed was the fact that as soon as he entered the place he put his walking-stick into the umbrella-stand over there by the door, close by where he stood, a most unusual thing for a casual caller to do, before even knowing whether you were in. This made me watch him closely. I perceived with increased interest that the stick was exactly of the same kind and pattern as one already standing there, also a curious thing. I kept my eyes carefully on those sticks, and was all the more interested and edified to see, when he left, that he took the *other* stick—not the one he came with—from the stand, and carried it away, leaving his own behind. I might have followed him, but I decided that more could be learned by staying, as, in fact, proved to be the case. This, by the by, is the stick he carried away with him. I took the liberty of fetching it back from Westminster, because I conceive it to be Ritier's property."

Hewitt produced the stick. It was an ordinary, thick Malacca cane, with a buck-horn handle and a silver band. Hewitt bent it across his knee and laid it on the table.

"Yes," Dixon answered, "that is Ritter's stick. I think I have often seen it in the stand. But what in the world—"

"One moment; I'll just fetch the stick Mirsky left behind." And Hewitt stepped across the corridor.

He returned with another stick, apparently an exact facsimile of the other, and placed it by the side of the other.

"When your assistants went into the inner room, I carried this stick off for a minute or two. I knew it was not Worsfold's, because there was an umbrella there with his initial on the handle. Look at this."

Martin Hewitt gave the handle a twist and rapidly unscrewed it from the top. Then it was seen that the stick was a mere tube of very thin metal, painted to appear like a Malacca cane.

"It was plain at once that this was no Malacca cane—it wouldn't bend. Inside it I found your tracings, rolled up tightly. You can get a marvelous quantity of thin tracing-paper into a small compass by tight rolling."

"And this—this was the way they were brought back!" the engineer exclaimed. "I see that clearly. But how did they get away? That's as mysterious as ever."

"Not a bit of it! See here. Mirsky gets hold of Ritter, and they agree to get your drawings and photograph them. Ritter is to let his confederate have the drawings, and Mirsky is to bring them back as soon as possible, so that they sha'n't be missed for a moment. Ritter habitually carries this Malacca cane, and the cunning of Mirsky at once suggests that this tube should be made in outward fac-simile. This morning Mirsky keeps the actual stick, and Ritter comes to the office with the tube. He seizes the first opportunity—probably when you were in this private room, and Worsfold was talking to you from the corridor—to get at the tracings, roll them up tightly, and put them in the tube, putting the tube back into the umbrella-stand. At half-past twelve, or whenever it was, Mirsky turns up for the first time with the actual stick and exchanges them, just as he afterward did when he brought the drawings back."

"Yes, but Mirsky came half an hour after they were—Oh, yes, I see. What a fool I was! I was forgetting. Of course, when I first missed the tracings, they were in this walking-stick, safe enough, and I was tearing my hair out within arm's reach of them!"

"Precisely. And Mirsky took them away before your very eyes. I expect Ritter was in a rare funk when he found that the drawings were missed. He calculated, no doubt, on your not wanting them for the hour or two they would be out of the office."

"How lucky that it struck me to jot a pencil-note on one of them! I might easily have made my note somewhere else, and then I should never have known that they had been away."

"Yes, they didn't give you any too much time to miss them. Well, I think the rest pretty clear. I brought the tracings in here, screwed up the sham stick and put it back. You identified the tracings and found none missing, and then my course was pretty clear, though it looked difficult. I knew you would be very naturally indignant with Ritter, so, as I wanted to manage him myself, I told you nothing of what he had actually done, for fear that, in your agitated state, you might burst out with something that would spoil my game. To Ritter I pretended to know nothing of the return of the drawings or *how* they had been stolen—the only things I did know with certainty. But I *did* pretend to know all about Mirsky—or Hunter—when, as a matter of fact, I knew nothing at all, except that he probably went under more than one name. That put Ritter into my hands completely. When he found the game was up, he began with a lying confession. Believing that the tracings were still in the stick and that we knew nothing of their return, he said that they had not been away, and that he would fetch them—as I had expected he would. I let him go for them alone, and, when he returned, utterly broken up by the discovery that they were not there, I had him altogether at my mercy. You see, if he had known that the drawings were all the time behind your book-case, he might have brazened it out, sworn that the drawings had been there all the time, and we could have done nothing with him. We couldn't have sufficiently frightened him by a threat of prosecution for theft, because there the things were in your possession, to his knowledge.

"As it was he answered the helm capitally: gave us Mirsky's address on the envelope, and wrote the letter that was to have got him out of the way while I committed burglary, if that disgraceful expedient had not been rendered unnecessary. On the whole, the case has gone very well."

"It has gone marvelously well, thanks to yourself. But what shall I do with Ritter?"

"Here's his stick—knock him downstairs with it, if you like. I should keep the tube, if I were you, as a memento. I don't suppose the respectable Mirsky will ever call to ask for it. But I should certainly kick Ritter out of doors—or out of window, if you like—without delay."

Mirsky was caught, and, after two remands at the police-court, was extradited on the charge of forging Russian notes. It came out that he had written to the embassy, as Hewitt had surmised, stating that he had certain valuable information to offer, and the letter which Hewitt had seen delivered was an acknowledgment, and a request for more definite particulars. This was what gave rise to the impression that Mirsky had himself informed the Russian authorities of his forgeries. His real intent was very different, but was never guessed.

"I wonder," Hewitt has once or twice observed, "whether, after all, it would not have paid the Russian authorities better on the whole if I had never investigated Mirsky's little note factory. The Dixon torpedo was worth a good many twenty-ruble notes."

5

THE QUINTON JEWEL AFFAIR

It was comparatively rarely that Hewitt came into contact with members of the regular criminal class—those, I mean, who are thieves, of one sort or another, by exclusive profession. Still, nobody could have been better prepared than Hewitt for encountering this class when it became necessary. By some means, which I never quite understood, he managed to keep abreast of the very latest fashions in the ever-changing slang dialect of the fraternity, and he was a perfect master of the more modern and debased form of Romany. So much so that frequently a gypsy who began (as they always do) by pretending that he understood nothing, and never heard of a gypsy language, ended by confessing that Hewitt could *rokker* better than most Romany *chals* themselves.

By this acquaintance with their habits and talk Hewitt was sometimes able to render efficient service in cases of especial importance. In the Quinton jewel affair Hewitt came into contact with a very accomplished thief.

The case will probably be very well remembered. Sir Valentine Quinton, before he married, had been as poor as only a man of rank with an old country establishment to keep up can be. His marriage, however, with the daughter of a wealthy financier had changed all that, and now the Quinton establishment was carried on on as lavish a scale as might be; and, indeed, the extravagant habits of Lady Quinton herself rendered it an extremely lucky thing that she had brought a fortune with her.

Among other things her jewels made quite a collection, and chief among them was the great ruby, one of the very few that were sent to this country to be sold (at an average price of somewhere about twenty thousand pounds apiece, I believe) by the Burmese king before the annexation of his country. Let but a ruby be of a great size and color, and no equally fine diamond can approach its value. Well, this great ruby (which was set in a pendant, by the by), together with a necklace, brooches, bracelets, ear-rings—indeed, the greater part of Lady Quinton's collection—were stolen. The robbery was effected at the usual time and in the usual way in cases of carefully planned jewelry robberies. The time was early evening—dinner-time, in fact—and an entrance had been made by the window to Lady Quinton's dressing-room, the door screwed up on the inside, and wires artfully stretched about the grounds below to overset anybody who might observe and pursue the thieves.

On an investigation by London detectives, however, a feature of singularity was brought to light. There had plainly been only one thief at work at Radcot Hall, and no other had been inside the grounds. Alone he had planted the wires, opened the window, screwed the door, and picked the lock of the safe. Clearly this was a thief of the most accomplished description.

Some few days passed, and, although the police had made various arrests, they appeared to be all mistakes, and the suspected persons were released one after another. I was talking of the robbery with Hewitt at lunch, and asked him if he had received any commission to hunt for the missing jewels.

"No," Hewitt replied, "I haven't been commissioned. They are offering an immense reward however—a very pleasant sum, indeed. I have had a short note from Radcot Hall informing me of the amount, and that's all. Probably they fancy that I may take the case up as a speculation, but that is a great mistake. I'm not a beginner, and I must be commissioned in a regular manner, hit or miss, if I am to deal with the case. I've quite enough commissions going now, and no time to waste hunting for a problematical reward."

But we were nearer a clue to the Quinton jewels than we then supposed.

We talked of other things, and presently rose and left the restaurant, strolling quietly toward home. Some little distance from the Strand, and near our own door, we passed an excited Irishman—without doubt an Irishman by appearance and talk—who was pouring a torrent of angry complaints in the ears of a policeman. The policeman obviously thought little of the man's grievances, and with an amused smile appeared to be advising him to go home quietly and think no more about it. We passed on and mounted our stairs. Something interesting in our conversation made me stop for a little while at Hewitt's office door on my way up, and, while I stood there, the Irishman we had seen in the street mounted the stairs. He was a poorly dressed but sturdy-looking fellow, apparently a laborer, in a badly-worn best suit of clothes. His agitation still held him, and without a pause he immediately burst out:

"Which of ye jintlemen will be Misther Hewitt, sor?"

"This is Mr Hewitt," I said. "Do you want him?"

"It's protecshin I want, sor—protecshin! I spake to the polis, an' they laff at me, begob. Foive days have I lived in London, an' 'tis nothin' but battle, murdher, an' suddhen death for me here all day an' ivery day! An' the polis say I'm dhrunk!"

He gesticulated wildly, and to me it seemed just possible that the police might be right.

"They say I'm drunk, sor," he continued, "but, begob, I b'lieve they think I'm mad. An' me being thracked an' folleyed an' dogged an' waylaid an' poisoned an' blandandhered an' kidnapped an' murdhered, an' for why I do not know!"

"And who's doing all this?"

"Sthrangers, sor—sthrangers. 'Tis a sthranger here I am mesilf, an' fwy they do it bates me, onless I do be so like the Prince av Wales or other crowned head they thry to slaughter me. They're layin' for me in the sthreet now, I misdoubt not, and fwat they may thry next I can tell no more than the Lord Mayor. An' the polis won't listen to me!"

This, I thought, must be one of the very common cases of mental hallucination which one hears of every day—the belief of the sufferer that he is surrounded by enemies and followed by spies. It is probably the most usual delusion of the harmless lunatic.

"But what have these people done?" Hewitt asked, looking rather interested, although amused. "What actual assaults have they committed, and when? And who told you to come here?"

"Who towld me, is ut? Who but the payler outside—in the street below! I explained to 'um, an' sez he: 'Ah, you go an' take a slape,' sez he; 'you go an' take a good slape, an' they'll be all gone whin ye wake up.' 'But they'll murdher me,' sez I. 'Oh, no!' sez he, smilin' behind av his ugly face. 'Oh, no, they won't; you take ut aisy, me frind, an' go home!' 'Take it aisy, is ut, an' go home!' sez I; 'why, that's just where they've been last, a-ruinationin' an' a-turnin' av the place upside down, an' me strook on the head onsensible a mile away. Take ut aisy, is ut, ye say, whin all the demons in this unholy place is jumpin' on me every minut in places promiscuous till I can't tell where to turn, descendin' an' vanishin' marvelious an' onaccountable? Take ut aisy, is ut?' sez I. 'Well, me frind,' sez he, 'I can't help ye; that's the marvelious an' onaccountable departmint up the stairs forninst ye. Misther Hewitt ut is,' sez he, 'that attinds to the onaccountable departmint, him as wint by a minut ago. You go an' bother him.' That's how I was towld, sor."

Hewitt smiled.

"Very good," he said; "and now what are these extraordinary troubles of yours? Don't declaim," he added, as the Irishman raised his hand and opened his mouth, preparatory to another torrent of complaint; "just say in ten words, if you can, what they've done to you."

"I will, sor. Wan day had I been in London, sor—wan day only, an' a low scutt thried to poison me dhrink; next day some udther thief av sin shoved me off av a railway platform undher a train, malicious and purposeful; glory be, he didn't kill me! but the very docther that felt me bones thried to pick me pockut, I du b'lieve. Sunday night I was grabbed outrageous in a darrk turnin', rowled on the groun', half strangled, an' me pockuts nigh ripped out av me trousies. An' this very blessed mornin' av light I was strook onsensible an' left a livin' corpse, an' my lodgin's penethrated an' all the thruck mishandled an' bruk up behind me back. Is that a panjandhery for the polis to laff at, sor?"

Had Hewitt not been there I think I should have done my best to quiet the poor fellow with a few soothing words and to persuade him to go home to his friends. His excited and rather confused manner, his fantastic story of a sort of general conspiracy to kill him, and the absurd reference to the doctor who tried to pick his pocket seemed to me plainly to confirm my first impression that he was insane. But Hewitt appeared strangely interested.

"Did they steal anything?" he asked.

"Divil a shtick but me door-key, an' that they tuk home an' lift in the door."

Hewitt opened his office door.

"Come in," he said, "and tell me all about this. You come, too, Brett."

The Irishman and I followed him into the inner office, where, shutting the door, Hewitt suddenly turned on the Irishman and exclaimed sharply: *"Then you've still got it?"*

He looked keenly in the man's eyes, but the only expression there was one of surprise.

"Got ut?" said the Irishman. "Got fwhat, sor? Is ut you're thinkin' I've got the horrors, as well as the polis?"

Hewitt's gaze relaxed. "Sit down, sit down!" he said. "You've still got your watch and money, I suppose, since you weren't robbed?"

"Oh, that? Glory be, I have ut still! though for how long—or me own head, for that matter—in this state of besiegement, I can not say."

"Now," said Hewitt, "I want a full, true, and particular account of yourself and your doings for the last week. First, your name?"

"Leamy's my name, sor—Michael Leamy."

"Lately from Ireland?"

"Over from Dublin this last blessed Wednesday, and a crooil bad poundherin' tit was in the boat, too—shpakin'av that same."

"Looking for work?"

"That is my purshuit at prisint, sor."

"Did anything noticeable happen before these troubles of yours began—anything here in London or on the journey?"

"Sure," the Irishman smiled, "part av the way I thraveled first-class by favor av the gyard, an' I got a small job before I lift the train."

"How was that? Why did you travel first-class part of the way?"

"There was a station fwhere we shtopped afther a long run, an' I got down to take the cramp out av me joints, an' take a taste av dhrink. I over-shtayed somehow, an', whin I got to the train, begob, it was on the move. There was a first-class carr'ge door opin right forninst me, an' into that the gyard crams me holus-bolus. There was a juce of a foine jintleman sittin' there, an' he stares at me umbrageous, but I was not dishcommoded, bein' onbashful by natur'. We thravelled along a heap av miles more, till we came near London. Afther we had shtopped at a station where they tuk tickets we wint ahead again, an' prisintly, as we rips through some udther station, up jumps the jintleman opposite, swearin' hard undher his tongue, an' looks out at the windy. 'I thought this train shtopped here,' sez he."

"Chalk Farm," observed Hewitt, with a nod.

"The name I do not know, sor, but that's fwhat he said. Then he looks at me onaisy for a little, an' at last he sez: 'Wud ye loike a small job, me good man, well paid?'

"'Faith,' sez I, ''tis that will suit me well.'

"'Then, see here,' sez he, 'I should have got out at that station, havin' particular business; havin' missed, I must sen' a telegrammer from Euston. Now, here's a bag,' sez he, 'a bag full of imporrtant papers for my solicitor—imporrtant to me, ye ondershtand, not worth the shine av a brass farden to a sowl else—an' I want 'em tuk on to him. Take you this bag,' he sez, 'an' go you straight out wid it at Euston an' get a cab. I shall stay in the station a bit to see to the telegrammer. Dhrive out av the station, across the road outside, an' wait there five minuts by the clock. Ye ondershtand? Wait five minuts, an, maybe I'll come an' join ye. If I don't 'twill be bekase I'm detained onexpected, an' then ye'll dhrive to my solicitor straight. Here's his address, if ye can read writin',' an' he put ut on a piece av paper. He gave me half-a-crown for the cab, an' I tuk his bag."

"One moment—have you the paper with the address now?"

"I have not, sor. I missed ut afther the blayguards overset me yesterday; but the solicitor's name was Hollams, an' a liberal jintleman wid his money he was, too, by that same token."

"What was his address?"

"'Twas in Chelsea, and 'twas Gold or Golden something, which I know by the good token av fwhat he gave me; but the number I misremember."

Hewitt turned to his directory. "Gold Street is the place, probably," he said, "and it seems to be a street chiefly of private houses. You would be able to point out the house if you were taken there, I suppose?"

"I should that, sor; indade, I was thinkin' av goin' there an' tellin' Misther Hollams all my throubles, him havin' been so kind."

"Now tell me exactly what instructions the man in the train gave you, and what happened?"

"He sez: 'You ask for Misther Hollams, an' see nobody else. Tell him ye've brought the sparks from Misther W.'"

I fancied I could see a sudden twinkle in Hewitt's eye, but he made no other sign, and the Irishman proceeded.

"'Sparks?' sez I. 'Yes, sparks,' sez he. 'Misther Hollams will know; 'tis our jokin' word for 'em; sometimes papers is sparks when they set a lawsuit ablaze,' and he laffed. 'But be sure ye say the *sparks from Misther W.*,' he sez again, 'bekase then he'll know ye're jinuine an' he'll pay ye han'some. Say Misther W. sez you're to have your reg'lars, if ye like. D'ye mind that?'

"'Ay,' sez I, 'that I'm to have my reg'lars.'

"Well, sor, I tuk the bag and wint out of the station, tuk the cab, an' did all as he towld me. I waited the foive minuts, but he niver came, so off I druv to Misther Hollams, and he threated me han'some, sor."

"Yes, but tell me exactly all he did."

"'Misther Hollams, sor?' sez I. 'Who are ye?' sez he. 'Mick Leamy, sor,' sez I, 'from Misther W. wid the sparks.' 'Oh,' sez he, 'thin come in.' I wint in. 'They're in here, are they?' sez he, takin' the bag. 'They are, sor,' sez I, 'an' Misther W. sez I'm to have me reg'lars.' 'You shall,' sez he. 'What shall we say, now— afinnip?' 'Fwhat's that, sor?' sez I. 'Oh,' sez he, 'I s'pose ye're a new hand; five quid—ondershtand that?'"

"Begob, I did ondershtand it, an' moighty plazed I was to have come to a place where they pay five-pun' notes for carryin' bags. So whin he asked me was I new to London an' shud I kape in the same line av business, I towld him I shud for certin, or any thin' else payin' like it. 'Right,' sez he; 'let me know whin ye've got any thin'—ye'll find me all right.' An' he winked frindly. 'Faith, that I know I shall, sor,' sez I, wid the money safe in me pockut; an' I winked him back, conjanial. 'I've a smart family about me,' sez he, 'an' I treat 'em all fair an' liberal.' An', saints, I thought it likely his family 'ud have all they wanted, seein' he was so free-handed wid a stranger. Thin he asked me where I was a livin' in London, and, when I towld him nowhere, he towld me av a room in Musson Street, here by Drury Lane, that was to let, in a house his fam'ly knew very well, an' I wint straight there an' tuk ut, an' there I do be stayin' still, sor."

I hadn't understood at first why Hewitt took so much interest in the Irishman's narrative, but the latter part of it opened my eyes a little. It seemed likely that Leamy had, in his innocence, been made a conveyer of stolen property. I knew enough of thieves' slang to know that "sparks" meant diamonds or other jewels; that "regulars" was the term used for a payment made to a brother thief who gave assistance in some small way, such as carrying the booty; and that the "family" was the time-honored expression for a gang of thieves.

"This was all on Wednesday, I understand," said Hewitt. "Now tell me what happened on Thursday—the poisoning, or drugging, you know?"

"Well, sor, I was walking out, an' toward the evenin' I lost mesilf. Up comes a man, seemin'ly a sthranger, and shmacks me on the showldher. 'Why, Mick!' sez he; 'it's Mick Leamy, I du b'lieve!'

"'I am that,' sez I, 'but you I do not know.'

"'Not know me?' sez he. 'Why, I wint to school wid ye.' An' wid that he hauls me off to a bar, blarneyin' and minowdherin', an' orders dhrinks.

"Can ye rache me a poipe-loight?' sez he, an' I turned to get ut, but, lookin' back suddent, there was that onblushin' thief av the warl' tippin' a paperful of phowder stuff into me glass."

"What did you do?" Hewitt asked.

"I knocked the dhirty face av him, sor, an' can ye blame me? A mane scutt, thryin' for to poison a well-manin' sthranger. I knocked the face av him, an' got away home."

"Now the next misfortune?"

"Faith, that was av a sort likely to turn out the last of all misfortunes. I wint that day to the Crystial Palace, bein' dishposed for a little sphort, seein' as I was new to London. Comin' home at night, there was a juce av a crowd on the station platform, consekins of a late thrain. Sthandin' by the edge av the platform at the fore end, just as thrain came in, some onvisible murdherer gives me a stupenjus drive in the back, and over I wint on the line, mid-betwixt the rails. The engine came up an' wint half over me widout givin' me a scratch, bekase av my centraleous situation, an' then the porther-men pulled me out, nigh sick wid fright, sor, as ye may guess. A jintleman in the crowd sings out: 'I'm a medical man!' an' they tuk me in the waitin'-room, an' he investigated me, havin' turned everybody else out av the room. There wuz no bones bruk, glory be! and the docthor-man he was tellin' me so, after feelin' me over, whin I felt his hand in me waistcoat pockut.

"'An' fwhat's this, sor?' sez I. 'Do you be lookin' for your fee that thief's way?'

"He laffed, and said: 'I want no fee from ye, me man, an' I did but feel your ribs,' though on me conscience he had done that undher me waistcoat already. An' so I came home."

"What did they do to you on Saturday?"

"Saturday, sor, they gave me a whole holiday, and I began to think less of things; but on Saturday night, in a dark place, two blayguards tuk me throat from behind, nigh choked me, flung me down, an' wint through all me pockuts in about a quarter av a minut."

"And they took nothing, you say?"

"Nothing, sor. But this mornin' I got my worst dose. I was trapesing along distreshful an' moighty sore, in a street just away off the Strand here, when I obsarved the docthor-man that was at the Crystal Palace station a-smilin' an' beckonin' at me from a door.

"'How are ye now?' sez he. 'Well,' sez I, 'I'm moighty sore an' sad bruised,' sez I. 'Is that so?' sez he. 'Sthep in here.' So I sthepped in, an' before I could wink there dhropped a crack on the back av me head that sent me off as unknowledgable as a corrpse. I knew no more for a while, sor, whether half an hour or an hour, an' thin I got up in a room av the place, marked 'To Let.' 'Twas a house full av offices, by the same token, like this. There was a sore bad lump on me head—see ut, sor?—an' the whole warl' was shpinnin' roun' rampageous. The things out av me pockuts were lyin' on the flure by me—all barrin' the key av me room. So that the demons had been through me posseshins again, bad luck to 'em."

"You are quite sure, are you, that everything was there except the key?" Hewitt asked.

"Certin, sor? Well, I got along to me room, sick an' sorry enough, an' doubtsome whether I might get in wid no key. But there was the key in the open door, an', by this an' that, all the shtuff in the room—chair, table, bed, an' all—was shtandin' on their heads twisty-ways, an' the bedclothes an' every thin' else; such a disgraceful stramash av conglomerated thruck as ye niver dhreamt av. The chist av drawers was lyin' on uts face, wid all the dhrawers out an' emptied on the flure. 'Twas as though an arrmy had been lootin', sor!"

"But still nothing was gone?"

"Nothin', so far as I investigated, sor. But I didn't shtay. I came out to spake to the polis, an' two av them laffed at me— wan afther another!"

"It has certainly been no laughing matter for you. Now, tell me—have you anything in your possession—documents, or valuables, or anything—that any other person, to your knowledge, is anxious to get hold of!"

"I have not, sor—divil a document! As to valuables, thim an' me is the cowldest av sthrangers."

"Just call to mind, now, the face of the man who tried to put powder in your drink, and that of the doctor who attended to you in the railway station. Were they at all alike, or was either like anybody you have seen before?"

Leamy puckered his forehead and thought.

"Faith," he said presently, "they were a bit alike, though one had a beard an' the udther whiskers only."

"Neither happened to look like Mr Hollams, for instance?"

Leamy started. "Begob, but they did! They'd ha' been mortal like him if they'd been shaved." Then, after a pause, he suddenly added: "Holy saints! is ut the fam'ly he talked av?"

Hewitt laughed. "Perhaps it is," he said. "Now, as to the man who sent you with the bag. Was it an old bag?"

"Bran' cracklin' new—a brown leather bag."

"Locked?"

"That I niver thried, sor. It was not my consarn."

"True. Now, as to this Mr W. himself." Hewitt had been rummaging for some few minutes in a portfolio, and finally produced a photograph, and held it before the Irishman's eye. "Is that like him?" he asked.

"Shure it's the man himself! Is he a friend av yours, sor?"

"No, he's not exactly a friend of mine," Hewitt answered, with a grim chuckle. "I fancy he's one of that very respectable *family* you heard about at Mr Hollams'. Come along with me now to Chelsea, and see if you can point out that house in Gold Street. I'll send for a cab."

He made for the outer office, and I went with him.

"What is all this, Hewitt?" I asked. "A gang of thieves with stolen property?"

Hewitt looked in my face and replied: "*It's the Quinton ruby!*"

"What! The ruby? Shall you take the case up, then?"

"I shall. It is no longer a speculation."

"Then do you expect to find it at Hollams' house in Chelsea?" I asked.

"No, I don't, because it isn't there—else why are they trying to get it from this unlucky Irishman? There has been bad faith in Hollams' gang, I expect, and Hollams has missed the ruby and suspects Leamy of having taken it from the bag."

"Then who is this Mr W. whose portrait you have in your possession?"

"See here!" Hewitt turned over a small pile of recent newspapers and selected one, pointing at a particular paragraph. "I kept that in my mind, because to me it seemed to be the most likely arrest of the lot," he said.

It was an evening paper of the previous Thursday, and the paragraph was a very short one, thus:

"The man Wilks, who was arrested at Euston Station yesterday, in connection with the robbery of Lady Quinton's jewels, has been released, nothing being found to incriminate him."

"How does that strike you?" asked Hewitt. "Wilks is a man well known to the police—one of the most accomplished burglars in this country, in fact. I have had no dealings with him as yet, but I found means, some time ago, to add his portrait to my little collection, in case I might want it, and today it has been quite useful."

The thing was plain now. Wilks must have been bringing his booty to town, and calculated on getting out at Chalk Farm and thus eluding the watch which he doubtless felt pretty sure would be kept (by telegraphic instruction) at Euston for suspicious characters arriving from the direction of Radcot. His transaction with Leamy was his only possible expedient to save himself from being hopelessly taken with the swag in his possession. The paragraph told me why Leamy had waited in vain for "Mr W." in the cab.

"What shall you do now?" I asked.

"I shall go to the Gold Street house and find out what I can as soon as this cab turns up."

There seemed a possibility of some excitement in the adventure, so I asked: "Will you want any help?"

Hewitt smiled. "I *think* I can get through it alone," he said.

"Then may I come to look on?" I said. "Of course I don't want to be in your way, and the result of the business, whatever it is, will be to your credit alone. But I am curious."

"Come, then, by all means. The cab will be a four-wheeler, and there will be plenty of room."

Gold Street was a short street of private houses of very fair size and of a half-vanished pretension to gentility. We drove slowly through, and Leamy had no difficulty in pointing out the house wherein he had been paid five pounds for carrying a bag. At the end the cab turned the corner and stopped, while Hewitt wrote a short note to an official of Scotland Yard.

"Take this note," he instructed Leamy, "to Scotland Yard in the cab, and then go home. I will pay the cabman now."

"I will, sor. An' will I be protected?"

"Oh, yes! Stay at home for the rest of the day, and I expect you'll be left alone in future. Perhaps I shall have something to tell you in a day or two; if I do, I'll send. Goodby."

The cab rolled off, and Hewitt and I strolled back along Gold Street. "I think," Hewitt said, "we will drop in on Mr Hollams for a few minutes while we can. In a few hours I expect the police will have him, and his house, too, if they attend promptly to my note."

"Have you ever seen him?"

"Not to my knowledge, though I may know him by some other name. Wilks I know by sight, though he doesn't know me."

"What shall we say?"

"That will depend on circumstances. I may not get my cue till the door opens, or even till later. At worst, I can easily apply for a reference as to Leamy, who, you remember, is looking for work."

But we were destined not to make Mr Hollams' acquaintance, after all. As we approached the house a great uproar was heard from the lower part giving on to the area, and suddenly a man, hatless, and with a sleeve of his coat nearly torn away burst through the door and up the area steps, pursued by two others. I had barely time to observe that one of the pursuers carried a revolver, and that both hesitated and retired on seeing that several people were about the street, when Hewitt, gripping my arm and exclaiming: "That's our man!" started at a run after the fugitive.

We turned the next corner and saw the man thirty yards before us, walking, and pulling up his sleeve at the shoulder, so as to conceal the rent. Plainly he felt safe from further molestation.

"That's Sim Wilks," Hewitt explained, as we followed, "the 'juce of a foine jintleman' who got Leamy to carry his bag, and the man who knows where the Quinton ruby is, unless I am more than usually mistaken. Don't stare after him, in case he looks round. Presently, when we get into the busier streets, I shall have a little chat with him."

But for some time the man kept to the back streets. In time, however, he emerged into the Buckingham Palace Road, and we saw him stop and look at a hat-shop. But after a general look over the window and a glance in at the door he went on.

"Good sign!" observed Hewitt; "got no money with him— makes it easier for us."

In a little while Wilks approached a small crowd gathered about a woman fiddler. Hewitt touched my arm, and a few quick steps took us past our man and to the opposite side of the crowd. When Wilks emerged, he met us coming in the opposite direction.

"What, Sim!" burst out Hewitt with apparent delight. "I haven't piped your mug for a stretch; I thought you'd fell. Where's your cady?"

Wilks looked astonished and suspicious. "I don't know you," he said. "You've made a mistake."

Hewitt laughed. "I'm glad you don't know me," he said. "If you don't, I'm pretty sure the reelers won't. I think I've faked my mug pretty well, and my clobber, too. Look here: I'll stand you a new cady. Strange blokes don't do that, eh?"

Wilks was still suspicious. "I don't know what you mean," he said. Then, after a pause, he added: "Who are you, then?"

Hewitt winked and screwed his face genially aside. "Hooky!" he said. "I've had a lucky touch and I'm Mr Smith till I've melted the pieces. You come and damp it."

"I'm off," Wilks replied. "Unless you're pal enough to lend me a quid," he added, laughing.

"I am that," responded Hewitt, plunging his hand in his pocket. "I'm flush, my boy, flush, and I've been wetting it pretty well today. I feel pretty jolly now, and I shouldn't wonder if I went home cannon. Only a quid? Have two, if you want 'em—or three; there's plenty more, and you'll do the same for me some day. Here y'are."

Hewitt had, of a sudden, assumed the whole appearance, manners, and bearing of a slightly elevated rowdy. Now he pulled his hand from his pocket and extended it, full of silver, with five or six sovereigns interspersed, toward Wilks.

"I'll have three quid," Wilks said, with decision, taking the money; "but I'm blowed if I remember you. Who's your pal?"

Hewitt jerked his hand in my direction, winked, and said, in a low voice: "He's all right. Having a rest. Can't stand Manchester," and winked again.

Wilks laughed and nodded, and I understood from that that Hewitt had very flatteringly given me credit for being "wanted" by the Manchester police.

We lurched into a public house, and drank a very little very bad whisky and water. Wilks still regarded us curiously, and I could see him again and again glancing doubtfully in Hewitt's face. But the loan of three pounds had largely reassured him. Presently Hewitt said:

"How about our old pal down in Gold Street? Do anything with him now? Seen him lately?"

Wilks looked up at the ceiling and shook his head.

"That's a good job. It 'ud be awkward if you were about there today, I can tell you."

"Why?"

"Never mind, so long as you're not there. I know something, if I *have* been away. I'm glad I haven't had any truck with Gold Street lately, that's all."

"D'you mean the reelers are on it?"

Hewitt looked cautiously over his shoulder, leaned toward Wilks, and said: "Look here: this is the straight tip. I know this — I got it from the very nark that's given the show away: By six o'clock No. 8 Gold Street will be turned inside out, like an old glove, and everyone in the place will be—" He finished the sentence by crossing his wrists like a handcuffed man. "What's more," he went on, "they know all about what's gone on there lately, and everybody that's been in or out for the last two moons will be wanted particular—and will be found, I'm told." Hewitt concluded with a confidential frown, a nod, and a wink, and took another mouthful of whisky. Then he added, as an afterthought: "So I'm glad you haven't been there lately."

Wilks looked in Hewitt's face and asked: "Is that straight?"

"*Is* it?" replied Hewitt with emphasis. "You go and have a look, if you ain't afraid of being smugged yourself. Only *I* shan't go near No. 8 just yet — I know that."

Wilks fidgeted, finished his drink, and expressed his intention of going. "Very well, if you *won't* have another—" replied Hewitt. But he had gone.

"Good!" said Hewitt, moving toward the door; "he has suddenly developed a hurry. I shall keep him in sight, but you had better take a cab and go straight to Euston. Take tickets to the nearest station to Radcot—Kedderby, I think it is—and look up the train arrangements. Don't show yourself too much, and keep an eye on the entrance. Unless I am mistaken, Wilks will be there pretty soon, and I shall be on his heels. If I *am* wrong, then you won't see the end of the fun, that's all."

Hewitt hurried after Wilks, and I took the cab and did as he wished. There was an hour and a few minutes, I found, to wait for the next train, and that time I occupied as best I might, keeping a sharp lookout across the quadrangle. Barely five minutes before the train was to leave, and just as I was beginning to think about the time of the next, a cab dashed up and Hewitt alighted. He hurried in, found me, and drew me aside into a recess, just as another cab arrived.

"Here he is," Hewitt said. "I followed him as far as Euston Road and then got my cabby to spurt up and pass him. He had had his mustache shaved off, and I feared you mightn't recognize him, and so let him see you."

From our retreat we could see Wilks hurry into the booking-office. We watched him through to the platform and followed. He wasted no time, but made the best of his way to a third-class carriage at the extreme fore end of the train.

"We have three minutes," Hewitt said, "and everything depends on his not seeing us get into this train. Take this cap. Fortunately, we're both in tweed suits."

He had bought a couple of tweed cricket caps, and these we assumed, sending our "bowler" hats to the cloak-room. Hewitt also put on a pair of blue spectacles, and then walked boldly up the platform and entered a first-class carriage. I followed close on his heels, in such a manner that a person looking from the fore end of the train would be able to see but very little of me.

"So far so good," said Hewitt, when we were seated and the train began to move off. "I must keep a lookout at each station, in case our friend goes off unexpectedly."

"I waited some time," I said; "where did you both go to?"

"First he went and bought that hat he is wearing. Then he walked some distance, dodging the main thoroughfares and keeping to the back streets in a way that made following difficult, till he came to a little tailor's shop. There he entered and came out in a quarter of an hour with his coat mended. This was in a street in Westminster. Presently he worked his way up to Tothill Street, and there he plunged into a barber's shop. I took a cautious peep at the window, saw two or three other customers also waiting, and took the opportunity to rush over to a 'notion' shop and buy these blue spectacles, and to a hatter's for these caps—of which I regret to observe that yours is too big. He was rather a long while in the barber's, and finally came out, as you saw him, with no mustache. This was a good indication. It made it plainer than ever that he had believed my warning as to the police descent on the house in Gold Street and its frequenters; which was right and proper, for what I told him was quite true. The rest you know. He cabbed to the station, and so did I."

"And now perhaps," I said, "after giving me the character of a thief wanted by the Manchester police, forcibly depriving me of my hat in exchange for this all-too-large cap, and rushing me off out of London without any definite idea of when I'm coming back, perhaps you'll tell me what we're after?"

Hewitt laughed. "You wanted to join in, you know," he said, "and you must take your luck as it comes. As a matter of fact there is scarcely anything in my profession so uninteresting and so difficult as this watching and following business. Often it lasts for weeks. When we alight, we shall have to follow

Wilks again, under the most difficult possible conditions, in the country. There it is often quite impossible to follow a man unobserved. It is only because it is the only way that I am undertaking it now. As to what we're after, you know that as well as I—the Quinton ruby. Wilks has hidden it, and without his help it would be impossible to find it. We are following him so that he will find it for us."

"He must have hidden it, I suppose, to avoid sharing with Hollams?"

"Of course, and availed himself of the fact of Leamy having carried the bag to direct Hollams's suspicion to him. Hollams found out by his repeated searches of Leamy and his lodgings, that this was wrong, and this morning evidently tried to persuade the ruby out of Wilks' possession with a revolver. We saw the upshot of that."

Kedderby Station was about forty miles out. At each intermediate stopping station Hewitt watched earnestly, but Wilks remained in the train. "What I fear," Hewitt observed, "is that at Kedderby he may take a fly. To stalk a man on foot in the country is difficult enough; but you *can't* follow one vehicle in another without being spotted. But if he's so smart as I think, he won't do it. A man traveling in a fly is noticed and remembered in these places."

He did *not* take a fly. At Kedderby we saw him jump out quickly and hasten from the station. The train stood for a few minutes, and he was out of the station before we alighted. Through the railings behind the platform we could see him walking briskly away to the right. From the ticket collector we ascertained that Radcot lay in that direction, three miles off.

To my dying day I shall never forget that three miles. They seemed three hundred. In the still country almost every footfall seemed audible for any distance, and in the long stretches of road one could see half a mile behind or before. Hewitt was cool and patient, but I got into a fever of worry, excitement, want of breath, and back-ache. At first, for a little, the road zigzagged, and then the chase was comparatively easy. We waited behind one bend till Wilks had passed the next, and then hurried in his trail, treading in the dustiest parts of the road or on the side grass, when there was any, to deaden the sound of our steps.

At the last of these short bends we looked ahead and saw a long, white stretch of road with the dark form of Wilks a couple of hundred yards in front. It would never do to let him get to the end of this great stretch before following, as he might turn off at some branch road out of sight and be lost. So we jumped the hedge and scuttled along as we best might on the other side, with backs bent, and our feet often many inches deep in wet clay. We had to make continual stoppages to listen and peep out, and on one occasion, happening, incautiously, to stand erect, looking after him, I was much startled to see Wilks, with his face toward me, gazing down the road. I ducked like lightning, and, fortunately, he seemed not to have observed me, but went on as before. He had probably heard some slight noise, but looked straight along the road for its explanation, instead of over the hedge. At hilly parts of the road there was extreme difficulty; indeed, on approaching a rise it was usually necessary to lie down under the hedge till Wilks had passed the top, since from the higher ground he could have seen us easily. This improved neither my clothes, my comfort, nor my temper. Luckily we never encountered the difficulty of a long and high wall, but once we were nearly betrayed by a man who shouted to order us off his field.

At last we saw, just ahead, the square tower of an old church, set about with thick trees. Opposite this Wilks paused, looked irresolutely up and down the road, and then went on. We crossed the road, availed ourselves of the opposite hedge, and followed. The village was to be seen some three or four hundred yards farther along the road, and toward it Wilks sauntered slowly. Before he actually reached the houses he stopped and turned back.

"The churchyard!" exclaimed Hewitt, under his breath. "Lie close and let him pass."

Wilks reached the churchyard gate, and again looked irresolutely about him. At that moment a party of children, who had been playing among the graves, came chattering and laughing toward and out of the gate, and Wilks walked hastily away again, this time in the opposite direction.

"That's the place, clearly," Hewitt said. "We must slip across quietly, as soon as he's far enough down the road. Now!"

We hurried stealthily across, through the gate, and into the churchyard, where Hewitt threw his blue spectacles away. It was now nearly eight in the evening, and the sun was setting. Once again Wilks approached the gate, and did not enter, because a laborer passed at the time. Then he came back and slipped through.

The grass about the graves was long, and under the trees it was already twilight. Hewitt and I, two or three yards apart, to avoid falling over one another in case of sudden movement, watched from behind gravestones. The form of Wilks stood out large and black against the fading light in the west as he stealthily approached through the long grass. A light cart came clattering along the road, and Wilks dropped at once and crouched on his knees till it had passed. Then, staring warily about him, he made straight for the stone behind which Hewitt waited.

I saw Hewitt's dark form swing noiselessly round to the other side of the stone. Wilks passed on and dropped on his knee beside a large, weather-worn slab that rested on a brick understructure a foot or so high. The long grass largely hid the bricks, and among it Wilks plunged his hand, feeling along the brick surface. Presently he drew out a loose brick, and laid it on the slab. He felt again in the place, and brought forth a small dark object. I saw Hewitt rise erect in the gathering dusk, and with extended arm step noiselessly toward the stooping man. Wilks made a motion to place the dark object in his pocket, but checked himself, and opened what appeared to be a lid, as though to make sure of the safety of the contents. The last light, straggling under the trees, fell on a brilliantly sparkling object within, and like a flash Hewitt's hand shot over Wilks' shoulder and snatched the jewel.

The man actually screamed—one of those curious sharp little screams that one may hear from a woman very suddenly alarmed. But he sprang at Hewitt like a cat, only to meet a straight drive of the fist that stretched him on his back across the slab. I sprang from behind my stone, and helped Hewitt to secure his wrists with a pocket-handkerchief. Then we marched him, struggling and swearing, to the village.

When, in the lights of the village, he recognized us, he had a perfect fit of rage, but afterward he calmed down, and admitted that it was a "very clean cop." There was some difficulty in finding the village constable, and Sir Valentine Quinton was dining out and did not arrive for at least an hour. In the interval Wilks grew communicative.

"How much d'ye think I'll get?" he asked.

"Can't guess," Hewitt replied. "And as we shall probably have to give evidence, you'll be giving yourself away if you talk too much."

"Oh, I don't care; that'll make no difference. It's a fair cop, and I'm in for it. You got at me nicely, lending me three quid. I never knew a reeler do that before. That blinded me. But was it kid about Gold Street?"

"No, it wasn't. Mr Hollams is safely shut up by this time, I expect, and you are avenged for your little trouble with him this afternoon."

"What did you know about that? Well, you've got it up nicely for me, I must say. S'pose you've been following me all the time?"

"Well, yes; I haven't been far off. I guessed you'd want to clear out of town if Hollams was taken, and I knew this"—Hewitt tapped his breast pocket—"was what you'd take care to get hold of first. You hid it, of course, because you knew that Hollams would probably have you searched for it if he got suspicious?"

"Yes, he did, too. Two blokes went over my pockets one night, and somebody got into my room. But I expected that, Hollams is such a greedy pig. Once he's got you under his thumb he don't give you half your makings, and, if you kick, he'll have you smugged. So that I wasn't going to give him *that* if I could help it. I s'pose it ain't any good asking how you got put on to our mob?"

"No," said Hewitt, "it isn't."

We didn't get back till the next day, staying for the night, despite an inconvenient want of requisites, at the Hall. There were, in fact, no late trains. We told Sir Valentine the story of the Irishman, much to his amusement.

"Leamy's tale sounded unlikely, of course," Hewitt said, "but it was noticeable that every one of his misfortunes pointed in the same direction—that certain persons were tremendously anxious to get at something they supposed he had. When he spoke of his adventure with the bag, I at once remembered Wilks' arrest and subsequent release. It was a curious coincidence, to say the least, that this should happen at the very station to which the proceeds of this robbery must come, if they came to London at all, and on the day following the robbery itself. Kedderby is one of the few stations on this line where no trains would stop after the time of the robbery, so that the thief would have to wait till the next day to get back. Leamy's recognition of Wilks' portrait made me feel pretty certain. Plainly, he had carried stolen property; the poor, innocent fellow's conversation with Hollams showed that, as, in fact, did the sum, five pounds, paid to him by way of 'regulars,' or customary toll, from the plunder of services of carriage. Hollams obviously took Leamy for a criminal friend of Wilks', because of his use of the thieves' expressions 'sparks' and 'regulars,' and suggested, in terms which Leamy misunderstood, that he should sell any plunder he might obtain to himself, Hollams. Altogether it would have been very curious if the plunder were *not* that from Radcot Hall, especially as no other robbery had been reported at the time.

"Now, among the jewels taken, only one was of a very pre-eminent value—the famous ruby. It was scarcely likely that Hollams would go to so much trouble and risk, attempting to drug, injuring, waylaying, and burgling the rooms of the unfortunate Leamy, for a jewel of small value—for any jewel, in fact, but the ruby. So that I felt a pretty strong presumption, at all events, that it was the ruby Hollams was after. Leamy had not had it, I was convinced, from his tale and his manner, and from what I judged of the man himself. The only other person was Wilks, and certainly he had a temptation to keep this to himself, and avoid, if possible, sharing with his London director, or principal; while the carriage of the bag by the Irishman gave him a capital opportunity to put suspicion on him, with the results seen. The most daring of Hollams' attacks on Leamy was doubtless the attempted maiming or killing at the railway station, so as to be able, in the character of a medical man, to search his pockets. He was probably desperate at the time, having, I have no doubt, been following Leamy about all day at the Crystal Palace without finding an opportunity to get at his pockets.

"The struggle and flight of Wilks from Hollams' confirmed my previous impressions. Hollams, finally satisfied that very morning that Leamy certainly had not the jewel, either on his person or at his lodging, and knowing, from having so closely watched him, that he had been nowhere where it could be disposed of, concluded that Wilks was cheating him, and attempted to extort the ruby from him by the aid of another ruffian and a pistol. The rest of my way was plain. Wilks, I knew, would seize the opportunity of Hollams' being safely locked up to get at and dispose of the ruby. I supplied him with funds and left him to lead us to his hiding-place. He did it, and I think that's all."

"He must have walked straight away from my house to the churchyard," Sir Valentine remarked, "to hide that pendant. That was fairly cool."

"Only a cool hand could carry out such a robbery single-handed," Hewitt answered. "I expect his tools were in the bag that Leamy carried, as well as the jewels. They must have been a small and neat set."

They were. We ascertained on our return to town the next day that the bag, with all its contents intact, including the tools, had been taken by the police at their surprise visit to No. 8 Gold Street, as well as much other stolen property.

Hollams and Wilks each got very wholesome doses of penal servitude, to the intense delight of Mick Leamy. Leamy himself, by the by, is still to be seen, clad in a noble uniform, guarding the door of a well-known London restaurant. He has not had any more five-pound notes for carrying bags, but knows London too well now to expect it.

6

THE STANWAY CAMEO MYSTERY

It is now a fair number of years back since the loss of the famous Stanway Cameo made its sensation, and the only person who had the least interest in keeping the real facts of the case secret has now been dead for some time, leaving neither relatives nor other representatives. Therefore no harm will be done in making the inner history of the case public; on the contrary, it will afford an opportunity of vindicating the professional reputation of Hewitt, who is supposed to have completely failed to make anything of the mystery surrounding the case. At the present time connoisseurs in ancient objects of art are often heard regretfully to wonder whether the wonderful cameo, so suddenly discovered and so quickly stolen, will ever again be visible to the public eye. Now this question need be asked no longer.

The cameo, as may be remembered from the many descriptions published at the time, was said to be absolutely the finest extant. It was a sardonyx of three strata—one of those rare sardonyx cameos in which it has been possible for the artist to avail himself of three different colors of superimposed stone—the lowest for the ground and the two others for the middle and high relief of the design. In size it was, for a cameo, immense, measuring seven and a half inches by nearly six. In subject it was similar to the renowned Gonzaga Cameo—now the property of the Czar of Russia—a male and a female head with imperial insignia; but in this case supposed to represent Tiberius Claudius and Messalina. Experts considered it probably to be the work of Athenion, a famous gem-cutter of the first Christian century, whose most notable other work now extant is a smaller cameo, with a mythological subject, preserved in the Vatican.

The Stanway Cameo had been discovered in an obscure Italian village by one of those traveling agents who scour all Europe for valuable antiquities and objects of art. This man had hurried immediately to London with his prize, and sold it to Mr Claridge of St. James Street, eminent as a dealer in such objects. Mr Claridge, recognizing the importance and value of the article, lost no opportunity of making its existence known, and very soon the Claudius Cameo, as it was at first usually called, was as famous as any in the world. Many experts in ancient art examined it, and several large bids were made for its purchase.

In the end it was bought by the Marquis of Stanway for five thousand pounds for the purpose of presentation to the British Museum. The marquis kept the cameo at his town house for a few days, showing it to his friends, and then returned it to Mr Claridge to be finally and carefully cleaned before passing into the national collection. Two nights after Mr Claridge's premises were broken into and the cameo stolen.

Such, in outline, was the generally known history of the Stanway Cameo. The circumstances of the burglary in detail were these: Mr Claridge had himself been the last to leave the premises at about eight in the evening, at dusk, and had locked the small side door as usual. His assistant, Mr Cutler, had left an hour and a half earlier. When Mr Claridge left, everything was in order, and the policeman on fixed-point duty just opposite, who bade Mr Claridge good-evening as he left, saw nothing suspicious during the rest of his term of duty, nor did his successors at the point throughout the night.

In the morning, however, Mr Cutler, the assistant, who arrived first, soon after nine o'clock, at once perceived that something unlooked-for had happened. The door, of which he had a key, was still fastened, and had not been touched; but in the room behind the shop Mr Claridge's private desk had been broken open, and the contents turned out in confusion. The door leading on to the staircase had also been forced. Proceeding up the stairs, Mr Cutler found another door open, leading from the top landing to a small room; this door had been opened by the simple expedient of unscrewing and taking off the lock, which had been on the inside. In the ceiling of this room was a trapdoor, and this was six or eight inches open, the edge resting on the half-wrenched-off bolt, which had been torn away when the trap was levered open from the outside.

Plainly, then, this was the path of the thief or thieves. Entrance had been made through the trapdoor, two more doors had been opened, and then the desk had been ransacked. Mr Cutler afterward explained that at this time he had no precise idea what had been stolen, and did not know where the cameo had been left on the previous evening. Mr Claridge had himself undertaken the cleaning, and had been engaged on it, the assistant said, when he left.

There was no doubt, however, after Mr Claridge's arrival at ten o'clock—the cameo was gone. Mr Claridge, utterly confounded at his loss, explained incoherently, and with curses on his own carelessness, that he had locked the precious article in his desk on relinquishing work on it the previous evening, feeling rather tired, and not taking the trouble to carry it as far as the safe in another part of the house.

The police were sent for at once, of course, and every investigation made, Mr Claridge offering a reward of five hundred pounds for the recovery of the cameo. The affair was scribbled off at large in the earliest editions of the evening papers, and by noon all the world was aware of the extraordinary theft of the Stanway Cameo, and many people were discussing the probabilities of the case, with very indistinct ideas of what a sardonyx cameo precisely was.

It was in the afternoon of this day that Lord Stanway called on Martin Hewitt. The marquis was a tall, upstanding man of spare figure and active habits, well known as a member of learned societies and a great patron of art. He hurried into Hewitt's private room as soon as his name had been announced, and, as soon as Hewitt had given him a chair, plunged into business.

"Probably you already guess my business with you, Mr Hewitt—you have seen the early evening papers? Just so; then I needn't tell you again what you already know. My cameo is gone, and I badly want it back. Of course the police are hard at work at Claridge's, but I'm not quite satisfied. I have been there myself for two or three hours, and can't see that they know any more about it than I do myself. Then, of course, the police, naturally and properly enough from their point of view, look first to find the criminal, regarding the recovery of the property almost as a secondary consideration. Now, from *my* point of view, the chief consideration is the property. Of course I want the thief caught, if possible, and properly punished; but still more I want the cameo."

"Certainly it is a considerable loss. Five thousand pounds—"

"Ah, but don't misunderstand me! It isn't the monetary value of the thing that I regret. As a matter of fact, I am indemnified for that already. Claridge has behaved most honorably—more than honorably. Indeed, the first intimation I had of the loss was a check from him for five thousand pounds, with a letter assuring me that the restoration to me of the amount I had paid was the least he could do to repair the result of what he called his unpardonable carelessness. Legally, I'm not sure that

I could demand anything of him, unless I could prove very flagrant neglect indeed to guard against theft."

"Then I take it, Lord Stanway," Hewitt observed, "that you much prefer the cameo to the money?"

"Certainly. Else I should never have been willing to pay the money for the cameo. It was an enormous price—perhaps much above the market value, even for such a valuable thing—but I was particularly anxious that it should not go out of the country. Our public collections here are not so fortunate as they should be in the possession of the very finest examples of that class of work. In short, I had determined on the cameo, and, fortunately, happen to be able to carry out determinations of that sort without regarding an extra thousand pounds or so as an obstacle. So that, you see, what I want is not the value, but the thing itself. Indeed, I don't think I can possibly keep the money Claridge has sent me; the affair is more his misfortune than his fault. But I shall say nothing about returning it for a little while; it may possibly have the effect of sharpening everybody in the search."

"Just so. Do I understand that you would like me to look into the case independently, on your behalf?"

"Exactly. I want you, if you can, to approach the matter entirely from my point of view—your sole object being to find the cameo. Of course, if you happen on the thief as well, so much the better. Perhaps, after all, looking for the one is the same thing as looking for the other?"

"Not always; but usually it is, or course; even if they are not together, they certainly *have* been at one time, and to have one is a very long step toward having the other. Now, to begin with, is anybody suspected?"

"Well, the police are reserved, but I believe the fact is they've nothing to say. Claridge won't admit that he suspects any one, though he believes that whoever it was must have watched him yesterday evening through the back window of his room, and must have seen him put the cameo away in his desk; because the thief would seem to have gone straight to the place. But I half fancy that, in his inner mind, he is inclined to suspect one of two people. You see, a robbery of this sort is different from others. That cameo would never be stolen, I imagine, with the view of its being sold—it is much too famous a thing; a man might as well walk about offering to sell the Tower of London. There are only a very few people who buy such things, and every one of them knows all about it. No dealer would touch it; he could never even show it, much less sell it, without being called to account. So that it really seems more likely that it has been taken by somebody who wishes to keep it for mere love of the thing—a collector, in fact—who would then have to keep it secretly at home, and never let a soul besides himself see it, living in the consciousness that at his death it must be found and this theft known; unless, indeed, an ordinary vulgar burglar has taken it without knowing its value."

"That isn't likely," Hewitt replied. "An ordinary burglar, ignorant of its value, wouldn't have gone straight to the cameo and have taken it in preference to many other things of more apparent worth, which must be lying near in such a place as Claridge's."

"True—I suppose he wouldn't. Although the police seem to think that the breaking in is clearly the work of a regular criminal—from the jimmy-marks, you know, and so on."

"Well, but what of the two people you think Mr Claridge suspects?"

"Of course I can't say that he does suspect them—I only fancied from his tone that it might be possible; he himself insists that he can't, in justice, suspect anybody. One of these men is Hahn, the traveling agent who sold him the cameo. This man's character does not appear to be absolutely irreproachable; no dealer trusts him very far. Of course Claridge doesn't say what he paid him for the cameo; these dealers are very reticent about their profits, which I believe are as often something like five hundred per cent as not. But it seems Hahn bargained to have something extra, depending on the amount Claridge could sell the carving for. According to the appointment he should have turned up this morning, but he hasn't been seen, and nobody seems to know exactly where he is."

"Yes; and the other person?"

"Well, I scarcely like mentioning him, because he is certainly a gentleman, and I believe, in the ordinary way, quite incapable of anything in the least degree dishonorable; although, of course, they say a collector has no conscience in the matter of his own particular hobby, and certainly Mr Wollett is as keen a collector as any man alive. He lives in chambers in the next turning past Claridge's premises—can, in fact, look into Claridge's back windows if he likes. He examined the cameo several times before I bought it, and made several high offers—appeared, in fact, very anxious indeed to get it. After I had bought it he made, I understand, some rather strong remarks about people like myself 'spoiling the market' by paying extravagant prices, and altogether cut up 'crusty,' as they say, at losing the specimen." Lord Stanway paused a few seconds, and then went on: "I'm not sure that I ought to mention Mr Woollett's name for a moment in connection with such a matter; I am personally perfectly certain that he is as incapable of anything like theft as myself. But I am telling you all I know."

"Precisely. I can't know too much in a case like this. It can do no harm if I know all about fifty innocent people, and may save me from the risk of knowing nothing about the thief. Now, let me see: Mr Wollett's rooms, you say, are near Mr Claridge's place of business? Is there any means of communication between the roofs?"

"Yes, I am told that it is perfectly possible to get from one place to the other by walking along the leads."

"Very good! Then, unless you can think of any other information that may help me, I think, Lord Stanway, I will go at once and look at the place."

"Do, by all means. I think I'll come back with you. Somehow, I don't like to feel idle in the matter, though I suppose I can't do much. As to more information, I don't think there is any."

"In regard to Mr Claridge's assistant, now: Do you know anything of him?"

"Only that he has always seemed a very civil and decent sort of man. Honest, I should say, or Claridge wouldn't have kept him so many years—there are a good many valuable things about at Claridge's. Besides, the man has keys of the place himself, and, even if he were a thief, he wouldn't need to go breaking in through the roof."

"So that," said Hewitt, "we have, directly connected with this cameo, besides yourself, these people: Mr Claridge, the dealer; Mr Cutler, the assistant in Mr Claridge's business; Hahn, who sold the article to Claridge, and Mr Woollett, who made bids for it. These are all?"

"All that I know of. Other gentlemen made bids, I believe, but I don't know them."

"Take these people in their order. Mr Claridge is out of the question, as a dealer with a reputation to keep up would be, even if he hadn't immediately sent you this five thousand pounds— more than the market value, I understand, of the cameo. The assistant is a reputable man, against whom nothing is known, who would never need to break in, and who must understand his business well enough to know that he could never attempt to sell the missing stone without instant detection. Hahn is a man of shady antecedents, probably clever enough to know as well as anybody how to dispose of such plunder—if it be possible to dispose of it at all; also, Hahn hasn't been to Claridge's today, although he had an appointment to take money. Lastly, Mr Woollett is a gentleman of the most honorable record, but a perfectly rabid collector, who had made every effort to secure the cameo before you bought it; who, moreover, could have seen Mr Claridge working in his back room, and who has perfectly easy access to Mr Claridge's roof. If we find it can't be none of these, then we must look where circumstances indicate."

There was unwonted excitement at Mr Claridge's place when Hewitt and his client arrived. It was a dull old building, and in the windows there was never more show than an odd blue china vase or two, or, mayhap, a few old silver shoe-buckles and a curious small sword. Nine men out of ten would have passed it without a glance; but the tenth at least would probably know it for a place famous through the world for the number and value of the old and curious objects of art that had passed through it.

On this day two or three loiterers, having heard of the robbery, extracted what gratification they might from staring at nothing between the railings guarding the windows. Within, Mr Claridge, a brisk, stout, little old man, was talking earnestly to a burly police-inspector in uniform, and Mr Cutler, who had seized the opportunity to attempt amateur detective work on his own account, was groveling perseveringly about the floor, among old porcelain and loose pieces of armor, in the futile hope of finding any clue that the thieves might have considerately dropped.

Mr Claridge came forward eagerly.

"The leather case has been found, I am pleased to be able to tell you, Lord Stanway, since you left."

"Empty, of course?"

"Unfortunately, yes. It had evidently been thrown away by the thief behind a chimney-stack a roof or two away, where the police have found it. But it is a clue, of course."

"Ah, then this gentleman will give me his opinion of it," Lord Stanway said, turning to Hewitt. "This, Mr Claridge, is

Mr Martin Hewitt, who has been kind enough to come with me here at a moment's notice. With the police on the one hand and Mr Hewitt on the other we shall certainly recover that cameo, if it is to be recovered, I think."

Mr Claridge bowed, and beamed on Hewitt through his spectacles. "I'm very glad Mr Hewitt has come," he said. "Indeed, I had already decided to give the police till this time tomorrow, and then, if they had found nothing, to call in Mr Hewitt myself."

Hewitt bowed in his turn, and then asked: "Will you let me see the various breakages? I hope they have not been disturbed."

"Nothing whatever has been disturbed. Do exactly as seems best. I need scarcely say that everything here is perfectly at your disposal. You know all the circumstances, of course?"

"In general, yes. I suppose I am right in the belief that you have no resident housekeeper?"

"No," Claridge replied, "I haven't. I had one housekeeper who sometimes pawned my property in the evening, and then another who used to break my most valuable china, till I could never sleep or take a moment's ease at home for fear my stock was being ruined here. So I gave up resident housekeepers. I felt some confidence in doing it because of the policeman who is always on duty opposite."

"Can I see the broken desk?"

Mr Claridge led the way into the room behind the shop. The desk was really a sort of work-table, with a lifting top and a lock. The top had been forced roughly open by some instrument which had been pushed in below it and used as a lever, so that the catch of the lock was torn away. Hewitt examined the damaged parts and the marks of the lever, and then looked out at the back window.

"There are several windows about here," he remarked, "from which it might be possible to see into this room. Do you know any of the people who live behind them?"

"Two or three I know," Mr Claridge answered, "but there are two windows—the pair almost immediately before us—belonging to a room or office which is to let. Any stranger might get in there and watch."

"Do the roofs above any of those windows communicate in any way with yours?"

"None of those directly opposite. Those at the left do; you may walk all the way along the leads."

"And whose windows are they?"

Mr Claridge hesitated. "Well," he said, "they're Mr Woollett's, an excellent customer of mine. But he's a gentleman, and—well, I really think it's absurd to suspect him."

"In a case like this," Hewitt answered, "one must disregard nothing but the impossible. Somebody—whether Mr Woollett himself or another person—could possibly have seen into this room from those windows, and equally possibly could have reached this room from that one. Therefore we must not forget Mr Woollett. Have any of your neighbors been burgled during the night? I mean that strangers anxious to get at your trap-door would probably have to begin by getting into some other house close by, so as to reach your roof."

"No," Mr Claridge replied; "there has been nothing of that sort. It was the first thing the police ascertained."

Hewitt examined the broken door and then made his way up the stairs with the others. The unscrewed lock of the door of the top back-room required little examination. In the room below the trapdoor was a dusty table on which stood a chair, and at the other side of the table sat Detective-Inspector Plummer, whom Hewitt knew very well, and who bade him "goodday" and then went on with his docket.

"This chair and table were found as they are now, I take it?" Hewitt asked.

"Yes," said Mr Claridge; "the thieves, I should think, dropped in through the trapdoor, after breaking it open, and had to place this chair where it is to be able to climb back."

Hewitt scrambled up through the trap-way and examined it from the top. The door was hung on long external barn-door hinges, and had been forced open in a similar manner to that practiced on the desk. A jimmy had been pushed between the frame and the door near the bolt, and the door had been pried open, the bolt being torn away from the screws in the operation.

Presently Inspector Plummer, having finished his docket, climbed up to the roof after Hewitt, and the two together went to the spot, close under a chimney-stack on the next roof but one, where the case had been found. Plummer produced the case, which he had in his coat-tail pocket, for Hewitt's inspection.

"I don't see anything particular about it; do you?" he said. "It shows us the way they went, though, being found just here."

"Well, yes," Hewitt said; "if we kept on in this direction, we should be going toward Mr Woollett's house, and *his* trap-door, shouldn't we!"

The inspector pursed his lips, smiled, and shrugged his shoulders. "Of course we haven't waited till now to find that out," he said.

"No, of course. And, as you say, I didn't think there is much to be learned from this leather case. It is almost new, and there isn't a mark on it." And Hewitt handed it back to the inspector.

"Well," said Plummer, as he returned the case to his pocket, "what's your opinion?"

"It's rather an awkward case."

"Yes, it is. Between ourselves—I don't mind telling you—I'm having a sharp lookout kept over there"—Plummer jerked his head in the direction of Mr Woollett's chambers—"because the robbery's an unusual one. There's only two possible motives—the sale of the cameo or the keeping of it. The sale's out of the question, as you know; the thing's only salable to those who would collar the thief at once, and who wouldn't have the thing in their places now for anything. So that it must be taken to keep, and that's a thing nobody but the maddest of collectors would do, just such persons as—" and the inspector nodded again toward Mr Woollett's quarters. "Take that with the other circumstances," he added, "and I think you'll agree it's worthwhile looking a little farther that way. Of course some of the work—taking off the lock and so on—looks rather like a regular burglar, but it's just possible that anyone badly wanting the cameo would like to hire a man who was up to the work."

"Yes, it's possible."

"Do you know anything of Hahn, the agent?" Plummer asked, a moment later.

"No, I don't. Have you found him yet?"

"I haven't yet, but I'm after him. I've found he was at Charing Cross a day or two ago, booking a ticket for the Continent. That and his failing to turn up today seem to make it worthwhile not to miss *him* if we can help it. He isn't the sort of man that lets a chance of drawing a bit of money go for nothing."

They returned to the room. "Well," said Lord Stanway, "what's the result of the consultation? We've been waiting here very patiently, while you two clever men have been discussing the matter on the roof."

On the wall just beneath the trapdoor a very dusty old tall hat hung on a peg. This Hewitt took down and examined very closely, smearing his fingers with the dust from the inside lining. "Is this one of your valuable and crusted old antiques?" he asked, with a smile, of Mr Claridge.

"That's only an old hat that I used to keep here for use in bad weather," Mr Claridge said, with some surprise at the question. "I haven't touched it for a year or more."

"Oh, then it couldn't have been left here by your last night's visitor," Hewitt replied, carelessly replacing it on the hook. "You left here at eight last night, I think?"

"Eight exactly—or within a minute or two."

"Just so. I think I'll look at the room on the opposite side of the landing, if you'll let me."

"Certainly, if you'd like to," Claridge replied; "but they haven't been there—it is exactly as it was left. Only a lumber-room, you see," he concluded, flinging the door open.

A number of partly broken-up packing-cases littered about this room, with much other rubbish. Hewitt took the lid of one of the newest-looking packing-cases, and glanced at the address label. Then he turned to a rusty old iron box that stood against a wall. "I should like to see behind this," he said, tugging at it with his hands. "It is heavy and dirty. Is there a small crowbar about the house, or some similar lever?"

Mr Claridge shook his head. "Haven't such a thing in the place," he said.

"Never mind," Hewitt replied, "another time will do to shift that old box, and perhaps, after all, there's little reason for moving it. I will just walk round to the police-station, I think, and speak to the constables who were on duty opposite during the night. I think, Lord Stanway, I have seen all that is necessary here."

"I suppose," asked Mr Claridge, "it is too soon yet to ask if you have formed any theory in the matter?"

"Well—yes, it is," Hewitt answered. "But perhaps I may be able to surprise you in an hour or two; but that I don't promise. By the by," he added suddenly, "I suppose you're sure the trap-door was bolted last night?"

"Certainly," Mr Claridge answered, smiling. "Else how could the bolt have been broken? As a matter of fact, I believe the trap hasn't been opened for months. Mr Cutler, do you remember when the trap-door was last opened?"

Mr Cutler shook his head. "Certainly not for six months," he said.

"Ah, very well; it's not very important," Hewitt replied.

As they reached the front shop a fiery-faced old gentleman bounced in at the street door, stumbling over an umbrella that stood in a dark corner, and kicking it three yards away.

"What the deuce do you mean," he roared at Mr Claridge, "by sending these police people smelling about my rooms and asking questions of my servants? What do you mean, sir, by treating me as a thief? Can't a gentleman come into this place to look at an article without being suspected of stealing it, when it disappears through your wretched carelessness? I'll ask my solicitor, sir, if there isn't a remedy for this sort of thing. And if I catch another of your spy fellows on my staircase, or crawling about my roof, I'll—I'll shoot him!"

"Really, Mr Woollett—" began Mr Claridge, somewhat abashed, but the angry old man would hear nothing.

"Don't talk to me, sir; you shall talk to my solicitor. And am I to understand, my lord"—turning to Lord Stanway—"that these things are being done with your approval?"

"Whatever is being done," Lord Stanway answered, "is being done by the police on their own responsibility, and entirely without prompting, I believe, by Mr Claridge—certainly without a suggestion of any sort from myself. I think that the personal opinion of Mr Claridge—certainly my own—is that anything like a suspicion of your position in this wretched matter is ridiculous. And if you will only consider the matter calmly—"

"Consider it calmly? Imagine yourself considering such a thing calmly, Lord Stanway. I *won't* consider it calmly. I'll—I'll—I won't have it. And if I find another man on my roof, I'll pitch him off!" And Mr Woollett bounced into the street again.

"Mr Woollett is annoyed," Hewitt observed, with a smile. "I'm afraid Plummer has a clumsy assistant somewhere."

Mr Claridge said nothing, but looked rather glum, for Mr Woollett was a most excellent customer.

Lord Stanwood and Hewitt walked slowly down the street, Hewitt staring at the pavement in profound thought. Once or twice Lord Stanway glanced at his face, but refrained from disturbing him. Presently, however, he observed: "You seem, at least, Mr Hewitt, to have noticed something that has set you thinking. Does it look like a clue?"

Hewitt came out of his cogitation at once. "A clue?" he said; "the case bristles with clues. The extraordinary thing to me is that Plummer, usually a smart man, doesn't seem to have seen one of them. He must be out of sorts, I'm afraid. But the case is decidedly a most remarkable one."

"Remarkable in what particular way?"

"In regard to motive. Now it would seem, as Plummer was saying to me just now on the roof, that there were only two possible motives for such a robbery. Either the man who took all this trouble and risk to break into Claridge's place must have desired to sell the cameo at a good price, or he must have desired to keep it for himself, being a lover of such things. But neither of these has been the actual motive."

"Perhaps he thinks he can extort a good sum from me by way of ransom?"

"No, it isn't that. Nor is it jealousy, nor spite, nor anything of that kind. I know the motive, I *think*—but I wish we could get hold of Hahn. I will shut myself up alone and turn it over in my mind for half an hour presently."

"Meanwhile, what I want to know is, apart from all your professional subtleties—which I confess I can't understand—can you get back the cameo?"

"That," said Hewitt, stopping at the corner of the street, "I am rather afraid I can not—nor anybody else. But I am pretty sure I know the thief."

"Then surely that will lead you to the cameo?"

"It *may*, of course; but, then, it is just possible that by this evening you may not want to have it back, after all."

Lord Stanway stared in amazement.

"Not want to have it back!" he exclaimed. "Why, of course I shall want to have it back. I don't understand you in the least; you talk in conundrums. Who is the thief you speak of?"

"I think, Lord Stanway," Hewitt said, "that perhaps I had better not say until I have quite finished my inquiries, in case of mistakes. The case is quite an extraordinary one, and of quite a different character from what one would at first naturally imagine, and I must be very careful to guard against the possibility of error. I have very little fear of a mistake, however, and I hope I may wait on you in a few hours at Piccadilly with news. I have only to see the policemen."

"Certainly, come whenever you please. But why see the policemen? They have already most positively stated that they saw nothing whatever suspicious in the house or near it."

"I shall not ask them anything at all about the house," Hewitt responded. "I shall just have a little chat with them—about the weather." And with a smiling bow he turned away, while Lord Stanway stood and gazed after him, with an expression that implied a suspicion that his special detective was making a fool of him.

In rather more than an hour Hewitt was back in Mr Claridge's shop. "Mr Claridge," he said, "I think I must ask you one or two questions in private. May I see you in your own room?"

They went there at once, and Hewitt, pulling a chair before the window, sat down with his back to the light. The dealer shut the door, and sat opposite him, with the light full in his face.

"Mr Claridge," Hewitt proceeded slowly, *"when did you first find that Lord Stanway's cameo was a forgery?"*

Claridge literally bounced in his chair. His face paled, but he managed to stammer sharply: "What—what—what d'you mean? Forgery? Do you mean to say I sell forgeries? Forgery? It wasn't a forgery!"

"Then," continued Hewitt in the same deliberate tone, watching the other's face the while, "if it wasn't a forgery, *why did you destroy it and burst your trapdoor and desk to imitate a burglary?*"

The sweat stood thick on the dealer's face, and he gasped. But he struggled hard to keep his faculties together, and ejaculated hoarsely: "Destroy it? What—what—I didn't—didn't destroy it!"

"Threw it into the river, then—don't prevaricate about details."

"No—no—it's a lie! Who says that? Go away! You're insulting me!" Claridge almost screamed.

"Come, come, Mr Claridge," Hewitt said more placably, for he had gained his point; "don't distress yourself, and don't attempt to deceive me—you can't, I assure you. I know everything you did before you left here last night—everything."

Claridge's face worked painfully. Once or twice he appeared to be on the point of returning an indignant reply, but hesitated, and finally broke down altogether.

"Don't expose me, Mr Hewitt!" he pleaded; "I beg you won't expose me! I haven't harmed a soul but myself. I've paid Lord Stanway every penny back, and I never knew the thing was a forgery till I began to clean it. I'm an old man, Mr Hewitt, and my professional reputation has been spotless until now. I beg you won't expose me."

Hewitt's voice softened. "Don't make an unnecessary trouble of it," he said. "I see a decanter on your sideboard—let me give you a little brandy and water. Come, there's nothing criminal, I believe, in a man's breaking open his own desk, or his own trap-door, for that matter. Of course I'm acting for Lord Stanway in this affair, and I must, in duty, report to him without reserve. But Lord Stanway is a gentleman, and I'll undertake he'll do nothing inconsiderate of your feelings, if you're disposed to be frank. Let us talk the affair over; tell me about it."

"It was that swindler Hahn who deceived me in the beginning," Claridge said. "I have never made a mistake with a cameo before, and I never thought so close an imitation was possible. I examined it most carefully, and was perfectly satisfied, and many experts examined it afterward, and were all equally deceived. I felt as sure as I possibly could feel that I had bought one of the finest, if not actually the finest, cameos known to exist. It was not until after it had come back from Lord Stanway's, and I was cleaning it the evening before last, that in course of my work it became apparent that the thing was nothing but a consummately clever forgery. It was made of three layers of molded glass, nothing more nor less. But the glass was treated in a way I had never before known of, and the surface had been cunningly worked on till it defied any ordinary examination. Some of the glass imitation cameos made in the latter part of the last century, I may tell you, are regarded as marvelous pieces of work, and, indeed, command very fair prices, but this was something quite beyond any of those.

"I was amazed and horrified. I put the thing away and went home. All that night I lay awake in a state of distraction, quite unable to decide what to do. To let the cameo go out of my possession was impossible. Sooner or later the forgery would be discovered, and my reputation—the highest in these matters in this country, I may safely claim, and the growth of nearly fifty years of honest application and good judgment—this reputation would be gone forever. But without considering this, there was the fact that I had taken five thousand pounds of Lord Stanway's money for a mere piece of glass, and that money I must, in mere common honesty as well as for my own sake, return. But how? The name of the Stanway Cameo had become a household word, and to confess that the whole thing was a sham would ruin my reputation and destroy all confidence—past, present, and future—in me and in my transactions. Either way spelled ruin. Even if I confided in Lord Stanway privately, returned his money, and destroyed the cameo, what then? The sudden disappearance of an article so famous would excite remark at once. It had been presented to the British Museum, and if it never appeared in that collection, and no news were to be got of it, people would guess at the truth at once. To make it known that I myself had been deceived would have availed nothing. It is my business *not* to be deceived; and to have it known that my most expensive specimens might be forgeries would equally mean ruin, whether I sold them cunningly as a rogue or ignorantly as a fool. Indeed, my pride, my reputation as a connoisseur, is a thing near to my heart, and it would be an unspeakable humiliation to me to have it known that I had been imposed on by such a forgery. What could I do? Every expedient seemed useless but one—the one I adopted. It was not straightforward, I admit; but, oh! Mr Hewitt, consider the temptation—and remember that it couldn't do a soul any harm. No matter who might be suspected, I knew there could not possibly be evidence to make them suffer. All the next day— yesterday—I was anxiously worrying out the thing in my mind and carefully devising the—the trick, I'm afraid you'll call it, that you by some extraordinary means have seen through. It seemed the only thing—what else was there? More I needn't tell you; you know it. I have only now to beg that you will use your best influence with Lord Stanway to save me from public derision and exposure. I will do anything—pay anything— anything but exposure, at my age, and with my position."

"Well, you see," Hewitt replied thoughtfully, "I've no doubt Lord Stanway will show you every consideration, and certainly I will do what I can to save you in the circumstances; though you must remember that you *have* done some harm—you have caused suspicions to rest on at least one honest man. But as to reputation, I've a professional reputation of my own. If I help to conceal your professional failure, I shall appear to have failed in *my* part of the business."

"But the cases are different, Mr Hewitt. Consider. You are not expected—it would be impossible—to succeed invariably; and there are only two or three who know you have looked into the case. Then your other conspicuous successes—"

"Well, well, we shall see. One thing I don't know, though—whether you climbed out of a window to break open the trapdoor, or whether you got up through the trap-door itself and pulled the bolt with a string through the jamb, so as to bolt it after you."

"There was no available window. I used the string, as you say. My poor little cunning must seem very transparent to you, I fear. I spent hours of thought over the question of the trapdoor—how to break it open so as to leave a genuine appearance, and especially how to bolt it inside after I had reached the roof. I thought I had succeeded beyond the possibility of suspicion; how you penetrated the device surpasses my comprehension. How, to begin with, could you possibly know that the cameo was a forgery? Did you ever see it?"

"Never. And, if I had seen it, I fear I should never have been able to express an opinion on it; I'm not a connoisseur. As a matter of fact, I *didn't* know that the thing was a forgery in the first place; what I knew in the first place was that it was *you* who had broken into the house. It was from that that I arrived at the conclusion, after a certain amount of thought, that the cameo must have been forged. Gain was out of the question. You, beyond all men, could never sell the Stanway Cameo again, and, besides, you had paid back Lord Stanway's money. I knew enough of your reputation to know that you would never incur the scandal of a great theft at your place for the sake of getting the cameo for yourself, when you might have kept it in the beginning, with no trouble and mystery. Consequently I had to look for another motive, and at first another motive seemed an impossibility. Why should you wish to take all this trouble to lose five thousand pounds? You had nothing to gain; perhaps you had something to save—your professional reputation, for instance. Looking at it so, it was plain that you were *suppressing* the cameo—burking it; since, once taken as you had taken it, it could never come to light again. That suggested the solution of the mystery at once—you had discovered, after the sale, that the cameo was not genuine."

"Yes, yes—I see; but you say you began with the knowledge that I broke into the place myself. How did you know that? I cannot imagine a trace—"

"My dear sir, you left traces everywhere. In the first place, it struck me as curious, before I came here, that you had sent off that check for five thousand pounds to Lord Stanway an hour or so after the robbery was discovered; it looked so much as though you were sure of the cameo never coming back, and were in a hurry to avert suspicion. Of course I understood that, so far as I then knew the case, you were the most unlikely person in the world, and that your eagerness to repay Lord Stanway might be the most creditable thing possible. But the point was worth remembering, and I remembered it.

"When I came here, I saw suspicious indications in many directions, but the conclusive piece of evidence was that old hat hanging below the trapdoor."

"But I never touched it; I assure you, Mr Hewitt, I never touched the hat; haven't touched it for months—"

"Of course. If you *had* touched it, I might never have got the clue. But we'll deal with the hat presently; that wasn't what struck me at first. The trapdoor first took my attention. Consider, now: Here was a trapdoor, most insecurely hung on *external* hinges; the burglar had a screwdriver, for he took off the door-lock below with it. Why, then, didn't he take this trap off by the hinges, instead of making a noise and taking longer time and trouble to burst the bolt from its fastenings? And why, if he were a stranger, was he able to plant his jimmy from the outside just exactly opposite the interior bolt? There was only one mark on the frame, and that precisely in the proper place.

"After that I saw the leather case. It had not been thrown away, or some corner would have shown signs of the fall. It had been put down carefully where it was found. These things, however, were of small importance compared with the hat. The hat, as you know, was exceedingly thick with dust—the accumulation of months. But, on the top side, presented toward the trapdoor, were a score or so of *raindrop marks*. That was all. They were new marks, for there was no dust over them; they had merely had time to dry and cake the dust they had fallen on. *Now, there had been no rain since a sharp shower just after seven o'clock last night.* At that time you, by your own statement, were in the place. You left at eight, and the rain was all over at ten minutes or a quarter past seven. The trapdoor, you also told me, had not been opened for months. The thing was plain. You, or somebody who was here when you were, had opened that trapdoor during, or just before, that shower. I said little then, but went, as soon as I had left, to the police-station. There I made perfectly certain that there had been no rain during the night by questioning the policemen who were on duty outside all the time. There had been none. I knew everything.

"The only other evidence there was pointed with all the rest. There were no rain-marks on the leather case; it had been put on the roof as an afterthought when there was no rain. A very poor afterthought, let me tell you, for no thief would throw away a useful case that concealed his booty and protected it from breakage, and throw it away just so as to leave a clue as to what direction he had gone in. I also saw, in the lumber-room, a number of packing-cases—one with a label dated two days back—which had been opened with an iron lever; and yet, when I made an excuse to ask for it, you said there was no such thing in the place. Inference, you didn't want me to compare it with the marks on the desks and doors. That is all, I think."

Mr Claridge looked dolorously down at the floor. "I'm afraid," he said, "that I took an unsuitable rôle when I undertook to rely on my wits to deceive men like you. I thought there wasn't a single vulnerable spot in my defense, but you walk calmly through it at the first attempt. Why did I never think of those raindrops?"

"Come," said Hewitt, with a smile, "that sounds unrepentant. I am going, now, to Lord Stanway's. If I were you, I think I should apologize to Mr Woollett in some way."

Lord Stanway, who, in the hour or two of reflection left him after parting with Hewitt, had come to the belief that he had employed a man whose mind was not always in order, received Hewitt's story with natural astonishment. For some time he was in doubt as to whether he would be doing right in acquiescing in anything but a straightforward public statement of the facts connected with the disappearance of the cameo, but in the end was persuaded to let the affair drop, on receiving an assurance from Mr Woollett that he unreservedly accepted the apology offered him by Mr Claridge.

As for the latter, he was at least sufficiently punished in loss of money and personal humiliation for his escapade. But the bitterest and last blow he sustained when the unblushing Hahn walked smilingly into his office two days later to demand the extra payment agreed on in consideration of the sale. He had been called suddenly away, he exclaimed, on the day he should have come, and hoped his missing the appointment had occasioned no inconvenience. As to the robbery of the cameo, of course he was very sorry, but "pishness was pishness," and he would be glad of a check for the sum agreed on. And the unhappy Claridge was obliged to pay it, knowing that the man had swindled him, but unable to open his mouth to say so.

The reward remained on offer for a long time; indeed, it was never publicly withdrawn, I believe, even at the time of Claridge's death. And several intelligent newspapers enlarged upon the fact that an ordinary burglar had completely baffled and defeated the boasted acumen of Mr Martin Hewitt, the well-known private detective.

7

THE AFFAIR OF THE TORTOISE

Very often Hewitt was tempted, by the fascination of some particularly odd case, to neglect his other affairs to follow up a matter that from a business point of view was of little or no value to him. As a rule, he had a sufficient regard for his own interests to resist such temptations, but in one curious case, at least, I believe he allowed it largely to influence him. It was certainly an extremely odd case—one of those affairs that, coming to light at intervals, but more often remaining unheard of by the general public, convince one that, after all, there is very little extravagance about Mr R.L. Stevenson's bizarre imaginings of doings in London in his "New Arabian Nights." "There is nothing in this world that is at all possible," I have often heard Martin Hewitt say, "that has not happened or is not happening in London." Certainly he had opportunities of knowing.

The case I have referred to occurred some time before my own acquaintance with him began—in 1878, in fact. He had called one Monday morning at an office in regard to something connected with one of those uninteresting, though often difficult, cases which formed, perhaps, the bulk of his practice, when he was informed of a most mysterious murder that had taken place in another part of the same building on the previous Saturday afternoon. Owing to the circumstances of the case, only the vaguest account had appeared in the morning papers, and even this, as it chanced, Hewitt had not read.

The building was one of a new row in a partly rebuilt street near the National Gallery. The whole row had been built by a speculator for the purpose of letting out in flats, suites of chambers, and in one or two cases, on the ground floors, offices. The rooms had let very well, and to desirable tenants, as a rule. The least satisfactory tenant, the proprietor reluctantly admitted, was a Mr Rameau, a black gentleman, single, who had three rooms on the top floor but one of the particular building that Hewitt was visiting. His rent was paid regularly, but his behavior had produced complaints from other tenants. He got uproariously drunk, and screamed and howled in unknown tongues. He fell asleep on the staircase, and ladies were afraid to pass. He bawled rough chaff down the stairs and along the corridors at butcher-boys and messengers, and played on errand-boys brutal practical jokes that ended in police-court summonses. He once had a way of sliding down the balusters, shouting: "Ho! ho! ho! yah!" as he went, but as he was a big, heavy man, and the balusters had been built for different treatment, he had very soon and very firmly been requested to stop it. He had plenty of money, and spent it freely; but it was generally felt that there was too much of the light-hearted savage about him to fit him to live among quiet people.

How much longer the landlord would have stood this sort of thing, Hewitt's informant said, was a matter of conjecture, for on the Saturday afternoon in question the tenancy had come to a startling full-stop. Rameau had been murdered in his room, and the body had, in the most unaccountable fashion, been secretly removed from the premises.

The strongest possible suspicion pointed to a man who had been employed in shoveling and carrying coals, cleaning windows, and chopping wood for several of the buildings, and who had left that very Saturday. The crime had, in fact, been committed with this man's chopper, and the man himself had been heard, again and again, to threaten Rameau, who, in his brutal fashion, had made a butt of him. This man was a Frenchman, Victor Goujon by name, who had lost his employment as a watchmaker by reason of an injury to his right hand, which destroyed its steadiness, and so he had fallen upon evil days and odd jobs.

He was a little man of no great strength, but extraordinarily excitable, and the coarse gibes and horse-play of the big black drove him almost to madness. Rameau would often, after some more than ordinarily outrageous attack, contemptuously fling Goujon a shilling, which the little Frenchman, although wanting a shilling badly enough, would hurl back in his face, almost weeping with impotent rage. "Pig! *Canaille!*" he would scream. "Dirty savage of Africa! Take your sheelin' to vere you 'ave stole it! *Voleur!* Pig!"

There was a tortoise living in the basement, of which Goujon had made rather a pet, and the black would sometimes use this animal as a missile, flinging it at the little Frenchman's head. On one such occasion the tortoise struck the wall so forcibly as to break its shell, and then Goujon seized a shovel and rushed at his tormentor with such blind fury that the latter made a bolt of it. These were but a few of the passages between Rameau and the fuel-porter, but they illustrate the state of feeling between them.

Goujon, after correspondence with a relative in France who offered him work, gave notice to leave, which expired on the day of the crime. At about three that afternoon a housemaid, proceeding toward Rameau's rooms, met Goujon as he was going away. Goujon bade her goodby, and, pointing in the direction of Rameau's rooms, said exultantly: "Dere shall be no more of the black savage for me; vit 'im I 'ave done for. Zut! I mock me of 'im! 'E vill never *tracasser* me no more." And he went away.

The girl went to the outer door of Rameau's rooms, knocked, and got no reply. Concluding that the tenant was out, she was about to use her keys, when she found that the door was unlocked. She passed through the lobby and into the sitting-room, and there fell in a dead faint at the sight that met her eyes. Rameau lay with his back across the sofa and his head — drooping within an inch of the ground. On the head was a fearful gash, and below it was a pool of blood.

The girl must have lain unconscious for about ten minutes. When she came to her senses, she dragged herself, terrified, from the room and up to the housekeeper's apartments, where, being an excitable and nervous creature, she only screamed "Murder!" and immediately fell in a fit of hysterics that lasted three-quarters of an hour. When at last she came to herself, she told her story, and, the hall-porter having been summoned, Rameau's rooms were again approached.

The blood still lay on the floor, and the chopper, with which the crime had evidently been committed, rested against the fender; but the body had vanished! A search was at once made, but no trace of it could be seen anywhere. It seemed impossible that it could have been carried out of the building, for the hall-porter must at once have noticed anybody leaving with so bulky a burden. Still, in the building it was not to be found.

When Hewitt was informed of these things on Monday, the police were, of course, still in possession of Rameau's rooms. Inspector Nettings, Hewitt was told, was in charge of the case, and as the inspector was an acquaintance of his, and was then in the rooms upstairs, Hewitt went up to see him.

Nettings was pleased to see Hewitt, and invited him to look around the rooms. "Perhaps you can spot something we have overlooked," he said. "Though it's not a case there can be much doubt about."

"You think it's Goujon, don't you?"

"Think? Well, rather! Look here! As soon as we got here on Saturday, we found this piece of paper and pin on the floor. We showed it to the housemaid, and then she remembered — she was too much upset to think of it before — that when she was in the room the paper was laying on the dead man's chest — pinned there, evidently. It must have dropped off when they removed the body. It's a case of half-mad revenge on Goujon's part, plainly. See it; you read French, don't you?"

The paper was a plain, large half-sheet of note-paper, on which a sentence in French was scrawled in red ink in a large, clumsy hand, thus:

puni par un vengeur de la tortue.

"*Puni par un vengeur de la tortue,*" Hewitt repeated musingly. "'Punished by an avenger of the tortoise,' That seems odd."

"Well, rather odd. But you understand the reference, of course. Have they told you about Rameau's treatment of Goujon's pet tortoise?"

"I think it was mentioned among his other pranks. But this is an extreme revenge for a thing of that sort, and a queer way of announcing it."

"Oh, he's mad — mad with Rameau's continual ragging and baiting," Nettings answered. "Anyway, this is a plain indication — plain as though he'd left his own signature. Besides, it's in his own language — French. And there's his chopper, too."

"Speaking of signatures," Hewitt remarked, "perhaps you have already compared this with other specimens of Goujon's writing?"

"I did think of it, but they don't seem to have a specimen to hand, and, anyway, it doesn't seem very important. There's 'avenger of the tortoise' plain enough, in the man's own language, and that tells everything. Besides, handwritings are easily disguised."

"Have you got Goujon?"

"Well, no; we haven't. There seems to be some little difficulty about that. But I expect to have him by this time tomorrow. Here comes Mr Styles, the landlord."

Mr Styles was a thin, querulous, and withered-looking little man, who twitched his eyebrows as he spoke, and spoke in short, jerky phrases.

"No news, eh, inspector, eh? eh? Found out nothing else, eh? Terrible thing for my property—terrible! Who's your friend?"

Nettings introduced Hewitt.

"Shocking thing this, eh, Mr Hewitt? Terrible! Comes of having anything to do with these bloodthirsty foreigners, eh? New buildings and all—character ruined. No one come to live here now, eh? Tenants—noisy savages—murdered by my own servants—terrible! *You* formed any opinion, eh?"

"I dare say I might if I went into the case."

"Yes, yes—same opinion as inspector's, eh? I mean an opinion of your own?" The old man scrutinized Hewitt's face sharply.

"If you'd like me to look into the matter—" Hewitt began.

"Eh? Oh, look into it! Well, I can't commission you, you know—matter for the police. Mischief's done. Police doing very well, I think—must be Goujon. But look about the place, certainly, if you like. If you see anything likely to serve *my* interests, tell me, and—and—perhaps I'll employ you, eh, eh? Good-afternoon."

The landlord vanished, and the inspector laughed. "Likes to see what he's buying, does Mr Styles," he said.

Hewitt's first impulse was to walk out of the place at once. But his interest in the case had been roused, and he determined, at any rate, to examine the rooms, and this he did very minutely. By the side of the lobby was a bathroom, and in this was fitted a tip-up washbasin, which Hewitt inspected with particular attention. Then he called the housekeeper, and made inquiries about Rameau's clothes and linen. The housekeeper could give no idea of how many overcoats or how much linen he had had. He had all a black's love of display, and was continually buying new clothes, which, indeed, were lying, hanging, littering, and choking up the bedroom in all directions. The housekeeper, however, on Hewitt's inquiring after such a garment in particular, did remember one heavy black ulster, which Rameau had very rarely worn—only in the coldest weather.

"After the body was discovered," Hewitt asked the housekeeper, "was any stranger observed about the place—whether carrying anything or not?"

"No, sir," the housekeeper replied. "There's been particular inquiries about that. Of course, after we knew what was wrong and the body was gone, nobody was seen, or he'd have been stopped. But the hall-porter says he's certain no stranger came or went for half an hour or more before that—the time about when the housemaid saw the body and fainted."

At this moment a clerk from the landlord's office arrived and handed Nettings a paper. "Here you are," said Nettings to Hewitt; "they've found a specimen of Goujon's handwriting at last, if you'd like to see it. I don't want it; I'm not a graphologist, and the case is clear enough for me anyway."

Hewitt took the paper. "This" he said, "is a different sort of handwriting from that on the paper. The red-ink note about the avenger of the tortoise is in a crude, large, clumsy, untaught style of writing. This is small, neat, and well formed—except that it is a trifle shaky, probably because of the hand injury."

"That's nothing," contended Nettings. "handwriting clues are worse than useless, as a rule. It's so easy to disguise and imitate writing; and besides, if Goujon is such a good penman as you seem to say, why, he could all the easier alter his style. Say now yourself, can any fiddling question of handwriting get over this thing about 'avenging the tortoise'—practically a written confession—to say nothing of the chopper, and what he said to the housemaid as he left?"

"Well," said Hewitt, "perhaps not; but we'll see. Meantime"—turning to the landlord's clerk—"possibly you will be good enough to tell me one or two things. First, what was Goujon's character?"

"Excellent, as far as we know. We never had a complaint about him except for little matters of carelessness—leaving coal-scuttles on the staircases for people to fall over, losing shovels, and so on. He was certainly a bit careless, but, as far as we could see, quite a decent little fellow. One would never have thought him capable of committing murder for the sake of a tortoise, though he was rather fond of the animal."

"The tortoise is dead now, I understand?"

"Yes."

"Have you a lift in this building?"

"Only for coals and heavy parcels. Goujon used to work it, sometimes going up and down in it himself with coals, and so on; it goes into the basement."

"And are the coals kept under this building?"

"No. The store for the whole row is under the next two houses—the basements communicate."

"Do you know Rameau's other name?"

"César Rameau he signed in our agreement."

"Did he ever mention his relations?"

"No. That is to say, he did say something one day when he was very drunk; but, of course, it was all rot. Someone told him not to make such a row—he was a beastly tenant—and he said he was the best man in the place, and his brother was Prime Minister, and all sorts of things. Mere drunken rant! I never heard of his saying anything sensible about relations. We know nothing of his connections; he came here on a banker's reference."

"Thanks. I think that's all I want to ask. You notice," Hewitt proceeded, turning to Nettings, "the only ink in this place is scented and violet, and the only paper is tinted and scented, too, with a monogram—characteristic of a an African with money. The paper that was pinned on Rameau's breast is in red ink on common and rather grubby paper, therefore it was written somewhere else and brought here. Inference, premeditation."

"Yes, yes. But are you an inch nearer with all these speculations? Can you get nearer than I am now without them?"

"Well, perhaps not," Hewitt replied. "I don't profess at this moment to know the criminal; you do. I'll concede you that point for the present. But you don't offer an opinion as to who removed Rameau's body—which I think I know."

"Who was it, then?"

"Come, try and guess that yourself. It wasn't Goujon; I don't mind letting you know that. But it was a person quite within your knowledge of the case. You've mentioned the person's name more than once."

Nettings stared blankly. "I don't understand you in the least," he said. "But, of course, you mean that this mysterious person you speak of as having moved the body committed the murder?"

"No, I don't. Nobody could have been more innocent of that."

"Well," Nettings concluded with resignation, "I'm afraid one of us is rather thick-headed. What will you do?"

"Interview the person who took away the body," Hewitt replied, with a smile.

"But, man alive, why? Why bother about the person if it isn't the criminal?"

"Never mind—never mind; probably the person will be a most valuable witness."

"Do you mean you think this person—whoever it is—saw the crime?"

"I think it very probable indeed."

"Well, I won't ask you any more. I shall get hold of Goujon; that's simple and direct enough for me. I prefer to deal with the heart of the case—the murder itself—when there's such clear evidence as I have."

"I shall look a little into that, too, perhaps," Hewitt said, "and, if you like, I'll tell you the first thing I shall do."

"What's that?"

"I shall have a good look at a map of the West Indies, and I advise you to do the same. Good morning."

Nettings stared down the corridor after Hewitt, and continued staring for nearly two minutes after he had disappeared. Then he said to the clerk, who had remained: "What was he talking about?"

"Don't know," replied the clerk. "Couldn't make head nor tail of it."

"I don't believe there *is* a head to it," declared Nettings; "nor a tail either. He's kidding us."

Nettings was better than his word, for within two hours of his conversation with Hewitt, Goujon was captured and safe in a cab bound for Bow Street. He had been stopped at Newhaven in the morning on his way to Dieppe, and was brought back to London. But now Nettings met a check.

Late that afternoon he called on Hewitt to explain matters. "We've got Goujon," he said, gloomily, "but there's a difficulty. He's got two friends who can swear an *alibi*. Rameau was seen alive at half-past one on Saturday, and the girl found him dead about three. Now, Goujon's two friends, it seems, were with him from one o'clock till four in the afternoon, with the exception of five minutes when the girl saw him, and then he left them to take a key or something to the housekeeper before finally leaving. They were waiting on the landing below when Goujon spoke to the housemaid, heard him speaking, and had seen him go all the way up to the housekeeper's room and back, as they looked up the wide well of the staircase. They are men employed near the place, and seem to have good characters. But perhaps we shall find something unfavorable about them. They were drinking with Goujon, it seems, by way of 'seeing him off.'"

"Well," Hewitt said, "I scarcely think you need trouble to damage these men's characters. They are probably telling the truth. Come, now, be plain. You've come here to get a hint as to whether my theory of the case helps you, haven't you?"

"Well, if you can give me a friendly hint, although, of course, I may be right, after all. Still, I wish you'd explain a bit as to what you meant by looking at a map and all that mystery. Nice thing for me to be taking a lesson in my own business after all these years! But perhaps I deserve it."

"See, now," quoth Hewitt, "you remember what map I told you to look at?"

"The West Indies."

"Right! Well, here you are." Hewitt reached an atlas from his bookshelf. "Now, look here: the biggest island of the lot on this map, barring Cuba, is Hayti. You know as well as I do that the western part of that island is peopled by the black republic of Hayti, and that the country is in a degenerate state of almost unexampled savagery, with a ridiculous show of civilization. There are revolutions all the time; the South American republics are peaceful and prosperous compared to Hayti. The state of the country is simply awful—read Sir Spenser St. John's book on it. President after president of the vilest sort forces his way to power and commits the most horrible and bloodthirsty excesses, murdering his opponents by the hundred and seizing their property for himself and his satellites, who are usually as bad, if not worse, than the president himself. Whole families—men, women, and children—are murdered at the instance of these ruffians, and, as a consequence, the most deadly feuds spring up, and the presidents and their followers are always themselves in danger of reprisals from others. Perhaps the very worst of these presidents in recent times has been the notorious Domingue, who was overthrown by an insurrection, as they all are sooner or later, and compelled to fly the country. Domingue and his nephews, one of whom was Chief Minister, while in power committed the cruellest bloodshed, and many members of the opposite party sought refuge in a small island lying just to the north of Hayti, but were sought out there and almost exterminated. Now, I will show you that island on the map. What is its name?"

"Tortuga."

"It is. 'Tortuga,' however, is only the old Spanish name; the Haytians speak French—Creole French. Here is a French atlas: now see the name of that island."

"La Tortue!"

"La Tortue it is—the tortoise. Tortuga means the same thing in Spanish. But that island is always spoken of in Hayti as La Tortue. Now, do you see the drift of that paper pinned to Rameau's breast?"

"Punished by an avenger of—or from—the tortoise or La Tortue—clear enough. It would seem that the dead man had something to do with the massacre there, and somebody from the island is avenging it. The thing's most extraordinary."

"And now listen. The name of Domingue's nephew, who was Chief Minister, was *Septimus Rameau*."

"And this was César Rameau—his brother, probably. I see. Well, this *is* a case."

"I think the relationship probable. Now you understand why I was inclined to doubt that Goujon was the man you wanted."

"Of course, of course! And now I suppose I must try to get a an African—the chap who wrote that paper. I wish he hadn't been such an ignorant savage. If he'd only have put the capitals to the words 'La Tortue,' I might have thought a little more about them, instead of taking it for granted that they meant that wretched tortoise in the basement of the house. Well, I've made a fool of a start, but I'll be after that savage now."

"And I, as I said before," said Hewitt, "shall be after the person that carried off Rameau's body. I have had something else to do this afternoon, or I should have begun already."

"You said you thought he saw the crime. How did you judge that?"

Hewitt smiled. "I think I'll keep that little secret to myself for the present," he said. "You shall know soon."

"Very well," Nettings replied, with resignation. "I suppose I mustn't grumble if you don't tell me everything. I feel too great a fool altogether over this case to see any farther than you show me." And Inspector Nettings left on his search; while Martin Hewitt, as soon as he was alone, laughed joyously and slapped his thigh.

There was a cab-rank and shelter at the end of the street where Mr Styles' building stood, and early that evening a man approached it and hailed the cabmen and the waterman. Anyone would have known the newcomer at once for a cabman taking a holiday. The brim of the hat, the bird's-eye neckerchief, the immense coat-buttons, and, more than all, the rolling walk and the wrinkled trousers, marked him out distinctly.

"Watcheer!" he exclaimed, affably, with the self-possessed nod only possible to cabbies and 'busmen. "I'm a-lookin' for a bilker. I'm told one o' the blokes off this rank carried 'im last Saturday, and I want to know where he went. I ain't 'ad a chance o' gettin' 'is address yet. Took a cab just as it got dark, I'm told. Tallish chap, muffled up a lot, in a long black overcoat. Any of ye seen 'im?"

The cabbies looked at one another and shook their heads; it chanced that none of them had been on that particular rank at that time. But the waterman said: "'Old on—I bet 'e's the bloke wot old Bill Stammers took. Yorkey was fust on the rank, but the bloke wouldn't 'ave a 'ansom—wanted a four-wheeler, so old Bill took 'im. Biggish chap in a long black coat, collar up an' muffled thick; soft wide-awake 'at, pulled over 'is eyes; and he was in a 'urry, too. Jumped in sharp as a weasel."

"Didn't see 'is face, did ye?"

"No—not an inch of it; too much muffled. Couldn't tell if he 'ad a face."

"Was his arm in a sling?"

"Ay, it looked so. Had it stuffed through the breast of his coat, like as though there might be a sling inside."

"That's 'im. Any of ye tell me where I might run across old Bill Stammers? He'll tell me where my precious bilker went to."

As to this there was plenty of information, and in five minutes Martin Hewitt, who had become an unoccupied cabman for the occasion, was on his way to find old Bill Stammers. That respectable old man gave him full particulars as to the place in the East End where he had driven his muffled fare on Saturday, and Hewitt then begun an eighteen, or twenty hours' search beyond Whitechapel.

At about three on Tuesday afternoon, as Nettings was in the act of leaving Bow Street Police Station, Hewitt drove up in a four-wheeler. Some prisoner appeared to be crouching low in the vehicle, but, leaving him to take care of himself, Hewitt hurried into the station and shook Nettings by the hand. "Well," he said, "have you got the murderer of Rameau yet?"

"No," Nettings growled. "Unless—well, Goujon's under remand still, and, after all, I've been thinking that he may know something—"

"Pooh, nonsense!" Hewitt answered. "You'd better let him go. Now, I *have* got somebody." Hewitt laughed and slapped the inspector's shoulder. "I've got the man who carried Rameau's body away!"

"The deuce you have! Where? Bring him in. We must have him—"

"All right, don't be in a hurry; he won't bolt." And Hewitt stepped out to the cab and produced his prisoner, who, pulling his hat farther over his eyes, hurried furtively into the station. One hand was stowed in the breast of his long coat, and below the wide brim of his hat a small piece of white bandage could be seen; and, as he lifted his face, it was seen to be that of a black.

"Inspector Nettings," Hewitt said ceremoniously, "allow me to introduce Mr César Rameau!"

Netting's gasped.

"What!" he at length ejaculated. "What! You—you're Rameau?"

The black looked round nervously, and shrank farther from the door.

"Yes," he said; "but please not so loud—please not loud. Zey may be near, and I'm 'fraid."

"You will certify, will you not," asked Hewitt, with malicious glee, "not only that you were not murdered last Saturday by Victor Goujon, but that, in fact, you were not murdered at all? Also, that you carried your own body away in the usual fashion, on your own legs."

"Yes, yes," responded Rameau, looking haggardly about; "but is not zis—zis room publique? I should not be seen."

"Nonsense!" replied Hewitt rather testily; "you exaggerate your danger and your own importance, and your enemies' abilities as well. You're safe enough."

"I suppose, then," Nettings remarked slowly, like a man on whose mind something vast was beginning to dawn, "I suppose—why, hang it, you must have just got up while that fool of a girl was screaming and fainting upstairs, and walked out. They say there's nothing so hard as a an African's skull skull, and yours has certainly made a fool of me. But, then, *somebody* must have chopped you over the head; who was it?"

"My enemies—my great enemies—enemies politique. I am a great man"—this with a faint revival of vanity amid his fear—"a great man in my countree. Zey have great secret clubsieties to kill me—me and my fren's; and one enemy coming in my rooms does zis—one, two"—he indicated wrist and head—"wiz a choppa."

Rameau made the case plain to Nettings, so far as the actual circumstances of the assault on himself were concerned. A black whom he had noticed near the place more than once during the previous day or two had attacked him suddenly in his rooms, dealing him two savage blows with a chopper. The first he had caught on his wrist, which was seriously damaged, as well as excruciatingly painful, but the second had taken effect on his head. His assailant had evidently gone away then, leaving him for dead; but, as a matter of fact, he was only stunned by the shock, and had, thanks to the adamantine thickness of the African skull and the ill-direction of the chopper, only a very bad scalp-wound, the bone being no more than grazed. He had lain insensible for some time, and must have come to his senses soon after the housemaid had left the room. Terrified at the knowledge that his enemies had found him out, his only thought was to get away and hide himself. He hastily washed and tied up his head, enveloped himself in the biggest coat he could find, and let himself down into the basement by the coal-lift, for fear of observation. He waited in the basement of one of the adjoining buildings till dark and then got away in a cab, with the idea of hiding himself in the East End. He had had very little money with him on his flight, and it was by reason of this circumstance that Hewitt, when he found him, had prevailed on him to leave his hiding-place, since it would be impossible for him to touch any of the large sums of money in the keeping of his bank so long as he was supposed to be dead. With much difficulty, and the promise of ample police protection, he was at last convinced that it would be safe to declare himself and get his property, and then run away and hide wherever he pleased.

Nettings and Hewitt strolled off together for a few minutes and chatted, leaving the wretched Rameau to cower in a corner among several policemen.

"Well, Mr Hewitt," Nettings said, "this case has certainly been a shocking beating for me. I must have been as blind as a bat when I started on it. And yet I don't see that you had a deal to go on, even now. What struck you first?"

"Well, in the beginning it seemed rather odd to me that the body should have been taken away, as I had been told it was, after the written paper had been pinned on it. Why should the murderer pin a label on the body of his victim if he meant carrying that body away? Who would read the label and learn of the nature of the revenge gratified? Plainly, that indicated that the person who had carried away the body was *not* the person who had committed the murder. But as soon as I began to examine the place I saw the probability that there was no murder, after all. There were any number of indications of this fact, and I can't understand your not observing them. First, although there was a good deal of blood on the floor just below where the housemaid had seen Rameau lying, there was none between that place and the door. Now, if the body had been dragged, or even carried, to the door, blood must have become smeared about the floor, or at least there would have been drops, but there were none, and this seemed to hint that the corpse might have come to itself, sat up on the sofa, stanched the wound, and walked out. I reflected at once that Rameau was a full-blooded African, and that a African head is very nearly invulnerable to anything short of bullets. Then, if the body had been dragged out—as such a heavy body must have been—

almost of necessity the carpet and rugs would show signs of the fact, but there were no such signs. But beyond these there was the fact that no long black overcoat was left with the other clothes, although the housekeeper distinctly remembered Rameau's possession of such a garment. I judged he would use some such thing to assist his disguise, which was why I asked her. *Why* he would want to disguise was plain, as you shall see presently. There were no towels left in the bathroom; inference, used for bandages. Everything seemed to show that the only person responsible for Rameau's removal was Rameau himself. Why, then, had he gone away secretly and hurriedly, without making complaint, and why had he stayed away? What reason would he have for doing this if it had been Goujon that had attacked him? None. Goujon was going to France. Clearly, Rameau was afraid of another attack from some implacable enemy whom he was anxious to avoid—one against whom he feared legal complaint or defense would be useless. This brought me at once to the paper found on the floor. If this were the work of Goujon and an open reference to his tortoise, why should he be at such pains to disguise his handwriting? He would have been already pointing himself out by the mere mention of the tortoise. And, if he could not avoid a shake in his natural, small handwriting, how could he have avoided it in a large, clumsy, slowly drawn, assumed hand? No, the paper was not Goujon's."

"As to the writing on the paper," Nettings interposed, "I've told you how I made that mistake. I took the readiest explanation of the words, since they seemed so pat, and I wouldn't let anything else outweigh that. As to the other things—the evidences of Rameau's having gone off by himself—well, I don't usually miss such obvious things; but I never thought of the possibility of the *victim* going away on the quiet and not coming back, as though *he'd* done something wrong. Comes of starting with a set of fixed notions."

"Well," answered Hewitt, "I fancy you must have been rather 'out of form,' as they say; everybody has his stupid days, and you can't keep up to concert pitch forever. To return to the case. The evidence of the chopper was very untrustworthy, especially when I had heard of Goujon's careless habits—losing shovels and leaving coal-scuttles on stairs. Nothing more likely than for the chopper to be left lying about, and a criminal who had calculated his chances would know the advantage to himself of using a weapon that belonged to the place, and leaving it behind to divert suspicion. It is quite possible, by the way, that the man who attacked Rameau got away down the coal-lift and out by an adjoining basement, just as did Rameau himself; this, however, is mere conjecture. The would-be murderer had plainly prepared for the crime: witness the previous preparation of the paper declaring his revenge, an indication of his pride at having run his enemy to earth at such a distant place as this—although I expect he was only in England by chance, for Haytians are not a persistently energetic race. In regard to the use of small instead of capital letters in the words 'La Tortue' on the paper, I observed, in the beginning, that the first letter of the whole sentence—the 'p' in 'puni'—was a small one. Clearly, the writer was an illiterate man, and it was at once plain that he may have made the same mistake with ensuing words.

"On the whole, it was plain that everybody had begun with a too ready disposition to assume that Goujon was guilty. Everybody insisted, too, that the body had been carried away—which was true, of course, although not in the sense intended—so I didn't trouble to contradict, or to say more than that I guessed who *had* carried the body off. And, to tell you the truth, I was a little piqued at Mr Styles' manner, and indisposed, interested in the case as I was, to give away my theories too freely.

"The rest of the job was not very difficult. I found out the cabman who had taken Rameau away—you can always get readier help from cabbies if you go as one of themselves, especially if you are after a bilker—and from him got a sufficiently near East End direction to find Rameau after inquiries. I ventured, by the way, on a rather long shot. I described my man to the cabman as having an injured arm or wrist—and it turned out a correct guess. You see, a man making an attack with a chopper is pretty certain to make more than a single blow, and as there appeared to have been only a single wound on the head, it seemed probable that another had fallen somewhere else—almost certainly on the arm, as it would be raised to defend the head. At Limehouse I found he had had his head and wrist attended to at a local medico's, and a big black in a fright, with a long black coat, a broken head, and a lame hand, is not so difficult to find in a small area. How I persuaded him up here you know already; I think I frightened him a little, too, by explaining how easily I had tracked him, and giving him a hint that others might do the same. He is in a great funk. He seems to have quite lost faith in England as a safe asylum."

The police failed to catch Rameau's assailant—chiefly because Rameau could not be got to give a proper description of him, nor to do anything except get out of the country in a hurry. In truth, he was glad to be quit of the matter with nothing worse than his broken head. Little Goujon made a wild storm about his arrest, and before he did go to France managed to extract twenty pounds from Rameau by way of compensation, in spite of the absence of any strictly legal claim against his old tormentor. So that, on the whole, Goujon was about the only person who derived any particular profit from the tortoise mystery.

Chronicles of Martin Hewitt

CONTENTS

1.	The Ivy Cottage Mystery	181
2.	The Nicobar Bullion Case	209
3.	The Holford Will Case	245
4.	The Case of the Missing Hand	275
5.	The Case of Laker, Absconded	307

1

THE IVY COTTAGE MYSTERY

I had been working double tides for a month: at night on my morning paper, as usual; and in the morning on an evening paper as *locum tenens* for another man who was taking a holiday. This was an exhausting plan of work, although it only actually involved some six hours' attendance a day, or less, at the two offices. I turned up at the headquarters of my own paper at ten in the evening, and by the time I had seen the editor, selected a subject, written my leader, corrected the slips, chatted, smoked, and so on, and cleared off, it was very usually one o'clock. This meant bed at two, or even three, after supper at the club.

This was all very well at ordinary periods, when any time in the morning would do for rising, but when I had to be up again soon after seven, and round at the evening paper office by eight, I naturally felt a little worn and disgusted with things by midday, after a sharp couple of hours' leaderette scribbling and paragraphing, with attendant sundries.

But the strain was over, and on the first day of comparative comfort I indulged in a midday breakfast and the first undisgusted glance at a morning paper for a month. I felt rather interested in an inquest, begun the day before, on the body of a man whom I had known very slightly before I took to living in chambers.

His name was Gavin Kingscote, and he was an artist of a casual and desultory sort, having, I believe, some small private means of his own. As a matter of fact, he had boarded in the same house in which I had lodged myself for a while, but as I was at the time a late homer and a fairly early riser, taking no regular board in the house, we never became much acquainted. He had since, I understood, made some judicious Stock Exchange speculations, and had set up house in Finchley.

Now the news was that he had been found one morning murdered in his smoking-room, while the room itself, with others, was in a state of confusion. His pockets had been rifled, and his watch and chain were gone, with one or two other small articles of value. On the night of the tragedy a friend had sat smoking with him in the room where the murder took place, and he had been the last person to see Mr Kingscote alive. A jobbing gardener, who kept the garden in order by casual work from time to time, had been arrested in consequence of footprints exactly corresponding with his boots, having been found on the garden beds near the French window of the smoking-room.

I finished my breakfast and my paper, and Mrs Clayton, the housekeeper, came to clear my table. She was sister of my late landlady of the house where Kingscote had lodged, and it was by this connection that I had found my chambers. I had not seen the housekeeper since the crime was first reported, so I now said:

"This is shocking news of Mr Kingscote, Mrs Clayton. Did you know him yourself?"

She had apparently only been waiting for some such remark to burst out with whatever information she possessed.

"Yes, sir," she exclaimed: "shocking indeed. Pore young feller! I see him often when I was at my sister's, and he was always a nice, quiet gentleman, so different from some. My sister, she's awful cut up, sir, I assure you. And what d'you think 'appened, sir, only last Tuesday? You remember Mr Kingscote's room where he painted the woodwork so beautiful with gold flowers, and blue, and pink? He used to tell my sister she'd always have something to remember him by. Well, two young fellers, gentlemen I can't call them, come and took that room (it being to let), and went and scratched off all the paint in mere wicked mischief, and then chopped up all the panels into sticks and bits! Nice sort o' gentlemen them! And then they bolted in the morning, being afraid, I s'pose, of being made to pay after treating a pore widder's property like that. That was only Tuesday, and the very next day the pore young gentleman himself's dead, murdered in his own 'ouse, and him going to be married an' all! Dear, dear! I remember once he said—"

Mrs Clayton was a good soul, but once she began to talk someone else had to stop her. I let her run on for a reasonable time, and then rose and prepared to go out. I remembered very well the panels that had been so mischievously destroyed. They made the room the showroom of the house, which was an old one. They were indeed less than half finished when I came away, and Mrs Lamb, the landlady, had shown them to me one day when Kingscote was out. All the walls of the room were panelled and painted white, and Kingscote had put upon them an eccentric but charming decoration, obviously suggested by some of the work of Mr Whistler. Tendrils, flowers, and butterflies in a quaint convention wandered thinly from panel to panel, giving the otherwise rather uninteresting room an unwonted atmosphere of richness and elegance. The lamentable jackasses who had destroyed this had certainly selected the best feature of the room whereon to inflict their senseless mischief.

I strolled idly downstairs, with no particular plan for the afternoon in my mind, and looked in at Hewitt's offices. Hewitt was reading a note, and after a little chat he informed me that it had been left an hour ago, in his absence, by the brother of the man I had just been speaking of.

"He isn't quite satisfied," Hewitt said, "with the way the police are investigating the case, and asks me to run down to Finchley and look round. Yesterday I should have refused, because I have five cases in progress already, but today I find that circumstances have given me a day or two. Didn't you say you knew the man?"

"Scarcely more than by sight. He was a boarder in the house at Chelsea where I stayed before I started chambers."

"Ah, well; I think I shall look into the thing. Do you feel particularly interested in the case? I mean, if you've nothing better to do, would you come with me?"

"I shall be very glad," I said. "I was in some doubt what to do with myself. Shall you start at once?"

"I think so. Kerrett, just call a cab. By the way, Brett, which paper has the fullest report of the inquest yesterday? I'll run over it as we go down."

As I had only seen one paper that morning, I could not answer Hewitt's question. So we bought various papers as we went along in the cab, and I found the reports while Martin Hewitt studied them. Summarised, this was the evidence given—

Sarah Dodson, general servant, deposed that she had been in service at Ivy Cottage, the residence of the deceased, for five months, the only other regular servant being the housekeeper and cook. On the evening of the previous Tuesday both servants retired a little before eleven, leaving Mr Kingscote with a friend in the smoking or sitting room. She never saw her master again alive. On coming downstairs the following morning and going to open the smoking-room windows, she was horrified to discover the body of Mr Kingscote lying on the floor of the room with blood about the head. She at once raised an alarm, and, on the instructions of the housekeeper, fetched a doctor, and gave information to the police. In answer to questions, witness stated she had heard no noise of any sort during the night, nor had anything suspicious occurred.

Hannah Carr, housekeeper and cook, deposed that she had been in the late Mr Kingscote's service since he had first taken Ivy Cottage—a period of rather more than a year. She had last seen the deceased alive on the evening of the previous Tuesday, at half-past ten, when she knocked at the door of the smoking-room, where Mr Kingscote was sitting with a friend, to ask if he would require anything more. Nothing was required, so witness shortly after went to bed. In the morning she was called by the previous witness, who had just gone downstairs, and found the body of deceased lying as described. Deceased's watch and chain were gone, as also was a ring he usually wore, and his pockets appeared to have been turned out. All the ground floor of the house was in confusion, and a bureau, a writing-table, and various drawers were open—a bunch of keys usually carried by deceased being left hanging at one keyhole. Deceased had drawn some money from the bank on the Tuesday, for current expenses; how much she did not know. She had not heard or seen anything suspicious during the night. Besides Dodson and herself, there were no regular servants; there was a charwoman, who came occasionally, and a jobbing gardener, living near, who was called in as required.

Mr James Vidler, surgeon, had been called by the first witness between seven and eight on Wednesday morning. He found the deceased lying on his face on the floor of the smoking-room, his feet being about eighteen inches from the window, and his head lying in the direction of the fireplace. He found three large contused wounds on the head, any one of which would probably have caused death. The wounds had all been inflicted, apparently, with the same blunt instrument—probably a club or life preserver, or other similar weapon. They could not have been done with the poker. Death was due to concussion of the brain, and deceased had probably been dead seven or eight hours when witness saw him. He had since examined the body more closely, but found no marks at all indicative of a struggle having taken place; indeed, from the position of the wounds and their severity, he should judge that the deceased had been attacked unawares from behind, and had died at once. The body appeared to be perfectly healthy.

Then there was police evidence, which showed that all the doors and windows were found shut and completely fastened, except the front door, which, although shut, was not bolted. There were shutters behind the French windows in the smoking-room, and these were found fastened. No money was found in the bureau, nor in any of the opened drawers, so that if any had been there, it had been stolen. The pockets were entirely empty, except for a small pair of nail scissors, and there was no watch upon the body, nor a ring. Certain footprints were found on the garden beds, which had led the police to take certain steps. No footprints were to be seen on the garden path, which was hard gravel.

Mr Alexander Campbell, stockbroker, stated that he had known deceased for some few years, and had done business for him. He and Mr Kingscote frequently called on one another, and on Tuesday evening they dined together at Ivy Cottage. They sat smoking and chatting till nearly twelve o'clock, when Mr Kingscote himself let him out, the servants having gone to bed. Here the witness proceeded rather excitedly: "That is all I know of this horrible business, and I can say nothing else. What the police mean by following and watching me—"

The Coroner: "Pray be calm, Mr Campbell. The police must do what seems best to them in a case of this sort. I am sure you would not have them neglect any means of getting at the truth."

Witness: "Certainly not. But if they suspect me, why don't they say so? It is intolerable that I should be—"

The Coroner: "Order, order, Mr Campbell. You are here to give evidence."

The witness then, in answer to questions, stated that the French windows of the smoking-room had been left open during the evening, the weather being very warm. He could not recollect whether or not deceased closed them before he left, but he certainly did not close the shutters. Witness saw nobody near the house when he left.

Mr Douglas Kingscote, architect, said deceased was his brother. He had not seen him for some months, living as he did in another part of the country. He believed his brother was fairly well off, and he knew that he had made a good amount by speculation in the last year or two. Knew of no person who would be likely to owe his brother a grudge, and could suggest no motive for the crime except ordinary robbery. His brother was to have been married in a few weeks. Questioned further on this point, witness said that the marriage was to have taken place a year ago, and it was with that view that Ivy Cottage, deceased's residence, was taken. The lady, however, sustained a domestic bereavement, and afterwards went abroad with her family: she was, witness believed, shortly expected back to England.

William Bates, jobbing gardener, who was brought up in custody, was cautioned, but elected to give evidence. Witness, who appeared to be much agitated, admitted having been in the garden of Ivy Cottage at four in the morning, but said that he had only gone to attend to certain plants, and knew absolutely nothing of the murder. He however admitted that he had no order for work beyond what he had done the day before. Being further pressed, witness made various contradictory statements, and finally said that he had gone to take certain plants away.

The inquest was then adjourned.

This was the case as it stood—apparently not a case presenting any very striking feature, although there seemed to me to be doubtful peculiarities in many parts of it. I asked Hewitt what he thought.

"Quite impossible to think anything, my boy, just yet; wait till we see the place. There are any number of possibilities. Kingscote's friend, Campbell, may have come in again, you know, by way of the window—or he may not. Campbell may have owed him money or something—or he may not. The anticipated wedding may have something to do with it—or, again, *that* may not. There is no limit to the possibilities, as far as we can see from this report—a mere dry husk of the affair. When we get closer we shall examine the possibilities by the light of more detailed information. One *probability* is that the wretched gardener is innocent. It seems to me that his was only a comparatively blameless manœuvre not unheard of at other times in his trade. He came at four in the morning to steal away the flowers he had planted the day before, and felt rather bashful when questioned on the point. Why should he trample on the beds, else? I wonder if the police thought to examine the beds for traces of rooting up, or questioned the housekeeper as to any plants being missing? But we shall see."

We chatted at random as the train drew near Finchley, and I mentioned *inter alia* the wanton piece of destruction perpetrated at Kingscote's late lodgings. Hewitt was interested.

"That was curious," he said, "very curious. Was anything else damaged? Furniture and so forth?"

"I don't know. Mrs Clayton said nothing of it, and I didn't ask her. But it was quite bad enough as it was. The decoration was really good, and I can't conceive a meaner piece of tomfoolery than such an attack on a decent woman's property."

Then Hewitt talked of other cases of similar stupid damage by creatures inspired by a defective sense of humour, or mere love of mischief. He had several curious and sometimes funny anecdotes of such affairs at museums and picture exhibitions, where the damage had been so great as to induce the authorities to call him in to discover the offender. The work was not always easy, chiefly from the mere absence of intelligible motive; nor, indeed, always successful. One of the anecdotes related to a case of malicious damage to a picture—the outcome of blind artistic jealousy—a case which had been hushed up by a large expenditure in compensation. It would considerably startle most people, could it be printed here, with the actual names of the parties concerned.

Ivy Cottage, Finchley, was a compact little house, standing in a compact little square of garden, little more than a third of an acre, or perhaps no more at all. The front door was but a dozen yards or so back from the road, but the intervening space was well treed and shrubbed. Mr Douglas Kingscote had not yet returned from town, but the housekeeper, an intelligent, matronly woman, who knew of his intention to call in Martin Hewitt, was ready to show us the house.

"*First*," Hewitt said, when we stood in the smoking-room, "I observe that somebody has shut the drawers and the bureau. That is unfortunate. Also, the floor has been washed and the carpet taken up, which is much worse. That, I suppose, was because the police had finished their examination, but it doesn't help me to make one at all. Has *anything*—anything *at all*—been left as it was on Tuesday morning?"

"Well, sir, you see everything was in such a muddle," the housekeeper began, "and when the police had done—"

"Just so. I know. You 'set it to rights,' eh? Oh, that setting to rights! It has lost me a fortune at one time and another. As to the other rooms, now, have they been set to rights?"

"Such as was disturbed have been put right, sir, of course."

"Which were disturbed? Let me see them. But wait a moment."

He opened the French windows, and closely examined the catch and bolts. He knelt and inspected the holes whereinto the bolts fell, and then glanced casually at the folding shutters. He opened a drawer or two, and tried the working of the locks with the keys the housekeeper carried. They were, the housekeeper explained, Mr Kingscote's own keys. All through the lower floors Hewitt examined some things attentively and closely, and others with scarcely a glance, on a system unaccountable to me. Presently, he asked to be shown Mr Kingscote's bedroom, which had not been disturbed, "set to rights," or slept in since the crime. Here, the housekeeper said, all drawers were kept unlocked but two—one in the wardrobe and one in the dressing-table, which Mr Kingscote had always been careful to keep locked. Hewitt immediately pulled both drawers open without difficulty. Within, in addition to a few odds and ends, were papers. All the contents of these drawers had been turned over confusedly, while those of the unlocked drawers were in perfect order.

"The police," Hewitt remarked, "may not have observed these matters. Any more than such an ordinary thing as *this*," he added, picking up a bent nail lying at the edge of a rug.

The housekeeper doubtless took the remark as a reference to the entire unimportance of a bent nail, but I noticed that Hewitt dropped the article quietly into his pocket.

We came away. At the front gate we met Mr Douglas Kingscote, who had just returned from town. He introduced himself, and expressed surprise at our promptitude both of coming and going.

"You can't have got anything like a clue in this short time, Mr Hewitt?" he asked.

"Well, no," Hewitt replied, with a certain dryness, "perhaps not. But I doubt whether a month's visit would have helped me to get anything very striking out of a washed floor and a houseful of carefully cleaned-up and 'set-to-rights' rooms.

Candidly, I don't think you can reasonably expect much of me. The police have a much better chance—they had the scene of the crime to examine. I have seen just such a few rooms as any one might see in the first well-furnished house he might enter. The trail of the housemaid has overlaid all the others."

"I'm very sorry for that; the fact was, I expected rather more of the police; and, indeed, I wasn't here in time entirely to prevent the clearing up. But still, I thought your well-known powers—"

"My dear sir, my 'well-known powers' are nothing but common sense assiduously applied and made quick by habit. That won't enable me to see the invisible."

"But can't we have the rooms put back into something of the state they were in? The cook will remember—"

"No, no. That would be worse and worse; that would only be the housemaid's trail in turn overlaid by the cook's. You must leave things with me for a little, I think."

"Then you don't give the case up?" Mr Kingscote asked anxiously.

"Oh, no! I don't give it up just yet. Do you know anything of your brother's private papers—as they were before his death?"

"I never knew anything till after that. I have gone over them, but they are all very ordinary letters. Do you suspect a theft of papers?"

Martin Hewitt, with his hands on his stick behind him, looked sharply at the other, and shook his head. "No," he said, "I can't quite say that."

We bade Mr Douglas Kingscote good-day, and walked towards the station. "Great nuisance, that setting to rights," Hewitt observed, on the way. "If the place had been left alone, the job might have been settled one way or another by this time. As it is, we shall have to run over to your old lodgings."

"My old lodgings?" I repeated, amazed. "Why my old lodgings?"

Hewitt turned to me with a chuckle and a wide smile. "Because we can't see the broken panel-work anywhere else," he said. "Let's see—Chelsea, isn't it?"

"Yes, Chelsea. But why—you don't suppose the people who defaced the panels also murdered the man who painted them?"

"Well," Hewitt replied, with another smile, "that would be carrying a practical joke rather far, wouldn't it? Even for the ordinary picture damager."

"You mean you *don't* think they did it, then? But what *do* you mean?"

"My dear fellow, I don't mean anything but what I say. Come now, this is rather an interesting case despite appearances, and it *has* interested me: so much, in fact, that I really think I forgot to offer Mr Douglas Kingscote my condolence on his bereavement. You see a problem is a problem, whether of theft, assassination, intrigue, or anything else, and I only think of it as one. The work very often makes me forget merely human sympathies. Now, you have often been good enough to express a very flattering interest in my work, and you shall have an opportunity of exercising your own common sense in the way I am always having to exercise mine. You shall see all my evidence (if I'm lucky enough to get any) as I collect it, and you shall make your own inferences. That will be a little exercise for you; the sort of exercise I should give a pupil if I had one. But I will give you what information I have, and you shall start fairly from this moment. You know the inquest evidence, such as it was, and you saw everything I did in Ivy Cottage?"

"Yes; I think so. But I'm not much the wiser."

"Very well. Now I will tell you. What does the whole case look like? How would you class the crime?"

"I suppose as the police do. An ordinary case of murder with the object of robbery."

"It is *not* an ordinary case. If it were, I shouldn't know as much as I do, little as that is; the ordinary cases are always difficult.

The assailant did not come to commit a burglary, although he was a skilled burglar, or one of them was, if more than one were concerned. The affair has, I think, nothing to do with the expected wedding, nor had Mr Campbell anything to do in it—at any rate, personally—nor the gardener. The criminal (or one of them) was known personally to the dead man, and was well-dressed: he (or again one of them, and I think there were two) even had a chat with Mr Kingscote before the murder took place. He came to ask for something which Mr Kingscote was unwilling to part with,—perhaps hadn't got. It was not a bulky thing. Now you have all my materials before you."

"But all this doesn't look like the result of the blind spite that would ruin a man's work first and attack him bodily afterwards."

"Spite isn't always blind, and there are other blind things besides spite; people with good eyes in their heads are blind sometimes, even detectives."

"But where did you get all this information? What makes you suppose that this was a burglar who didn't want to burgle, and a well-dressed man, and so on?"

Hewitt chuckled and smiled again.

"I saw it—saw it, my boy, that's all," he said. "But here comes the train."

On the way back to town, after I had rather minutely described Kingscote's work on the boarding-house panels, Hewitt asked me for the names and professions of such fellow lodgers in that house as I might remember. "When did you leave yourself?" he ended.

"Three years ago, or rather more. I can remember Kingscote himself; Turner, a medical student—James Turner, I think; Harvey Challitt, diamond merchant's articled pupil—he was a bad egg entirely, he's doing five years for forgery now; by the bye he had the room we are going to see till he was marched off, and Kingscote took it—a year before I left; there was Norton—don't know what he was; 'something in the City,' I think; and

Carter Paget, in the Admiralty Office. I don't remember any more at this moment; there were pretty frequent changes. But you can get it all from Mrs Lamb, of course."

"Of course; and Mrs Lamb's exact address is—what?"

I gave him the address, and the conversation became disjointed. At Farringdon station, where we alighted, Hewitt called two hansoms. Preparing to enter one, he motioned me to the other, saying, "You get straight away to Mrs Lamb's at once. She may be going to burn that splintered wood, or to set things to rights, after the manner of her kind, and you can stop her. I must make one or two small inquiries, but I shall be there half an hour after you."

"Shall I tell her our object?"

"Only that I may be able to catch her mischievous lodgers—nothing else yet." He jumped into the hansom and was gone.

I found Mrs Lamb still in a state of indignant perturbation over the trick served her four days before. Fortunately, she had left everything in the panelled room exactly as she had found it, with an idea of the being better able to demand or enforce reparation should her lodgers return. "The room's theirs, you see, sir," she said, "till the end of the week, since they paid in advance, and they may come back and offer to make amends, although I doubt it. As pleasant-spoken a young chap as you might wish, he seemed, him as come to take the rooms. 'My cousin,' says he, 'is rather an invalid, havin' only just got over congestion of the lungs, and he won't be in London till this evening late. He's comin' up from Birmingham,' he ses, 'and I hope he won't catch a fresh cold on the way, although of course we've got him muffled up plenty.' He took the rooms, sir, like a gentleman, and mentioned several gentlemen's names I knew well, as had lodged here before; and then he put down on that there very table, sir."—Mrs Lamb indicated the exact spot with her hand, as though that made the whole thing much more wonderful—"he put down on that very table a week's rent in advance, and ses, 'That's always the best sort of reference, Mrs Lamb, I think,' as kind-mannered as anything—and never 'aggled about the amount nor nothing. He only had a little black bag, but he said his cousin had all the luggage coming in the train, and as there was so much p'r'aps they wouldn't get it here till next day. Then he went out and came in with his cousin at eleven that night—Sarah let 'em in her own self—and in the morning they was gone—and this!" Poor Mrs Lamb, plaintively indignant, stretched her arm towards the wrecked panels.

"If the gentleman as you say is comin' on, sir," she pursued, "can do anything to find 'em, I'll prosecute 'em, that I will, if it costs me ten pound. I spoke to the constable on the beat, but he only looked like a fool, and said if I knew where they were I might charge 'em with wilful damage, or county court 'em. Of course I know I can do that if I knew where they were, but how can I find 'em? Mr Jones he said his name was; but how many Joneses is there in London, sir?"

I couldn't imagine any answer to a question like this, but I condoled with Mrs Lamb as well as I could. She afterwards went on to express herself much as her sister had done with regard to Kingscote's death, only as the destruction of her panels loomed larger in her mind, she dwelt primarily on that. "It might almost seem," she said, "that somebody had a deadly spite on the pore young gentleman, and went breakin' up his paintin' one night, and murderin' him the next!"

I examined the broken panels with some care, having half a notion to attempt to deduce something from them myself, if possible. But I could deduce nothing. The beading had been taken out, and the panels, which were thick in the centre but bevelled at the edges, had been removed and split up literally into thin firewood, which lay in a tumbled heap on the hearth and about the floor. Every panel in the room had been treated in the same way, and the result was a pretty large heap of sticks, with nothing whatever about them to distinguish them from other sticks, except the paint on one face, which I observed in many cases had been scratched and scraped away. The rug was drawn half across the hearth, and had evidently been used to deaden the sound of chopping. But mischief—wanton and stupid mischief—was all I could deduce from it all.

Mr Jones's cousin, it seemed, only Sarah had seen, as she admitted him in the evening, and then he was so heavily muffled that she could not distinguish his features, and would never be able to identify him. But as for the other one, Mrs Lamb was ready to swear to him anywhere.

Hewitt was long in coming, and internal symptoms of the approach of dinner-time (we had had no lunch) had made themselves felt before a sharp ring at the doorbell foretold his arrival. "I have had to wait for answers to a telegram," he said in explanation, "but at any rate I have the information I wanted. And these are the mysterious panels, are they?"

Mrs Lamb's true opinion of Martin Hewitt's behaviour as it proceeded would have been amusing to know. She watched in amazement the antics of a man who purposed finding out who had been splitting sticks by dint of picking up each separate stick and staring at it. In the end he collected a small handful of sticks by themselves and handed them to me, saying, "Just put these together on the table, Brett, and see what you make of them."

I turned the pieces painted side up, and fitted them together into a complete panel, joining up the painted design accurately. "It is an entire panel," I said.

"Good. Now look at the sticks a little more closely, and tell me if you notice anything peculiar about them—any particular in which they differ from all the others."

I looked. "Two adjoining sticks," I said, "have each a small semi-circular cavity stuffed with what seems to be putty. Put together it would mean a small circular hole, perhaps a knot-hole, half an inch or so in diameter, in the panel, filled in with putty, or whatever it is."

"A *knot-hole?*" Hewitt asked, with particular emphasis.

"Well, no, not a knot-hole, of course, because that would go right through, and this doesn't. It is probably less than half an inch deep from the front surface."

"Anything else? Look at the whole appearance of the wood itself. Colour, for instance."

"It is certainly darker than the rest."

"So it is." He took the two pieces carrying the puttied hole, threw the rest on the heap, and addressed the landlady. "The Mr Harvey Challitt who occupied this room before Mr Kingscote, and who got into trouble for forgery, was the Mr Harvey Challitt who was himself robbed of diamonds a few months before on a staircase, wasn't he?"

"Yes, sir," Mrs Lamb replied in some bewilderment. "He certainly was that, on his own office stairs, chloroformed."

"Just so, and when they marched him away because of the forgery, Mr Kingscote changed into his rooms?"

"Yes, and very glad I was. It was bad enough to have the disgrace brought into the house, without the trouble of trying to get people to take his very rooms, and I thought—"

"Yes, yes, very awkward, very awkward!" Hewitt interrupted rather impatiently. "The man who took the rooms on Monday, now—you'd never seen him before, had you?"

"No, sir."

"Then is *that* anything like him?" Hewitt held a cabinet photograph before her.

"Why—why—law, yes, that's *him!*"

Hewitt dropped the photograph back into his breast pocket with a contented "Um," and picked up his hat. "I think we may soon be able to find that young gentleman for you, Mrs Lamb. He is not a very respectable young gentleman, and perhaps you are well rid of him, even as it is. Come, Brett," he added, "the day hasn't been wasted, after all."

We made towards the nearest telegraph office. On the way I said, "That puttied-up hole in the piece of wood seems to have influenced you. Is it an important link?"

"Well—yes," Hewitt answered, "it is. But all those other pieces are important, too."

"But why?"

"Because there are no holes in them." He looked quizzically at my wondering face, and laughed aloud. "Come," he said, "I won't puzzle you much longer. Here is the post-office. I'll send my wire, and then we'll go and dine at Luzatti's."

He sent his telegram, and we cabbed it to Luzatti's. Among actors, journalists, and others who know town and like a good dinner, Luzatti's is well known. We went upstairs for the sake of quietness, and took a table standing alone in a recess just inside the door. We ordered our dinner, and then Hewitt began:

"Now tell me what *your* conclusion is in this matter of the Ivy Cottage murder."

"Mine? I haven't one. I'm sorry I'm so very dull, but I really haven't."

"Come, I'll give you a point. Here is the newspaper account (torn sacrilegiously from my scrapbook for your benefit) of the robbery perpetrated on Harvey Challitt a few months before his forgery. Read it."

"Oh, but I remember the circumstances very well. He was carrying two packets of diamonds belonging to his firm downstairs to the office of another firm of diamond merchants on the ground-floor. It was a quiet time in the day, and halfway down he was seized on a dark landing, made insensible by chloroform, and robbed of the diamonds—five or six thousand pounds' worth altogether, of stones of various smallish individual values up to thirty pounds or so. He lay unconscious on the landing till one of the partners, noticing that he had been rather long gone, followed and found him. That's all, I think."

"Yes, that's all. Well, what do you make of it?"

"I'm afraid I don't quite see the connection with this case."

"Well, then, I'll give you another point. The telegram I've just sent releases information to the police, in consequence of which they will probably apprehend Harvey Challitt and his confederate, Henry Gillard, *alias* Jones, for the murder of Gavin Kingscote. Now, then."

"Challitt! But he's in gaol already."

"Tut, tut, consider. Five years' penal was his dose, although for the first offence, because the forgery was of an extremely dangerous sort. You left Chelsea over three years ago yourself, and you told me that his difficulty occurred a year before. That makes four years, at least. Good conduct in prison brings a man out of a five years' sentence in that time or a little less, and, as a matter of fact, Challitt was released rather more than a week ago."

"Still, I'm afraid I don't see what you are driving at."

"Whose story is this about the diamond robbery from Harvey Challitt?"

"His own."

"Exactly. His own. Does his subsequent record make him look like a person whose stories are to be accepted without doubt or question?"

"Why, no. I think I see—no, I don't. You mean he stole them himself? I've a sort of dim perception of your drift now, but still I can't fix it. The whole thing's too complicated."

"It is a little complicated for a first effort, I admit, so I will tell you. This is the story. Harvey Challitt is an artful young man, and decides on a theft of his firm's diamonds. He first prepares a hiding-place somewhere near the stairs of his office, and when the opportunity arrives he puts the stones away, spills his chloroform, and makes a smell—possibly sniffs some, and actually goes off on the stairs, and the whole thing's done. He is carried into the office—the diamonds are gone. He tells of the attack on the stairs, as we have heard, and he is believed. At a suitable opportunity he takes his plunder from the hiding-place, and goes home to his lodgings. What is he to do with those diamonds? He can't sell them yet, because the robbery is publicly notorious, and all the regular jewel buyers know him.

"Being a criminal novice, he doesn't know any regular receiver of stolen goods, and if he did would prefer to wait and get full value by an ordinary sale. There will always be a danger of detection so long as the stones are not securely hidden, so he proceeds to hide them. He knows that if any suspicion were aroused his rooms would be searched in every likely place, so he looks for an unlikely place. Of course, he thinks of taking out a panel and hiding them behind that. But the idea is so obvious that it won't do; the police would certainly take those panels out to look behind them. Therefore he determines to hide them *in* the panels. See here—he took the two pieces of wood with the filled hole from his tail pocket and opened his penknife—the putty near the surface is softer than that near the bottom of the hole; two different lots of putty, differently mixed, perhaps, have been used, therefore, presumably, at different times."

"But to return to Challitt. He makes holes with a centre-bit in different places on the panels, and in each hole he places a diamond, embedding it carefully in putty. He smooths the surface carefully flush with the wood, and then very carefully paints the place over, shading off the paint at the edges so as to leave no signs of a patch. He doesn't do the whole job at once, creating a noise and a smell of paint, but keeps on steadily, a few holes at a time, till in a little while the whole wainscoting is set with hidden diamonds, and every panel is apparently sound and whole."

"But, then—there was only one such hole in the whole lot."

"Just so, and that very circumstance tells us the whole truth. Let me tell the story first—I'll explain the clue after. The diamonds lie hidden for a few months—he grows impatient. He wants the money, and he can't see a way of getting it. At last he determines to make a bolt and go abroad to sell his plunder. He knows he will want money for expenses, and that he may not be able to get rid of his diamonds at once. He also expects that his suddenly going abroad while the robbery is still in people's minds will bring suspicion on him in any case, so, in for a penny in for a pound, he commits a bold forgery, which, had it been successful, would have put him in funds and enabled him to leave the country with the stones. But the forgery is detected, and he is haled to prison, leaving the diamonds in their wainscot setting.

"Now we come to Gavin Kingscote. He must have been a shrewd fellow—the sort of man that good detectives are made of. Also he must have been pretty unscrupulous. He had his suspicions about the genuineness of the diamond robbery, and kept his eyes open. What indications he had to guide him we don't know, but living in the same house a sharp fellow on the look-out would probably see enough. At any rate, they led him to the belief that the diamonds were in the thief's rooms, but not among his movables, or they would have been found after the arrest. Here was his chance. Challitt was out of the way for years, and there was plenty of time to take the house to pieces if it were necessary. So he changed into Challitt's rooms.

"How long it took him to find the stones we shall never know. He probably tried many other places first, and, I expect, found the diamonds at last by pricking over the panels with a needle. Then came the problem of getting them out without attracting attention. He decided not to trust to the needle, which might possibly leave a stone or two undiscovered, but to split up each panel carefully into splinters so as to leave no part unexamined. Therefore he took measurements, and had a number of panels made by a joiner of the exact size and pattern of those in the room, and announced to his landlady his intention of painting her panels with a pretty design. This to account for the wet paint, and even for the fact of a panel being out of the wall, should she chance to bounce into the room at an awkward moment. All very clever, eh?"

"Very."

"Ah, he was a smart man, no doubt. Well, he went to work, taking out a panel, substituting a new one, painting it over, and chopping up the old one on the quiet, getting rid of the splinters out of doors when the booty had been extracted. The decoration progressed and the little heap of diamonds grew. Finally, he came to the last panel, but found that he had used all his new panels and hadn't one left for a substitute. It must have been at some time when it was difficult to get hold of the joiner—Bank Holiday, perhaps, or Sunday, and he was impatient. So he scraped the paint off, and went carefully over every part of the surface—experience had taught him by this that all the holes were of the same sort—and found one diamond. He took it out, refilled the hole with putty, painted the old panel and put it back. *These* are pieces of that old panel—the only old one of the lot.

"Nine men out of ten would have got out of the house as soon as possible after the thing was done, but he was a cool hand and stayed. That made the whole thing look a deal more genuine than if he had unaccountably cleared out as soon as he had got his room nicely decorated. I expect the original capital for those Stock Exchange operations we heard of came out of those diamonds. He stayed as long as suited him, and left when he set up housekeeping with a view to his wedding. The rest of the story is pretty plain. You guess it, of course?"

"Yes," I said, "I think I can guess the rest, in a general sort of way—except as to one or two points."

"It's all plain—perfectly. See here! Challitt, in gaol, determines to get those diamonds when he comes out. To do that without being suspected it will be necessary to hire the room. But he knows that he won't be able to do that himself, because the landlady, of course, knows him, and won't have an ex-convict in the house. There is no help for it; he must have a confederate, and share the spoil. So he makes the acquaintance of another convict, who seems a likely man for the job, and whose sentence expires about the same time as his own. When they come out, he arranges the matter with this confederate, who is a well-mannered (and pretty well-known) housebreaker, and the latter calls at Mrs Lamb's house to look for rooms. The very room itself happens to be to let, and of course it is taken, and Challitt (who is the invalid cousin) comes in at night muffled and unrecognisable.

"The decoration on the panel does not alarm them, because, of course, they suppose it to have been done on the old panels and over the old paint. Challitt tries the spots where diamonds were left—there are none—there is no putty even. Perhaps, think they, the panels have been shifted and interchanged in the painting, so they set to work and split them all up as we have seen, getting more desperate as they go on. Finally they realize that they are done, and clear out, leaving Mrs Lamb to mourn over their mischief.

"They know that Kingscote is the man who has forestalled them, because Gillard (or Jones), in his chat with the landlady, has heard all about him and his painting of the panels. So the next night they set off for Finchley. They get into Kingscote's garden and watch him let Campbell out. While he is gone, Challitt quietly steps through the French window into the smoking-room, and waits for him, Gillard remaining outside.

"Kingscote returns, and Challitt accuses him of taking the stones. Kingscote is contemptuous—doesn't care for Challitt, because he knows he is powerless, being the original thief himself; besides, knows there is no evidence, since the diamonds are sold and dispersed long ago. Challitt offers to divide the plunder with him—Kingscote laughs and tells him to go; probably threatens to throw him out, Challitt being the smaller man. Gillard, at the open window, hears this, steps in behind, and quietly knocks him on the head. The rest follows as a matter of course. They fasten the window and shutters, to exclude observation; turn over all the drawers, etc., in case the jewels are there; go to the best bedroom and try there, and so on. Failing (and possibly being disturbed after a few hours' search by the noise of the acquisitive gardener), Gillard, with the instinct of an old thief, determines they shan't go away with nothing, so empties Kingscote's pockets and takes his watch and chain and so on. They go out by the front door and shut it after them. *Voilà tout.*"

I was filled with wonder at the prompt ingenuity of the man who in these few hours of hurried inquiry could piece together so accurately all the materials of an intricate and mysterious affair such as this; but more, I wondered where and how he had collected those materials.

"There is no doubt, Hewitt," I said, "that the accurate and minute application of what you are pleased to call your common sense has become something very like an instinct with you. What did you deduce from? You told me your conclusions from the examination of Ivy Cottage, but not how you arrived at them."

"They didn't leave me much material downstairs, did they? But in the bedroom, the two drawers which the thieves found locked were ransacked—opened probably with keys taken from the dead man. On the floor I saw a bent French nail; here it is. You see, it is twice bent at right angles, near the head and near the point, and there is the faint mark of the pliers that were used to bend it. It is a very usual burglars' tool, and handy in experienced hands to open ordinary drawer locks. Therefore,

I knew that a professional burglar had been at work. He had probably fiddled at the drawers with the nail first, and then had thrown it down to try the dead man's keys.

"But I knew this professional burglar didn't come for a burglary, from several indications. There was no attempt to take plate, the first thing a burglar looks for. Valuable clocks were left on mantelpieces, and other things that usually go in an ordinary burglary were not disturbed. Notably, it was to be observed that no doors or windows were broken, or had been forcibly opened; therefore, it was plain that the thieves had come in by the French window of the smoking-room, the only entrance left open at the last thing. *Therefore*, they came in, or one did, knowing that Mr Kingscote was up, and being quite willing—presumably anxious—to see him. Ordinary burglars would have waited till he had retired, and then could have got through the closed French window as easily almost as if it were open, notwithstanding the thin wooden shutters, which would never stop a burglar for more than five minutes. Being anxious to see him, they—or again, *one* of them—presumably knew him. That they had come to *get* something was plain, from the ransacking. As, in the end, they *did* steal his money, and watch, but did *not* take larger valuables, it was plain that they had no bag with them—which proves not only that they had not come to burgle, for every burglar takes his bag, but that the thing they came to get was not bulky. Still, they could easily have removed plate or clocks by rolling them up in a table-cover or other wrapper, but such a bundle, carried by well-dressed men, would attract attention—therefore it was probable that they were well dressed. Do I make it clear?"

"Quite—nothing seems simpler now it is explained—that's the way with difficult puzzles."

"There was nothing more to be got at the house. I had already in my mind the curious coincidence that the panels at Chelsea had been broken the very night before that of the murder, and determined to look at them in any case. I got from you the name of the man who had lived in the panelled room before Kingscote, and at once remembered it (although I said nothing about it) as that of the young man who had been chloroformed for his employer's diamonds. I keep things of that sort in my mind, you see—and, indeed, in my scrapbook. You told me yourself about his imprisonment, and there I was with what seemed now a hopeful case getting into a promising shape.

"You went on to prevent any setting to rights at Chelsea, and I made enquiries as to Challitt. I found he had been released only a few days before all this trouble arose, and I also found the name of another man who was released from the same establishment only a few days earlier. I knew this man (Gillard) well, and knew that nobody was a more likely rascal for such a crime as that at Finchley. On my way to Chelsea I called at my office, gave my clerk certain instructions, and looked up my scrap-book. I found the newspaper account of the chloroform business, and also a photograph of Gillard—I keep as many of these things as I can collect. What I did at Chelsea you know. I saw that one panel was of old wood and the rest new. I saw the hole in the old panel, and I asked one or two questions. The case was complete."

We proceeded with our dinner. Presently I said: "It all rests with the police now, of course?"

"Of course. I should think it very probable that Challitt and Gillard will be caught. Gillard, at any rate, is pretty well known. It will be rather hard on the surviving Kingscote, after engaging me, to have his dead brother's diamond transactions publicly exposed as a result, won't it? But it can't be helped. *Fiat justitia*, of course."

"How will the police feel over this?" I asked. "You've rather cut them out, eh?"

"Oh, the police are all right. They had not the information I had, you see; they knew nothing of the panel business. If

Mrs Lamb had gone to Scotland Yard instead of to the policeman on the beat, perhaps I should never have been sent for."

The same quality that caused Martin Hewitt to rank as mere "common-sense" his extraordinary power of almost instinctive deduction, kept his respect for the abilities of the police at perhaps a higher level than some might have considered justified.

We sat some little while over our dessert, talking as we sat, when there occurred one of those curious conjunctions of circumstances that we notice again and again in ordinary life, and forget as often, unless the importance of the occasion fixes the matter in the memory. A young man had entered the dining-room, and had taken his seat at a corner table near the back window. He had been sitting there for some little time before I particularly observed him. At last he happened to turn his thin, pale face in my direction, and our eyes met. It was Challitt—the man we had been talking of!

I sprang to my feet in some excitement.

"That's the man!" I cried. "Challitt!"

Hewitt rose at my words, and at first attempted to pull me back. Challitt, in guilty terror, saw that we were between him and the door, and turning, leaped upon the sill of the open window, and dropped out. There was a fearful crash of broken glass below, and everybody rushed to the window.

Hewitt drew me through the door, and we ran downstairs. "Pity you let out like that," he said, as he went. "If you'd kept quiet we could have sent out for the police with no trouble. Never mind—can't help it."

Below, Challitt was lying in a broken heap in the midst of a crowd of waiters. He had crashed through a thick glass skylight and fallen, back downward, across the back of a lounge. He was taken away on a stretcher unconscious, and, in fact, died in a week in hospital from injuries to the spine.

During his periods of consciousness he made a detailed statement, bearing out the conclusions of Martin Hewitt with the most surprising exactness, down to the smallest particulars. He and Gillard had parted immediately after the crime, judging it safer not to be seen together. He had, he affirmed, endured agonies of fear and remorse in the few days since the fatal night at Finchley, and had even once or twice thought of giving himself up. When I so excitedly pointed him out, he knew at once that the game was up, and took the one desperate chance of escape that offered. But to the end he persistently denied that he had himself committed the murder, or had even thought of it till he saw it accomplished. That had been wholly the work of Gillard, who, listening at the window and perceiving the drift of the conversation, suddenly beat down Kingscote from behind with a life-preserver. And so Harvey Challitt ended his life at the age of twenty-six.

Gillard was never taken. He doubtless left the country, and has probably since that time become "known to the police" under another name abroad. Perhaps he has even been hanged, and if he has been, there was no miscarriage of justice, no matter what the charge against him may have been.

2

THE *NICOBAR* BULLION CASE

I.

The whole voyage was an unpleasant one, and Captain Mackrie, of the Anglo-Malay Company's steamship *Nicobar*, had at last some excuse for the ill-temper that had made him notorious and unpopular in the company's marine staff. Although the fourth and fifth mates in the seclusion of their berth ventured deeper in their search for motives, and opined that the "old man" had made a deal less out of this voyage than usual, the company having lately taken to providing its own stores; so that "makings" were gone clean and "cumshaw" (which means commission in the trading lingo of the China seas) had shrunk small indeed. In confirmation they adduced the uncommonly long face of the steward (the only man in the ship satisfied with the skipper), whom the new regulations hit with the same blow. But indeed the steward's dolor might well be credited to the short passenger list, and the unpromising aspect of the few passengers in the eyes of a man accustomed to gauge one's tip-yielding capacity a month in advance. For the steward it was altogether the wrong time of year, the wrong sort of voyage, and certainly the wrong sort of passengers. So that doubtless the confidential talk of the fourth and fifth officers was mere youthful scandal. At any rate, the captain had prospect of a good deal in private trade home, for he had been taking curiosities and Japanese oddments aboard (plainly for sale in London) in a way that a third steward would have been ashamed of, and which, for a captain, was a scandal and an ignominy; and he had taken pains to insure well for the lot. These things the fourth and fifth mates often spoke of, and more than once made a winking allusion to, in the presence of the third mate and the chief engineer, who laughed and winked too, and sometimes said as much to the second mate, who winked without laughing; for of such is the tittle-tattle of shipboard.

The *Nicobar* was bound home with few passengers, as I have said, a small general cargo, and gold bullion to the value of £200,000 — the bullion to be landed at Plymouth, as usual. The presence of this bullion was a source of much conspicuous worry on the part of the second officer, who had charge of the bullion-room. For this was his first voyage on his promotion from third officer, and the charge of £200,000 worth of gold bars was a thing he had not been accustomed to. The placid first officer pointed out to him that this wasn't the first shipment of bullion the world had ever known, by a long way, nor the largest. Also that every usual precaution was taken, and the keys were in the captain's cabin; so that he might reasonably be as easy in his mind as the few thousand other second officers who had had charge of hatches and special cargo since the world began. But this did not comfort Brasyer. He fidgeted about when off watch, considering and puzzling out the various means by which the bullion-room might be got at, and fidgeted more when on watch, lest somebody might be at that moment putting into practice the ingenious dodges he had thought of. And he didn't keep his fears and speculations to himself. He bothered the first officer with them, and when the first officer escaped he explained the whole thing at length to the third officer.

"Can't think what the company's about," he said on one such occasion to the first mate, "calling a tin-pot bunker like that a bullion-room."

"Skittles!" responded the first mate, and went on smoking.

"Oh, that's all very well for you who aren't responsible," Brasyer went on, "but I'm pretty sure something will happen some day; if not on this voyage on some other. Talk about a strong room! Why, what's it made of?"

"Three-eighths boiler plate."

"Yes, three-eighths boiler plate—about as good as a sixpenny tin money box. Why, I'd get through that with my grandmother's scissors!"

"All right; borrow 'em and get through. *I* would if I had a grandmother."

"There it is down below there out of sight and hearing, nice and handy for anybody who likes to put in a quiet hour at plate cutting from the coal bunker next door—always empty, because it's only a seven-ton bunker, not worth trimming. And the other side's against the steward's pantry. What's to prevent a man shipping as steward, getting quietly through while he's supposed to be bucketing about among his slops and his crockery, and strolling away with the plunder at the next port? And then there's the carpenter. *He's* always messing about somewhere below, with a bag full of tools. Nothing easier than for him to make a job in a quiet corner, and get through the plates."

"But then what's he to do with the stuff when he's got it? You can't take gold ashore by the hundredweight in your boots."

"Do with it. Why, dump it, of course. Dump it overboard in a quiet port and mark the spot. Come to that, he could desert clean at Port Said—what easier place?—and take all he wanted. You know what Port Said's like. Then there are the firemen—oh, *anybody* can do it!" And Brasyer moved off to take another peep under the hatchway.

The door of the bullion-room was fastened by one central patent lock and two padlocks, one above and one below the other lock. A day or two after the conversation recorded above, Brasyer was carefully examining and trying the lower of the padlocks with a key, when a voice immediately behind him asked sharply, "Well, sir, and what are you up to with that padlock?"

Brasyer started violently and looked round. It was Captain Mackrie.

"There's—that is—I'm afraid these are the same sort of padlocks as those in the carpenter's stores," the second mate replied, in a hurry of explanation. "I—I was just trying, that's all; I'm afraid the keys fit."

"Just you let the carpenter take care of his own stores, will you, Mr Brasyer? There's a Chubb's lock there as well as the padlocks, and the key of that's in my cabin, and I'll take care doesn't go out of it without my knowledge. So perhaps you'd best leave off experiments till you're asked to make 'em, for your own sake. That's enough now," the captain added, as Brasyer appeared to be ready to reply; and he turned on his heel and made for the steward's quarters.

Brasyer stared after him ragefully. "Wonder what *you* want down here," he muttered under his breath. "Seems to me one doesn't often see a skipper as thick with the steward as that." And he turned off growling towards the deck above.

"Hanged if I like that steward's pantry stuck against the side of the bullion-room," he said later in the day to the first officer. "And what does a steward want with a lot of boiler-maker's tools aboard? You know he's got them."

"In the name of the prophet, rats!" answered the first mate, who was of a less fussy disposition. "What a fatiguing creature you are, Brasyer! Don't you know the man's a boiler-maker by regular trade, and has only taken to stewardship for the last year or two? That sort of man doesn't like parting with his tools, and as he's a widower, with no home ashore, of course he has to carry all his traps aboard. Do shut up, and take your proper rest like a Christian. Here, I'll give you a cigar; it's all right—Burman; stick it in your mouth, and keep your jaw tight on it."

But there was no soothing the second officer. Still he prowled about the after orlop deck, and talked at large of his anxiety for the contents of the bullion-room. Once again, a few days later, as he approached the iron door, he was startled by the appearance of the captain coming, this time, *from* the steward's pantry. He fancied he had heard tapping, Brasyer explained, and had come to investigate. But the captain turned him back with even less ceremony than before, swearing he would give charge of the bullion-room to another officer if Brasyer persisted in his eccentricities. On the first deck the second officer was met by the carpenter, a quiet, sleek, soft-spoken man, who asked him for the padlock and key he had borrowed from the stores during the week. But Brasyer put him off, promising to send it back later. And the carpenter trotted away to a job he happened to have, singularly enough, in the hold, just under the after orlop deck, and below the floor of the bullion-room.

As I have said, the voyage was in no way a pleasant one. Everywhere the weather was at its worst, and scarce was Gibraltar passed before the Lascars were shivering in their cotton trousers, and the Seedee boys were buttoning tight such old tweed jackets as they might muster from their scanty kits. It was January. In the Bay the weather was tremendous, and the *Nicobar* banged and shook and pitched distractedly across in a howling world of thunderous green sea, washed within and without, above and below. Then, in the Chops, as night fell, something went, and there was no more steerage-way, nor, indeed, anything else but an aimless wallowing. The screw had broken.

The high sea had abated in some degree, but it was still bad. Such sail as the steamer carried, inadequate enough, was set, and shift was made somehow to worry along to Plymouth—or to Falmouth if occasion better served—by that means. And so the *Nicobar* beat across the Channel on a rather better, though anything but smooth, sea, in a black night, made thicker by a storm of sleet, which turned gradually to snow as the hours advanced.

The ship laboured slowly ahead, through a universal blackness that seemed to stifle. Nothing but a black void above, below, and around, and the sound of wind and sea; so that one coming before a deck-light was startled by the quiet advent of the large snowflakes that came like moths as it seemed from nowhere. At four bells—two in the morning—a foggy light appeared away on the starboard bow—it was the Eddystone light—and an hour or two later, the exact whereabouts of the ship being a thing of much uncertainty, it was judged best to lay her to till daylight. No order had yet been given, however, when suddenly there were dim lights over the port quarter, with a more solid blackness beneath them. Then a shout and a thunderous crash, and the whole ship shuddered, and in ten seconds had belched up every living soul from below. The *Nicobar's* voyage was over—it was a collision.

The stranger backed off into the dark, and the two vessels drifted apart, though not till some from the *Nicobar* had jumped aboard the other. Captain Mackrie's presence of mind was wonderful, and never for a moment did he lose absolute command of every soul on board. The ship had already begun to settle down by the stern and list to port. Life-belts were served out promptly. Fortunately there were but two women among the passengers, and no children. The boats were lowered without a mishap, and presently two strange boats came as near as they dare from the ship (a large coasting steamer, it afterwards appeared) that had cut into the *Nicobar*. The last of the passengers were being got off safely, when Brasyer, running anxiously to the captain, said:—

"Can't do anything with that bullion, can we, sir? Perhaps a box or two—"

"Oh, damn the bullion!" shouted Captain Mackrie. "Look after the boat, sir, and get the passengers off. The insurance companies can find the bullion for themselves."

But Brasyer had vanished at the skipper's first sentence. The skipper turned aside to the steward as the crew and engine-room staff made for the remaining boats, and the two spoke quietly together. Presently the steward turned away as if to execute an order, and the skipper continued in a louder tone:—

"They're the likeliest stuff, and we can but drop 'em, at worst. But be slippy—she won't last ten minutes."

She lasted nearly a quarter of an hour. By that time, however, everybody was clear of her, and the captain in the last boat was only just near enough to see the last of her lights as she went down.

II.

The day broke in a sulky grey, and there lay the *Nicobar*, in ten fathoms, not a mile from the shore, her topmasts forlornly visible above the boisterous water. The sea was rough all that day, but the snow had ceased, and during the night the weather calmed considerably. Next day Lloyd's agent was steaming about in a launch from Plymouth, and soon a salvage company's tug came up and lay to by the emerging masts. There was every chance of raising the ship as far as could be seen, and a diver went down from the salvage tug to measure the breach made in the *Nicobar's* side, in order that the necessary oak planking or sheeting might be got ready for covering the hole, preparatory to pumping and raising. This was done in a very short time, and the necessary telegrams having been sent, the tug remained in its place through the night, and prepared for the sending down of several divers on the morrow to get out the bullion as a commencement.

Just at this time Martin Hewitt happened to be engaged on a case of some importance and delicacy on behalf of Lloyd's Committee, and was staying for a few days at Plymouth. He heard the story of the wreck, of course, and speaking casually with Lloyd's agent as to the salvage work just beginning, he was told the name of the salvage company's representative on the tug, Mr Percy Merrick—a name he immediately recognised as that of an old acquaintance of his own. So that on the day when the divers were at work in the bullion-room of the sunken *Nicobar*, Hewitt gave himself a holiday, and went aboard the tug about noon.

Here he found Merrick, a big, pleasant man of thirty-eight or so. He was very glad to see Hewitt, but was a great deal puzzled as to the results of the morning's work on the wreck. Two cases of gold bars were missing.

"There was £200,000 worth of bullion on board," he said, "that's plain and certain. It was packed in forty cases, each of £5,000 value. But now there are only thirty-eight cases! Two are gone clearly. I wonder what's happened?"

"I suppose your men don't know anything about it?" asked Hewitt.

"No, they're all right. You see, it's impossible for them to bring anything up without its being observed, especially as they have to be unscrewed from their diving-dresses here on deck. Besides, bless you, I was down with them."

"Oh! Do you dive yourself, then?"

"Well, I put the dress on sometimes, you know, for any such special occasion as this. I went down this morning. There was no difficulty in getting about on the vessel below, and I found the keys of the bullion-room just where the captain said I would, in his cabin. But the locks were useless, of course, after being a couple of days in salt water. So we just burgled the door with crowbars, and then we saw that we might have done it a bit more easily from outside. For that coasting-steamer cut clean into the bunker next the bullion-room, and ripped open the sheet of boiler-plate dividing them."

"The two missing cases couldn't have dropped out that way, of course?"

"Oh, no. We looked, of course, but it would have been impossible. The vessel has a list the other way—to starboard—and the piled cases didn't reach as high as the torn part. Well, as I said, we burgled the door, and there they were, thirty-eight sealed bullion cases, neither more nor less, and they're down below in the after-cabin at this moment. Come and see."

Thirty-eight they were; pine cases bound with hoop-iron and sealed at every joint, each case about eighteen inches by a foot, and six inches deep. They were corded together, two and two, apparently for convenience of transport.

"Did you cord them like this yourself?" asked Hewitt.

"No, that's how we found 'em. We just hooked 'em on a block and tackle, the pair at a time, and they hauled 'em up here aboard the tug."

"What have you done about the missing two—anything?"

"Wired off to headquarters, of course, at once. And I've sent for Captain Mackrie—he's still in the neighbourhood, I believe—and Brasyer, the second officer, who had charge of the bullion-room. They may possibly know something. Anyway, *one* thing's plain. There were forty cases at the beginning of the voyage, and now there are only thirty-eight."

There was a pause; and then Merrick added, "By the by, Hewitt, this is rather your line, isn't it? You ought to look up these two cases."

Hewitt laughed. "All right," he said; "I'll begin this minute if you'll commission me."

"Well," Merrick replied slowly, "of course I can't do that without authority from headquarters. But if you've nothing to do for an hour or so there is no harm in putting on your considering cap, is there? Although, of course, there's nothing to go upon as yet. But you might listen to what Mackrie and Brasyer have to say. Of course I don't know, but as it's a £10,000 question probably it might pay you, and if you *do* see your way to anything I'd wire and get you commissioned at once."

There was a tap at the door and Captain Mackrie entered. "Mr Merrick?" he said interrogatively, looking from one to another.

"That's myself, sir," answered Merrick.

"I'm Captain Mackrie, of the *Nicobar*. You sent for me, I believe. Something wrong with the bullion I'm told, isn't it?"

Merrick explained matters fully. "I thought perhaps you might be able to help us, Captain Mackrie. Perhaps I have been wrongly informed as to the number of cases that should have been there?"

"No; there were forty right enough. I think though—perhaps I might be able to give you a sort of hint."—and Captain Mackrie looked hard at Hewitt.

"This is Mr Hewitt, Captain Mackrie," Merrick interposed. "You may speak as freely as you please before him. In fact, he's sort of working on the business, so to speak."

"Well," Mackrie said, "if that's so, speaking between ourselves, I should advise you to turn your attention to Brasyer. He was my second officer, you know, and had charge of the stuff."

"Do you mean," Hewitt asked, "that Mr Brasyer might give us some useful information?"

Mackrie gave an ugly grin. "Very likely he might," he said, "if he were fool enough. But I don't think you'd get much out of him direct. I meant you might watch him."

"What, do you suppose he was concerned in any way with the disappearance of this gold?"

"I should think—speaking, as I said before, in confidence and between ourselves—that it's very likely indeed. I didn't like his manner all through the voyage."

"Why?"

"Well, he was so eternally cracking on about his responsibility, and pretending to suspect the stokers and the carpenter, and one person and another, of trying to get at the bullion cases—that that alone was almost enough to make one suspicious. He protested so much, you see. He was so conscientious and diligent himself, and all the rest of it, and everybody else was such a desperate thief, and he was so sure there would be some of that bullion missing some day that—that—well, I don't know if I express his manner clearly, but I tell you I didn't like it a bit. But there was something more than that. He was eternally smelling about the place, and peeping in at the steward's pantry—which adjoins the bullion-room on one side, you know—and nosing about in the bunker on the other side. And once I actually caught him fitting keys to the padlocks—keys he'd borrowed from the carpenter's stores. And every time his excuse was that he fancied he heard somebody else trying to get in to the gold, or something of that sort; every time I caught him below on the orlop deck that was his excuse—happened to have heard something or suspected something or somebody every time. Whether or not I succeed in conveying my impressions to you, gentlemen, I can assure you that I regarded his whole manner and actions as very suspicious throughout the voyage, and I made up my mind I wouldn't forget it if by chance anything *did* turn out wrong. Well, it has, and now I've told you what I've observed. It's for you to see if it will lead you anywhere."

"Just so," Hewitt answered. "But let me fully understand, Captain Mackrie. You say that Mr Brasyer had charge of the bullion-room, but that he was trying keys on it from the carpenter's stores. Where were the legitimate keys then?"

"In my cabin. They were only handed out when I knew what they were wanted for. There was a Chubb's lock between the two padlocks, but a duplicate wouldn't have been hard for

Brasyer to get. He could easily have taken a wax impression of my key when he used it at the port where we took the bullion aboard."

"Well, and suppose he had taken these boxes, where do you think he would keep them?"

Mackrie shrugged his shoulders and smiled. "Impossible to say," he replied. "He might have hidden 'em somewhere on board, though I don't think that's likely. He'd have had a deuce of a job to land them at Plymouth, and would have had to leave them somewhere while he came on to London. Bullion is always landed at Plymouth, you know, and if any were found to be missing, then the ship would be overhauled at once, every inch of her; so that he'd have to get his plunder ashore somehow before the rest of the gold was unloaded—almost impossible. Of course, if he's done that it's somewhere below there now, but that isn't likely. He'd be much more likely to have 'dumped' it—dropped it overboard at some well-known spot in a foreign port, where he could go later on and get it. So that you've a deal of scope for search, you see. Anywhere under water from here to Yokohama;" and Captain Mackrie laughed.

Soon afterward he left, and as he was leaving a man knocked at the cabin door and looked in to say that Mr Brasyer was on board. "You'll be able to have a go at him now," said the captain. "Good-day."

"There's the steward of the *Nicobar* there too, sir," said the man after the captain had gone, "and the carpenter."

"Very well, we'll see Mr Brasyer first," said Merrick, and the man vanished. "It seems to have got about a bit," Merrick went on to Hewitt. "I only sent for Brasyer, but as these others have come, perhaps they've got something to tell us."

Brasyer made his appearance, overflowing with information. He required little assurance to encourage him to speak openly before Hewitt, and he said again all he had so often said before on board the *Nicobar*. The bullion-room was a mere tin box, the whole thing was as easy to get at as anything could be, he didn't wonder in the least at the loss—he had prophesied it all along.

The men whose movements should be carefully watched, he said, were the captain and the steward. "Nobody ever heard of a captain and a steward being so thick together before," he said. "The steward's pantry was next against the bullion-room, you know, with nothing but that wretched bit of three-eighths boiler plate between. You wouldn't often expect to find the captain down in the steward's pantry, would you, thick as they might be. Well, that's where I used to find him, time and again. And the steward kept boiler-makers' tools there! That I can swear to. And he's been a boiler-maker, so that, likely as not, he could open a joint somewhere and patch it up again neatly so that it wouldn't be noticed. He was always messing about down there in his pantry, and once I distinctly heard knocking there, and when I went down to see, whom should I meet? Why, the skipper, coming away from the place himself, and he bullyragged me for being there and sent me on deck. But before that he bullyragged me because I had found out that there were other keys knocking about the place that fitted the padlocks on the bullion-room door. Why should he slang and threaten me for looking after these things and keeping my eye on the bullion-room, as was my duty? But that was the very thing that he didn't like. It was enough for him to see me anxious about the gold to make him furious. Of course his character for meanness and greed is known all through the company's service—he'll do anything to make a bit."

"But have you any positive idea as to what has become of the gold?"

"Well," Brasyer replied, with a rather knowing air, "I don't think they've dumped it."

"Do you mean you think it's still in the vessel—hidden somewhere?"

"No, I don't. I believe the captain and the steward took it ashore, one case each, when we came off in the boats."

"But wouldn't that be noticed?"

"It needn't be, on a black night like that. You see, the parcels are not so big—look at them, a foot by a foot and a half by six inches or so, roughly. Easily slipped under a big coat or covered up with anything. Of course they're a bit heavy—eighty or ninety pounds apiece altogether—but that's not much for a strong man to carry—especially in such a handy parcel, on a black night, with no end of confusion on. Now you just look here—I'll tell you something. The skipper went ashore last in a boat that was sent out by the coasting steamer that ran into us. That ship's put into dock for repairs and her crew are mostly having an easy time ashore. Now I haven't been asleep this last day or two, and I had a sort of notion there might be some game of this sort on, because when I left the ship that night I thought we might save a little at least of the stuff, but the skipper wouldn't let me go near the bullion-room, and that seemed odd. So I got hold of one of the boat's crew that fetched the skipper ashore, and questioned him quietly—pumped him, you know—and he assures me that the skipper *did* have a rather small, heavy sort of parcel with him. What do you think of that? Of course, in the circumstances, the man couldn't remember any very distinct particulars, but he thought it was a sort of square wooden case about the size I've mentioned. But there's something more." Brasyer lifted his forefinger and then brought it down on the table before him—"something more. I've made inquiries at the railway station and I find that two heavy parcels were sent off yesterday to London—deal boxes wrapped in brown paper, of just about the right size. And the paper got torn before the things were sent off, and the clerk could see that the boxes inside were fastened with hoop-iron—like those!" and the second officer pointed triumphantly to the boxes piled at one side of the cabin.

"Well done!" said Hewitt. "You're quite a smart detective. Did you find out who brought the parcels, and who they were addressed to?"

"No, I couldn't get quite as far as that. Of course the clerk didn't know the names of the senders, and not knowing me, wouldn't tell me exactly where the parcels were going. But I got quite chummy with him after a bit, and I'm going to meet him presently—he has the afternoon off, and we're going for a stroll. I'll find something more, I'll bet you!"

"Certainly," replied Hewitt, "find all you can—it may be very important. If you get any valuable information you'll let us know at once, of course. Anything else, now?"

"No, I don't think so; but I think what I've told you is pretty well enough for the present, eh? I'll let you know some more soon."

Brasyer went, and Norton, the steward of the old ship, was brought into the cabin. He was a sharp-eyed, rather cadaverous-looking man, and he spoke with sepulchral hollowness. He had heard, he said, that there was something wrong with the chests of bullion, and came on board to give any information he could. It wasn't much, he went on to say, but the smallest thing might help. If he might speak strictly confidentially he would suggest that observation be kept on Wickens, the carpenter. He (Norton) didn't want to be uncharitable, but his pantry happened to be next the bullion-room, and he had heard Wickens at work for a very long time just below—on the under side of the floor of the bullion-room, it seemed to him, although, of course, he *might* have been mistaken. Still, it was very odd that the carpenter always seemed to have a job just at that spot. More, it had been said—and he (Norton) believed it to be true—that Wickens, the carpenter, had in his possession, and kept among his stores, keys that fitted the padlocks on the bullion-room door. That, it seemed to him, was a very suspicious circumstance. He didn't know anything more definite, but offered his ideas for what they were worth, and if his suspicions proved unfounded nobody would be more pleased than himself. But—but—and the steward shook his head doubtfully.

"Thank you, Mr Norton," said Merrick, with a twinkle in his eye; "we won't forget what you say. Of course, if the stuff is found in consequence of any of your information, you won't lose by it."

The steward said he hoped not, and he wouldn't fail to keep his eye on the carpenter. He had noticed Wickens was in the tug, and he trusted that if they were going to question him they would do it cautiously, so as not to put him on his guard. Merrick promised they would.

"By the bye, Mr Norton," asked Hewitt, "supposing your suspicions to be justified, what do you suppose the carpenter would do with the bullion?"

"Well, sir," replied Norton, "I don't think he'd keep it on the ship. He'd probably dump it somewhere."

The steward left, and Merrick lay back in his chair and guffawed aloud. "This grows farcical," he said, "simply farcical. What a happy family they must have been aboard the *Nicobar*! And now here's the captain watching the second officer, and the second officer watching the captain and the steward, and the steward watching the carpenter! It's immense. And now we're going to see the carpenter. Wonder whom *he* suspects?"

Hewitt said nothing, but his eyes twinkled with intense merriment, and presently the carpenter was brought into the cabin.

"Good-day to you, gentlemen," said the carpenter in a soft and deferential voice, looking from one to the other. "Might I 'ave the honour of addressin' the salvage gentlemen?"

"That's right," Merrick answered, motioning him to a seat. "This is the salvage shop, Mr Wickens. What can we do for you?"

The carpenter coughed gently behind his hand. "I took the liberty of comin', gentlemen, consekins o' 'earin' as there was some bullion missin'. P'raps I'm wrong."

"Not at all. We haven't found as much as we expected, and I suppose by this time nearly everybody knows it. There are two cases wanting. You can't tell us where they are, I suppose?"

"Well, sir, as to that—no. I fear I can't exactly go as far as that. But if I am able to give vallable information as may lead to recovery of same, I presoom I may without offence look for some reasonable small recognition of my services?"

"Oh, yes," answered Merrick, "that'll be all right, I promise you. The company will do the handsome thing, of course, and no doubt so will the underwriters."

"Presoomin' I may take that as a promise—among gentlemen"—this with an emphasis—"I'm willing to tell something."

"It's a promise, at any rate as far as the company's concerned," returned Merrick. "I'll see it's made worth your while—of course, providing it leads to anything."

"Purvidin' that, sir, o' course. Well, gentlemen, my story ain't a long one. All I've to say was what I 'eard on board, just before she went down. The passengers was off, and the crew was gettin' into the other boats when the skipper turns to the steward an' speaks to him quiet-like, not observin', gentlemen, as I was agin 'is elbow, so for to say. ''Ere, Norton,' 'e sez, or words to that effeck, 'why shouldn't we try gettin' them things ashore with us—you know, the cases—eh? I've a notion we're pretty close inshore,' 'e sez, 'and there's nothink of a sea now. You take one, anyway, and I'll try the other,' 'e says, 'but don't make a flourish.' Then he sez, louder, 'cos o' the steward goin' off, 'They're the likeliest stuff, and at worst we can but drop 'em. But look sharp,' 'e says. So then I gets into the nearest boat, and that's all I 'eard."

"That was all?" asked Hewitt, watching the man's face sharply.

"All?" the carpenter answered with some surprise. "Yes, that was all; but I think it's pretty well enough, don't you? It's plain enough what was meant—him and the steward was to take two cases, one apiece, on the quiet, and they was the likeliest stuff aboard, as he said himself. And now there's two cases o' bullion missin'. Ain't that enough?"

The carpenter was not satisfied till an exact note had been made of the captain's words. Then after Merrick's promise on behalf of the company had been renewed, Wickens took himself off.

"Well," said Merrick, grinning across the table at Hewitt, "this is a queer go, isn't it? What that man says makes the skipper's case look pretty fishy, doesn't it? What he says, and what Brasyer says, taken together, makes a pretty strong case—I should say makes the thing a certainty. But what a business! It's likely to be a bit serious for someone, but it's a rare joke in a way. Wonder if Brasyer will find out anything more? Pity the skipper and steward didn't agree as to whom they should pretend to suspect. *That's* a mistake on their part."

"Not at all," Hewitt replied. "*If* they are conspiring, and know what they're about, they will avoid seeming to be both in a tale. The bullion is in bars, I understand?"

"Yes, five bars in each case; weight, I believe, sixteen pounds to a bar."

"Let me see," Hewitt went on, as he looked at his watch; "it is now nearly two o'clock. I must think over these things if I am to do anything in the case. In the meantime, if it could be managed, I should like enormously to have a turn underwater in a diving-dress. I have always had a curiosity to see under the sea. Could it be managed now?"

"Well," Merrick responded, "there's not much fun in it, I can assure you; and it's none the pleasanter in this weather. You'd better have a try later in the year if you really want to—unless you think you can learn anything about this business by smelling about on the *Nicobar* down below?"

Hewitt raised his eyebrows and pursed his lips.

"I *might* spot something," he said; "one never knows. And if I do anything in a case I always make it a rule to see and hear everything that can possibly be seen or heard, important or not. Clues lie where least expected. But beyond that, probably I may never have another chance of a little experience in a diving-dress. So if it can be managed I'd be glad."

"Very well, you shall go, if you say so. And since it's your first venture, I'll come down with you myself. The men are all ashore, I think, or most of them. Come along."

Hewitt was put in woollens and then in India-rubbers. A leaden-soled boot of twenty pounds' weight was strapped on each foot, and weights were hung on his back and chest.

"That's the dress that Gullen usually has," Merrick remarked. "He's a very smart fellow; we usually send him first to make measurements and so on. An excellent man, but a bit too fond of the diver's lotion."

"What's that?" asked Hewitt.

"Oh, you shall try some if you like, afterwards. It's a bit too heavy for me; rum and gin mixed, I think."

A red nightcap was placed on Martin Hewitt's head, and after that a copper helmet, secured by a short turn in the segmental screw joint at the neck. In the end he felt a vast difficulty in moving at all. Merrick had been meantime invested with a similar rig-out, and then each was provided with a communication cord and an incandescent electric lamp. Finally, the front window was screwed on each helmet, and all was ready.

Merrick went first over the ladder at the side, and Hewitt with much difficulty followed. As the water closed over his head, his sensations altered considerably. There was less weight to carry; his arms in particular felt light, though slow in motion. Down, down they went slowly, and all round about it was fairly light, but once on the sunken vessel and among the lower decks, the electric lamps were necessary enough. Once or twice Merrick spoke, laying his helmet against Hewitt's for the purpose, and instructing him to keep his air-pipe, lifeline, and lamp connection from fouling something at every step. Here and there shadowy swimming shapes came out of the gloom, attracted by their lamps, to dart into obscurity again with a twist of the tail. The fishes were exploring the *Nicobar*. The hatchway of the lower deck was open, and down this they passed to the orlop deck. A little way along this they came to a door standing open, with a broken lock hanging to it. It was the door of the bullion-room, which had been forced by the divers in the morning.

Merrick indicated by signs how the cases had been found piled on the floor. One of the sides of the room of thin steel was torn and thrust in the length of its whole upper half, and when they backed out of the room and passed the open door they stood in the great breach made by the bow of the strange coasting vessel. Steel, iron, wood, and everything stood in rents and splinters, and through the great gap they looked out into the immeasurable ocean. Hewitt put up his hand and felt the edge of the bullion-room partition where it had been torn. It was just such a tear as might have been made in cardboard.

They regained the upper deck, and Hewitt, placing his helmet against his companion's, told him that he meant to have a short walk on the ocean bed. He took to the ladder again, where it lay over the side, and Merrick followed him.

The bottom was of that tough, slimy sort of clay-rock that is found in many places about our coasts, and was dotted here and there with lumps of harder rock and clumps of curious weed. The two divers turned at the bottom of the ladder, walked a few steps, and looked up at the great hole in the *Nicobar's* side. Seen from here it was a fearful chasm, laying open hold, orlop, and lower deck.

Hewitt turned away, and began walking about. Once or twice he stood and looked thoughtfully at the ground he stood on, which was fairly flat. He turned over with his foot a whitish, clean-looking stone about as large as a loaf. Then he wandered on slowly, once or twice stopping to examine the rock beneath him, and presently stooped to look at another stone nearly as large as the other, weedy on one side only, standing on the edge of a cavity in the claystone. He pushed the stone into the hole, which it filled, and then he stood up.

Merrick put his helmet against Hewitt's, and shouted—

"Satisfied now? Seen enough of the bottom?"

"In a moment!" Hewitt shouted back; and he straightway began striding out in the direction of the ship. Arrived at the bows, he turned back to the point he started from, striding off again from there to the white stone he had kicked over, and from there to the vessel's side again. Merrick watched him in intense amazement, and hurried, as well as he might, after the light of Hewitt's lamp. Arrived for the second time at the bows of the ship, Hewitt turned and made his way along the side to the ladder, and forthwith ascended, followed by Merrick. There was no halt at the deck this time, and the two made there way up and up into the lighter water above, and so to the world of air.

On the tug, as the men were unscrewing them from there waterproof prisons, Merrick asked Hewitt—

"Will you try the 'lotion' now?"

"No," Hewitt replied, "I won't go quite so far as that. But I *will* have a little whisky, if you've any in the cabin. And give me a pencil and a piece of paper."

These things were brought, and on the paper Martin Hewitt immediately wrote a few figures and kept it in his hand.

"I might easily forget those figures," he observed.

Merrick wondered, but said nothing.

Once more comfortably in the cabin, and clad in his usual garments, Hewitt asked if Merrick could produce a chart of the parts thereabout.

"Here you are," was the reply, "coast and all. Big enough, isn't it? I've already marked the position of the wreck on it in pencil. She lies pointing north by east as nearly exact as anything."

"As you've begun it," said Hewitt, "I shall take the liberty of making a few more pencil marks on this." And with that he spread out the crumpled note of figures, and began much ciphering and measuring. Presently he marked certain points on a spare piece of paper, and drew through them two lines forming an angle. This angle he transferred to the chart, and, placing a ruler over one leg of the angle, lengthened it out till it met the coastline.

"There we are," he said musingly. "And the nearest village to that is Lostella—indeed, the only coast village in that neighbourhood." He rose. "Bring me the sharpest-eyed person on board," he said; "that is, if he were here all day yesterday."

"But what's up? What's all this mathematical business over? Going to find that bullion by rule of three?"

Hewitt laughed. "Yes, perhaps," he said, "but where's your sharp lookout? I want somebody who can tell me everything that was visible from the deck of this tug all day yesterday."

"Well, really I believe the very sharpest chap is the boy. He's most annoyingly observant sometimes. I'll send for him."

He came—a bright, snub-nosed, impudent-looking young ruffian.

"See here, my boy," said Merrick, "polish up your wits and tell this gentleman what he asks."

"Yesterday," said Hewitt, "no doubt you saw various pieces of wreckage floating about?"

"Yessir."

"What were they?"

"Hatch-gratings mostly—nothin' much else. There's some knockin' about now."

"I saw them. Now, remember. Did you see a hatch-grating floating yesterday that was different from the others? A painted one, for instance—those out there now are not painted, you know."

"Yes sir, I see a little white 'un painted, bobbin' about away beyond the foremast of the *Nicobar*."

"You're sure of that?"

"Certain sure, sir—it was the only painted thing floatin'. And today it's washed away somewheres."

"So I noticed. You're a smart lad. Here's a shilling for you—keep your eyes open and perhaps you'll find a good many more shillings before you're an old man. That's all."

The boy disappeared, and Hewitt turned to Merrick and said, "I think you may as well send that wire you spoke of. If I get the commission I think I may recover that bullion. It may take some little time, or, on the other hand, it may not. If you'll write the telegram at once, I'll go in the same boat as the messenger. I'm going to take a walk down to Lostella now—it's only two or three miles along the coast, but it will soon be getting dark."

"But what sort of a clue have you got? I didn't—"

"Never mind," replied Hewitt, with a chuckle. "Officially, you know, I've no right to a clue just yet—I'm not commissioned. When I am I'll tell you everything."

Hewitt was scarcely ashore when he was seized by the excited Brasyer. "Here you are," he said. "I was coming aboard the tug again. I've got more news. You remember I said I was going out with that railway clerk this afternoon, and meant pumping him? Well, I've done it and rushed away—don't know what he'll think's up. As we were going along we saw Norton, the steward, on the other side of the way, and the clerk recognised him as one of the men who brought the cases to be sent off; the other was the skipper, I've no doubt, from his description. I played him artfully, you know, and then he let out that both the cases were addressed to Mackrie at his address in London! He looked up the entry, he said, after I left when I first questioned him, feeling curious. That's about enough, I think, eh? I'm off to London now—I believe Mackrie's going tonight. I'll have him! Keep it dark!" And the zealous second officer dashed off without waiting for a reply. Hewitt looked after him with an amused smile, and turned off towards Lostella.

III.

It was about eleven the next morning when Merrick received the following note, brought by a boatman:—

> "DEAR MERRICK,—Am I commissioned? If not, don't trouble, but if I am, be just outside Lostella, at the turning before you come to the Smack Inn, at two o'clock. Bring with you a light cart, a policeman—or two perhaps will be better—and a man with a spade. There will probably be a little cabbage-digging. Are you fond of the sport?—Yours, MARTIN HEWITT.
> "P.S.—*Keep all your men aboard*; bring the spade artist from the town."

Merrick was off in a boat at once. His principals had replied to his telegram after Hewitt's departure the day before, giving him a free hand to do whatever seemed best. With some little difficulty he got the policemen, and with none at all he got a light cart and a jobbing man with a spade. Together they drove off to the meeting-place.

It was before the time, but Martin Hewitt was there, waiting. "You're quick," he said, "but the sooner the better. I gave you the earliest appointment I thought you could keep, considering what you had to do."

"Have you got the stuff, then?" Merrick asked anxiously.

"No, not exactly yet. But I've got this," and Hewitt held up the point of his walking-stick. Protruding half an inch or so from it was the sharp end of a small gimlet, and in the groove thereof was a little white wood, such as commonly remains after a gimlet has been used.

"Why, what's that?"

"Never mind. Let us move along—I'll walk. I think we're about at the end of the job—it's been a fairly lucky one, and quite simple. But I'll explain after."

Just beyond the Smack Inn, Hewitt halted the cart, and all got down. They looped the horse's reins round a hedge-stake and proceeded the small remaining distance on foot, with the policemen behind, to avoid a premature scare. They turned up a lane behind a few small and rather dirty cottages facing the sea, each with its patch of kitchen garden behind. Hewitt led the way to the second garden, pushed open the small wicket gate and walked boldly in, followed by the others.

Cabbages covered most of the patch, and seemed pretty healthy in their situation, with the exception of half a dozen—singularly enough, all together in a group. These were drooping, yellow, and wilted, and towards these Hewitt straightway walked. "Dig up those wilted cabbages," he said to the jobbing man. "They're really useless now. You'll probably find something else six inches down or so."

The man struck his spade into the soft earth, wherein it stopped suddenly with a thud. But at this moment a gaunt, slatternly woman, with a black eye, a handkerchief over her head, and her skirt pinned up in front, observing the invasion from the back door of the cottage, rushed out like a maniac and attacked the party valiantly with a broom. She upset the jobbing man over his spade, knocked off one policeman's helmet, lunged into the other's face with her broom, and was making her second attempt to hit Hewitt (who had dodged), when Merrick caught her firmly by the elbows from behind, pressed them together, and held her. She screamed, and people came from other cottages and looked on. "Peter! Peter!" the woman screamed, "come 'ee, come'ee here! Davey! They're come!"

A grimy child came to the cottage door, and seeing the woman thus held, and strangers in the garden, set up a piteous howl. Meantime the digger had uncovered two wooden boxes, each eighteen inches long or so, bound with hoop-iron and sealed. One had been torn partly open at the top, and the broken wood roughly replaced. When this was lifted, bars of yellow metal were visible within.

The woman still screamed vehemently, and struggled. The grimy child retreated, and then there appeared at the door, staggering hazily and rubbing his eyes, a shaggy, unkempt man, in shirt and trousers. He looked stupidly at the scene before him, and his jaw dropped.

"Take that man," cried Hewitt. "He's one!" And the policeman promptly took him, so that he had handcuffs on his wrists before he had collected his faculties sufficiently to begin swearing.

Hewitt and the other policeman entered the cottage. In the lower two rooms there was nobody. They climbed the few narrow stairs, and in the front room above they found another man, younger, and fast asleep. "He's the other," said Hewitt. "Take *him*." And this one was handcuffed before he woke.

Then the recovered gold was put into the cart, and with the help of the village constable, who brought his own handcuffs for the benefit and adornment of the lady with the broom, such a procession marched out of Lostella as had never been dreamed of by the oldest inhabitant in his worst nightmare, nor recorded in the whole history of Cornwall.

"Now," said Hewitt, turning to Merrick, "we must have that fellow of yours—what's his name—Gullen, isn't it? The one that went down to measure the hole in the ship. You've kept him aboard, of course?"

"What, Gullen?" exclaimed Merrick. "Gullen? Well, as a matter of fact he went ashore last night and hasn't come back. But you don't mean to say—"

"I *do*," replied Hewitt. "And now you've lost him."

IV.

"But tell me all about it now we've a little time to ourselves," asked Merrick an hour or two later, as they sat and smoked in the after-cabin of the salvage tug. "We've got the stuff, thanks to you, but I don't in the least see how *they* got it, nor how you found it out."

"Well, there didn't seem to be a great deal either way in the tales told by the men from the *Nicobar*. They cancelled one another out, so to speak, though it seemed likely that there might be something in them in one or two respects. Brasyer, I could see, tried to prove too much. If the captain and the steward were conspiring to rob the bullion-room, why should the steward trouble to cut through the boiler-plate walls when the captain kept the keys in his cabin? And if the captain had been stealing the bullion, why should he stop at two cases when he had all the voyage to operate in and forty cases to help himself to? Of course the evidence of the carpenter gave some colour to the theory, but I think I can imagine a very reasonable explanation of that.

"You told me, of course, that you were down with the men yourself when they opened the bullion-room door and got out the cases, so that there could be no suspicion of *them*. But at the same time you told me that the breach in the *Nicobar's* side had laid open the bullion-room partition, and that you might more easily have got the cases out that way. You told me, of course, that the cases couldn't have *fallen* out that way because of the list of the vessel, the position of the rent in the boiler-plate, and so on. But I reflected that the day before a diver had been down alone—in fact, that his business had been with the very hole that extended partly to the bullion-room: he had to measure it. That diver might easily have got at the cases through the breach. But then, as you told me, a diver can't bring things up from below unobserved. This diver would know this, and might therefore hide the booty below. So that I made up my mind to have a look under water before I jumped to any conclusion.

"I didn't think it likely that he had hidden the cases, mind you. Because he would have had to dive again to get them, and would have been just as awkwardly placed in fetching them to the light of day then as ever. Besides, he couldn't come diving here again in the company's dress without some explanation. So what more likely than that he would make some ingenious arrangement with an accomplice, whereby he might make the gold in some way accessible to him?

"We went under water. I kept my eyes open, and observed, among other things, that the vessel was one of those well-kept 'swell' ones on which all the hatch gratings and so on are in plain oak or teak, kept holystoned. This (with the other things) I put by in my mind in case it should be useful. When we went over the side and looked at the great gap, I saw that it would have been quite easy to get at the broken bullion-room partition from outside."

"Yes," remarked Merrick, "it would be no trouble at all. The ladder goes down just by the side of the breach, and anyone descending by that might just step off at one side on to the jagged plating at the level of the after orlop, and reach over into the bullion safe."

"Just so. Well, next I turned my attention to the seabed, which I was extremely pleased to see was of soft, slimy claystone. I walked about a little, getting farther and farther away from the vessel as I went, till I came across that clean stone which I turned over with my foot. Do you remember?"

"Yes."

"Well, that was noticeable. It was the only clean, bare stone to be seen. Every other was covered with a green growth, and to most clumps of weed clung. The obvious explanation of this was that the stone was a newcomer—lately brought from dry land—from the shingle on the sea-shore, probably, since it was washed so clean. Such a stone could not have come a mile out to sea by itself. Somebody had brought it in a boat and thrown it over, and whoever did it didn't take all that trouble for nothing. Then its shape told a tale; it was something of the form, rather exaggerated, of a loaf—the sort that is called a 'cottage'—the most convenient possible shape for attaching to a line and lowering. But the line had gone, so somebody must have been down there to detach it. Also it wasn't unreasonable to suppose that there might have been a hook on the end of that line. This, then, was a theory. Your man had gone down alone to take his measurement, had stepped into the broken side, as you have explained he could, reached into the bullion-room, and lifted the two cases. Probably he unfastened the cord, and brought them out one at a time for convenience in carrying. Then he carried the cases, one at a time, as I have said, over to that white stone which lay there sunk with the hook and line attached by previous arrangement with some confederate. He detached the rope from the stone—it was probably fixed by an attached piece of cord, tightened round the stone with what you call a timber-hitch, easily loosened—replaced the cord round the two cases, passed the hook under the cord, and left it to be pulled up from above. But then it could not have been pulled up there in broad daylight, under your very noses. The confederates would wait till night. That meant that the other end of the rope was attached to some floating object, so that it might be readily recovered. The whole arrangement was set one night to be carried away the next."

"But why didn't Gullen take more than two cases?"

"He couldn't afford to waste the time, in the first place. Each case removed meant another journey to and from the vessel, and you were waiting above for his measurements. Then he was probably doubtful as to weight. Too much at once wouldn't easily be drawn up, and might upset a small boat.

"Well, so much for the white stone. But there was more; close by the stone I noticed (although I think you didn't) a mark in the claystone. It was a triangular depression or pit, sharp at the bottom — just the hole that would be made by the sharp impact of the square corner of a heavy box, if shod with iron, as the bullion cases are. This was one important thing. It seemed to indicate that the boxes had not been lifted directly up from the seabed, but had been dragged sideways — at all events at first — so that a sharp corner had turned over and dug into the claystone! I walked a little farther and found more indications — slight scratches, small stones displaced, and so on, that convinced me of this, and also pointed out the direction in which the cases had been dragged. I followed the direction, and presently arrived at another stone, rather smaller than the clean one. The cases had evidently caught against this, and it had been displaced by their momentum, and perhaps by a possible wrench from above. The green growth covered the part which had been exposed to the water, and the rest of the stone fitted the hole beside it, from which it had been pulled. Clearly these things were done recently, or the sea would have wiped out all the traces in the soft claystone. The rest of what I did under water of course you understood."

"I suppose so: you took the bearings of the two stones in relation to the ship by pacing the distances."

"That is so. I kept the figures in my head till I could make a note of them, as you saw, on paper. The rest was mere calculation. What I judged had happened was this. Gullen had arranged with somebody, identity unknown, but certainly somebody with a boat at his disposal, to lay the line, and take it up the following night. Now anything larger than a rowing boat could not have got up quite so close to you in the night (although your tug was at the other end of the wreck) without a risk of being seen. *But* no rowing boat could have *dragged* those cases forcibly along the bottom; they would act as an anchor to it. Therefore this was what had happened. The thieves had come in a large boat—a fishing smack, lugger, or something of that sort—with a small boat in tow. The sailing boat had lain to at a convenient distance, *in the direction in which it was afterwards to go*, so as to save time if observed, and a man had put off quietly in the small boat to pick up the float, whatever it was. There must have been a lot of slack line on this for the purpose, as also for the purpose of allowing the float to drift about fairly freely, and not attract attention by remaining in one place. The man pulled off to the sailing boat, and took the float and line aboard. Then the sailing boat swung off in the direction of home, and the line was hauled in with the plunder at the end of it."

"One would think you had seen it all—or done it," Merrick remarked, with a laugh.

"Nothing else could have happened, you see. That chain of events is the only one that will explain the circumstances. A rapid grasp of the whole circumstances and a perfect appreciation of each is more than half the battle in such work as this. Well, you know I got the exact bearings of the wreck on the chart, worked out from that the lay of the two stones with the scratch marks between, and then it was obvious that a straight line drawn through these and carried ahead would indicate, approximately, at any rate, the direction the thieves' vessel had taken. The line fell on the coast close by the village of Lostella—indeed that was the only village for some few miles either way. The indication was not certain, but it was likely, and the only one available, therefore it must be followed up."

"And what about the painted hatch? How did you guess that?"

"Well, I saw there were hatch-gratings belonging to the *Nicobar* floating about, and it seemed probable that the thieves would use for a float something similar to the other wreckage in the vicinity, so as not to attract attention. Nothing would be more likely than a hatch-grating. But then, in small vessels, such as fishing-luggers and so on, fittings are almost always painted—they can't afford to be such holystoning swells as those on the *Nicobar*. So I judged the grating might be painted, and this would possibly have been noticed by some sharp person. I made the shot, and hit. The boy remembered the white grating, which had gone—'washed away,' as he thought. That was useful to me, as you shall see.

"I made off toward Lostella. The tide was low and it was getting dusk when I arrived. A number of boats and smacks were lying anchored on the beach, but there were few people to be seen. I began looking out for smacks with white-painted fittings in them. There are not so many of these among fishing vessels—brown or red is more likely, or sheer colourless dirt over paint unrecognisable. There were only two that I saw last night. The first *might* have been the one I wanted, but there was nothing to show it. The second *was* the one. She was half-decked and had a small white-painted hatch. I shifted the hatch and found a long line, attached to the grating at one end and carrying a hook at the other! They had neglected to unfasten their apparatus—perhaps had an idea that there might be a chance of using it again in a few days. I went to the transom and read the inscription, '*Rebecca*. Peter and David Garthew, Lostella.' Then my business was to find the Garthews.

"I wandered about the village for some little time, and presently got hold of a boy. I made a simple excuse for asking about the Garthews—wanted to go for a sail tomorrow. The boy, with many grins, confided to me that both of the Garthews were 'on the booze.' I should find them at the Smack Inn, where they had been all day, drunk as fiddlers. This seemed a likely sort of thing after the haul they had made. I went to the Smack Inn, determined to claim old friendship with the Garthews, although I didn't know Peter from David. There they were — one sleepy drunk, and the other loving and crying drunk. I got as friendly as possible with them under the circumstances, and at closing time stood another gallon of beer and carried it home for them, while they carried each other. I took care to have a good look round in the cottage. I even helped Peter's 'old woman'—the lady with the broom—to carry them up to bed. But nowhere could I see anything that looked like a bullion-case or a hiding-place for one. So I came away, determined to renew my acquaintance in the morning, and to carry it on as long as might be necessary; also to look at the garden in the daylight for signs of burying. With that view I fixed that little gimlet in my walking-stick, as you saw.

"This morning I was at Lostella before ten, and took a look at the Garthews' cabbages. It seemed odd that half a dozen, all in a clump together, looked withered and limp, as though they had been dug up hastily, the roots broken, perhaps, and then replanted. And altogether these particular cabbages had a dissipated, leaning-different-ways look, as though *they* had been on the loose with the Garthews. So, seeing a grubby child near the back door of the cottage, I went towards him, walking rather unsteadily, so as, if I were observed, to favour the delusion that I was not yet quite got over last night's diversions. 'Hullo, my b-boy,' I said, 'hullo, li'l b-boy, look here,' and I plunged my hand into my trousers' pocket and brought it out full of small change. Then, making a great business of selecting him a penny, I managed to spill it all over the dissipated cabbages. It was easy then, in stooping to pick up the change, to lean heavily on my stick and drive it through the loose earth. As I had expected, there was a box below. So I gouged away with my walking-stick while I collected my coppers, and finally swaggered off, after a few civil words with the 'old woman,' carrying with me evident proof that it was white wood recently buried there. The rest you saw for yourself. I think you and I may congratulate each other on having dodged that broom. It hit all the others."

"What I'm wild about," said Merrick, "is having let that scoundrel Gullen get off. He's an artful chap, without a doubt. He saw us go over the side, you know, and after you had gone he came into the cabin for some instructions. Your pencil notes and the chart were on the table, and no doubt he put two and two together (which was more than I could, not knowing what had happened), and concluded to make himself safe for a bit. He had no leave that night—he just pulled away on the quiet. Why didn't you give me the tip to keep him?"

"That wouldn't have done. In the first place, there was no legal evidence to warrant his arrest, and ordering him to keep aboard would have aroused his suspicions. I didn't know at the time how many days, or weeks, it would take me to find the bullion, if I ever found it, and in that time Gullen might have communicated in some way with his accomplices, and so spoilt the whole thing. Yes, certainly he seems to have been fairly smart in his way. He knew he would probably be sent down first, as usual, alone to make measurements, and conceived his plan and made his arrangements forthwith."

"But now what I want to know is what about all those *Nicobar* people watching and suspecting one another? More especially what about the cases the captain and the steward are said to have fetched ashore?"

Hewitt laughed. "Well," he said, "as to that, the presence of the bullion seems to have bred all sorts of mutual suspicion on board the ship. Brasyer was over-fussy, and his continual chatter started it probably, so that it spread like an infection. As to the captain and the steward, of course I don't know anything but that their rescued cases were not bullion cases. Probably they were doing a little private trading—it's generally the case when captain and steward seem unduly friendly for their relative positions—and perhaps the cases contained something specially valuable: vases or bronzes from Japan, for instance; possibly the most valuable things of the size they had aboard. Then, if they had insured their things, Captain Mackrie (who has the reputation of a sharp and not very scrupulous man) might possibly think it rather a stroke of business to get the goods and the insurance money too, which would lead him to keep his parcels as quiet as possible. But that's as it may be."

The case was much as Hewitt had surmised. The zealous Brasyer, posting to London in hot haste after Mackrie, spent some days in watching him. At last the captain and the steward with their two boxes took a cab and went to Bond Street, with Brasyer in another cab behind them. The two entered a shop, the window of which was set out with rare curiosities and much old silver and gold. Brasyer could restrain himself no longer. He grabbed a passing policeman, and rushed with him into the shop. There they found the captain and the steward with two small packing cases opened before them, trying to sell—a couple of very ancient-looking Japanese bronze figures, of that curious old workmanship and varied colour of metal that in genuine examples mean nowadays high money value.

Brasyer vanished: there was too much chaff for him to live through in the British mercantile marine after this adventure. The fact was, the steward had come across the bargain, but had not sufficient spare cash to buy, so he called in the aid of the captain, and they speculated in the bronzes as partners. There was much anxious inspection of the prizes on the way home, and much discussion as to the proper price to ask. Finally, it was said, they got three hundred pounds for the pair.

Now and again Hewitt meets Merrick still. Sometimes Merrick says, "Now, I wonder after all whether or not some of those *Nicobar* men who were continually dodging suspiciously about that bullion-room *did* mean having a dash at the gold if there were a chance?" And Hewitt replies, "I wonder."

3

THE HOLFORD WILL CASE

At one time, in common, perhaps, with most people, I took a sort of languid, amateur interest in questions of psychology, and was impelled thereby to plunge into the pages of the many curious and rather abstruse books which attempt to deal with phenomena of mind, soul and sense. Three things of the real nature of which, I am convinced, no man will ever learn more than we know at present—which is nothing.

From these I strayed into the many volumes of *Transactions* of the Psychical Research Society, with an occasional by-excursion into mental telepathy and theosophy; the last, a thing whereof my Philistine intelligence obstinately refused to make head or tail.

It was while these things were occupying part of my attention that I chanced to ask Hewitt whether, in the course of his divers odd and out-of-the-way experiences, he had met with any such weird adventures as were detailed in such profusion in the books of "authenticated" spooks, doppelgangers, poltergeists, clairvoyance, and so forth.

"Well," Hewitt answered, with reflection, "I haven't been such a wallower in the uncanny as some of the worthy people who talk at large in those books of yours, and, as a matter of fact, my little adventures, curious as some of them may seem, have been on the whole of the most solid and matter-of-fact description. One or two things have happened that perhaps your 'psychical' people might be interested in, but they've mostly been found to be capable of a disappointingly simple explanation. One case of some genuine psychological interest, however, I have had; although there's nothing even in that which isn't a matter of well-known scientific possibility." And he proceeded to tell me the story that I have set down here, as well as I can, from recollection.

I think I have already said, in another place, that Hewitt's professional start as a private investigator dated from his connection with the famous will case of Bartley v. Bartley and others, in which his then principals, Messrs. Crellan, Hunt & Crellan, chiefly through his exertions established their extremely high reputation as solicitors. It was ten years or so after this case that Mr Crellan senior—the head of the firm— retired into private life, and by an odd chance Hewitt's first meeting with him after that event was occasioned by another will difficulty.

These were the terms of the telegram that brought Hewitt again into personal relations with his old principal:—

> *"Can you run down at once on a matter of private business? I will be at Guildford to meet eleven thirty-five from Waterloo. If later or prevented please wire. Crellan."*

The day and the state of Hewitt's engagements suited, and there was full half an hour to catch the train. Taking, therefore, the small travelling-bag that always stood ready packed in case of any sudden excursion that presented the possibility of a night from home, he got early to Waterloo, and by half-past twelve was alighting at Guildford Station. Mr Crellan, a hale, white-haired old gentleman, wearing gold-rimmed spectacles, was waiting with a covered carriage.

"How d'ye do, Mr Hewitt, how d'ye do?" the old gentleman exclaimed as soon as they met, grasping Hewitt's hand, and hurrying him toward the carriage. "I'm glad you've come, very glad. It isn't raining, and you might have preferred something more open, but I brought the brougham because I want to talk privately. I've been vegetating to such an extent for the last few years down here that any little occurrence out of the ordinary excites me, and I'm sure I couldn't have kept quiet till we had got indoors. It's been bad enough, keeping the thing to myself, already."

The door shut, and the brougham started. Mr Crellan laid his hand on Hewitt's knee, "I hope," he said, "I haven't dragged you away from any important business?"

"No," Hewitt replied, "you have chosen a most excellent time. Indeed, I did think of making a small holiday today, but your telegram—"

"Yes, yes. Do you know, I was almost ashamed of having sent it after it had gone. Because, after all, the matter is, probably, really a very simple sort of affair that you can't possibly help me in. A few years ago I should have thought nothing of it, nothing at all. But as I have told you, I've got into such a dull, vegetable state of mind since I retired and have nothing to do that a little thing upsets me, and I haven't mental energy enough to make up my mind to go to dinner sometimes. But you're an old friend, and I'm sure you'll forgive my dragging you all down here on a matter that will, perhaps, seem ridiculously simple to you, a man in the thick of active business. If I hadn't known you so well I wouldn't have had the impudence to bother you. But never mind all that. I'll tell you.

"Do you ever remember my speaking of an intimate friend, a Mr Holford? No. Well, it's a long time ago, and perhaps I never happened to mention him. He was a most excellent man—old fellow, like me, you know; two or three years older, as a matter of fact. We were chums many years ago; in fact, we lodged in the same house when I was an articled clerk and he was a student at Guy's. He retired from the medical profession early, having come into a fortune, and came down here to live at the house we're going to; as a matter of fact, Wedbury Hall.

"When I retired I came down and took up my quarters not far off, and we were a very excellent pair of old chums till last Monday—the day before yesterday—when my poor old friend died. He was pretty well in years—seventy-three—and a man can't live for ever. But I assure you it has upset me terribly, made a greater fool of me than ever, in fact, just when I ought to have my wits about me.

"The reason I particularly want my wits just now, and the reason I have requisitioned yours, is this: that I can't find poor old Holford's will. I drew it up for him years ago, and by it I was appointed his sole executor. I am perfectly convinced that he cannot have destroyed it, because he told me everything concerning his affairs. I have always been his only adviser, in fact, and I'm sure he would have consulted me as to any change in his testamentary intentions before he made it. Moreover, there are reasons why I know he could not have wished to die intestate."

"Which are—?" queried Hewitt as Mr Crellan paused in his statement.

"Which are these: Holford was a widower, with no children of his own. His wife, who has been dead nearly fifteen years now, was a most excellent woman, a model wife, and would have been a model mother if she had been one at all. As it was she adopted a little girl, a poor little soul who was left an orphan at two years of age. The child's father, an unsuccessful man of business of the name of Garth, maddened by a sudden and ruinous loss, committed suicide, and his wife died of the shock occasioned by the calamity.

"The child, as I have said, was taken by Mrs Holford and made a daughter of, and my old friend's daughter she has been ever since, practically speaking. The poor old fellow couldn't possibly have been more attached to a daughter of his own, and on her part she couldn't possibly have been a better daughter than she was. She stuck by him night and day during his last illness, until she became rather ill herself, although of course there was a regular nurse always in attendance.

"Now, in his will, Mr Holford bequeathed rather more than half of his very large property to this Miss Garth; that is to say, as residuary legatee, her interest in the will came to about that. The rest was distributed in various ways. Holford had largely spent the leisure of his retirement in scientific pursuits. So there were a few legacies to learned societies; all his servants were remembered; he left me a certain number of his books; and there was a very fair sum of money for his nephew, Mr Cranley Mellis, the only near relation of Mr Holford's still living. So that you see what the loss of this will may mean. Miss Garth, who was to have taken the greater part of her adoptive father's property, will not have one shilling's worth of claim on the estate and will be turned out into the world without a cent. One or two very old servants will be very awkwardly placed, too, with nothing to live on, and very little prospect of doing more work."

"Everything will go to this nephew," said Hewitt, "of course?"

"Of course. That is unless I attempt to prove a rough copy of the will which I may possibly have by me. But even if I have such a thing and find it, long and costly litigation would be called for, and the result would probably be all against us."

"You say you feel sure Mr Holford did not destroy the will himself?"

"I am quite sure he would never have done so without telling me of it; indeed, I am sure he would have consulted me first. Moreover, it can never have been his intention to leave Miss Garth utterly unprovided for; it would be the same thing as disinheriting his only daughter."

"Did you see him frequently?"

"There's scarcely been a day when I haven't seen him since I have lived down here. During his illness—it lasted a month—I saw him every day."

"And he said nothing of destroying his will?"

"Nothing at all. On the contrary, soon after his first seizure—indeed, on the first visit at which I found him in bed—he said, after telling me how he felt, 'Everything's as I want it, you know, in case I go under.' That seemed to me to mean his will was still as he desired it to be."

"Well, yes, it would seem so. But counsel on the other side (supposing there were another side) might quite as plausibly argue that he meant to die intestate, and had destroyed his will so that everything should be as he wanted it, in that sense. But what do you want me to do—find the will?"

"Certainly, if you can. It seemed to me that you, with your clever head, might be able to form a better judgment than I as to what has happened and who is responsible for it. Because if the will *has* been taken away, someone has taken it."

"It seems probable. Have you told anyone of your difficulty?"

"Not a soul. I came over as soon as I could after Mr Holford's death, and Miss Garth gave me all the keys, because, as executor, the case being a peculiar one, I wished to see that all was in order, and, as you know, the estate is legally vested in the executor from the death of the testator, so that I was responsible for everything; although, of course, if there is no will I'm not executor. But I thought it best to keep the difficulty to myself till I saw you."

"Quite right. Is this Wedbury Hall?"

The brougham had passed a lodge gate, and approached, by a wide drive, a fine old red brick mansion carrying the heavy stone dressings and copings distinctive of early eighteenth century domestic architecture.

"Yes," said Mr Crellan, "this is the place. We will go straight to the study, I think, and then I can explain details."

The study told the tale of the late Mr Holford's habits and interests. It was half a library, half a scientific laboratory—pathological curiosities in spirits, a retort or two, test tubes on the writing-table, and a fossilized lizard mounted in a case, balanced the many shelves and cases of books disposed about the walls. In a recess between two bookcases stood a heavy, old-fashioned mahogany bureau.

"Now it was in that bureau," Mr Crellan explained, indicating it with his finger, "that Mr Holford kept every document that was in the smallest degree important or valuable. I have seen him at it a hundred times, and he always maintained it was as secure as any iron safe. That may not have been altogether the fact, but the bureau is certainly a tremendously heavy and strong one. Feel it."

Hewitt took down the front and pulled out a drawer that Mr Crellan unlocked for the purpose.

"Solid Spanish mahogany an inch thick," was his verdict, "heavy, hard, and seasoned; not the sort of thing you can buy nowadays. Locks, Chubb's patent, early pattern, but not easily to be picked by anything short of a blast of gunpowder. If there are no marks on this bureau it hasn't been tampered with."

"Well," Mr Crellan pursued, "as I say, *that* was where Mr Holford kept his will. I have often seen it when we have been here together, and this was the drawer, the top on the right, that he kept it in. The will was a mere single sheet of foolscap, and was kept, folded of course, in a blue envelope."

"When did you yourself last actually see the will?"

"I saw it in my friend's hand two days before he took to his bed. He merely lifted it in his hand to get at something else in the drawer, replaced it, and locked the drawer again."

"Of course there are other drawers, bureaux, and so on, about the place. You have examined them carefully, I take it?"

"I've turned out ever possible receptacle for that will in the house, I positively assure you, and there isn't a trace of it."

"You've thought of secret drawers, I suppose?"

"Yes. There are two in the bureau which I always knew of. Here they are." Mr Crellan pressed his thumb against a partition of the pigeon-holes at the back of the bureau and a strip of mahogany flew out from below, revealing two shallow drawers with small ivory catches in lieu of knobs. "Nothing there at all. And this other, as I have said, was the drawer where the will was kept. The other papers kept in the same drawer are here as usual."

"Did anybody else know where Mr Holford kept his will?"

"Everybody in the house, I should think. He was a frank, above-board sort of man. His adopted daughter knew, and the butler knew, and there was absolutely no reason why all the other servants shouldn't know; probably they did."

"First," said Hewitt, "we will make quite sure there are no more secret drawers about this bureau. Lock the door in case anybody comes."

Hewitt took out every drawer of the bureau, and examined every part of each before he laid it aside. Then he produced a small pair of silver callipers and an ivory pocket-rule and went over every inch of the heavy framework, measuring, comparing, tapping, adding, and subtracting dimensions. In the end he rose to his feet satisfied. "There is most certainly nothing concealed there," he said.

The drawers were put back, and Mr Crellan suggested lunch. At Hewitt's suggestion it was brought to the study.

"So far," Hewitt said, "we arrive at this: either Mr Holford has destroyed his will, or he has most effectually concealed it, or somebody has stolen it. The first of these possibilities you don't favour."

"I don't believe it is a possibility for a moment. I have told you why; and I knew Holford so well, you know. For the same reasons I am sure he never concealed it."

"Very well, then. Somebody has stolen it. The question is, who?"

"That is so."

"It seems to me that everyone in this house had a direct and personal interest in preserving that will. The servants have all something left them, you say, and without the will that goes, of course. Miss Garth has the greatest possible interest in the will. The only person I have heard of as yet who would benefit by its loss or destruction would be the nephew, Mr Mellis. There are no other relatives, you say, who would benefit by intestacy?"

"Not one."

"Well, what do you think yourself, now? Have you any suspicions?"

Mr Crellan shrugged his shoulders. "I've no more right to suspicions than you have, I suppose," he said. "Of course, if there are to be suspicions they can only point one way. Mr Mellis is the only person who can gain by the disappearance of this will."

"Just so, Now, what do you know of him?"

"I don't know much of the young man," Mr Crellan said slowly. "I must say I never particularly took to him. He is rather a clever fellow, I believe. He was called to the bar some time ago, and afterwards studied medicine, I believe, with the idea of priming himself for a practice in medical jurisprudence. He took a good deal of interest in my old friend's researches, I am told—at any rate he *said* he did; he may have been thinking of his uncle's fortune. But they had a small tiff on some medical question. I don't know exactly what it was, but Mr Holford objected to something—a method of research or something of that kind—as being dangerous and unprofessional. There was no actual rupture between them, you understand, but Mellis's visits slacked off, and there was a coolness."

"Where is Mr Mellis now?"

"In London, I believe."

"Has he been in this house between the day you last saw the will in that drawer and yesterday, when you failed to find it?"

"Only once. He came to see his uncle two days before his death—last Saturday, in fact. He didn't stay long."

"Did you see him?"

"Yes."

"What did he do?"

"Merely came into the room for a few minutes—visitors weren't allowed to stay long—spoke a little to his uncle, and went back to town."

"Did he do nothing else, or see anybody else?"

"Miss Garth went out of the room with him as he left, and I should think they talked for a little before he went away, to judge by the time she was gone; but I don't know."

"You are sure he went then?"

"I saw him in the drive as I looked from the window."

"Miss Garth, you say, has kept all the keys since the beginning of Mr Holford's illness?"

"Yes, until she gave them up to me yesterday. Indeed, the nurse, who is rather a peppery customer, and was jealous of Miss Garth's presence in the sick room all along, made several difficulties about having to go to her for everything."

"And there is no doubt of the bureau having been kept locked all the time?"

"None at all. I have asked Miss Garth that—and, indeed, a good many other things—without saying why I wanted the information."

"How are Mr Mellis and Miss Garth affected toward one another—are they friendly?"

"Oh, yes. Indeed, some while ago I rather fancied that Mellis was disposed to pay serious addresses in that quarter. He may have had a fancy that way, or he may have been attracted by the young lady's expectations. At any rate, nothing definite seems to have come of it as yet. But I must say—between ourselves, of course—I have more than once noticed a decided air of agitation, shyness perhaps, in Miss Garth when Mr Mellis has been present. But, at any rate, that scarcely matters. She is twenty-four years of age now, and can do as she likes. Although, if I had anything to say in the matter—well, never mind."

"You, I take it, have known Miss Garth a long time?"

"Bless you, yes. Danced her on my knee twenty years ago. I've been her 'Uncle Leonard' all her life."

"Well, I think we must at least let Miss Garth know of the loss of the will. Perhaps, when they have cleared away these plates, she will come here for a few minutes."

"I'll go and ask her," Mr Crellan answered, and having rung the bell, proceeded to find Miss Garth.

Presently he returned with the lady. She was a slight, very pale young woman; no doubt rather pretty in ordinary, but now not looking her best. She was evidently worn and nervous from anxiety and want of sleep, and her eyes were sadly inflamed. As the wind slammed a loose casement behind her she started nervously, and placed her hand to her head.

"Sit down at once, my dear," Mr Crellan said; "sit down. This is Mr Martin Hewitt, whom I have taken the liberty of inviting down here to help me in a very important matter. The fact is, my dear," Mr Crellan added gravely, "I can't find your poor father's will."

Miss Garth was not surprised. "I thought so," she said mildly, "when you asked me about the bureau yesterday."

"Of course I need not say, my dear, what a serious thing it may be for you if that will cannot be found. So I hope you'll try and tell Mr Hewitt here anything he wants to know as well as you can, without forgetting a single thing. I'm pretty sure that he will find it for us if it is to be found."

"I understand, Miss Garth," Hewitt asked, "that the keys of that bureau never left your possession during the whole time of Mr Holford's last illness, and that the bureau was kept locked?"

"Yes, that is so."

"Did you ever have occasion to go to the bureau yourself?"

"No, I have not touched it."

"Then you can answer for it, I presume, that the bureau was never unlocked by *anyone* from the time Mr Holford placed the keys in your hands till you gave them to Mr Crellan?"

"Yes, I am sure of that."

"Very good. Now is there any place on the whole premises that you can suggest where this will may possibly be hidden?"

"There is no place that Mr Crellan doesn't know of, I'm sure."

"It is an old house, I observe," Hewitt pursued. "Do you know of any place of concealment in the structure—any secret doors, I mean, you know, or sliding panels, or hollow door frames, and so forth?"

Miss Garth shook her head. "There is not a single place of the sort you speak of in the whole building, so far as I know," she said, "and I have lived here almost all my life."

"You knew the purport of Mr Holford's will, I take it, and understand what its loss may mean to yourself?"

"Perfectly."

"Now I must ask you to consider carefully. Take your mind back to two or three days before Mr Holford's illness began, and tell me if you can remember any single fact, occurrence, word, or hint from that day to this in any way bearing on the will or anything connected with it?"

Miss Garth shook her head thoughtfully. "I can't remember the thing being mentioned by anybody, except perhaps by the nurse, who is rather a touchy sort of woman, and once or twice took it upon herself to hint that my recent anxiety was chiefly about my poor father's money. And that once, when I had done some small thing for him, my father—I have always called him father, you know—said that he wouldn't forget it, or that I should be rewarded, or something of that sort. Nothing else that I can remember in the remotest degree concerned the will."

"Mr Mellis said nothing about it, then?"

Miss Garth changed colour slightly, but answered, "No, I only saw him to the door."

"Thank you, Miss Garth, I won't trouble you any further just now. But if you *can* remember anything more in the course of the next few hours it may turn out to be of great service."

Miss Garth bowed and withdrew. Mr Crellan shut the door behind her and returned to Hewitt. "*That* doesn't carry us much further," he said. "The more certain it seems that the will cannot have been got at, the more difficult our position is from a legal point of view. What shall we do now?"

"Is the nurse still about the place?"

"Yes, I believe so."

"Then I'll speak to her."

The nurse came in response to Mr Crellan's summons: a sharp-featured, pragmatical woman of forty-five. She took the seat offered her, and waited for Hewitt's questions.

"You were in attendance on Mr Holford, I believe, Mrs Turton, since the beginning of his last illness?"

"Since October 24th."

"Were you present when Mr Mellis came to see his uncle last Saturday?"

"Yes."

"Can you tell me what took place?"

"As to what the gentleman said to Mr Holford," the nurse replied, bridling slightly, "of course I don't know anything, it not being my business and not intended for my ears. Mr Crellan was there, and knows as much as I do, and so does Miss Garth. I only know that Mr Mellis stayed for a few minutes and then went out of the room with Miss Garth."

"How long was Miss Garth gone?"

"I don't know, ten minutes or a quarter of an hour, perhaps."

"Now Mrs Turton, I want you to tell me in confidence—it is very important—whether you, at any time, heard Mr Holford during his illness say anything of his wishes as to how his property was to be left in case of his death?"

The nurse started and looked keenly from Hewitt to Mr Crellan and back again.

"Is it the will you mean?" she asked sharply.

"Yes. Did he mention it?"

"You mean you can't find the will, isn't that it?"

"Well, suppose it is, what then?"

"Suppose won't do," the nurse answered shortly; "I *do* know something about the will, and I believe you can't find it."

"I'm sure, Mrs Turton, that if you know anything about the will you will tell Mr Crellan in the interests of right and justice."

"And who's to protect me against the spite of those I shall offend if I tell you?"

Mr Crellan interposed.

"Whatever you tell us, Mrs Turton," he said, "will be held in the strictest confidence, and the source of our information shall not be divulged. For that I give you my word of honour. And, I need scarcely add, I will see that you come to no harm by anything you may say."

"Then the will *is* lost. I may understand that?"

Hewitt's features were impassive and impenetrable. But in Mr Crellan's disturbed face the nurse saw a plain answer in the affirmative.

"Yes," she said, "I see that's the trouble. Well, I know who took it."

"Then who was it?"

"*Miss Garth!*"

"Miss Garth! Nonsense!" cried Mr Crellan, starting upright. "Nonsense!"

"It may be nonsense," the nurse replied slowly, with a monotonous emphasis on each word. "It may be nonsense, but it's a fact. I saw her take it."

Mr Crellan simply gasped. Hewitt drew his chair a little nearer.

"If you saw her take it," he said gently, closely watching the woman's face the while, "then, of course, there's no doubt."

"I tell you I saw her take it," the nurse repeated. "What was in it, and what her game was in taking it, I don't know. But it was in that bureau, wasn't it?"

"Yes—probably."

"In the right hand top drawer?"

"Yes."

"A white paper in a blue envelope?"

"Yes."

"Then I saw her take it, as I said before. She unlocked that drawer before my eyes, took it out, and locked the drawer again."

Mr Crellan turned blankly to Hewitt, but Hewitt kept his eyes on the nurse's face.

"When did this occur?" he asked, "and how?"

"It was on Saturday night, rather late. Everybody was in bed but Miss Garth and myself, and she had been down to the dining-room for something. Mr Holford was asleep, so as I wanted to re-fill the water-bottle, I took it up and went. As I was passing the door of this room that we are in now, I heard a noise, and looked in at the door, which was open. There was a candle on the table which had been left there earlier in the evening. Miss Garth was opening the top right hand drawer of *that* bureau"—Mrs Turton stabbed her finger spitefully toward the piece of furniture, as though she owed it a personal grudge—"and I saw her take out a blue foolscap envelope, and as the flap was open, I could see the enclosed paper was white. She shut the drawer, locked it, and came out of the room with the envelope in her hand."

"And what did you do?"

"I hurried on, and she came away without seeing me, and went in the opposite direction — toward the small staircase."

"Perhaps," Mr Crellan ventured at a blurt, "perhaps she was walking in her sleep?"

"That she wasn't!" the nurse replied, "for she came back to Mr Holford's room almost as soon as I returned there, and asked some questions about the medicine — which was nothing new, for I must say she was very fond of interfering in things that were part of my business."

"That is quite certain, I suppose," Hewitt remarked — "that she could not have been asleep?"

"Quite certain. She talked for about a quarter of an hour, and wanted to kiss Mr Holford, which might have wakened him, before she went to bed. In fact, I may say we had a disagreement."

Hewitt did not take his steady gaze from the nurse's face for some seconds after she had finished speaking. Then he only said, "Thank you, Mrs Turton. I need scarcely assure you, after what Mr Crellan has said, that your confidence shall not be betrayed. I think that is all, unless you have more to tell us."

Mrs Turton bowed and rose. "There is nothing more," she said, and left the room.

As soon as she had gone, "Is Mrs Turton at all interested in the will," Hewitt asked.

"No, there is nothing for her. She is a newcomer, you see. Perhaps," Mr Crellan went on, struck by an idea, "she may be jealous, or something. She seems a spiteful woman — and really, I can't believe her story for a moment."

"Why?"

"Well, you see, it's absurd. Why should Miss Garth go to all this trouble to do herself an injury — to make a beggar of herself? And besides, she's not in the habit of telling barefaced lies. She distinctly assured us, you remember, that she had never been to the bureau for any purpose whatever."

"But the nurse has an honest character, hasn't she?"

"Yes, her character is excellent. Indeed, from all accounts, she is a very excellent woman, except for a desire to govern everybody, and a habit of spite if she is thwarted. But, of course, that sort of thing sometimes leads people rather far."

"So it does," Hewitt replied. "But consider now. Is it not possible that Miss Garth, completely infatuated with Mr Mellis, thinks she is doing a noble thing for him by destroying the will and giving up her whole claim to his uncle's property? Devoted women do just such things, you know."

Mr Crellan stared, bent his head to his hand, and considered. "So they do, so they do," he said. "Insane foolery. Really, it's the sort of thing I can imagine her doing—she's honour and generosity itself. But then those lies," he resumed, sitting up and slapping his leg; "I can't believe she'd tell such tremendous lies as that for anybody. And with such a calm face, too—I'm sure she couldn't."

"Well, that's as it may be. You can scarcely set a limit to the lengths a woman will go on behalf of a man she loves. I suppose, by the bye, Miss Garth is not exactly what you would call a 'strong-minded' woman?"

"No, she's not that. She'd never get on in the world by herself. She's a good little soul, but nervous—very; and her month of anxiety, grief, and want of sleep seems to have broken her up."

"Mr Mellis knows of the death, I suppose?"

"I telegraphed to him at his chambers in London the first thing yesterday—Tuesday—morning, as soon as the telegraph office was open. He came here (as I've forgotten to tell you as yet) the first thing this morning—before I was over here myself, in fact. He had been staying not far off—at Ockham, I think—and the telegram had been sent on. He saw Miss Garth, but couldn't stay, having to get back to London. I met him going away as I came, about eleven o'clock. Of course I said nothing about the fact that I couldn't find the will, but he will probably be down again soon, and may ask questions."

"Yes," Hewitt replied. "And speaking of that matter, you can no doubt talk with Miss Garth on very intimate and familiar terms?"

"Oh yes—yes; I've told you what old friends we are."

"I wish you could manage, at some favourable opportunity today, to speak to her alone, and without referring to the will in any way, get to know, as circumspectly and delicately as you can, how she stands in regard to Mr Mellis. Whether he is an accepted lover, or likely to be one, you know. Whatever answer you may get, you may judge, I expect, by her manner how things really are."

"Very good—I'll seize the first chance. Meanwhile what to do?"

"Nothing, I'm afraid, except perhaps to examine other pieces of furniture as closely as we have examined this bureau."

Other bureaux, desks, tables, and chests were examined fruitlessly. It was not until after dinner that Mr Crellan saw a favourable opportunity of sounding Miss Garth as he had promised. Half an hour later he came to Hewitt in the study, more puzzled than ever.

"There's no engagement between them," he reported, "secret or open, nor ever has been. It seems, from what I can make out, going to work as diplomatically as possible, that Mellis *did* propose to her, or something very near it, a time ago, and was point-blank refused. Altogether, Miss Garth's sentiment for him appears to be rather dislike than otherwise."

"That rather knocks a hole in the theory of self-sacrifice, doesn't it?" Hewitt remarked. "I shall have to think over this, and sleep on it. It's possible that it may be necessary tomorrow for you to tax Miss Garth, point-blank, with having taken away the will. Still, I hope not."

"I hope not, too," Mr Crellan said, rather dubious as to the result of such an experiment. "She has been quite upset enough already. And, by the by, she didn't seem any the better or more composed after Mellis' visit this morning."

"Still, *then* the will was gone."

"Yes."

And so Hewitt and Mr Crellan talked on late into the evening, turning over every apparent possibility and finding reason in none. The household went to bed at ten, and, soon after, Miss Garth came to bid Mr Crellan goodnight. It had been settled that both Martin Hewitt and Mr Crellan should stay the night at Wedbury Hall.

Soon all was still, and the ticking of the tall clock in the hall below could be heard as distinctly as though it were in the study, while the rain without dropped from eaves and sills in regular splashes. Twelve o'clock struck, and Mr Crellan was about to suggest retirement, when the sound of a light footstep startled Hewitt's alert ear. He raised his hand to enjoin silence, and stepped to the door of the room, Mr Crellan following him.

There was a light over the staircase, seven or eight yards away, and down the stairs came Miss Garth in dressing gown and slippers; she turned at the landing and vanished in a passage leading to the right.

"Where does that lead to?" Hewitt whispered hurriedly.

"Toward the small staircase—other end of house," Mr Crellan replied in the same tones.

"Come quietly," said Hewitt, and stepped lightly after Miss Garth, Mr Crellan at his heels.

She was nearing the opposite end of the passage, walking at a fair pace and looking neither to right nor left. There was another light over the smaller staircase at the end. Without hesitation Miss Garth turned down the stairs till about half down the flight, and then stopped and pressed her hand against the oak wainscot.

Immediately the vertical piece of framing against which she had placed her hand turned on central pivots top and bottom, revealing a small recess, three feet high and little more than six inches wide. Miss Garth stooped and felt about at the bottom of this recess for several seconds. Then with every sign of extreme agitation and horror she withdrew her hand empty, and sank on the stairs. Her head rolled from side to side on her shoulders, and beads of perspiration stood on her forehead. Hewitt with difficulty restrained Mr Crellan from going to her assistance.

Presently, with a sort of shuddering sigh, Miss Garth rose, and after standing irresolute for a moment, descended the flight of stairs to the bottom. There she stopped again, and pressing her hand to her forehead, turned and began to re-ascend the stairs.

Hewitt touched his companion's arm, and the two hastily but noiselessly made their way back along the passage to the study. Miss Garth left the open framing as it was, reached the top of the landing, and without stopping proceeded along the passage and turned up the main staircase, while Hewitt and Mr Crellan still watched her from the study door.

At the top of the flight she turned to the right, and up three or four more steps toward her own room. There she stopped, and leaned thoughtfully on the handrail.

"Go up," whispered Hewitt to Mr Crellan, "as though you were going to bed. Appear surprised to see her; ask if she isn't well, and, if you can, manage to repeat that question of mine about secret hiding-places in the house."

Mr Crellan nodded and started quickly up the stairs. Halfway up he turned his head, and, as he went on, "Why, Nelly, my dear," he said, "what's the matter? Aren't you well?"

Mr Crellan acted his part well, and waiting below, Hewitt heard this dialogue:

"No, uncle, I don't feel very well, but it's nothing. I think my room seems close. I can scarcely breathe."

"Oh, it isn't close tonight. You'll be catching cold, my dear. Go and have a good sleep; you mustn't worry that wise little head of yours, you know. Mr Hewitt and I have been making quite a night of it, but I'm off to bed now."

"I hope they've made you both quite comfortable, uncle?"

"Oh, yes; capital, capital. We've been talking over business, and, no doubt, we shall put that matter all in order soon. By the by, I suppose since you saw Mr Hewitt you haven't happened to remember anything more to tell him?"

"No."

"You still can't remember any hiding-places or panels, or that sort of thing in the wainscot or anywhere?"

"No, I'm sure I don't know of any, and I don't believe for a moment that any exist."

"Quite sure of that, I suppose?"

"Oh yes."

"All right. Now go to bed. You'll catch *such* a cold in these draughty landings. Come, I won't move a step till I see your door shut behind you. Goodnight."

"Goodnight, uncle."

Mr Crellan came downstairs again with a face of blank puzzlement.

"I wouldn't have believed it," he assured Martin Hewitt; "positively I wouldn't have believed she'd have told such a lie, and with such confidence, too. There's something deep and horrible here, I'm afraid. What does it mean?"

"We'll talk of that afterwards," Hewitt replied. "Come now and take a look at that recess."

They went, quietly still, to the small staircase, and there, with a candle, closely examined the recess. It was a mere box, three feet high, a foot or a little more deep, and six or seven inches wide. The piece of oak framing, pivoted to the stair at the bottom and to a horizontal piece of framing at the top, stood edge forward, dividing the opening down the centre. There was nothing whatever in the recess.

Hewitt ascertained that there was no catch, the plank simply remaining shut by virtue of fitting tightly, so that nothing but pressure on the proper part was requisite to open it. He had closed the plank and turned to speak to Mr Crellan, when another interruption occurred.

On each floor the two staircases were joined by passages, and the ground-floor passage, from the foot of the flight they were on, led to the entrance hall. Distinct amid the loud clicking of the hall clock, Hewitt now heard a sound, as of a person's foot shifting on a stone step.

Mr Crellan heard it too, and each glanced at the other. Then Hewitt, shading the candle with his hand, led the way to the hall. There they listened for several seconds—almost an hour—it seemed—and then the noise was repeated. There was no doubt of it. It was at the other side of the front door.

In answer to Hewitt's hurried whispers, Mr Crellan assured him that there was no window from which, in the dark, a view could be got of a person standing outside the door. Also that any other way out would be equally noisy, and would entail the circuit of the house. The front door was fastened by three heavy bolts, an immense old-fashioned lock, and a bar. It would take nearly a minute to open at least, even if everything went easily. But, as there was no other way, Hewitt determined to try it. Handing the candle to his companion, he first lifted the bar, conceiving that it might be done with the least noise. It went easily, and, handling it carefully, Hewitt let it hang from its rivet without a sound. Just then, glancing at Mr Crellan, he saw that he was forgetting to shade the candle, whose rays extended through the fanlight above the door, and probably through the wide crack under it. But it was too late. At the same moment the light was evidently perceived from outside; there was a hurried jump from the steps, and for an instant a sound of running on gravel. Hewitt tore back the bolts, flung the door open, and dashed out into the darkness, leaving Mr Crellan on the doorstep with the candle.

Hewitt was gone, perhaps, five or ten minutes, although to Mr Crellan—standing there at the open door in a state of high nervous tension, and with no notion of what was happening or what it all meant—the time seemed an eternity. When at last Hewitt reached the door again, "What was it?" asked Mr Crellan, much agitated. "Did you see? Have you caught them?"

Hewitt shook his head.

"I hadn't a chance," he said. "The wall is low over there, and there's a plantation of trees at the other side. But I think—yes, I begin to think—that I may possibly be able to see my way through this business in a little while. See this?"

On the top step in the sheltered porch there remained the wet prints of two feet. Hewitt took a letter from his pocket, opened it out, spread it carefully over the more perfect of the two marks, pressed it lightly and lifted it. Then, when the door was shut, he produced his pocket scissors, and with great care cut away the paper round the wet part, leaving a piece, of course, the shape of a boot sole.

"Come," said Hewitt, "we may get at something after all. Don't ask me to tell you anything now; I don't know anything, as a matter of fact. I hope this is the end of the night's entertainment, but I'm afraid the case is rather an unpleasant business. There is nothing for us to do now but to go to bed, I think. I suppose there's a handy man kept about the place?"

"Yes, he's gardener and carpenter and carpet-beater, and so on."

"Good! Where's his sanctum? Where does he keep his shovels and carpet sticks?"

"In the shed by the coach house, I believe. I think it's generally unlocked."

"Very good. We've earned a night's rest, and now we'll have it."

The next morning, after breakfast, Hewitt took Mr Crellan into the study.

"Can you manage," he said, "to send Miss Garth out for a walk this morning—with somebody?"

"I can send her out for a ride with the groom—unless she thinks it wouldn't be the thing to go riding so soon after her bereavement."

"Never mind, that will do. Send her at once, and see that she goes. Call it doctor's orders; say she must go for her health's sake—anything."

Mr Crellan departed, used his influence, and in half an hour Miss Garth had gone.

"I was up pretty early this morning," Hewitt remarked on Mr Crellan's return to the study, "and, among other things, I sent a telegram to London. Unless my eyes deceive me, a boy with a peaked cap—a telegraph boy, in fact—is coming up the drive this moment. Yes, he is. It is probably my answer."

In a few minutes a telegram was brought in. Hewitt read it and then asked,—

"Your friend Mr Mellis, I understand, was going straight to town yesterday morning?"

"Yes."

"Read that, then."

Mr Crellan took the telegram and read:

"Mellis did not sleep at chambers last night. Been out of town for some days past. Kerrett."

Mr Crellan looked up.

"Who's Kerrett?" he asked.

"Lad in my office; sharp fellow. You see, Mellis didn't go to town after all. As a matter of fact, I believe he was nearer this place than we thought. You said he had a disagreement with his uncle because of scientific practices which the old gentleman considered 'dangerous and unprofessional,' I think?"

"Yes, that was the case."

"Ah, then the key to all the mystery of the will is in this room."

"Where?"

"There." Hewitt pointed to the bookcases. "Read Bernheim's *Suggestive Therapeutics*, and one or two books of Heidenhain's and Björnström's and you'll see the thing more clearly than you can without them; but that would be rather a long sort of job, so—but why, who's this? Somebody coming up the drive in a fly, isn't it?"

"Yes," Mr Crellan replied, looking out of the window. Presently he added, "It's Cranley Mellis."

"Ah," said Hewitt, "he won't trouble us for a little. I'll bet you a penny cake he goes first by himself to the small staircase and tries that secret recess. If you get a little way along the passage you will be able to see him; but that will scarcely matter—I can see you don't guess now what I am driving at."

"I don't in the least."

"I told you the names of the books in which you could read the matter up; but that would be too long for the present purpose. The thing is fairly well summarised, I see, in that encyclopædia there in the corner. I have put a marker in volume seven. Do you mind opening it at that place and seeing for yourself?"

Mr Crellan, doubtful and bewildered, reached the volume. It opened readily, and in the place where it opened lay a blue foolscap envelope. The old gentleman took the envelope, drew from it a white paper, stared first at the paper, then at Hewitt, then at the paper again, let the volume slide from his lap, and gasped,—

"Why—why—it's the will!"

"Ah, so I thought," said Hewitt, catching the book as it fell. "But don't lose this place in the encyclopædia. Read the name of the article. What is it?"

Mr Crellan looked absent-mindedly at the title, holding the will before him all the time. Then, mechanically, he read aloud the word, "*Hypnotism*."

"Hypnotism it is," Hewitt answered. "A dangerous and terrible power in the hands of an unscrupulous man."

"But—but how? I don't understand it. This—this is the real will, I suppose?"

"Look at it; you know best."

Mr Crellan looked.

"Yes," he said, "this certainly is the will. But where did it come from? It hasn't been in this book all the time, has it?"

"No. Didn't I tell you I put it there myself as a marker? But come, you'll understand my explanation better if I first read you a few lines from this article. See here now:—

'Although hypnotism has power for good when properly used by medical men, it is an exceedingly dangerous weapon in the hands of the unskilful or unscrupulous. Crimes have been committed by persons who have been hypnotised. Just as a person when hypnotised is rendered extremely impressionable, and therefore capable of receiving beneficial suggestions, so he is nearly as liable to receive suggestions for evil; and it is quite possible for an hypnotic subject, while under hypnotic influence, to be impressed with the belief that he is to commit some act after the influence is removed, and that act he is safe to commit, acting at the time as an automaton. Suggestions may be thus made of which the subject, in his subsequent uninfluenced moments, has no idea, but which he will proceed to carry out automatically at the time appointed. In the case of a complete state of hypnotism the subject has subsequently no recollection whatever of what has happened. Persons whose will or nerve power has been weakened by fear or other similar causes can be hypnotised without consent on their part.'"

"There now, what do you make of that?"

"Why, do you mean that Miss Garth has been hypnotised by—by—Cranley Mellis?"

"I think that is the case; indeed, I am pretty sure of it. Notice, on the occasion of each of his last two visits, he was alone with Miss Garth for some little time. On the evening following each of those visits she does something which she afterwards knows nothing about—something connected with the disappearance of this will, the only thing standing between Mr Mellis and the whole of his uncle's property. Who could have been in a weaker nervous state than Miss Garth has been lately? Remember, too, on the visit of last Saturday, while Miss Garth says she only showed Mellis to the door, both you and the nurse speak of their being gone some little time. Miss Garth must have forgotten what took place then, when Mellis hypnotised her, and impressed on her the suggestion that she should take Mr Holford's will that night, long after he—Mellis—had gone, and when he could not be suspected of knowing anything of it. Further, that she should, at that time when her movements would be less likely to be observed, secrete that will in a place of hiding known only to himself."

"Dear, dear, what a rascal! Do you really think he did that?"

"Not only that, but I believe he came here yesterday morning while you were out to get the will from the recess. The recess, by the bye, I expect he discovered by accident on one of his visits (he has been here pretty often, I suppose, altogether), and kept the secret in case it might be useful. Yesterday, not finding the will there, he hypnotised Miss Garth once again, and conveyed the suggestion that, at midnight last night, she should take the will from wherever she had put it and pass it to him under the front door."

"What, do you mean it was he you chased across the grounds last night?"

"That is a thing I am pretty certain of. If we had Mr Mellis's boot here we could make sure by comparing it with the piece of paper I cut out, as you will remember, in the entrance hall. As we have the will, though, that will scarcely be necessary. What he will do now, I expect, will be to go to the recess again on the vague chance of the will being there now, after all, assuming that his second dose of mesmerism has somehow miscarried. If Miss Garth were here he might try his tricks again, and that is why I got you to send her out."

"And where did you find the will?"

"Now you come to practical details. You will remember that I asked about the handyman's tool-house? Well, I paid it a visit at six o'clock this morning, and found therein some very excellent carpenter's tools in a chest. I took a selection of them to the small staircase, and took out the tread of a stair—the one that the pivoted framing-plank rested on."

"And you found the will there?"

"The will, as I rather expected when I examined the recess last night, had slipped down a rather wide crack at the end of the stair timber, which, you know, formed, so to speak, the floor of the recess. The fact was, the stair-tread didn't quite reach as far as the back of the recess. The opening wasn't very distinct to see, but I soon felt it with my fingers. When Miss Garth, in her hypnotic condition on Saturday night, dropped the will into the recess, it shot straight to the back corner and fell down the slit. That was why Mellis found it empty, and why Miss Garth also found it empty on returning there last night under hypnotic influence. You observed her terrible state of nervous agitation when she failed to carry out the command that haunted her. It was frightful. Something like what happens to a suddenly awakened somnambulist, perhaps. Anyway, that is all over. I found the will under the end of the stair-tread, and here it is. If you will come to the small staircase now you shall see where the paper slipped out of sight. Perhaps we shall meet Mr Mellis."

"He's a scoundrel," said Mr Crellan. "It's a pity we can't punish him."

"That's impossible, of course. Where's your proof? And if you had any I'm not sure that a hypnotist is responsible at law for what his subject does. Even if he were, moving a will from one part of the house to another is scarcely a legal crime. The explanation I have given you accounts entirely for the disturbed manner of Miss Garth in the presence of Mellis. She merely felt an indefinite sense of his power over her. Indeed, there is all the possibility that, finding her an easy subject, he had already practised his influence by way of experiment. A hypnotist, as you will see in the books, has always an easier task with a person he has hypnotised before."

As Hewitt had guessed, in the corridor they met Mr Mellis. He was a thin, dark man of about thirty-five, with large, bony features, and a slight stoop. Mr Crellan glared at him ferociously.

"Well, sir, and what do you want?" he asked.

Mr Mellis looked surprised. "Really, that's a very extraordinary remark, Mr Crellan," he said. "This is my late uncle's house. I might, with at least as much reason, ask you what you want."

"I'm here, sir, as Mr Holford's executor."

"Appointed by will?"

"Yes."

"And is the will in existence?"

"Well—the fact is—we couldn't find it—"

"Then, what do you mean, sir, by calling yourself an executor with no will to warrant you?" interrupted Mellis. "Get out of this house. If there's no will, I administer."

"But there *is* a will," roared Mr Crellan, shaking it in his face. "There is a will. I didn't say we hadn't found it yet, did I? There *is* a will, and here it is in spite of all your diabolical tricks, with your scoundrelly hypnotism and secret holes, and the rest of it! Get out of this place, sir, or I'll have you thrown out of the window!"

Mr Mellis shrugged his shoulders with an appearance of perfect indifference. "If you've a will appointing you executor it's all right, I suppose, although I shall take care to hold you responsible for any irregularities. As I don't in the least understand your conduct, unless it is due to drink, I'll leave you." And with that he went.

Mr Crellan boiled with indignation for a minute, and then turning to Hewitt, "I say, I hope it's all right," he said, "connecting him with all this queer business?"

"We shall soon see," replied Hewitt, "if you'll come and look at the pivoted plank."

They went to the small staircase, and Hewitt once again opened the recess. Within lay a blue foolscap envelope, which Hewitt picked up. "See," he said, "it is torn at the corner. He has been here and opened it. It's a fresh envelope, and I left it for him this morning, with the corner gummed down a little so that he would have to tear it in opening. This is what was inside," Hewitt added, and laughed aloud as he drew forth a rather crumpled piece of white paper. "It was only a childish trick after all," he concluded, "but I always liked a small practical joke on occasion." He held out the crumpled paper, on which was inscribed in large capital letters the single word—"SOLD."

4

THE CASE OF THE MISSING HAND

I think I have recorded in another place Hewitt's frequent aphorism that "there is nothing in this world that is at all possible that has not happened or is not happening in London." But there are many strange happenings in this matter-of-fact country and in these matter-of-fact times that occur far enough from London. Fantastic crimes, savage revenges, mediæval superstitions, horrible cruelty, though less in sight, have been no more extinguished by the advent of the nineteenth century than have the ancient races who practised them in the dark ages. Some of the races have become civilized, and some of the savageries are heard of no more. But there are survivals in both cases. I say these things having in my mind a particular case that came under the personal notice of both Hewitt and myself—an affair that brought one up standing with a gasp and a doubt of one's era.

My good uncle, the Colonel, was not in the habit of gathering large house parties at his place at Ratherby, partly because the place was not a great one, and partly because the Colonel's gout was. But there was an excellent bit of shooting for two or three guns, and even when he was unable to leave the house himself, my uncle was always pleased if some good friend were enjoying a good day's sport in his territory. As to myself, the good old soul was in a perpetual state of offence because I visited him so seldom, though whenever my scant holidays fell in a convenient time of the year I was never insensible to the attractions of the Ratherby stubble. More than once had I sat by the old gentleman when his foot was exceptionally troublesome, amusing him with accounts of some of the doings of Martin Hewitt, and more than once had my uncle expressed his desire to meet Hewitt himself, and commissioned me with an invitation to be presented to Hewitt at the first likely opportunity, for a joint excursion to Ratherby. At length I persuaded Hewitt to take a fortnight's rest, coincident with a little vacation of my own, and we got down to Ratherby within a few days past September the 1st, and before a gun had been fired at the Colonel's bit of shooting. The Colonel himself we found confined to the house with his foot on the familiar rest, and though ourselves were the only guests, we managed to do pretty well together. It was during this short holiday that the case I have mentioned arose.

When first I began to record some of the more interesting of Hewitt's operations, I think I explained that such cases as I myself had not witnessed I should set down in impersonal narrative form, without intruding myself. The present case, so far as Hewitt's work was concerned, I saw, but there were circumstances which led up to it that we only fully learned afterwards. These circumstances, however, I shall put in their proper place—at the beginning.

The Fosters were a fairly old Ratherby family, of whom Mr John Foster had died by an accident at the age of about forty, leaving a wife twelve years younger than himself and three children, two boys and one girl, who was the youngest. The boys grew up strong, healthy, out-of-door young ruffians, with all the tastes of sportsmen, and all the qualities, good and bad, natural to lads of fairly well-disposed character allowed a great deal too much of their own way from the beginning.

Their only real bad quality was an unfortunate knack of bearing malice, and a certain savage vindictiveness towards such persons as they chose to consider their enemies. With the louts of the village they were at unceasing war, and, indeed, once got into serious trouble for peppering the butcher's son (who certainly was a great blackguard) with sparrow-shot. At the usual time they went to Oxford together, and were fraternally sent down together in their second year, after enjoying a spell of rustication in their first. The offence was never specifically mentioned about Ratherby, but was rumoured of as something particularly outrageous.

It was at this time, sixteen years or thereabout after the death of their father, that Henry and Robert Foster first saw and disliked Mr Jonas Sneathy, a director of penny banks and small insurance offices. He visited Ranworth (the Fosters' home) a great deal more than the brothers thought necessary, and, indeed, it was not for lack of rudeness on their part that Mr Sneathy failed to understand, as far as they were concerned, his room was preferred to his company.

But their mother welcomed him, and in the end it was announced that Mrs Foster was to marry again, and that after that her name would be Mrs Sneathy.

Hereupon there were violent scenes at Ranworth. Henry and Robert Foster denounced their prospective father-in-law as a fortune-hunter, a snuffler, a hypocrite. They did not stop at broad hints as to the honesty of his penny banks and insurance offices, and the house straightway became a house of bitter strife. The marriage took place, and it was not long before Mr Sneathy's real character became generally obvious. For months he was a model, if somewhat sanctimonious husband, and his influence over his wife was complete. Then he discovered that her property had been strictly secured by her first husband's will, and that, willing as she might be, she was unable to raise money for her new husband's benefit, and was quite powerless to pass to him any of her property by deed of gift. Hereupon the man's nature showed itself. Foolish woman as Mrs Sneathy might be, she was a loving, indeed, an infatuated wife; but Sneathy repaid her devotion by vulgar derision, never hesitating to state plainly that he had married her for his own profit, and that he considered himself swindled in the result. More, he even proceeded to blows and other practical brutality of a sort only devisable by a mean and ugly nature. This treatment, at first secret, became open, and in the midst of it Mr Sneathy's penny banks and insurance offices came to a grievous smash all at once, and everybody wondered how Mr Sneathy kept out of gaol.

Keep out of gaol he did, however, for he had taken care to remain on the safe side of the law, though some of his co-directors learnt the taste of penal servitude. But he was beggared, and lived, as it were, a mere pensioner in his wife's house. Here his brutality increased to a frightful extent, till his wife, already broken in health in consequence, went in constant fear of her life, and Miss Foster passed a life of weeping misery. All her friends' entreaties, however, could not persuade Mrs Sneathy to obtain a legal separation from her husband. She clung to him with the excuse—for it was no more—that she hoped to win him to kindness by submission, and with a pathetic infatuation that seemed to increase as her bodily strength diminished.

Henry and Robert, as may be supposed, were anything but silent in these circumstances. Indeed, they broke out violently again and again, and more than once went near permanently injuring their worthy father-in-law. Once especially, when Sneathy, absolutely without provocation, made a motion to strike his wife in their presence, there was a fearful scene. The two sprang at him like wild beasts, knocked him down and dragged him to the balcony with the intention of throwing him out of the window. But Mrs Sneathy impeded them, hysterically imploring them to desist.

"If you lift your hand to my mother," roared Henry, gripping Sneathy by the throat till his fat face turned blue, and banging his head against the wall, "if you lift your hand to my mother again I'll chop it off—I will! I'll chop it off and drive it down your throat!"

"We'll do worse," said Robert, white and frantic with passion, "we'll hang you—hang you to the door! You're a proved liar and thief, and you're worse than a common murderer. I'd hang you to the front door for twopence!"

For a few days Sneathy was comparatively quiet, cowed by their violence. Then he took to venting redoubled spite on his unfortunate wife, always in the absence of her sons, well aware that she would never inform them. On their part, finding him apparently better behaved in consequence of their attack, they thought to maintain his wholesome terror, and scarcely passed him without a menace, taking a fiendish delight in repeating the threats they had used during the scene, by way of keeping it present to his mind.

"Take care of your hands, sir," they would say. "Keep them to yourself, or, by George, we'll take 'em off with a billhook!"

But his revenge for all this Sneathy took unobserved on their mother. Truly a miserable household.

Soon, however, the brothers left home, and went to London by way of looking for a profession. Henry began a belated study of medicine, and Robert made a pretence of reading for the bar. Indeed, their departure was as much as anything a consequence of the earnest entreaty of their sister, who saw that their presence at home was an exasperation to Sneathy, and aggravated her mother's secret sufferings. They went, therefore; but at Ranworth things became worse.

Little was allowed to be known outside the house, but it was broadly said that Mr Sneathy's behaviour had now become outrageous beyond description. Servants left faster than new ones could be found, and gave their late employer the character of a raving maniac. Once, indeed, he committed himself in the village, attacking with his walking-stick an inoffensive tradesman who had accidentally brushed against him, and immediately running home. This assault had to be compounded for by a payment of fifty pounds. And then Henry and Robert Foster received a most urgent letter from their sister requesting their immediate presence at home.

They went at once, of course, and the servants' account of what occurred was this. When the brothers arrived Mr Sneathy had just left the house. The brothers were shut up with their mother and sister for about a quarter of an hour, and then left them and came out to the stable yard together. The coachman (he was a new man, who had only arrived the day before) overheard a little of their talk as they stood by the door.

Mr Henry said that "the thing must be done, and at once. There are two of us, so that it ought to be easy enough." And afterwards Mr Robert said, "You'll know best how to go about it, as a doctor." After which Mr Henry came towards the coachman and asked in what direction Mr Sneathy had gone. The coachman replied that it was in the direction of Ratherby Wood, by the winding footpath that led through it. But as he spoke he distinctly with the corner of his eye saw the other brother take a halter from a hook by the stable door and put it into his coat pocket.

So far for the earlier events, whereof I learned later bit by bit. It was on the day of the arrival of the brothers Foster at their old home, and, indeed, little more than two hours after the incident last set down, that news of Mr Sneathy came to Colonel Brett's place, where Hewitt and I were sitting and chatting with the Colonel. The news was that Mr Sneathy had committed suicide—had been found hanging, in fact, to a tree in Ratherby Wood, just by the side of the footpath.

Hewitt and I had of course at this time never heard of Sneathy, and the Colonel told us what little he knew. He had never spoken to the man, he said—indeed, nobody in the place outside Ranworth would have anything to do with him. "He's certainly been an unholy scoundrel over those poor people's banks," said my uncle, "and if what they say's true, he's been about as bad as possible to his wretched wife. He must have been pretty miserable, too, with all his scoundrelism, for he was a completely ruined man, without a chance of retrieving his position, and detested by everybody. Indeed, some of his recent doings, if what I have heard is to be relied on, have been very much those of a madman. So that, on the whole, I'm not much surprised. Suicide's about the only crime, I suppose, that he has never experimented with till now, and, indeed, it's rather a service to the world at large—his only service, I expect."

The Colonel sent a man to make further inquiries, and presently this man returned with the news that now it was said that Mr Sneathy had not committed suicide, but had been murdered. And hard on the man's heels came Mr Hardwick, a neighbour of my uncle's and a fellow J. P. He had had the case reported to him, it seemed, as soon as the body had been found, and had at once gone to the spot. He had found the body hanging—*and with the right hand cut off*.

"It's a murder, Brett," he said, "without doubt—a most horrible case of murder and mutilation. The hand is cut off and taken away, but whether the atrocity was committed before or after the hanging of course I can't say. But the missing hand makes it plainly a case of murder, and not suicide. I've come to consult you about issuing a warrant, for I think there's no doubt as to the identity of the murderers."

"That's a good job," said the Colonel, "else we should have had some work for Mr Martin Hewitt here, which wouldn't be fair, as he's taking a rest. Whom do you think of having arrested?"

"The two young Fosters. It's plain as it can be—and a most revolting crime too, bad as Sneathy may have been. They came down from London today and went out deliberately to it, it's clear. They were heard talking of it, asked as to the direction in which he had gone, and followed him—and with a rope."

"Isn't that rather an unusual form of murder—hanging?" Hewitt remarked.

"Perhaps it is," Mr Hardwick replied; "but it's the case here plain enough. It seems, in fact, that they had a way of threatening to hang him and even to cut off his hand if he used it to strike their mother. So that they appear to have carried out what might have seemed mere idle threats in a diabolically savage way. Of course they *may* have strangled him first and hanged him after, by way of carrying out their threat and venting their spite on the mutilated body. But that they did it is plain enough for me. I've spent an hour or two over it, and feel I am certainly more than justified in ordering their apprehension. Indeed, they were with him at the time, as I have found by their tracks on the footpath through the wood."

The Colonel turned to Martin Hewitt. "Mr Hardwick, you must know," he said, "is by way of being an amateur in your particular line—and a very good amateur, too, I should say, judging by a case or two I have known in this county."

Hewitt bowed, and laughingly expressed a fear lest Mr Hardwick should come to London and supplant him altogether. "This seems a curious case," he added. "If you don't mind, I think I should like to take a glance at the tracks and whatever other traces there may be, just by way of keeping my hand in."

"Certainly," Mr Hardwick replied, brightening. "I should of all things like to have Mr Hewitt's opinions on the observations I have made—just for my own gratification. As to his opinion—there can be no room for doubt; the thing is plain."

With many promises not to be late for dinner, we left my uncle and walked with Mr Hardwick in the direction of Ratherby Wood. It was an unfrequented part, he told us, and by particular care he had managed, he hoped, to prevent the rumour spreading to the village yet, so that we might hope to find the trails not yet overlaid. It was a man of his own, he said, who, making a short cut through the wood, had come upon the body hanging, and had run immediately to inform him. With this man he had gone back, cut down the body, and made his observations. He had followed the trail backward to Ranworth, and there had found the new coachman, who had once been in his own service. From him he had learned the doings of the brothers Foster as they left the place, and from him he had ascertained that they had not then returned. Then, leaving his man by the body, he had come straight to my uncle's.

Presently we came on the footpath leading from Ranworth across the field to Ratherby Wood. It was a mere trail of bare earth worn by successive feet amid the grass. It was damp, and we all stooped and examined the footmarks that were to be seen on it. They all pointed one way—towards the wood in the distance.

"Fortunately it's not a greatly frequented path," Mr Hardwick said. "You see, there are the marks of three pairs of feet only, and as first Sneathy and then both of the brothers came this way, these footmarks must be theirs. Which are Sneathy's is plain—they are these large flat ones. If you notice, they are all distinctly visible in the centre of the track, showing plainly that they belong to the man who walked alone, which was Sneathy. Of the others, the marks of the *outside* feet—the left on the left side and the right on the right—are often not visible. Clearly they belong to two men walking side by side, and more often than not treading, with their outer feet, on the grass at the side. And where these happen to drop on the same spot as the marks in the middle they cover them. Plainly they are the footmarks of Henry and Robert Foster, made as they followed Sneathy. Don't you agree with me Mr Hewitt?"

"Oh yes, that's very plain. You have a better pair of eyes than most people, Mr Hardwick, and a good idea of using them, too.

We will go into the wood now. As a matter of fact I can pretty clearly distinguish most of the other footmarks—those on the grass; but that's a matter of much training."

We followed the footpath, keeping on the grass at its side, in case it should be desirable to refer again to the foot-tracks. For some little distance into the wood the tracks continued as before, those of the brothers overlaying those of Sneathy. Then there was a difference. The path here was broader and muddy, because of the proximity of trees, and suddenly the outer footprints separated, and no more overlay the larger ones in the centre, but proceeded at an equal distance on either side of them.

"See there," cried Mr Hardwick, pointing triumphantly to the spot, "this is where they over took him, and walked on either side. The body was found only a little farther on—you could see the place now if the path didn't zigzag about so."

Hewitt said nothing, but stooped and examined the tracks at the sides with great care and evident thought, spanning the distances between them comparatively with his arms. Then he rose and stepped lightly from one mark to another, taking care not to tread on the mark itself. "Very good," he said shortly on finishing his examination. "We'll go on."

We went on, and presently came to the place where the body lay. Here the ground sloped from the left down towards the right, and a tiny streamlet, a mere trickle of a foot or two wide, ran across the path. In rainy seasons it was probably wider, for all the earth and clay had been washed away for some feet on each side, leaving flat, bare and very coarse gravel, on which the trail was lost. Just beyond this, and to the left, the body lay on a grassy knoll under the limb of a tree, from which still depended a part of the cut rope. It was not a pleasant sight. The man was a soft, fleshy creature, probably rather under than over the medium height, and he lay there, with his stretched neck and protruding tongue, a revolting object. His right arm lay by his side, and the stump of the wrist was clotted with black blood. Mr Hardwick's man was still in charge, seemingly little pleased with his job, and a few yards off stood a couple of countrymen looking on.

Hewitt asked from which direction these men had come, and having ascertained and noticed their footmarks, he asked them to stay exactly where they were, to avoid confusing such other tracks as might be seen. Then he addressed himself to his examination. "*First*," he said, glancing up at the branch, that was scarce a yard above his head, "this rope has been here for some time."

"Yes," Mr Hardwick replied, "it's an old swing rope. Some children used it in the summer, but it got partly cut away, and the odd couple of yards has been hanging since."

"Ah," said Hewitt, "then if the Fosters did this they were saved some trouble by the chance, and were able to take their halter back with them — and so avoid *one* chance of detection." He very closely scrutinised the top of a tree stump, probably the relic of a tree that had been cut down long before, and then addressed himself to the body.

"When you cut it down," he said, "did it fall in a heap?"

"No, my man eased it down to some extent."

"Not on to its face?"

"Oh no. On to its back, just as it is now." Mr Hardwick saw that Hewitt was looking at muddy marks on each of the corpse's knees, to one of which a small leaf clung, and at one or two other marks of the same sort on the fore part of the dress. "That seems to show pretty plainly," he said, "that he must have struggled with them and was thrown forward, doesn't it?"

Hewitt did not reply, but gingerly lifted the right arm by its sleeve. "Is either of the brothers Foster left-handed?" he asked.

"No, I think not. Here, Bennett, you have seen plenty of their doings — cricket, shooting, and so on — do you remember if either is left-handed?"

"Nayther, sir," Mr Hardwick's man answered. "Both on 'em's right-handed."

Hewitt lifted the lapel of the coat and attentively regarded a small rent in it. The dead man's hat lay near, and after a few glances at that, Hewitt dropped it and turned his attention to the hair. This was coarse and dark and long, and brushed straight back with no parting.

"This doesn't look very symmetrical, does it?" Hewitt remarked, pointing to the locks over the right ear. They were shorter just there than on the other side, and apparently very clumsily cut, whereas in every other part the hair appeared to be rather well and carefully trimmed. Mr Hardwick said nothing, but fidgeted a little, as though he considered that valuable time was being wasted over irrelevant trivialities.

Presently, however, he spoke. "There's very little to be learned from the body, is there?" he said. "I think I'm quite justified in ordering their arrest, eh? — indeed, I've wasted too much time already."

Hewitt was groping about among some bushes behind the tree from which the corpse had been taken. When he answered, he said, "I don't think I should do anything of the sort just now, Mr Hardwick. As a matter of fact, I *fancy*" — this word with an emphasis — "that the brothers Foster may not have seen this man Sneathy at all today."

"Not seen him? Why, my dear sir, there's no question of it. It's certain, absolutely. The evidence is positive. The fact of the threats and of the body being found treated so is pretty well enough, I should think. But that's nothing — look at those footmarks. They've walked along with him, one each side, without a possible doubt; plainly they were the last people with him, in any case. And you don't mean to ask anybody to believe that the dead man, even if he hanged himself, cut off his own hand first. Even if you do, where's the hand? And even putting aside all these considerations, each a complete case in itself, the Fosters *must* at least have seen the body as they came past, and yet nothing has been heard of them yet. Why didn't they spread the alarm? They went straight away in the opposite direction from home—there are their footmarks, which you've not seen yet, beyond the gravel."

Hewitt stepped over to where the patch of clean gravel ceased, at the opposite side to that from which we had approached the brook, and there, sure enough, were the now familiar footmarks of the brothers leading away from the scene of Sneathy's end. "Yes," Hewitt said, "I see them. Of course, Mr Hardwick, you'll do what seems right in your own eyes, and in any case not much harm will be done by the arrest beyond a terrible fright for that unfortunate family. Nevertheless, if you care for my impression, it is, as I have said, that the Fosters have not seen Sneathy today."

"But what about the hand?"

"As to that I have a conjecture, but as yet it is only a conjecture, and if I told it you would probably call it absurd—certainly you'd disregard it, and perhaps quite excusably. The case is a complicated one, and, if there is anything at all in my conjecture, one of the most remarkable I have ever had to do with. It interests me intensely, and I shall devote a little time now to following up the theory I have formed. You have, I suppose, already communicated with the police?"

"I wired to Shopperton at once, as soon as I heard of the matter. It's a twelve miles drive, but I wonder the police have not arrived yet. They can't be long; I don't know where the village constable has got to, but in any case *he* wouldn't be much good. But as to your idea that the Fosters can't be suspected—well, nobody could respect your opinion, Mr Hewitt, more than myself, but really, just think. The notion's impossible—fiftyfold impossible. As soon as the police arrive I shall have that trail followed and the Fosters apprehended. I should be a fool if I didn't."

"Very well, Mr Hardwick," Hewitt replied; "you'll do what you consider your duty, of course, and quite properly, though I *would* recommend you to take another glance at those three trails in the path. I shall take a look in this direction." And he turned up by the side of the streamlet, keeping on the gravel at its side.

I followed. We climbed the rising ground, and presently, among the trees, came to the place where the little rill emerged from the broken ground in the highest part of the wood. Here the clean ground ceased, and there was a large patch of wet clayey earth. Several marks left by the feet of cattle were there, and one or two human footmarks. Two of these (a pair), the newest and the most distinct, Hewitt studied carefully, and measured each direction.

"Notice these marks," he said. "They may be of importance or they may not—that we shall see. Fortunately they are very distinctive—the right boot is a badly worn one, and a small tag of leather, where the soul is damaged, is doubled over and trodden into the soft earth. Nothing could be luckier. Clearly they are the most recent footsteps in this direction— from the main road, which lies right ahead, through the rest of the wood."

"Then you think somebody else has been on the scene of the tragedy, beside the victim and the brothers?" I said.

"Yes, I do. But hark; there is a vehicle in the road. Can you see between the trees? Yes, it is the police cart. We shall be able to report its arrival to Mr Hardwick as we go down."

We turned and walked rapidly down the incline to where we had come from. Mr Hardwick and his man were still there, and another rustic had arrived to gape. We told Mr Hardwick that he might expect the police presently, and proceeded along the gravel skirting the stream, toward the lower part of the wood.

Here Hewitt proceeded very cautiously, keeping a sharp look-out on either side for footprints on the neighbouring soft ground. There were none, however, for the gravel margin of the stream made a sort of footpath of itself, and the trees and undergrowth were close and thick on each side. At the bottom we emerged from the wood on a small piece of open ground skirting a lane, and here, just by the side of the lane, where the stream fell into a trench, Hewitt suddenly pounced on another footmark. He was unusually excited.

"See," he said, "here it is—the right foot with its broken leather, and the corresponding left foot on the damp edge of the lane itself. He—the man with the broken shoe—has walked on the hard gravel all the way down from the source of the stream, and his is the only trail unaccounted for near the body. Come, Brett, we've an adventure on foot. Do you care to let your uncle's dinner go by the board, and follow?"

"Can't we go back and tell him?"

"No—there's no time to lose; we must follow up this man—or at least I must. You go or stay, of course, as you think best."

I hesitated a moment, picturing to myself the excellent Colonel as he would appear after waiting dinner an hour or two for us, but decided to go. "At any rate," I said, "if the way lies along the roads we shall probably meet somebody going in the direction of Ratherby who will take a message. But what is your theory? I don't understand at all. I must say everything Hardwick said seemed to me to be beyond question. There were the tracks to prove that the three had walked together to the spot, and that the brothers had gone on alone; and every other circumstance pointed the same way. Then, what possible motive could anybody else about here have for such a crime? Unless, indeed, it were one of the people defrauded by Sneathy's late companies."

"The motive," said Hewitt, "is, I fancy, a most extraordinary—indeed, a weird one. A thing as of centuries ago. Ask me no questions—I think you will be a little surprised before very long. But come, we must move." And we mended our pace along the lane.

The lane, by the bye, was hard and firm, with scarcely a spot where a track might be left, except in places at the sides; and at these places Hewitt never gave a glance. At the end the lane turned into a by-road, and at the turning Hewitt stopped and scrutinised the ground closely. There was nothing like a recognisable footmark to be seen; but almost immediately Hewitt turned off to the right, and we continued our brisk march without a glance at the road.

"How did you judge which way to turn then?" I asked.

"Didn't you see?" replied Hewitt; "I'll show you at the next turning."

Half a mile farther on the road forked, and here Hewitt stooped and pointed silently to a couple of small twigs, placed crosswise, with the longer twig of the two pointing down the branch of the road to the left. We took the branch to the left, and went on.

"Our man's making a mistake," Hewitt observed. "He leaves his friends' messages lying about for his enemies to read."

We hurried forward with scarcely a word. I was almost too bewildered by what Hewitt had said and done to formulate anything like a reasonable guess as to what our expedition tended, or even to make an effective inquiry—though, after what Hewitt had said, I knew that would be useless. Who was this mysterious man with the broken shoe? what had he to do with the murder of Sneathy? what did the mutilation mean? and who were his friends who left him signs and messages by means of crossed twigs?

We met a man, by whom I sent a short note to my uncle, and soon after we turned into a main road. Here again, at the corner, was the curious message of twigs. A cartwheel had passed over and crushed them, but it had not so far displaced them as to cause any doubt that the direction to take was to the right. At an inn a little farther along we entered, and Hewitt bought a pint of Irish whisky and a flat bottle to hold it in, as well as a loaf of bread and some cheese, which we carried away wrapped in paper.

"This will have to do for our dinner," Hewitt said as we emerged.

"But we're not going to drink a pint of common whisky between us?" I asked in some astonishment.

"Never mind," Hewitt answered with a smile. "Perhaps we'll find somebody to help us—somebody not so fastidious as yourself as to quality."

Now we hurried—hurried more than ever, for it was beginning to get dusk, and Hewitt feared a difficulty in finding and reading the twig signs in the dark. Two more turnings we made, each with its silent direction—the crossed twigs. To me there was something almost weird and creepy in this curious hunt for the invisible and incomprehensible, guided faithfully and persistently at every turn by this now unmistakable signal. After the second turning we broke into a trot along a long, winding lane, but presently Hewitt's hand fell on my shoulder, and we stopped. He pointed ahead, where some large object, round a bend of the hedge was illuminated as though by a light from below.

"We will walk now," Hewitt said. "Remember that we are on a walking tour, and have come along here entirely by accident."

We proceeded at a swinging walk, Hewitt whistling gaily. Soon we turned the bend, and saw that the large object was a travelling van drawn up with two others on a space of grass by the side of the lane. It was a gipsy encampment, the caravan having apparently only lately stopped, for a man was still engaged in tugging at the rope of a tent that stood near the vans. Two or three sullen-looking ruffians lay about a fire which burned in the space left in the middle of the encampment. A woman stood at the door of one van with a large kettle in her hand, and at the foot of the steps below her a more pleasant-looking old man sat on an inverted pail. Hewitt swung towards the fire from the road, and with an indescribable mixture of slouch, bow, and smile addressed the company generally with "*Kooshto bock, pals!*"

The men on the ground took no notice, but continued to stare doggedly before them. The man working at the tent looked round quickly for a moment, and the old man on the bucket looked up and nodded.

Quick to see the most likely friend, Hewitt at once went up to the old man, extending his hand, "*Sarshin, daddo?*" he said; "*Dell mandy tooty's varst.*"

The old man smiled and shook hands, though without speaking. Then Hewitt proceeded, producing the flat bottle of whisky, "*Tatty for pawny, chals. Dell mandy the pawny, and lell posh the tatty.*"

The whisky did it. We were Romany ryes in twenty minutes or less, and had already been taking tea with the gipsies for half the time. The two or three we had found about the fire were still reserved, but these, I found, were only half-gipsies, and understood very little Romany. One or two others, however, including the old man, were of purer breed, and talked freely, as did one of the women. They were Lees, they said, and expected to be on Wirksby racecourse in three days' time. We, too, were *pirimengroes*, or travellers, Hewitt explained, and might look to see them on the course.

Then he fell to telling gipsy stories, and they to telling others back, to my intense mystification. Hewitt explained afterwards that they were mostly stories of poaching, with now and again a horse-coping anecdote thrown in. Since then I have learned enough of Romany to take my part in such a conversation, but at the time a word or two here and there was all I could understand. In all this talk the man we had first noticed stretching the tent-rope took very little interest, but lay, with his head away from the fire, smoking his pipe. He was a much darker man than any other present—had, in fact, the appearance of a man of even a swarthier race than that of the others about us.

Presently, in the middle of a long and, of course, to me unintelligible story by the old man, I caught Hewitt's eye. He lifted one eyebrow almost imperceptibly, and glanced for a single moment at his walking-stick. Then I saw that it was pointed toward the feet of the very dark man, who had not yet spoken. One leg was thrown over the others as he lay, with the soles of his shoes presented toward the fire, and in its glare I saw—that the right sole was worn and broken, and that a small triangular tag of leather was doubled over beneath in just the place we knew of from the prints in Ratherby Wood.

I could not take my eyes off that man with his broken shoe. There lay the secret, the whole mystery of the fantastic crime in Ratherby Wood centred in that shabby ruffian. What was it?

But Hewitt went on, talking and joking furiously. The men who were not speaking mostly smoked gloomily, but whenever one spoke, he became animated and lively. I had attempted once or twice to join in, though my efforts were not particularly successful, except in inducing one man to offer me tobacco from his box—tobacco that almost made me giddy in the smell. He tried some of mine in exchange, and though he praised it with native politeness, and smoked the pipe through, I could see that my Hignett mixture was poor stuff in his estimation, compared with the awful tobacco in his own box.

Presently the man with the broken shoe got up, slouched over to his tent, and disappeared. Then said Hewitt (I translate):

"You're not all Lees here, I see?"

"Yes, *pal*, all Lees."

"But *he's* not a Lee?" and Hewitt jerked his head towards the tent.

"Why not a Lee, *pal*? We be Lees, and he is with us. Thus he is a Lee."

"Oh yes, of course. But I know he is from over the *pawny*. Come, I'll guess the *tem* he comes from—it's from Roumania, eh? Perhaps the Wallachian part?"

The men looked at one another, and then the old Lee said:

"You're right, pal. You're cleverer than we took you for. That is what they calls his *tem*. He is a petulengro, and he comes with us to shoe the *gries* and mend the *vardoes*. But he is with us, and so he is a Lee."

The talk and the smoke went on, and presently the man with the broken shoe returned, and lay down again. Then, when the whisky had all gone, and Hewitt, with some excuse that I did not understand, had begged a piece of cord from one of the men, we left in a chorus of *kooshto rardies*.

By this time it was nearly ten o'clock. We walked briskly till we came back again to the inn where we had bought the whisky. Here Hewitt, after some little trouble, succeeded in hiring a village cart, and while the driver was harnessing the horse, cut a couple of short sticks from the hedge. These, being each divided into two, made four short, stout pieces of something less than six inches long apiece. Then Hewitt joined them together in pairs, each pair being connected from centre to centre by about nine or ten inches of the cord he had brought from the gipsies' camp. These done, he handed one pair to me. "Handcuffs," he explained, "and no bad ones either. See—you use them so." And he passed the cord round my wrist, gripping the two handles, and giving them a slight twist that sufficiently convinced me of the excruciating pain that might be inflicted by a vigorous turn, and the utter helplessness of a prisoner thus secured in the hands of captors prepared to use their instruments.

"Whom are these for?" I asked. "The man with the broken shoe?"

Hewitt nodded.

"Yes," he said. "I expect we shall find him out alone about midnight. You know how to use these now."

It was fully eleven before the cart was ready and we started. A quarter of a mile or so from the gipsy encampment Hewitt stopped the cart and gave the driver instructions to wait. We got through the hedge, and made our way on the soft ground behind it in the direction of the vans and the tent.

"Roll up your handkerchief," Hewitt whispered, "into a tight pad. The moment I grab him, ram it into his mouth—*well* in, mind, so that it doesn't easily fall out. Probably he will be stooping—that will make it easier; we can pull him suddenly backward. Now be quiet."

We kept on till nothing but the hedge divided us from the space whereon stood the encampment. It was now nearer twelve o'clock than eleven, but the time we waited seemed endless. But time is not eternity after all, and at last we heard a move in the tent. A minute after, the man we sought was standing before us. He made straight for a gap in the hedge which we had passed on our way, and we crouched low and waited. He emerged on our side of the hedge with his back towards us, and began walking, as we had walked, behind the hedge, but in the opposite direction. We followed.

He carried something in his hand that looked like a large bundle of sticks and twigs, and he appeared to be as anxious to be secret as we ourselves. From time to time he stopped and listened; fortunately there was no moon, or in turning about, as he did once or twice, he would probably have observed us. The field sloped downward just before us, and there was another hedge at right angles, leading down to a slight hollow. To this hollow the man made his way, and in the shade of the new hedge we followed. Presently he stopped suddenly, stooped, and deposited his bundle on the ground before him. Crouching before it, he produced matches from his pocket, struck one, and in a moment had a fire of twigs and small branches, that sent up a heavy white smoke. What all this portended I could not imagine, but a sense of the weirdness of the whole adventure came upon me unchecked. The horrible corpse in the wood, with its severed wrist, Hewitt's enigmatical forebodings, the mysterious tracking of the man with the broken shoe, the scene round the gipsies' fire, and now the strange behaviour of this man, whose connection with the tragedy was so intimate and yet so inexplicable—all these things contributed to make up a tale of but a few hours' duration, but of an inscrutable impressiveness that I began to feel in my nerves.

The man bent a thin stick double, and using it as a pair of tongs, held some indistinguishable object over the flames before him. Excited as I was, I could not help noticing that he bent and held the stick with his left hand. We crept stealthily nearer, and as I stood scarcely three yards behind him and looked over his shoulder, the form of the object stood out clear and black against the dull red of the flame. It was a *human hand*.

I suppose I may have somehow betrayed my amazement and horror to my companion's sharp eyes, for suddenly I felt his hand tightly grip my arm just above the elbow. I turned, and found his face close by mine and his finger raised warningly. Then I saw him produce his wrist-grip and make a motion with his palm toward his mouth, which I understood to be intended to remind me of the gag. We stepped forward.

The man turned his horrible cookery over and over above the crackling sticks, as though to smoke and dry it in every part. I saw Hewitt's hand reach out toward him, and in a flash we had pulled him back over his heels and I had driven the gag between his teeth as he opened his mouth. We seized his wrists in the cords at once, and I shall never forget the man's look of ghastly, frantic terror as he lay on the ground. When I knew more I understood the reason of this.

Hewitt took both wristholds in one hand and drove the gag entirely into the man's mouth, so that he almost choked. A piece of sacking lay near the fire, and by Hewitt's request I dropped that awful hand from the wooden twigs upon it and rolled it up in a parcel—it was, no doubt, what the sacking had been brought for. Then we lifted the man to his feet and hurried him in the direction of the cart. The whole capture could not have occupied thirty seconds, and as I stumbled over the rough field at the man's left elbow I could only think of the thing as one thinks of a dream that one knows all the time *is* a dream.

But presently the man, who had been walking quietly, though gasping, sniffing and choking because of the tightly rolled handkerchief in his mouth—presently he made a sudden dive, thinking doubtless to get his wrists free by surprise. But Hewitt was alert, and gave them a twist that made him roll his head with a dismal, stifled yell, and with the opening of his mouth, by some chance the gag fell away. Immediately the man roared aloud for help.

"Quick," said Hewitt, "drag him along—they'll hear in the vans. Bring the hand!"

I seized the fallen handkerchief and crammed it over the man's mouth as well as I might, and together we made as much of a trot as we could, dragging the man between us, while Hewitt checked any reluctance on his part by a timely wrench of the wristholds. It was a hard two hundred and fifty yards to the lane even for us—for the gipsy it must have been a bad minute and a half indeed. Once more as we went over the uneven ground he managed to get out a shout, and we thought we heard a distinct reply from somewhere in the direction of the encampment.

We pulled him over a stile in a tangle; and dragged and pushed him through a small hedge-gap all in a heap. Here we were but a short distance from the cart, and into that we flung him without wasting time or tenderness, to the intense consternation of the driver, who, I believe, very nearly set up a cry for help on his own account. Once in the cart, however, I seized the reins and the whip myself and, leaving Hewitt to take care of the prisoner, put the turn-out along toward Ratherby at as near ten miles an hour as it could go.

We made first for Mr Hardwick's, but he, we found, was with my uncle, so we followed him. The arrest of the Fosters had been effected, we learned, not very long after we had left the wood, as they returned by another route to Ranworth. We brought our prisoner into the Colonel's library, where he and Mr Hardwick were sitting.

"I'm not quite sure what we can charge him with unless it's anatomical robbery," Hewitt remarked, "but here's the criminal."

The man only looked down, with a sulkily impenetrable countenance. Hewitt spoke to him once or twice, and at last he said, in a strange accent, something that sounded like "*kekin jin-navvy.*"

"*Keck jin?*" asked Hewitt, in the loud, clear tone one instinctively adopts in talking to a foreigner, "*Keckeno jinny?*"

The man understood and shook his head, but not another word would he say or another question answer.

"He's a foreign gipsy," Hewitt explained, "just as I thought—a Wallachian, in fact. Theirs is an older and purer dialect than that of the English gipsies, and only some of the root-words are alike. But I think we can make him explain tomorrow that the Fosters at least had nothing to do with, at any rate, cutting off Sneathy's hand. Here it is, I think." And he gingerly lifted the folds of sacking from the ghastly object as it lay on the table, and then covered it up again.

"But what—what does it all mean?" Mr Hardwick said in bewildered astonishment. "Do you mean this man was an accomplice?"

"Not at all—the case was one of suicide, as I think you'll agree, when I've explained. This man simply found the body hanging and stole the hand."

"But what in the world for?"

"For the HAND OF GLORY. Eh?" He turned to the gipsy and pointed to the hand on the table: "*Yag-varst*, eh?"

There was a quick gleam of intelligence in the man's eye, but he said nothing. As for myself I was more than astounded. Could it be possible that the old superstition of the Hand of Glory remained alive in a practical shape at this day?

"You know the superstition, of course," Hewitt said. "It did exist in this country in the last century, when there were plenty of dead men hanging at crossroads, and so on. On the Continent, in some places, it has survived later. Among the Wallachian gipsies it has always been a great article of belief, and the superstition is quite active still. The belief is that the right hand of a hanged man, cut off and dried over the smoke of certain wood and herbs, and then provided with wicks at each finger made of the dead man's hair, becomes, when lighted at each wick (the wicks are greased, of course), a charm, whereby a thief may walk without hindrance where he pleases in a strange house, push open all doors and take what he likes. Nobody can stop him, for everybody the Hand of Glory approaches is made helpless, and can neither move nor speak. You may remember there was some talk of 'thieves' candles' in connection with the horrible series of Whitechapel murders not long ago. That is only one form of the cult of the Hand of Glory."

"Yes," my uncle said, "I remember reading so. There is a story about it in the Ingoldsby Legends, too, I believe."

"There is—it is called 'The Hand of Glory,' in fact. You remember the spell, 'Open lock to the dead man's knock,' and so on. But I think you'd better have the constable up and get this man into safe quarters for the night. He should be searched, of course. I expect they will find on him the hair I noticed to have been cut from Sneathy's head."

The village constable arrived with his iron handcuffs in substitution for those of cord which had so sorely vexed the wrists of our prisoner, and marched him away to the little lock-up on the green.

Then my uncle and Mr Hardwick turned on Martin Hewitt with doubts and many questions:

"Why do you call it suicide?" Mr Hardwick asked. "It is plain the Fosters were with him at the time from the tracks. Do you mean to say that they stood there and watched Sneathy hang himself without interfering?"

"No, I don't," Hewitt replied, lighting a cigar. "I think I told you that they never saw Sneathy."

"Yes, you did, and of course that's what they said themselves when they were arrested. But the thing's impossible. Look at the tracks!"

"The tracks are exactly what revealed to me that it was *not* impossible," Hewitt returned. "I'll tell you how the case unfolded itself to me from the beginning. As to the information you gathered from the Ranworth coachman, to begin with. The conversation between the Fosters which he overheard might well mean something less serious than murder. What did they say? They had been sent for in a hurry and had just had a short consultation with their mother and sister. Henry said that 'the thing must be done at once'; also that as there were two of them it should be easy. Robert said that Henry, as a doctor, would know best what to do.

"Now you, Colonel Brett, had been saying—before we learned these things from Mr Hardwick—that Sneathy's behaviour of late had become so bad as to seem that of a madman. Then there was the story of his sudden attack on a tradesman in the village, and equally sudden running away—exactly the sort of impulsive, wild thing that madmen do. Why then might it not be reasonable to suppose that Sneathy *had* become mad—more especially considering all the circumstances of the case, his commercial ruin and disgrace and his horrible life with his wife and her family?—had become suddenly much worse and quite uncontrollable, so that the two wretched women left alone with him were driven to send in haste for Henry and Robert to help them? That would account for all.

"The brothers arrive just after Sneathy had gone out. They are told in a hurried interview how affairs stand, and it is decided that Sneathy must be at once secured and confined in an asylum before something serious happens. He has just gone out—something terrible may be happening at this moment. The brothers determine to follow at once and secure him wherever he may be. Then the meaning of their conversation is plain. The thing that 'must be done, and at once,' is the capture of Sneathy and his confinement in an asylum. Henry, as a doctor, would 'know what to do' in regard to the necessary formalities. And they took a halter in case a struggle should ensue and it were found necessary to bind him. Very likely, wasn't it?"

"Well, yes," Mr Hardwick replied, "it certainly is. It never struck me in that light at all."

"That was because you believed, to begin with, that a murder had been committed, and looked at the preliminary circumstances which you learned after in the light of your conviction. But now, to come to my actual observations. I saw the footmarks across the fields, and agreed with you (it was indeed obvious) that Sneathy had gone that way first, and that the brothers had followed, walking over his tracks. This state of the tracks continued until well into the wood, when suddenly the tracks of the brothers opened out and proceeded on each side of Sneathy's. The simple inference would seem to be, of course, the one you made—that the Fosters had here overtaken Sneathy, and walked one at each side of him.

"But of this I felt by no means certain. Another very simple explanation was available, which might chance to be the true one. It was just at the spot where the brothers' tracks separated that the path became suddenly much muddier, because of the closer overhanging of the trees at the spot. The path was, as was to be expected, wettest in the middle. It would be the most natural thing in the world for two well-dressed young men, on arriving here, to separate so as to walk one on each side of the mud in the middle.

"On the other hand, a man in Sneathy's state (assuming him, for the moment, to be mad and contemplating suicide) would walk straight along the centre of the path, taking no note of mud or anything else. I examined all the tracks very carefully, and my theory was confirmed. The feet of the brothers had everywhere alighted in the driest spots, and the steps were of irregular lengths—which meant, of course, that they were picking their way; while Sneathy's footmarks had never turned aside even for the dirtiest puddle. Here, then, were the rudiments of a theory.

"At the watercourse, of course, the footmarks ceased, because of the hard gravel. The body lay on a knoll at the left—a knoll covered with grass. On this the signs of footmarks were almost undiscoverable, although I am often able to discover tracks in grass that are invisible to others. Here, however, it was almost useless to spend much time in examination, for you and your man had been there, and what slight marks there might be would be indistinguishable one from another.

"Under the branch from which the man had hung there was an old tree stump, with a flat top, where the tree had been sawn off. I examined this, and it became fairly apparent that Sneathy had stood on it when the rope was about his neck—his muddy footprint was plain to see; the mud was not smeared about, you see, as it probably would have been if he had been stood there forcibly and pushed off. It was a simple, clear footprint—another hint at suicide.

"But then arose the objection that you mentioned yourself. Plainly the brothers Foster were following Sneathy, and came this way. Therefore, if he hanged himself before they arrived, it would seem that they must have come across the body. But now I examined the body itself. There was mud on the knees, and clinging to one knee was a small leaf. It was a leaf corresponding to those on the bush behind the tree, and it was not a dead leaf, so must have been just detached.

"After my examination of the body I went to the bush, and there, in the thick of it, were, for me, sufficiently distinct knee-marks, in one of which the knee had crushed a spray of the bush against the ground, and from that spray a leaf was missing. Behind the knee-marks were the indentations of boot-toes in the soft, bare earth under the bush, and thus the thing was plain. The poor lunatic had come in sight of the dangling rope, and the temptation to suicide was irresistible. To people in a deranged state of mind the mere sight of the means of self-destruction is often a temptation impossible to withstand. But at that moment he must have heard the steps—probably the voices—of the brothers behind him on the winding path. He immediately hid in the bush till they had passed. It is probable that seeing who the men were, and conjecturing that they were following him—thinking also, perhaps, of things that had occurred between them and himself—his inclination to self-destruction became completely ungovernable, with the result that you saw.

"But before I inspected the bush I noticed one or two more things about the body. You remember I inquired if either of the brothers Foster was left-handed, and was assured that neither was. But clearly the hand had been cut off by a left-handed man, with a large, sharply pointed knife. For well away to the *right* of where the wrist had hung the knife-point had made a tiny triangular rent in the coat, so that the hand must have been held in the mutilator's right hand, while he used the knife with his left—clearly a left-handed man.

"But most important of all about the body was the jagged hair over the right ear. Everywhere else the hair was well cut and orderly—here it seemed as though a good piece had been, so to speak, *sawn* off. What could anybody want with a dead man's right hand and certain locks of his hair? Then it struck me suddenly—the man was hanged; it was the Hand of Glory!

"Then you will remember I went, at your request, to see the footprints of the Fosters on the part of the path *past* the watercourse. Here again it was muddy in the middle, and the two brothers had walked as far apart as before, although nobody had walked between them. A final proof, if one were needed, of my theory as to the three lines of footprints.

"Now I was to consider how to get at the man who had taken his hand. He should be punished for the mutilation, but beyond that he would be required as a witness. Now all the foot-tracks in the vicinity had been accounted for. There were those of the brothers and of Sneathy, which we have been speaking of; those of the rustics looking on, which, however, stopped a little way off, and did not interfere with our sphere of observation; those of your man, who had cut straight through the wood when he first saw the body, and had come back the same way with you; and our own, which we had been careful to keep away from the others. Consequently there was *no* track of the man who had cut off the hand; therefore it was certain that he must have come along the hard gravel by the watercourse, for that was the only possible path which would not tell the tale. Indeed, it seemed quite a likely path through the wood for a passenger to take, coming from the high ground by the Shopperton road.

"Brett and I left you and traversed the watercourse, both up and down. We found a footprint at the top, left lately by a man with a broken shoe. Right down to the bottom of the watercourse where it emerged from the wood there was no sign on either side of this man having left the gravel. (Where the body was, as you will remember, he would simply have stepped off the gravel on to the grass, which I thought it useless to examine, as I have explained.) But at the bottom, by the lane, the footprint appeared again.

"This then was the direction in which I was to search for a left-handed man with a broken-soled shoe, probably a gipsy—and most probably a foreign gipsy—because a foreign gipsy would be the most likely still to hold the belief in the Hand of Glory. I conjectured the man to be a straggler from a band of gipsies—one who probably had got behind the caravan and had made a short cut across the wood after it; so at the end of the lane I looked for a *patrin*. This is a sign that gipsies leave to guide stragglers following up. Sometimes it is a heap of dead leaves, sometimes a few stones, sometimes a mark on the ground, but more usually a couple of twigs crossed, with the longer twig pointing the road.

"Guided by these *patrins* we came in the end on the gipsy camp just as it was settling down for the night. We made ourselves agreeable (as Brett will probably describe to you better than I can), we left them, and after they had got to sleep we came back and watched for the gentleman who is now in the lock-up. He would, of course, seize the first opportunity of treating his ghastly trophy in the prescribed way, and I guessed he would choose midnight, for that is the time the superstition teaches that the hand should be prepared. We made a few small preparations, collared him, and now you've got him. And I should think the sooner you let the brothers Foster go the better."

"But why didn't you tell me all the conclusions you had arrived at at the time?" asked Mr Hardwick.

"Well, really," Hewitt replied, with a quiet smile, "you were so positive, and some of the traces I relied on were so small, that it would probably have meant a long argument and a loss of time. But more than that, confess, if I had told you bluntly that Sneathy's hand had been taken away to make a mediæval charm to enable a thief to pass through a locked door and steal plate calmly under the owner's nose, what *would* you have said?"

"Well, well, perhaps I *should* have been a little sceptical. Appearances combined so completely to point to the Fosters as murderers that any other explanation almost would have seemed unlikely to me, and *that*—well no, I confess, I shouldn't have believed in it. But it is a startling thing to find such superstitions alive now-a-days."

"Yes, perhaps it is. Yet we find survivals of the sort very frequently. The Wallachians, however, are horribly superstitious still—the gipsies among them are, of course, worse. Don't you remember the case reported a few months ago, in which a child was drowned as a sacrifice in Wallachia in order to bring rain? And that was not done by gipsies either. Even in England, as late as 1865, a poor paralysed Frenchman was killed by being 'swum' for witchcraft—that was in Essex. And less atrocious cases of belief in wizardry occur again and again even now."

Then Mr Hardwick and my uncle fell into a discussion as to how the gipsy in the lock-up could be legally punished. Mr Hardwick thought it should be treated as a theft of a portion of a dead body, but my uncle fancied there was a penalty for mutilation of a dead body *per se*, though he could not point to the statute. As it happened, however, they were saved the trouble of arriving at a decision, for in the morning he was discovered to have escaped. He had been left, of course, with free hands, and had occupied the night in wrenching out the bars at the top of the back wall of the little prison-shed (it had stood on the green for a hundred and fifty years) and climbing out. He was not found again, and a month or two later the Foster family left the district entirely.

5

THE CASE OF LAKER, ABSCONDED

There were several of the larger London banks and insurance offices from which Hewitt held a sort of general retainer as detective adviser, in fulfilment of which he was regularly consulted as to the measures to be taken in different cases of fraud, forgery, theft, and so forth, which it might be the misfortune of the particular firms to encounter. The more important and intricate of these cases were placed in his hands entirely, with separate commissions, in the usual way. One of the most important companies of the sort was the General Guarantee Society, an insurance corporation which, among other risks, took those of the integrity of secretaries, clerks, and cashiers. In the case of a cash-box elopement on the part of any person guaranteed by the society, the directors were naturally anxious for a speedy capture of the culprit, and more especially of the booty, before too much of it was spent, in order to lighten the claim upon their funds, and in work of this sort Hewitt was at times engaged, either in general advice and direction, or in the actual pursuit of the plunder and the plunderer.

Arriving at his office a little later than usual one morning, Hewitt found an urgent message awaiting him from the General Guarantee Society, requesting his attention to a robbery which had taken place on the previous day. He had gleaned some hint of the case from the morning paper, wherein appeared a short paragraph, which ran thus: —

SERIOUS BANK ROBBERY. — In the course of yesterday a clerk employed by Messrs. Liddle, Neal & Liddle, the well-known bankers, disappeared, having in his possession a large sum of money, the property of his employers—a sum reported to be rather over £15,000. It would seem that he had been entrusted to collect the money in his capacity of "walk-clerk" from various other banks and trading concerns during the morning, but failed to return at the usual time. A large number of the notes which he received had been cashed at the Bank of England before suspicion was aroused. We understand that Detective-Inspector Plummer, of Scotland Yard, has the case in hand.

The clerk, whose name was Charles William Laker, had, it appeared from the message, been guaranteed in the usual way by the General Guarantee Society, and Hewitt's presence at the office was at once desired, in order that steps might quickly be taken for the man's apprehension, and in the recovery, at any rate, of as much of the booty as possible.

A smart hansom brought Hewitt to Threadneedle Street in a bare quarter of an hour, and there a few minutes' talk with the manager, Mr Lyster, put him in possession of the main facts of the case, which appeared to be simple. Charles William Laker was twenty-five years of age, and had been in the employ of Messrs. Liddle, Neal & Liddle for something more than seven years—since he left school, in fact—and until the previous day there had been nothing in his conduct to complain of. His duties as walk-clerk consisted in making a certain round, beginning at about half-past ten each morning. There were a certain number of the more important banks between which and Messrs. Liddle, Neal & Liddle there were daily transactions, and a few smaller semi-private banks and merchant firms acting as financial agents, with whom there was business intercourse of less importance and regularity; and each of these, as necessary, he visited in turn, collecting cash due on bills and other instruments of a like nature. He carried a wallet, fastened securely to his person by a chain, and this wallet contained the bills and the cash. Usually at the end of his round, when all his bills had been converted into cash, the wallet held very large sums. His work and responsibilities, in fine, were those common to walk-clerks in all banks.

On the day of the robbery he had started out as usual—possibly a little earlier than was customary—and the bills and other securities in his possession represented considerably more than £15,000. It had been ascertained that he had called in the usual way at each establishment.

Assembling the greatest detectives all together

Covering the full range and history of detective fiction.
From Zadig, *The Moonstone*, and Dupin through Sherlock Holmes, Loveday Brooke, Montague Egg, Lord Peter Wimsey, *The Thinking Machine*, Father Brown down to Solar Pons.

For more details and a full list of titles:
visit https://www.hachetteindia.com/home/yellowbacks

WELCOME BACK TO THE GOLDEN AGE